DEATH ON DEMAND

DEATH ON DEMAND

A DETECTIVE INSPECTOR ROLAND BENITO THRILLER

INGER GAMMELGAARD MADSEN

Translated from Danish by Sinéad Quirke Køngerskov

Published in 2023 by Podium Publishing, ULC
www.podiumaudio.com

DEATH ON DEMAND

Kila lenye mwanzo halikosi
kuwa na mwisho.

Everything that begins
must also come to an end.

—Traditional Swahili saying

1

——————

It smelled of autumn and earth from the newly ploughed fields. Not all the farmers were finished. In a distant field, a tractor drove with dust and a flock of screaming, hungry gulls in its wake. The hot summer, which had only begun in mid-August, had continued through September and into early October, making jackets and coats unnecessary despite the season.

After a loud quarrel about a Nintendo Wii game that Mikkel thought Lukas was too small for, Mum had sent them out to play in the clement weather. They pedalled off, wheels spinning at high speed. But to them, they weren't bikes. In their imagination, they were horses moving forward at a wild gallop.

"*Bang*, you're dead!" cried Lukas behind his brother, who angrily turned to face him on the saddle.

"You're not supposed to shoot me. You wanted to be a ninja!"

"So? Can ninjas not shoot cops!" Lukas sulked.

"Not a cop like me; I'm like a cop on TV." Mikkel, who was nine years old, could follow the news a bit and thought that cops were cool with their weapons and helmets, but for a six-year-old like Lukas, the ninjas from movies were much more exciting.

Suddenly, both bikes braked so hard that the gravel clouded around them. Lukas's bike skidded, and he only avoided crashing by setting one foot firmly on the ground in time. Ahead, they saw the trees around the bog. The leaves were changing in the beautiful golden brown and violet shades of autumn.

"We'd better turn around, Mikkel. We're not to go down to the bog without Mummy or Daddy."

"Argh, stop! That was only when we were babies. You're not a baby anymore, are you?"

Lukas grumbled even more and no longer looked like a dangerous bad guy, despite the headband and toy weapon stuck down in his belt, which really only served to hold up the oversized trousers that had once been Mikkel's around his thin body.

"But Mummy says it's dangerous. The Bog Woman could drag us into the water and drown us!" Lukas rubbed his finger nervously under the freckled nose that was red from the sun and the wind. His blue eyes searched Mikkel's in the hope of seeing the same horror he was feeling.

Mikkel laughed, uncertain. "Rubbish! There's no such thing as bog women. Come on!" He threw his bike in the grass.

Hesitantly, Lukas did the same. He could smell the water from the bog. The wind swirled some withered leaves in a martial arts dance around his feet. A gasp was drowned out by the rustling of the leaves, but Mikkel heard it anyway. He smiled, all adult-like. "Stop it; nothing is going to happen. It's just a bog!" He was already in between the trees.

"But the Bog Woman is real, Mikkel. When she's brewing something, that's when there's white fog down by the trees," murmured Lukas. But he followed his big brother anyway, as he kept a vigilant eye on whether the Bog Woman was behind the next tree. His heart pounded in his chest, and his shortness of breath wasn't only due to the fast bike ride. He approached Mikkel, who was standing by the water's edge, looking down into the murky, brown liquid full of green duck food.

"Come on. It's not dangerous. Look, there's a fish! Maybe it's a big pike!"

Lukas had just started in reception class, and the teacher had told them something about a pike. It could get very big and very old, she had said. Curiosity overtook anxiety. He ventured up beside Mikkel, but his eyes shone with fear. There were no fish.

"It's gone again. Maybe it was the Bog Woman?" teased Mikkel as he started to laugh.

Lukas could suddenly see the joke and laughed along. The bog wasn't as scary as he'd imagined after all. He'd only been here once before, with Daddy, but that was years ago—when he'd been a baby.

The birds were singing in the treetops, and occasionally they heard small plops in the water from fish or frogs leaping. Lukas began to relax and grew brave enough to walk around on his own. There was a lot to look at by the water's edge, and it didn't look like the kind of place where a bog woman would live. She'd drown in the dark liquid. His logic had almost convinced him when he spotted something at the water's edge. It seemed like a foot. Was it her—the Bog Woman?

"Mikkel . . . ! Mikkel . . . !" he called cautiously. "I found the Bog Woman."

"Stop, Lukas!"

Mikkel approached cautiously, as if in doubt. He'd also spotted what could be a brown foot sticking halfway out of the water under the branches of a bush that had only a few leaves left. Most of them were in the water, and some were the same colour as the foot—or whatever it was. An animal? A dead fish? He pulled himself together. He was, after all, the oldest and wisest. "It's not the Bog Woman. It's—something else." He found a stone and threw it into the bush. It hit something. He found another one and took aim again. Suddenly, the foot seemed to move in the water. They stepped back, startled.

The stone had punctured the brown leathery surface, and something yellowish had appeared. The blow had turned the object so it protruded more above the water, and now they could both see what it was. It *was* a human foot.

Mikkel threw the stone as if it were burning his hand, and quickly pulled his brother out of the shade of the trees and into the sun.

"Come on!" His voice shook.

"What is it, Mikkel? Is it the Bog Woman?" Lukas began to cry.

"Don't say anything to Mum and Dad about this," threatened Mikkel as they fled from the bog trees on their bikes at very high speed.

Lukas cried even louder.

2

The autopsy room at the Institute of Forensic Medicine was not his favourite place. The sight of the little girl found strangled in a dumpster a few years earlier had given him sleepless nights for a long time afterwards. She'd lain like a white doll on the sterile steel table. Some images never disappeared from his mind. They played repeatedly, like a horror film you couldn't turn off or turn your head away from.

The Institute of Forensic Medicine had moved to new, larger, and better premises at Skejby University Hospital the previous autumn. The move was viewed with both sadness and joy. Forensic pathologist Henry Leander had spent much of his thirty-one-year working life at the old Municipal Hospital, which was now called Aarhus Hospital, but he often complained about having to share the space with their pathologists. He was standing bent over the table, engrossed in his work, when Roland Benito came in. He straightened up and sent his old friend his usual magnificent smile, which pulled his white handlebar moustache up towards his ears.

"Welcome, Inspector," he said cheerfully, concentrating again on his work.

Roland was late. He'd just returned from a well-deserved summer holiday in his home country and hadn't yet shaken off the southern Italian spirit. He quickly greeted the other obligatory autopsy attendees gathered in a small cluster at an appropriate distance from the steel table. Only Steen

Dahl, a photographer from the Forensics Department ventured closer with his camera. His eyes shone with disgust over his face mask.

The body immediately put Roland in mind of a bog find, which, of course, it was. He pulled a handkerchief out of his pocket and held it to his nose until Leander handed him a mask. The air filtration system, which was a vast improvement on the one at the old institute, couldn't combat the sweet smell of death that he associated with stinking rubbish on the streets of Naples. But despite everything, the smell in the autopsy room wasn't as bad as it could have been, because almost only skin and bones remained of the body. The decomposing gases had long since evaporated— they were what stank unbearably.

"Are we any closer to identifying the body, the cause of death, or the time of death? Have we got ourselves a new Grauballe Man?" he asked.

They'd gathered early in the morning at the find site at the bog and, together with forensic scientists and digging equipment, had got the brown corpse out of the water and laid it on a stretcher, so Leander could carry out a post-mortem examination and record his observations on a Dictaphone.

Leander shook his head without looking at Roland. "I don't think we're going that far back in time. It doesn't look like a sacrifice to the gods. The cause of death appears to be a hard blow to the back of the head. Perhaps several." Gently, he turned the brown skull that had remnants of scalp and hair, the original colour of which could only be guessed at, so the back of the head faced Roland and the others present. He pointed to a hole in the cranium with a white-gloved hand. "It appears to be a hard, heavy object that ruptured the back of the head with violent force. I'd say in the weight of about one to three kilos."

He moved a little to the side so Roland could move closer.

"Murder?"

"That would be my guess."

Roland bent down and took a closer look at the hole in the skull. He straightened up and studied the rest of the hollow body. The brown leather skin was sunken around the bones, which manifested as yellowy protrusions in some places. It was hard to recognise the colour of the sparse cloth- ing that was left. It had been rinsed away or dissolved in the bog water. The face consisted only of empty eye sockets, a triangular hole where the nose had sat, and a series of yellowish teeth with very long tooth necks that were exposed in the jaw. He got the impression that the skull was laughing and instead looked at the forensic pathologist.

"A woman?"

Leander nodded and gently turned the corpse's head back, touching it only with his fingertips, as if not to wake the dead. He had a very special relationship with them. When he was alone, he spoke to them as if they were still alive, lamented their fate and comforted them by telling them the perpetrator would be found when the body had given him the information it always hid.

"The pelvis suggests a woman. A woman who has given birth. I judge her to be around thirty years old. I've sent some teeth to the odontologist for confirmation. The teeth can help with the identification, too. We may forget about fingerprints."

Everyone looked at the victim's fingers, where only the bones were left at the fingertips.

"She has nothing on her that can tell us who she is, and she's been lying in the swamp for a long time," Leander continued impassively.

"How long?"

Leander looked at Roland over the edge of his glasses. "Twenty years at least."

He stood for a moment staring at the corpse without taking it in, as the words penetrated. "So, you're saying we're dealing with a murder committed all the way back in the eighties?" He looked into Leander's blue-grey eyes.

"Looks like it. There must be a cold case with a missing woman. You'll get a more accurate year when I get the results of the analyses."

"Why did the body not come to the surface before—and why right now? Our bogs are teeming with ornithologists, so why has no one discovered her?" Kurt Olsen finally got his voice back. He had been appointed chief superintendent of the new police district and had seen a bit of everything.

"The decomposition gases do cause a corpse in water to rise to the surface, but it falls to the bottom again as soon as the gases evaporate. That happened a long time ago. Why she surfaced now is hard to say. Maybe because of the warm autumn or something completely different and unknown," Leander answered.

"The body should have completely decomposed after so many years, right?" Olsen scratched his neck, which had red spots that always appeared when he was under pressure.

"She's well preserved after all those years in the bog. That's because bog bodies aren't exposed to bacteria due to the acid that the plants produce. Throwing a body into the water before the bacteria have spread—for example, if it's been refrigerated—gives the best possibilities for preservation."

"So you mean, she might have been thrown—frozen—into the bog?" Roland ran a hand through his dark hair, which had faded slightly in the strong southern Italian sun, and he looked at Leander again.

He nodded. "Maybe she was kept somewhere cold before she was thrown into the bog. The intestines are well preserved, which indicates that they didn't have time to decay before the acid in the bog was able to take effect. The acidic, oxygen-poor water and perhaps low temperature also played roles. The water may have been very cold—maybe a winter's day—there are several possibilities."

The familiar lurch in his stomach and the bitter taste in his mouth surfaced, and Roland knew he would soon have to get out of here. Several years on the job, however, had hardened him a little more than when he saw his first corpse at an autopsy as a young cadet. He'd tried to pull himself together, but eventually, he'd sacrificed his lunch on the floor as well as the forensic pathologist's shoes in front of all the other police cadets, who'd been green around the gills, too, and had made strained swallowing movements.

"Two boys found the body in the bog, I understand," Olsen said, interrupting Roland's memories.

"Three days ago, yes. It is, of course, strictly forbidden to go down to the bog, so they'd kept their visit secret. But the youngest was terrified and dreamed that the Bog Woman came and took him, so in the end, he broke down and told his mother about their horrific find."

Olsen shook his head. "Poor boys. But such is life. What's forbidden is always the most exciting."

"But could excitement also have enticed our victim? Or what was she doing in the bog?" Roland sighed.

Leander occupied himself with his work again. He was digging something out of the fracture in the skull with a pair of long tweezers. Despite new technology, tweezers, scissors, and a scalpel were still the forensic pathologist's most important tools. "I hope we get an ID soon," he mumbled absently as he slowly pulled an item out and held the tweezers up against the bright, cold light. Everyone moved a little closer and narrowed their eyes over their face masks to get a better view.

"What is it?" asked the institute officer impatiently; he'd given up guessing, like the others.

Roland leaned in over Leander's shoulder and got closer. "Is that wood?"

"A pointed, polished piece of wood. Very hard wood. It was well protected inside the skull. Maybe a piece of the murder weapon," Leander replied. Steen Dahl's camera flash dazzled them for a brief second. Henry Leander put the piece of wood into a small bag and handed it to Gert Schmidt, the head of Forensics, who was unusually silent, but now thanked him and promised, in his loud voice, to take care of the matter as soon as possible.

Roland looked for the packet of cigarettes in his pocket as soon as he was outside the morgue. For over a year, since the ban, smoking had not been permitted at the police station. He still hadn't got used to it when, like now, he needed a cigarette more than ever. But his hand found only a packet of nicotine gum.

3

The recently hired intern, Nicolaj, sat clicking a ballpoint pen; Britt was blowing bubbles with her chewing gum and letting them explode with a provocative pop, while her transistor radio was playing louder than usual. Mads Dam's chair was empty. He was out somewhere—where, no one knew. Most likely he was sitting in a pub without a smoking ban in the city centre. Overall, the editorial staff was marked by the absence of editor Ivan Thygesen, who was on sick leave, and "when the cat's away . . ."

Despite Anne feeling more at ease by not having Thygesen's darting eyes in his ruddy face watching her from the other side of the glass pane that divided the editorial floor from his small office, all the ambient office sounds grated on her nervous system and stalled her concentration. She'd called her contact at the police station several times to hear news of the bog body, but no one wanted to tell her anything, so she was waiting for the press conference. Her irritation grew and grew. This time, she hadn't got the scoop on the find in the bog before all the other journalists. Her informant, who had illegal equipment for eavesdropping on police radios, had been arrested in the spring and locked up for possession of hash. Fortunately, he hadn't mentioned anything about her or their collaboration. She didn't have anything to do with hash anymore. All ties to the clique in Nørrebro were broken. She hadn't spoken to any of them during the two years she'd lived in Aarhus. Didn't care at all about their actions anymore—which mostly resembled petty vandalism. But she hadn't given up everything; the Nørrebro accent clearly cut through when she snarled for some peace and quiet and got up to get coffee. Britt popped another bubble of gum and looked indignantly at her.

"Well, here we seem to have the female version of Ivan the Terrible," she said dryly. The intern laughed. He was playing with some images in Photoshop, which he claimed to be an expert at using. Anne fleetingly remarked he hadn't come much further in retouching the bad photos from one of AGF's matches, which Mads Dam—the sports editor—was in the process of writing up when not sitting in a pub. But when you also had to stare dreamily out the window and click a ballpoint pen, it was a bit of a challenge to get it all done. Had it been the news photographer, Kamilla, dealing with the image, it would have been retouched long ago. Kamilla had been employed by the paper at the beginning of the year after working as a freelance photographer for years. But she had today off. Something about her mother being in the hospital. As if Kamilla hadn't suffered enough.

"Have you come to a standstill in your boggy case?" Britt asked, showing a little more team spirit as she sat down again at her computer with a plastic mug of lukewarm coffee. She turned down the music a bit, and Anne gloated to herself at having managed to command a little respect from the staff. They'd been on the receiving end of her fiery temper several times. Or maybe it was because of her past, which everyone now knew. Maybe it was more fear than respect.

"How cool is a bog body. My uncle is crazy about birds and is a member of the Danish Ornithological Society—he's an observer. He counts them— the birds! He's probably often lurked by the water's edge in that bog with his binoculars with no idea that there was a rotten old corpse just below him," said Nicolaj, laughing, before Anne could answer. She looked at him angrily. He was kind of cute with cheeky green eyes, curly red hair, and freckles on skin that was as fair as her own. Yet there was something about him that irritated her. Maybe it was the fact that she'd been appointed his internship supervisor because crime was Nicolaj's greatest interest, and so he would be shadowing her for his six months at the *Daily News*. She was the one who had to coach and guide him and give him an overview of his strengths and weaknesses. If he had plans of writing about crime, he'd soon be alleviated of what was "cool" about a rotten corpse.

"Yeah, it's a little hard to move on when no one wants to disclose anything." She took a sip of the coffee and ignored Nicolaj. "The only thing I know is that it seems to be a murder that was committed years ago. If I knew how many years ago, I could start searching for old missing person cases from that year, but how far do I have to go back?"

Britt stretched so her ample bosom almost spilled over the edge of the overly low-cut blouse. Nicolaj's eyes gave it a brief glance, which he quickly and blushingly retracted. Anne smiled behind the computer screen. It was quite a new thing for Thygesen to finally hire employees of the opposite sex. When she'd started at the paper, all the journalists had been women and pure babes—like Britt—but when Bertha had finished college, she got a job at *Ekstra Bladet* and had moved to Copenhagen. Tove had gone on maternity leave and never returned to the precarious newspaper industry. No new student had been hired, and Mads Dam had been hired to replace Tove, as there was a lack of someone with a flair for sports. How Thygesen thought to hire *him* out of all the qualified people who'd applied for the job, she'd never understood; apparently, they were old friends. Or perhaps he was the only one who would accept the salary. The industry was squeezed. Newspaper wars had raged without a clear victor, and more wars would undoubtedly come. Newspaper groups merged and pushed the small ones out to capture the entire market for themselves—including the local fodder. Ivan Thygesen had prepared them several times for the fact that the paper might have to close, but the *Daily News* had held on even better with the help of the various ad revenues from loyal advertisers. The ads almost overshadowed the journalistic material and were sometimes even used as front pages in times where news was slow.

"Maybe this bog body person wasn't missed and was never wanted," Britt suggested when she had finished stretching, and knocked a cigarette out of its packet, even though the staff usually followed the smoking ban at the paper. She waved her arms with the cigarette hanging between her lips as Anne looked reproachfully at her. "To hell with it, Health and Safety isn't coming here," she defended herself, flicking a disposable lighter with the Opel logo.

Anne shook her head. "Hmm, is it someone who wasn't missed?" she said. "I'm sure there's a missing person report in one of those old cases that just needs to be dug up." The chime of the phone on Thygesen's desk interrupted her. They all looked at each other.

"Just let it ring," Britt said, resuming work on the keyboard.

"We can't do that. Maybe it's about the press conference at the police station. They don't know that Thygesen is on sick leave, do they?" Anne got up, shaking her head disapprovingly again.

The stench of cigars and stale old pub lingered in Thygesen's office. She didn't believe he could leave the cigars alone when he sat here on his own late at night. The sun shone in through the window, which needed a good wiping, highlighting the dust in the frame. The cleaning staff had also been cut, so the editorial staff had to keep the office clean themselves. She knocked over a jar of chewed pencils and promotional pens as she leaned over the desk and picked up the phone. If they'd upgraded the system after the lightning strike last summer, she could have picked it up on her own phone at the touch of a button.

"Editor Thygesen's phone," she said as she picked up the jar, collected the pencils, and placed them in it again. The tower of City Hall could just be glimpsed on the horizon through the dirty window. She heard only gentle breathing coming through the receiver.

"Hello, who am I talking to?" she said, tempted to hang up.

"Who am *I* talking to? I will only speak to the person in charge at the *Daily News*!" The voice sounded as if the speaker were holding his nose or had asthma. She smelled something important.

"Unfortunately, the editor-in-chief is ill. Is there anything I can help you with? I'm a journalist. Anne Larsen."

Long silence.

"You who wrote about the murder of the girl? The one they found in the dumpster?"

Now she hesitated.

"Yes, that was me."

"Good, I can use you, too. I think I know something about the body in the bog," the voice continued. "If my suspicions are true, there will be more murders."

4

Roland had just hung up after talking to Gert Schmidt from Forensics when Detective Sergeant Mikkel Jensen entered his office. "Was that Gert?" he asked, as if he'd been listening at the door.

Roland nodded. "It was a tip on the murder weapon." He accepted the Coca-Cola that Mikkel had brought to him from the canteen. They had a mutual agreement in the department to buy something for each other if they went out or to the canteen. He tossed his chewing gum in the bin and took a sip of the Coke that tasted weird on top of the liquorice-flavoured Nicotinell.

Mikkel noisily pulled a chair in front of the desk and sat down. He ripped open a bag of marshmallows with his teeth. The three o'clock slump. Roland looked at him as he stuffed the first pink foam-like sweet into his mouth. Everyone had their vice. His own were Italian red wine and cigarettes. Mikkel's was marshmallows, though it didn't quite tie in with his masculine exterior—his almost clean-shaven head, young face, and powerful jawbone. Salty liquorice or strong Piratos were more a match for that. He wondered when a ban on consuming sugar in public places would come in because, it too, was unhealthy.

"Black ebony," he said.

"Wha'?" Mikkel couldn't hide his true Aarhusian ancestry.

"The murder weapon. Gert Schmidt says it's ebony. African ebony," he explained patiently.

"Are we looking for someone from Africa?" Mikkel asked with a naïve expression as he chewed.

"Who knows? The ebony is of very fine quality and beautifully worked. A souvenir, perhaps. But it could be from anywhere."

"African souvenirs can also be bought here. Online, for example," said Mikkel.

Roland had been on a couple of computer courses, but using the computer for something other than what he was supposed to do at work didn't occur to him at all. It was different for young people; they used the computer and the internet for pretty much everything. Even his granddaughter, Marianna, who had just turned seven, could operate the keyboard and mouse better than he could.

"I hardly think a murderer would intentionally go online and buy a souvenir carved from ebony to use as a murder weapon. It's more likely it was at the scene and was the quickest and easiest thing to get hold of."

"Yeah, well, I actually came for the missing persons reports," said Mikkel, as if they shouldn't be wasting time chatting about insignificant things like souvenirs.

"We don't have any missing persons from that time who weren't found—in Aarhus, that is. But I searched the entire country and I got something." Mikkel looked at him with his bright eyebrows raised to demonstrate the importance of the result.

"Yes?" Roland shook a new piece of chewing gum out of the box.

"A woman from Silkeborg was reported missing in 1983. She was never found. It could be her."

"Does the age match?"

"Yep. Thirty-two and a nursing assistant."

Roland nodded absently. A woman from Silkeborg. But why would she end up in a bog in Mundelstrup? He picked up the phone and called the Institute of Forensic Medicine to find out whether there were any results from the odontologist, but there was nothing yet. Annoyed, he hung up.

Mikkel got up and threw the empty sweet bag in Roland's bin. "When's the press conference? The journalists are swarming."

A deeper wrinkle formed on Roland's forehead. Journalists. Vultures, as he called them. They hovered over them like black shadows, lurking for news that would raise the sales figures of their needy newspapers. The body found in the bog was certainly an event they'd longed for, and the battle over who would be first to break the macabre news had set in. Involuntarily, he thought of the reporter at the *Daily News* whom he'd gone head-to-head with during the investigation of the Gitte murder a few years ago. Reluctantly, he had to admit that they'd had a useful collaboration and that she'd helped them a lot with the investigation, along with the bright photographer whose name he no longer remembered. But the journalist's name was Anne Larsen. He remembered that and briefly wondered whether she was still working for the *Daily News*. If she was, it probably wouldn't be long before he'd send her scurrying.

"We need to be surer of the ID before we go to the press," Roland said.

"But they just make stuff up, and that, we know, can be much worse," Mikkel advised.

Roland nodded and looked towards the door as it was pushed open and hit the chair Mikkel was sitting in. There wasn't exactly a whole lot of space in his office. Chief Superintendent Kurt Olsen stood in the doorway. Hair cut, freshly shaved, and in a clean shirt. He looked much more turned out than usual. There were rumours he and his wife were back together again, but what had changed the man the most—the shave or the wife—wasn't easy to say.

"We've called a press conference for late afternoon—we have to," he said briefly, as if he, too, had been listening at the door.

"Shouldn't we confirm whether it really is the missing woman from Silkeborg first," suggested Roland. "Pathology and Forensics should notify us soon."

A young woman apologised and squeezed past Kurt Olsen in the doorway. The office began to feel crowded.

Isabella Munch was one of the newly employed young women in the police force. She'd just been transferred to CID. Only now had Roland realised how much officers of the opposite sex had been missed in his department. Female intuition had been in short supply. He often used Irene's, but there were limits to how much he could tell his wife about criminal cases. In some cases, it wasn't appropriate and broke his duty of confidentiality, but Irene was better suited for the purpose than most other police wives by virtue of her profession as a social worker and former police secretary. Now female intuition was always on hand, and he could make use of it whenever he wanted. And as a plus, Roland took a little pleasure in watching the masculine Mikkel blush as the fair-haired officer with the ponytail looked up at him and smiled as she walked closely by to hand Roland a piece of paper.

"I've examined the case from back then more closely. Central and West Jutland Police were very cooperative. The search was called off in 1984 after four months of no significant leads. She has a son, Sebastian Juhl. He lives on Klostergade and works as a mechanic at a garage in Hasselager. I found the addresses; they're there," she continued and disappeared as fast as she had appeared.

He asked Kurt Olsen to delay the press conference, took his coat from the back of the chair, and waved to Mikkel to come with him.

"We're going to Klostergade," he announced tersely.

Reluctantly, Mikkel followed. "But the son can't say whether it's his mother who's been found in the bog. It's impossible for him to identify her, anyway," he mumbled on the way down in the lift.

"ID'ing her seems to be dragging out, so we have to follow the leads we can. Maybe the son can tell us something."

5

She was stopped in the hallway.

"Annemette Knudsen?"

"Yes."

"She's just in the shower, but she won't be long. You can get a cup of coffee over there while you're waiting." The woman nodded at a collection of differently coloured insulated coffee pots and mugs standing on a small table in the middle of a sofa arrangement.

Annemette nodded and sat down on a light grey sofa with brown coffee stains and waited. She watched the woman, who quickly disappeared into the hallway. She hadn't seen her before, so she must be new. But Annemette already knew all about the coffee pots. She came here as often as she could. But she should have called first. That's what she usually did.

The sun shone in through a tall window, casting dazzling light over the polished floor and the white walls. She looked at the abstract paintings. Not because she hadn't seen them before, but because she didn't know what else to do. Smoking wasn't allowed. She'd read the newspaper on the table this morning and had had her fill of coffee, too. Nora was ill again, so she was dealing with the payroll on her own. But she was grateful. Grateful that she had got the job despite her age. When the money had run out, it had been hard to afford everything. She hadn't been prepared for it. But it had to happen one day—given the way she'd lived. She had never allowed herself to go without.

The woman walked past again with a stack of towels in her arms and announced that now she was ready. Annemette got up. Why hadn't she just gone in? Why hadn't she just gone to her in the bathroom? She could easily have done that, even if the new employee had asked her to wait. She wondered about her unfamiliar passivity as she walked past closed doors down the long hallway. The door to her room stood open. The closer she got, the more her heart pounded. Annemette felt it could be heard as she reached the door and stood looking at her without entering. The young woman hadn't yet spotted her guest. Her long hair was wet and jet-black. Her eyes were black, too. They were facing the window and expressionlessly fixed on something out on the horizon. The sunlight made her olive skin appear pale. Her father was Spanish. A mistake from a summer holiday twenty years earlier.

"Hey, Kit." She entered cautiously and sat down on the opposite side of the table. "Happy Birthday."

"Hi. I didn't know if you'd come."

"Of course I'd come for your birthday! We have to celebrate it."

"It's *been* celebrated—with muffins and hot chocolate. That's why I had to have a shower. I spilled the hot chocolate." Kit tried to smile, but there were tears in her eyes.

Annemette stroked her cheek. "Don't worry about that. It was just hot chocolate."

"I burned myself actually!"

She pulled her hand away sharply and stuck it into a Salling carrier bag instead. "I have a present for you." She laid it on the table and waited anxiously while Kit gently unwrapped it with a small shy smile.

"What have you brought now? You didn't need to do that. Can you afford it?"

It took a long time to unwrap. Annemette waited calmly, but under the table, her foot tapped impatiently. God, she wanted a cigarette. Before the paper was completely unwrapped, she held the jumper up in front of Kit. The smile slowly died in her dark eyes, too.

"Don't you like it? Can you see what the sequins are?"

"Yeah. Butterflies. It's nice. Really. But when am I supposed to wear it? When would I need to look *so* nice?"

"Nonsense. You can wear it often. It's not so nice that you couldn't wear it every day."

Kit gently touched the sequins. There was the expression in her eyes that Annemette had never cared for. It was one of those days. One of those days she had a hard time dealing with.

"Why didn't you just let me die back then?"

"No, now stop it!"

"I know you were offered the choice. Why didn't you just say they should take it?"

Annemette gathered the noisy wrapping paper and stuffed it into the empty plastic bag. "Who says such nonsense? Where do you get those thoughts from?"

"Grandma told me. She said you had to make the decision. That was when she actually wanted to come and visit me."

"Grandma is sick. She walks very badly now—that's the only reason she doesn't come to visit. You know that very well."

"Then why didn't you get her and bring her with you?"

Annemette let the question hang.

"And I made the right decision back then, didn't I?" Otherwise, you wouldn't be celebrating a birthday today, would you?"

"And that would have been better. Anything would have been better than this!"

"You mustn't say that, honey."

Her pulse increased and her stomach cramped. She shouldn't have skipped lunch.

"Do they not bring coffee and cake on these occasions?" She tried to hide the irritation in her voice.

"They're having a party for me tonight. Are you coming?" Kit looked at her pleadingly.

"You know well I can't." She took hold of both of her hands, which were lying limply on the table. "I have to work."

Kit tore her hand away and looked angrily at Annemette until she let go of the other one. "You should have let me die, then you wouldn't have had to work so much. Then the job in the office would have been enough. Then you could have come."

"Yes, but then you wouldn't be here, and there'd be no party." She smiled and tried to sound teasing. Sometimes that was what was needed. "And it means you're going to need your nice new jumper tonight. You'll have fun with all your friends."

"Friends! Are you calling them friends? Well, where are my friends now? Tell me!"

"Honey, you can understand that they . . ." She stopped when it dawned on her that the sentence would be catastrophically misunderstood. She got up and started putting on her coat with Kit's eyes on all her movements. It hurt inside, and she was ashamed to be looking forward to standing outside in the sunshine again and breathing the clean air. Out in another world. Her world.

"Will you ring me tomorrow to hear how the party went?" There was a movement around Kit's lips, which had been given a layer of shiny lip gloss for the occasion.

Annemette took it as a smile and breathed a sigh of relief. "Of course. Have fun tonight and be happy that you've turned twenty. It's the best age of your life." Maybe that last sentence was misplaced—outright painful—but it was said now.

"Yes, it's the age to have fun and live life." The smile was there this time, but it was ironic and bitter. "Can I wave to you?"

"Of course you can. I have to go now."

She walked around behind Kit and pushed the wheelchair to the window.

When she looked up at the window from the car park and waved back, she thought Kit wasn't the biggest mistake she had ever made.

6

No one opened the door on Klostergade, so they assumed Sebastian Juhl was still at work.

The car repair shop was well hidden by the road into a yard. If the sign OLE HANSSON'S GARAGE hadn't been so prominently displayed outside the gate, they never would have found it. And notably, it was painted with strong red, yellow, and blue colours—not exactly tasteful—as Mikkel Jensen expressed with a grimace when he spotted it. "Apparently, it's here," he commented dryly, driving in over the pavement and parking.

The garage was a low-rise building that looked more like a chicken coop than a car repair shop, except for the dilapidated cars parked behind it, although they could easily have housed chickens. But the man who immediately came out into the sunlight was undoubtedly a mechanic and not a poultry breeder. He was absolutely filthy, and he was drying the oil off his fingers with a coloured rag while observing them with narrow eyes from his fat unshaven face, topped with hair that was combed forward to hide a budding bald spot.

"Criminal Investigation Department," Roland said, showing him his badge. "We would like to speak with Sebastian Juhl."

"Ole Hansson," the mechanic introduced himself, so they knew at once it was the owner himself they were talking to. "Sebastian is off today," he continued without showing any particular curiosity about what the police would want to talk to one of his employees about.

"Does anyone know where he is? There was no one at his residence," Roland said.

"How should I know. I don't know what my mechanics do in their spare time."

Ole Hansson continued wiping his fingers on the rag while chewing gum. Probably for giving up smoking was Roland's first thought, until he spotted the glow from a cigarette inside the dark workshop. Smoking was banned at the station, but apparently not here among the petrol and oil fumes.

"May we look around a bit?" he asked, displaying more politeness than Jensen, who was already on his way into the workshop.

"What's it about?" Hansson finally asked.

"How long has Sebastian worked here?"

"Six years, I think it must be now. He was an apprentice here. As soon as he graduated, he was offered a job. Sebastian's a skilled mechanic." Ole Hansson looked at Roland sceptically as he followed them into the garage, which was lit only by the work lamps. There were no windows, and there was the stench of petrol. Everything seemed dirty. Car tyres were stacked in the corner, and there were used car engines everywhere. On one wall hung an oil-stained picture of a sexy pin-up from *Rapportpigen*. Two mechanics in the garage were engrossed in their work. One was working in the garage pit under a relatively new Fiat, the other one was working on the undercarriage of a rusty white van suspended in a lift. The latter had a lit cigarette dangling between his plump lips under a black moustache. He quickly threw it on the floor and stepped out of the glow when he spotted the two strangers in nice clothes. They could be from Health and Safety. He resumed his work and no longer looked at them.

"Do either of you know if Sebastian had any plans today?" shouted Ole Hansson. Something negative was mumbled from the pit, and the guy at the lift shrugged and shook his head.

"Can we talk for a moment?" Roland nodded towards an enclosed room with dirty glass panes facing the garage, which he assumed was the office. He glimpsed a coffee machine and a newer flat-screen TV.

Ole Hansson nodded and opened the door to the office. It stank of petrol here, too. Roland felt a headache coming on. Mikkel stayed out in the garage, observing the work on the undercarriage. He tinkered with old cars in his spare time, so that was probably what they were talking about, the inspector guessed.

"Do you know anything about Sebastian's family?" asked Roland, politely declining the coffee offered to him. He could tell by the smell it had been boiling for a long time. Ole Hansson poured his into a large oil-stained mug and took a sip.

"Not much. It's not something he's ever talked about. But why all these questions? Is Sebastian involved in something?"

"Not as far as we know. It's about his mother."

Ole Hansson shook his head and gave a supercilious smile. "As far as I know, his mother disappeared when he wasn't that old. Poor boy. Do you have the right Sebastian?"

Roland nodded slowly. He was more confident now than when they'd arrived. "What else has he said about his parents? For example, do you know what his mother did?"

"No, no one asked him about his mother. Like I said, it's not something he ever talked about, and what good would it have done? She disappeared—didn't she?" Now the curiosity was evident in the man's fat face, and Roland was about to say something when the phone vibrated in his pocket.

As usual, Gert Schmidt shouted so loud that he had to go to a corner of the office for fear that Ole Hansson might overhear. "The victim has been identified. It's the nursing assistant from Silkeborg who disappeared in 1983. The odontologist confirmed it," Gert said.

Roland thanked him and quickly hung up. "I think we have to move on. Thank you for your help." He left the office and called Mikkel over. The sun dazzled them when they stepped out into the yard.

"The woman has been identified. It's her, so now we have to find the son. We have to give him the terrible message, and we have to be certain about how much he knows about his mother's disappearance."

DS Jensen nodded and followed him reluctantly to the car. The work in the garage apparently interested him more.

There was still no response when they rang the doorbell of the apartment on Klostergade again.

"Damn it! Olsen is insisting on a press conference this afternoon! We *need* to talk to the son before then." He knocked hard on the door—maybe the doorbell for these old apartments wasn't working. A young girl on her way up the stairs looked down at them from the floor above and asked if they were there to visit Sebastian. She told them he was on his way. She'd just met him on the pavement as he'd been helping one of the elderly residents out of a taxi. Roland mumbled an incomprehensible thank-you and looked impatiently at his watch. They waited politely in the stairwell, which smelled of old vinyl and brown soap. Then they heard voices from the ground floor and heavy, dragging steps. Shortly afterwards, an old woman appeared on the staircase with a young man holding her arm, supporting her up the uneven stairwell. He helped the old woman up the steps to the next floor and only let go of her arm when her crooked fingers had a firm grasp of the banisters. She thanked her neighbour and continued her shuffle up the stairs towards the next floor, where the young girl stood waiting for her. Roland and Mikkel looked knowingly at each other. They had more experience of young people's disrespect, of assaults on the elderly in their own homes, and cases of pensioners being raped and, occasionally, brutal robbery-murders.

"Would you like to talk to me?" Sebastian asked with a carefree smile as he stuck the key in the lock of his apartment. Roland's stomach shrank at the thought that he was about to ruin this young gentleman's day. They accompanied him into a cosy apartment, which, according to the door sign, was a bachelor pad, but still neat and tidy. The bed in the bedroom was made, and coloured pillows adorned the bedspread. The counter in the small, cramped kitchen was clean and wiped down. There was no build-up of washing-up, just a single used coffee cup. The living room was tidy, too, without looking uninhabited. A bowl of fresh fruit stood on the middle of a round dining table, indicating a healthy diet.

"Is it about the car I have for sale? I thought you were coming tomorrow," Sebastian said cheerfully, hanging his keys in a small, brushed steel cabinet.

"Unfortunately, no." Roland showed his badge and saw that a nerve was beginning to twitch almost imperceptibly in Sebastian's eyelid. He sat down and gestured that they could do the same. He was in his mid-thirties. The tanned skin made the light hair appear even lighter and the blue eyes deeper. They reminded Roland of a sled dog's eyes. He had seen them in a documentary about Finland. Siberian Husky, apparently. The chin and cheeks were covered in light stubble, without looking untidy. Roland had shaved that morning, but still had dark stubble that didn't look neat.

Sebastian took a red apple from the fruit bowl and began tossing it from hand to hand in small quick movements while he looked at the detectives intently. "It's been a long time since I've had a visit from the police," he said.

Roland took that as a good sign.

"It's about your mother."

Sebastian abruptly stopped throwing the apple and for a moment looked genuinely surprised. "Mother?" The word was vague and almost incomprehensible, as if it were a word he hadn't uttered for a long time.

Roland felt sorry for the lad. The unhappy expression that suddenly appeared in his eyes couldn't be forced whenever it suited.

"I know you weren't very old when your mother disappeared. But do you remember anything from that day?" His question made Sebastian look directly at him.

"I was only eight years old. I was in school."

The eye contact was so intense that Roland felt uncomfortable. It was as though Sebastian was looking deep into his soul, and it wasn't something he cared for. It was rare for him to be the first to break eye contact.

"So you don't know what your mother was going to do that day at all. You lived in Silkeborg—was she going to Aarhus?"

Sebastian watched Mikkel, who was quietly walking around and looking at the apartment and who hadn't said a word. It suited Roland, as Mikkel's direct manner meant he didn't always say the right thing. But now he returned to the living room with a picture in his hand.

"Is that your mother?" Mikkel asked. The compassion in his voice forced Roland to look at him in wonder.

Sebastian nodded and looked away quickly. The woman in the picture was probably in her late twenties. Only a few years younger than when she was killed. There was no doubt who the son looked like. His eyes particularly.

"I was questioned at the time, but as I said before, I was in school, and she never told me what she was doing. She went on a lot of house calls— but what do I know?"

The word *mother* had again disappeared from the son's vocabulary. He referred to her in an almost hostile way. But it was only natural that the mother's disappearance felt like a betrayal to an eight-year-old boy. He still didn't know her fate.

Sebastian looked at the apple in his hand as if it were a crystal ball that could tell him why his mother had disappeared.

"They said she probably ran away with a man and didn't care about me." His voice was hoarse.

"Who said that, Sebastian?"

"Everyone. Even the police, after some time had passed, and they still hadn't found her." Sebastian's intense eyes hit him again; there was reproach in them now, too.

"Do you think that, too?" asked Mikkel, who had sat down on the edge of the table. Sebastian shook his head and didn't notice Mikkel nodding tellingly to his superior. It was time for them to reveal why they had come.

"I'm sorry to have to tell you we found your mother. She is dead."

Sebastian emitted a half-suffocated sob. He dropped the apple as he hid his face in his hands. It rolled under the table and stopped at Roland's shoes. He stared at it. This part of the job was the one he liked the least.

7

The bedroom was exactly as she remembered it. The window stood open, and the breeze made the white lace curtains flutter slightly. She could glimpse the spire of the cathedral as a veiled shadow through the thin curtain. A fly sat on the windowsill, brushing its wings. There'd also been a fly on the back of the pew in front of her in the church when the pastor had said those nice words about her grandmother as she lay in the white coffin with all the flowers. She hadn't dared to turn her head to look at it. It was already hard enough to hold back the tears.

The door to the adjoining living room was closed, but the soft voices penetrated anyway, sometimes even a loud laugh that seemed inappropriate and offensive to her. She clenched the handkerchief hard in her hands. It hadn't been used. There were no more tears left. Since receiving the news of her grandmother's death, she had cried every night. Unnoticed and silent, so Peter didn't hear. He would just think she still hadn't settled in and that that was what was wrong again.

She glanced over the familiar things in the bedroom. Everything evoked memories. Time had come to a standstill in the apartment. Nothing had changed since she'd spent all her holidays here as a child. Her hand ran absently across the bedspread that her grandmother had crocheted from white cotton yarn. She'd worked for a long time on that blanket. And there in the bed beside it—in Grandad's bed—she had slept safely next to her grandmother after long, exciting adventures that sent her into a dream world with good fairies and princesses. Grandad's photo was on the bedside table in a silver frame. He looked at her mildly, but she didn't remember him. He died when she was only two years old. But Gran had told her so much about him that he stood vividly in front of her in her mind's eye. Her glasses lay on the bedside table, too, as if she would come back and get them at any time. But the fact was, she would never need them again and would never come back. Her face smiled out from behind the glass in a frame on the wall by the window. Her old, wise eyes looked at her almost apologetically, as if she regretted that she, too, had now left her. She felt the lump in her throat again. Of course, Peter was right about Elina becoming an old lady who had experienced a lot in her long life. But that didn't make her miss her less. Although she hadn't seen much of her lately, after she had moved to Italy with Peter, the knowledge that she was at home in Denmark, and that she could call and talk to her about anything whenever she wanted, had given her a sense of security—a safety net—that had now disappeared. It was as if a bond had been broken. A bond that meant something. A bond that had also connected her with her mother.

Her eyes stopped at another small picture on the bedside table. She took it and slid a finger down over the face behind the glass. She didn't remember her from anything other than this picture and the few others that existed. Now that she herself had grown up, she could well see the resemblance that everyone else talked about. The wavy dark hair surrounding a narrow face and the smiling brown eyes. The picture had been taken before her mother had fallen ill. Once the cancer took hold of her body, it had gone fast. She'd died that December. That year, they hadn't held Christmas together. As she sat looking at the picture, she thought she could remember it. Remember how something important disappeared out of her life and the loneliness she experienced for the first time. That nothing would be the same again. She replaced the photo on the bedside table when she heard the bedroom door open.

"There you are, Sabrina! Everyone's gone now. You didn't say goodbye." Her father sat down heavily next to her on the bed, so she fell against him as the mattress gave way under his weight. He put an arm around her shoulder and awkwardly rubbed her arm. His eyes lingered briefly on his mother-in-law's picture on the wall, but there was no love in them. Sabrina looked at his tormented face; his eyes were now focused on the floor. It looked as if he were counting every single loop in the old multicoloured rag rug.

"What happened between you and Gran?" she asked gently. "Why did you hate each other? Does it have anything to do with Mum?"

Gustav Hjort looked into his daughter's worried eyes. Seeing their striking resemblance to her mother's pained him. It had been months since he'd last seen Sabrina. He had almost forgotten those eyes and her mother, but now he felt his stomach clenching again and had to clear his throat a few times before answering. "We didn't hate each other, Sabrina. You have to believe that." He looked down at the rug again. Her brown eyes affected him too strongly. They had the same intense glow as Josefine's. They could look at him in the same reproachful way that hers had done. He sat uneasily on the bed, loosened his bloody tie, and didn't know how to explain. Why did she suddenly have to start asking about that after all these years?

"You know how mothers-in-law can be a nuisance sometimes! Elina was one of those." He tried to make light and laugh, but the laughter sounded hollow.

Sabrina's eyes grew even darker and shiny. "Gran wasn't like that. That I do know. How can you say such a thing about her, today of all days?"

She got up and smoothed her black skirt. It annoyed her that she'd fallen foul of him again so soon. During the entire flight from Milan, she had told herself that it wasn't to happen, but why couldn't he answer her? More than ever, she wanted to know what had divided the family. What had gone wrong? Was it just because Gustav married Carola far too soon after her mother's death? She stood with her arms crossed by the open window. The warm air smelled so different to what she'd been trying to get used to for the last six months in Milan.

Gustav walked behind her and gently laid his hands on her shoulders, a gesture he anticipated might be unwelcome. "It's great to have you home again, Sabrina. Even if the circumstances aren't . . ."

He quickly pulled his hands away as the door to the living room opened and a slender woman, skilfully made-up and clothed in black from head to toe, looked around until she caught sight of them by the window. The unnaturally white teeth lit up her tanned face. Confidently, she approached them in high heels.

"I didn't see you in the church at all, Sabrina. Nice to see you. Naturally, I was very sorry to hear about your grandmother," she said in her slightly hoarse voice, which men probably found sexy, as she took her husband's arm. She leaned into him affectionately and looked at Sabrina as if there were something she would like to change. But Sabrina was no longer affected by that look. She was used to it. Carola always found something she didn't like about her: her clothes, her hair, her colouring, her chubby figure. When she was a child, her stepmother had tried to dress her in uncomfortable little princess dresses and put bows in her hair to impose her idea of a beautiful child on the ugly daughter who accompanied her father, but it never took long for the bows to hang and the silk dresses to become dirty. Eventually, Carola gave up and instead developed an expression in her eyes every time she looked at Sabrina. Carola and Gustav hadn't had any children themselves. Why, she didn't know. They never spoke about that kind of thing. Their private life was a closed book to the outside world. Carola had a son from a previous marriage to an English naval officer, but he was three years older than Sabrina and had lived with his father in England, so she had only met him a few times when she wasn't that old. He himself had become something within the navy and sailed—as far as she knew—with a corvette in the Persian Gulf.

"It was a beautiful funeral," Carola said as the silence began to press. Gustav put his arm around her slender waist, and Sabrina had to reluctantly admit that they made a beautiful couple, even though they were both well on in years. She nodded and again felt the tears trying to take control, but she swallowed and held them back. Carola had never seen her cry.

"Won't you come and have dinner with us?" asked Gustav. "I'm excited to hear how you're doing in Italy."

"Have you settled in?" interrupted Carola. "You came home quickly, I understand from Peter."

It annoyed her that Peter had talked to Carola about such a private thing, that he talked to her at all, but she just nodded and pushed her hair behind her ears. "Yes, things are going better. I'll never learn the language, but I manage."

"You have to give it some time. For Peter's sake, I mean. Being a product engineer at Grundfos is his big chance." Carola smiled forcefully and glanced at Gustav. Sabrina realised that this was something they had discussed before. Yes, it was Peter's big chance. But what about her? She missed her job at Skovdal Hospice—she had taken a year's leave to follow her husband. Without knowing the language, her training as a clinical dietitian wasn't worth much in Italy, despite the many hospices in Milan. But now, fortunately, only six months remained, then they would return home to Denmark when Peter's posting, which was part of a long-term career plan, would be over. She could have chosen to stay at home, but Peter wanted her to come along, and a little break from everyday life with sick and dying people had been much needed at the time. But now she only wanted to return to Denmark and her job, and there had never been a question about her travelling home to attend Elina's funeral, even though Peter couldn't come.

"I'm sure Johanne has made something delicious for us. Won't you, Sabrina, so we can talk?" Gustav tried again and grabbed her arm as if he intended to pull her with him against her will, but she shook her head.

"Thanks, but no, Dad. I'm going to stay here a little longer. I promised Emma I'd help empty the apartment early tomorrow. I might sleep here tonight."

"You have to eat something." Gustav looked at her pleadingly. She wanted so badly to be with her father, but she wouldn't entertain Carola's criticism and reproaches. Not today. She kissed him on the cheek and inhaled the scent of his exclusive aftershave, no doubt chosen by Carola.

"Just go now, Dad. I'll order a pizza."

Carola grimaced but said nothing, clearly relieved, as she pulled away with her husband. He sent Sabrina a long look from the doorway before closing the door.

8

He laid his head back and enjoyed the rays of the afternoon sun on his face. It no longer had the intense heat of summer now in early October, but it was unbelievable that he could sit here in only a thick jumper. The other café patrons were also more or less dressed for summer. If this really was global warming, it suited him fine. Some of the girls were airing their bare legs, enabling him to look far up their tanned thighs. Aarhus River trickled in front of him, reflecting the light. The hum of voices was making him drowsy. Or was it the second draft beer? He closed his eyes but knew they were still there. He could hear their voices. Not what they were talking about, but that didn't matter as long as he knew they hadn't gone. The warmth of the sun on his face sent his thoughts back in time. His thoughts had begun to dwell on only one thing. His childhood.

The same sun had warmed his face that day. He had come home late from school. The front door had been open in the summer heat. He loved her voice. She was happy when she sang. She stood by the stove with her back to him, cooking. He didn't bother to disturb her. She was singing "What's Another Year"—the year's Eurovision winner. As she turned her profile towards him to reach for something in the fridge, he saw a cigarette hanging between her red lips as she sang. She only smoked when she knew no one was watching. Another good reason not to disturb her. She usually got angry when she was caught out. He sat down on the stairs with his eyes closed and listened to her singing as the sun's rays dried the sweat on his forehead and the blood under his nose. It would ruin her good mood that he'd been fighting at school again. There were holes in both trouser knees from when the big boys threw him down on the schoolyard's asphalt, his shirt was torn up under one sleeve, and he had got a nosebleed. It was always because of her that he ended up fighting, but she didn't know that. The boys from Year Nine had called her a whore and said she stripped in the nightclub where she worked at night, but he knew it was a lie. His mother would never do that. The school inspector had called him into his office with its brown furniture, reeking of cigar smoke, and threatened to tell his mother about all the fights, but she could never know. She mustn't be upset again. He had begged him not to say anything and promised he would never fight again. But he hadn't started it. It was the kids who had insulted his mother.

They had been alone for two years since his father had died in an accident at the construction site. He had been just five years old and couldn't remember the episode too well. Only that when he had been alive, everything was different. Mum was always at home looking after him and Dad. Sometimes he was allowed to stand on a chair and help her cook before Dad came home from work. Not dangerous things like cutting with a knife, but he could stir a pot with a spoon or tenderise meat with the meat hammer—that was the most fun. She'd always been happy back then. But when he died, she'd locked herself inside the bedroom, and a social worker had made sure he was placed with another family. He had missed her. But after a year, she was totally changed, and she brought him back to the little house where he had spent most of his safe childhood. She had worked as a waitress and could support them both. But she had also got a boyfriend who wasn't his dad. He hated him. They called him the African because he was always travelling to Africa. When he heard the noisy engine of the rusty red sports car, he might as well have shut himself in his room, because then his mum had no time for anyone else and became so embarrassing.

An unusual scent wafted from the kitchen to the stairs. They were going to have something special to eat today. Not the usual Wednesday dinner. Not fish and vegetables, but something more delicious. The hunger manifested itself as an empty hole in his stomach. But then he heard her open a bottle of wine and the sound of the glasses as she took them out of the cupboard. The hairs on his neck rose. The expectation died. It wasn't him she was cooking for. *He* was coming to dinner.

He jumped when he heard the hum of a car engine. He quickly opened his eyes. The sound that had pulled him back to reality came from a taxi collecting some drunk guests from the café. Then he realised their voices were gone. A waiter was removing the empty cups and wiping the table. He spotted them just before they disappeared around the corner by the Magasin department store towards the pedestrianised Immervad. He reached out for the waiter and grabbed his sleeve so hard he almost dropped the tray stacked with glasses and cups. He paid for his draft beers and quickly followed after them.

9

Emma was a lot younger than Sabrina's mother, her deceased sister. Sabrina had always loved her aunt's straightforward and unpredictable way of being. She smiled when Emma—even before they had sat down at a vacant table—had received and answered two text messages on a sleek silver-coloured mobile phone with such tiny keys that even she wouldn't be able to hit them. But Emma's small, thick thumbs moved quickly on them like a teenager's. "My granddaughter's texting me," she explained with a tired smile, continuing to type as she sat down. The red-rimmed eyes showed that she had cried a lot over the last few days.

Sabrina just nodded. She didn't know Emma's family very well; they didn't get together that much. She lived a little outside Ribe and was only staying in Aarhus until they'd finished cleaning Gran's apartment. She was booked into Hotel Cabinn next to Aarhus Theatre for as long as it would take. Her husband, Kaj, had stayed at home. They had a farm with piglets to see to.

"No, this is really taking too long," Emma exclaimed as soon as she had put her phone in her bag. "Where's that waiter gone?"

They both looked towards the café, where two waiters were jogging back and forth between the café's open door and the tables along the river. There were a lot of people. The sun was shining and warm, like a summer's day; most people had finished work and were enjoying a cup of coffee or a beer before going home. Only the staff of the various shops were looking enviously at the sun. It would be a few more hours before it was their turn. People crowded in and out of the Magasin's main entrance.

"They're busy, Emma. Have we time to wait?"

Emma got up impatiently. She was a petite, strong lady, but she knew how to dress, so it wasn't the first thing you noticed. The sun made her white bob glow like silver, and her little eyes were defiant. She put her bag under her arm and straightened up. "No, Sabrina. We have so much to do. If we have to wait hours for a cup of coffee, we won't get anything else done today." She disappeared into the hustle and bustle of the café with small quick steps and the bag clutched under her arm as if she feared someone were going to steal it from her here in the big city. Sabrina smiled again. She was also certainly going to have to wait inside, too.

She leaned back in the increasingly uncomfortable café chair, whose backrest bore into her spine, and watched the passers-by. Considering the season, people were lightly dressed. She enjoyed the smell from the café. One fragrant cup of espresso or cappuccino after another was carried past her. The atmosphere made her think of Italy and Peter. She missed him now that she was away from him. But wasn't that often the case—that you had to get away from someone to realise that you couldn't do without them? Did he feel the same way, or what was he doing all alone in Milan? They were supposed to be at a dinner with his colleagues from Grundfos. That was the first thing he'd complained about when she wanted to go home to Denmark for the funeral. A party was more important to him than a death in the family. Or rather, his career was more important. She watched a couple walk by, arms around each other's waists, and stared enviously at them. It was a long time since she and Peter had walked like that. She had gradually come to feel that it was a matter of course that she walked beside him when it was convenient for him. Otherwise, she could walk the streets of Milan on her own, looking at exclusive shop windows displaying fashion she would never be able to afford. Many times over the last few months she had downright regretted accompanying him. And now she was sitting here missing him after only two days. How could she live without him for a whole year? She put a hand on her stomach where the sun was warming it. And then there was that thing she hadn't told him. Peter had always insisted there would be no children before he had qualified as a product engineer and could earn the salary he deserved. He expected her to take the pill, but she had forgotten that night. Why had it been so easy for her when so many others couldn't have children? It was a gift, but would Peter see it that way, too? The only one she had been able to talk to about that kind of thing had been—Gran.

Emma came back surprisingly quickly to the table with a tray bearing a small coffee and a large cappuccino. There were wrapped chocolates on each of the saucers. Sabrina immediately got up to help. "That was fast! What did you do about the queue in there?" she asked, impressed.

Emma smiled secretively, twisting around her elbows and pointing them at her.

Sabrina laughed and sat down. It was almost like being with Gran again. She could always make her laugh, too. "Thanks for remembering I wanted a cappuccino," she said. "You're *content* with plain coffee, I see."

Emma scowled at Sabrina's big cup with its white foam and chocolate sprinkles. "Yes. I don't want any of that fatty whipped cream in my coffee." She wrinkled her nose and concentrated on her cup.

"It's not whipped cream, Emma. It's frothed milk. And it wouldn't surprise me if it was skimmed milk at that. In Italy, milk seems fattier without necessarily being so."

"Are you getting used to your new country?" Emma asked curiously, looking at her with narrowed eyes caused by the sun shining straight down on their table.

"I'm coming home again, so I wouldn't exactly call it my new country. To be honest, I don't like Milan. But one weekend we drove to southern Italy and visited Positano. That was lovely. Almost no cars. The sea and the Mediterranean atmosphere. The only thing that was missing was a mandolin being played under the balconies in the evening." She smiled absently. Peter hadn't seemed so stressed and had shown a romantic side that Sabrina rarely saw. She was convinced that was where their child had been conceived.

They sat in silence as she unwrapped the chocolate and Emma stirred sugar into her coffee.

The work on the waterfront of Aarhus River was long finished. The big project had been completed, and there probably weren't many Aarhusians who didn't think it was worth all the detours and rubble.

Emma stared out over the water. It wasn't hard to guess who she was thinking about.

"I'm going to miss her a lot, too," Sabrina said, tasting the cappuccino. It wasn't half as good as the ones she was used to enjoying at Bar del Corso on Corso Vittorio Emanuele, but that wasn't the fault of the coffee beans. In Italy, everything in a cappuccino tasted different—the water, the milk, the sugar.

Emma ate her chocolate and continued to look out at the water, which flowed quietly and glistened in the sun behind the sparse barrier. "Elina loved sitting here and people-watching—did you know that? She probably sat on this chair often, enjoying a cup of coffee and making up stories about people." Emma smiled, though her eyes were dull as she looked at her. "You were the biggest fan of her storytelling when you were a kid."

"I enjoyed them," Sabrina admitted.

"Her imagination never failed her. Unfortunately, I didn't see much of her when I was a child because I was so much younger than her. Elina started working at fourteen years old—that's how it was then in poor families. But I liked when she was home during the holidays and we could be together. I enjoyed her funny stories, too. They always had good endings."

Sabrina nodded. "Gran was a good person." She looked at Emma for a long time before she decided to ask. Emma reminded Sabrina of her mum, Josefine, in so many ways. Thoughts had plagued her all night while she slept in her grandad's bed with all the memories. It annoyed her that Peter had rented out their apartment on Dalgas Avenue to a young couple for the year they were in Italy, but the rent was good money, and it was pretty much what she lived off as she couldn't work in Italy. She'd considered a hotel room while staying in Aarhus, but why spend money on that when her gran's lovely apartment on Store Torv was empty? She certainly didn't want to stay with her father and Carola.

"Do you know what happened between Dad and Gran, Emma? Does it have anything to do with my mum?" she asked carefully.

"I clearly remember when Josefine died. Your mum was very ill, Sabrina. It affected us all deeply. I don't know whether Elina was angry with your dad because he married her so quickly. Carola—isn't that her name? She never mentioned it. She wouldn't talk about your mother in general, after we buried her. Oh, Sabrina, you were so young . . ." Emma took her hand and squeezed it hard.

"I don't remember the funeral. I actually can't remember Mum, either. Only brief glimpses that, I think, might just be things I've been told."

"You were only four years old. How are you supposed to remember her, dear? Josefine was a lovely person. You're a lot like her both inside and out. She had the same dark hair and eyes as you. But she was very thin in the end. Unrecognisable. Before her illness, she was a little chubby. But you've lost a lot of weight, Sabrina. A little too much, I think. You have to have some meat on your bones in case you get sick."

Sabrina was mortified and put a hand on her stomach again. The diet wouldn't last. She'd lost over ten kilos when she started studying to be a dietitian and gained more knowledge about healthy eating. That was before she'd met Peter. He probably wouldn't have noticed her otherwise. He was very critical in terms of diet and appearance in general. He would never fall for a fat girl.

"But, of course, you can't be a chubby thing like me when you work in your profession," commented Emma, self-effacingly, making a show of putting the last piece of chocolate into her mouth.

"Not all dietitians are thin." Sabrina laughed.

"Do you miss your job? I mean—is it not nice to be away from all those dying and sick people who . . ."

"I miss my job!" Sabrina interrupted, looking insistently at Emma. "Seeing such sick people who still have the will to live is so life-affirming, and helping to make their last days worth living is indescribable."

Emma nodded and was silent for a long time.

"Have any of the sick ever asked you to end their suffering?" she asked in a slightly hoarse and uncertain voice.

"Do you mean euthanasia? No, hospice patients rarely have that thought. Many people feel significantly better when they come to us. In fact, sometimes we have to send the dying home because they are no longer dying. A study from Hospice Forum Denmark showed that, in some places, every fifth person is sent home again to make room for sicker patients. That's food for thought, isn't it? Not to mention that it's against the law to take someone else's life—that applies to everyone, including doctors and nurses."

Her voice didn't sound entirely convincing. She remembered an episode a few years earlier where a patient had asked one of the nurses to give her enough morphine so she wouldn't wake up. The nurse had talked with the patient for a long time and learned that she didn't actually want to die but felt sorry for her husband who visited her faithfully every single day. The nurse had broken down in the coffee room afterwards and told Sabrina about the episode and other experiences she had had in the ICU she'd worked at before moving to Skovdal Hospice. She didn't know it at the time—she thought what happened was normal procedure. On a night shift, she witnessed a doctor give a patient so much morphine that he died shortly afterwards. They stood and watched. Later, she found out that the increased dose of morphine in the drip had never been noted, and when she asked the doctor why, he replied it was best for the next of kin. She hadn't dared stand up to her boss for fear of being fired. Euthanasia brings shame on hospitals—more than is realised, though it happens for many reasons—pity, mercy, or sheer cynicism.

"If there is no hope of regaining health, is it not the best for everyone? The patient doesn't feel anything when a morphine drip is increased," Emma continued, despite entering an area of debate that they would never agree on.

"We don't use morphine drips at Skovdal Hospice. There is far too much disagreement about how it should be done, when it should be administered, and when the dose should be increased. It's always an educated decision. Morphine is administered subcutaneously—under the skin—to patients in a lot of pain. A morphine pump is used, which means that the patient is more conscious and can enjoy their time with their relatives and vice versa during the last of the time they have together. No one has the right to play God." Her tone signalled the end of their debate and was in time with the sound of an engine from a white taxi—plastered with company advertisements—that was picking up a bunch of drunk people who were probably heading into the city to party.

"Well, we need to be getting on. Elina held onto everything, so there's a lot to go through. I've paid," said Emma, linking Sabrina's arm as they started walking. They turned the corner at Immervad. But they didn't notice the man following them.

10

Roland sighed in relief as he slumped down into the office chair, causing the gas cartridge to let out a moaning sound under his weight. Despite missing the cigarettes, he had to admit that the air in the office was fresher after he gave them up. He was allowed to smoke in his one-person office, but he chose to show solidarity and keep his small office smoke-free, too. He'd often had plans to quit smoking, and now there was a good reason. Smokers were no longer well liked. Incidentally, he thought, the Danish rule about being allowed to smoke in small one-person offices and in small bars and restaurants was a mistake. If you were going to do it, you should do it properly—like in Sweden—with a complete smoking ban. Breathing smoke in small venues was worse than breathing smoke in large areas, he had told Irene in anger. Irene had never smoked and couldn't see the problem. She said he should think of all the passive smokers and how, as a law enforcer, he should be a pioneer. So, that's what he became, no matter how difficult it was to replace the smoke with tough chewing gum.

The window had been left open while he was at the press conference, and now he could smell the seawater from the harbour. His sense of smell had improved. He poured half a cup of coffee into a plastic cup and took a mouthful. His sense of taste had improved, too, but the coffee served by the police canteen was still lousy. Irene had offered to make a thermos of coffee from his own Italian blend of beans so he could bring that to work, but that would be like mocking the canteen. They had to put up with so much else besides bad coffee. For example, the amalgamation of municipalities with Viborg as the capital and political power centre in the new Central Denmark Region now meant they had to adapt to functioning in a much larger police district—and the police reform that had been adopted by a broad majority in parliament to provide more police on the streets and modernise the seventy-year-old organisation. The department had been modernised with new phones and technical systems that didn't work. And now they—the police—had to face citizens, politicians, and the press about things not yet working as they should. Restructuring and reforms took time and weren't going to happen overnight. Undoubtedly, there were also those who were deliberately impeding the reforms laid out in the politicians' high-flying plans—plans that had not been backed up with any great financial help. Either way, it hadn't got any better. Never had they been so far behind with cases, and there was neither time nor human resources for basic crimes like theft. Roland envied the older staff who had accepted a severance package if they weren't in favour of the impending job or workplace changes. At the age of fifty-five, he wasn't one of the chosen. More people than expected had taken the opportunity, and it wasn't easy to fill their positions with new officers. The new police section was divided into three so-called pillars consisting of "agencies of emergency preparedness," where the traffic police, anti-riot police, alarm centre, and control centre were now organised. The "local police," whose remit was civilian crimes, such as burglary, robbery, theft, reportings, and preventive work was the second pillar. "Investigation"—to which he belonged—was the third main pillar. In addition to major financial cases, drugs, and organised and gang crimes, the third main pillar included crimes such as murder, sexual crimes, and cybercrime. In other words, all the cases that were previously investigated by the Criminal Investigation Department. That term was no longer to be used. It no longer existed in the new leadership positions. However, as a regular officer, he could choose to keep his title as a detective inspector. Future officers in his position would now be called police assistants, which didn't sound particularly authoritative to his ears. It was all nonsense. The title meant nothing. Officers, who weren't even trained for it, were on the streets to meet the demand for more police visibility. And many of the talented young cadets had left due to the poor pay. They could earn more in other professions—and without the threats to their lives that a police job brought with it nowadays. No one respected the badge anymore. Kim Ansager complained that his wife, who worked as a graphic designer at an advertising agency, earned much more than he did. And all she did was draw logos for various companies and shampoo brands.

Anyway, the press had more things to think about than police reform and the "the force's lack of action." A twenty-five-year-old corpse in a bog was, after all, more exciting and marketable. He had seen Anne Larsen from the *Daily News* in the middle of the press conference flock, but she was unusually silent. They had only made eye contact once, where he caught the glimpse of a friendly smile on her face, which otherwise always looked serious thanks to the scar on one of her eyebrows.

The chief superintendent had been very generous with information. It was something new he had come up with, as he believed involving the press would benefit the investigation—and, thereby, the public—in solving such an old murder case. Someone out there had to know something. He also referred to cold cases, which clearly demonstrated that solving cases happened more quickly when the press was involved and could garner information from the public. And that was exactly how it was; journalists believed they were little detectives who had to fix everything they felt the police couldn't figure out for themselves. And this was why he didn't like involving them too much. Again, he thought of Anne Larsen, who had gone her own way as a detective in the Gitte murder. Something good had come out of that situation—some journalists had more flair for it than others.

He sat in silence, mentally preparing for the meeting with his staff. They were to work on hypotheses, which meant he needed to come up with something before the meeting started. After all, he was the head of the investigation. He typed *bog body* and deleted it again with the most-used key—the *le* in *delete* was almost worn away—and wrote *corpse in the bog* instead. It seemed unethical to call it a bog body now that they knew who the victim was. *Victim knew killer—or random murder?* Maybe they could ignore the context of twenty-five years ago. Murderers with no connection to their victims had become more common in the years that followed. The global world. Yes, it was good for some things, but open borders, better and cheaper travel options, and access to communication over the internet also allowed crime to travel more freely. A murderer could travel from a foreign land—for example, Africa—kill someone in Denmark, and be back in their home country before the police had time to get the results of any DNA analyses. A murder where the killer knew their victim and vice versa was probably more likely in a small community in 1983. The victim could have become one of the statistics' "unreported figures"—the hidden and unsolved murders with the perps still at large. If the two boys hadn't ventured into the swamp in Mundelstrup . . . With a murder-solving rate of 95 per cent, Denmark was doing well. He didn't want to think about Italy's rate—in Naples alone . . . He immediately shooed the thought out of his head and gave up on writing any more. He had no doubt at all that was possible to commit the perfect crime. Without a corpse, a murder weapon, and a motive, there was no case. What were the suicide statistics concealing? Or deaths from overdose? People who had simply disappeared—of which the woman in the bog was one. They soon forgot when a natural explanation for their disappearance or death had swiftly been found and the case dropped or closed. Earlier, the intelligence services intervened in these cases once the local police had given up. Nothing was investigated; they just waited for the missing person—or a body—to appear. The case from Silkeborg was a good example. He was also certain there were innocent convicts in Danish prisons. Some had reported themselves for whatever reason even though they were innocent. Planted evidence, murders of justice, errors on the part of the investigators and technicians, undiscovered evidence that could clear the convicted person . . .

He stretched his back and legs, then got up and turned on the printer. It rumbled and groaned a few times and then started spitting out paper. He gathered the pages together in a pile. He'd have to hear what the others would want to say on the matter. Only one thing was sure—there was a lot to be done.

Three quick raps on the door followed by a bang as it was opened before he had a chance to answer made Roland look angrily at DS Kim Ansager, whose bespectacled face appeared apologetically in the doorway.

"Sorry about butting in, but that journalist is here. She wants to talk to you. You know the one . . ."

He knew exactly who Kim meant. Plus, he could see her thin figure standing behind the DS, stepping from foot to foot impatiently.

"This had better be important," he grumbled, quickly putting the prints in a drawer and shutting down his computer.

Without an invitation, Anne Larsen sat on the chair in front of his desk. She had lost more weight, and the face under her jet-black hair seemed extra pale.

"This had better be important," he repeated.

"It is. Thanks for the press conference, by the way. It was good—it's rare to get so much information." She smiled.

He mumbled something inaudible. Had it been only up to him, the press wouldn't have received half as much information. "So, what do you want then? There can't be anything you need to know," he said sarcastically.

"No. There's nothing. But there is something *you* need to know."

The power struggle had already begun.

"May I?" she asked, taking the insulated coffee pot from the desk and a cup from the stack that stood on the sideboard by the window.

"Of course." It was too late to say no anyway. "I have to leave in ten minutes, so I don't have long. What don't I know?" There was half an hour until the meeting, but she didn't need to know that. "What have you done with your photographer today?" he asked quickly to cover up the lie, despite her not seeing through it.

"Kamilla? She's in the hospital with her sick mother," Anne Larsen replied in a tone that implied the photographer was sitting in a café drinking coffee.

Roland was silent and irritated; he watched her as she made herself comfortable in the chair again now with the coffee, which she drank without showing any signs of disgust.

"I got a call yesterday morning at the paper. They actually wanted to talk to the person in charge, but Thygesen is on sick leave. The man sounded like he was holding his nose and said he knew something about the body in the bog," she continued.

He leaned back in his chair and looked at her with an indulgent smile. "You know that these kinds of cases bring out lunatics. He just wanted to be in the paper."

Anne shook her head and drank some more coffee. "That's what I thought at first, and I didn't think there was anything to it until after the press conference. He said he had a hunch about who the body was, and that if his hunch was right, there would be more murders. It almost sounded like he was expecting a massacre!"

"That's enough for you to feature him in a long article, too—no?" Roland was still smiling. He took a piece of chewing gum when he got the urge for a cigarette.

"Yes, if that was what he wanted. But he wants to remain anonymous."

"That's worse!"

"Yes, his info would be of no use except that . . ."

Anne Larsen had done it again—it always tormented him when she came up with something interesting. She took an artful pause and wanted to see his eyes pleading with her to move on.

"What?" he said after the pause as she provocatively looked down at the black coffee in the plastic cup, drumming on it with her nails like fanfare before the grand finale. His voice trembled with a hint of trepidation, which irritated him even more because he knew she was enjoying it.

"You don't mean he *actually* knew who the murder victim was?" He now had the upper hand and saw the disappointment on her face.

"Exactly. How could he know it was her long before the press conference—long before the results from Forensics?"

He caught himself chewing a little too energetically on the gum. "Did you get a name? Did you hear any sounds in the background that could tell us where he was calling from?"

"Nothing, no. But it sounded like there was muted traffic in the background—of course, that's everywhere today. And, unfortunately, I think he's too smart to call from a traceable mobile given that he thought of making his voice unrecognisable."

"Damn! That's the most important lead we have so far," he exclaimed, seeing how proud Anne Larsen clearly was. But it must have hurt her. She could have chosen to keep the information to herself and publish it as a front-page scoop, but she had chosen to go to him. She had also realised it was better to collaborate than to compete, in line with Kurt Olsen's new vision. Or maybe it was because they had been so generous with their own information.

"You didn't arrange to talk to him again?"

"I suggested it, but he wouldn't promise anything, so it's entirely up to him."

They met in the briefing room. Everyone arrived on time and took a seat around the table, which was covered with mugs and insulated coffee and tea pots. Kurt Olsen sat at the end of the table sorting images from Forensics. DS Niels Nyborg had been on patrol and had brought pastries with him. He served them by tearing open the bag up the middle, making sugar fly out all over the table.

"Imagine that foreigners call these 'Danishes.' What do they take us for?" asked Dan Vang, who believed you shouldn't eat sugar. New girl-friend, apparently.

Roland instilled silence by starting to write on the board.

He wrote *Body in the bog*. From there he drew a line and wrote the name of the victim, then he drew another line and wrote *Sebastian Juhl, son*. In one corner he wrote *Victim knew killer—or random murder?* then he turned to the small group of trusted staff and made eye contact with Isa-bella Munch; she smiled at him. Oh, how uplifting it was to have a female officer. He cleared his throat.

"This is what we have to go on. But I've just had a journalist visit the *Daily News*. She got a call from an unknown man. He knew the identity of the body—before either the forensic pathologist or odontologist. However, I don't know what connection he has to the case." He wrote *Unknown wit-ness—perp?* randomly on the board. Kurt Olsen handed him the macabre photos of the nursing assistant's earthly remains, which he also placed on the white board, as well as a picture of the wooden tip that Leander had found in the skull.

"The murderer may have a connection to Africa. Maybe it was only a holiday, and it's a souvenir he brought home. The murder weapon appears to be a large, heavy object of black African ebony."

"Maybe the victim or killer lived with someone who travelled there," Kim posited, and Roland nodded.

"You're using the past tense, Kim, and that's our biggest problem. All this happened twenty-five years ago, and most of the leads are gone. She went missing in 1983. According to her son, the police considered it a case of a woman running away with her boyfriend, so the search probably wasn't very intense. Either way, she was never found."

"Yeah, well—who searches a bog?" Dan mumbled as he scowled with disgust at Mikkel, who took a bite of pastry, leaving a ring of sugar around his mouth, which he rinsed down with coffee.

"The murderer probably had that thought, too. We'll start by concentrating on the circle of friends and the residents living around the bog that year. We have to start with a broad investigation, as we have nothing to go on. It wouldn't have been easy to transport a corpse there unseen unless the murderer lived close by or it happened at night. Kim, your patience and expertise in research make you ideal for reviewing the old reports. Involve our colleagues from the Central and West Jutland Police as much as possible. Get hold of Arne Svendsen. Say hello from me." He sat down and ate a pastry all the while followed by Dan's reproachful stare. Whether it was his praise of Kim or his craving for sugar that evoked the reproach, he could only guess. It was rare that Dan Vang was praised.

"Could it have been one of the deceased's patients? She was a nursing assistant," Isabella Munch suggested, and Roland nodded a little too eagerly.

"We need to find her patients—especially those she visited the last day she was alive.

"I've actually talked to my colleagues in Silkeborg about just that," said Kim. "There was nothing about it in the old report, and, unfortunately, there are no records of where the various nursing assistants were at certain times and days back then. They don't keep that kind of information so far back."

"Good work, Kim; we won't waste any more time on that. But they have to be found somehow. Unfortunately, the son couldn't help us much—he was only eight when all this happened."

"Could he be the one who called the journalist?" Kurt Olsen was chewing, too, but it was probably Stimorol rather than nicotine gum. He was not going to do without his beloved Stanwell pipe, which was normally an extension of his right hand. He took advantage of the ban loophole and puffed away in his private office.

"The young man seemed horrified to hear about his mother's death, so I doubt it very much," Roland replied, looking at Mikkel, who had also witnessed Sebastian's reaction. He nodded his head and agreed with his superior.

"I'm wondering why a nursing assistant from Silkeborg would have patients here in Aarhus. Does that not seem strange?" said Isabella. *That wonderful female intuition.* Roland frowned and nodded.

"Yes, you're right. I thought the same thing myself," he lied. "Niels, can you look into that. We need to know what a nursing assistant from Silkeborg was doing here in Aarhus."

"Can we rule out that the body was transported from Silkeborg to the bog? I mean, that she was murdered in her own home and brought here. That would exclude her patients." Kurt Olsen rolled up his sleeves and seemed convinced of his theory. Roland was only convinced that there were many possibilities with facts to go on.

"How long does it take to drive from Silkeborg to Mundelstrup?" he asked into the air.

"It depends on whether you're driving with the siren on," said Dan, earning a hard blow on the arm from Niels.

"A murderer doesn't drive with a bloody siren, you numbskull."

Dan Vang blushed as it dawned on him what the question had inferred. Roland shook his head slightly. Vang would soon have clocked up four years on the force, and it was only due to the lack of officers that he hadn't yet been fired. He was not sharp, and many serious conversations with his superiors hadn't improved his attitude to his work, which apparently lay only in the uniform and arms.

"It's about forty kilometres from Silkeborg to Mundelstrup—could it be done in a little over half an hour?" said Niels Nyborg, who had family in the city.

"If we assume that it happened on a cold winter's day with freezing temperatures, being transported for that long could explain why the body was cold when it was thrown into the bog. According to the autopsy report, the intestines were well preserved in the acidic bog water. They even think her last meal was beef, but it's not one hundred per cent confirmed," said Roland.

Kurt Olsen got up and stood with his hands in his trouser pockets as he studied the pictures of the body. "But who keeps a corpse and drives it so far? Isn't it about getting rid of it as soon as possible?" He turned to face the table where everyone was staring at him.

"Do we not have a time of death at all?" Nyborg asked, eagerly turning his pen between his slender fingers.

"Unfortunately not. The age of the corpse makes it complicated, so they are still working on it." Roland sighed and straightened up in his chair. "But we need to get cracking on this. The unknown man the journalist spoke to warned of several murders if he was right—and so far, he was."

A chill ran down his spine. What if it wasn't a warning, but a threat!

11

They were nearly through. It was late afternoon, and with small breaks, it had taken the entire day to clear the apartment. *A long life really acquires a lot*, she had thought several times. She got up and pushed back her hair. Her back hurt from the unfamiliar position she'd been sitting in to clean out the kitchen cupboards. The apartment was already rented out again and the new tenant was moving in on the first of the month; everything had to be out so it could be painted. Elina had lived here for years, and it hadn't really been kept up, so it really needed sorting out.

Out of breath, Emma pulled some cardboard boxes. "To think she saved letters from so far back." She sighed. "It says 1983 on the postmark on the top envelope." She dumped the boxes down on the stack of the others that were to be carried down to the skip.

"Do you want to throw them out?" Sabrina asked in disbelief, dragging a box of old, worn pots and pans to the pile. She pulled it across the floor with a scraping sound.

"What else would you do with them?" Emma looked at her watch and pulled down the blouse that had crept up over her round buttocks.

"You go, Emma. I'll do the rest."

She smiled gratefully. "Do you mean it? It's actually best that I go home for the weekend. Kaj has called me several times. He's missing me on the farm. It wouldn't surprise me if he hasn't had anything other than the food I prepared for him before I left."

Sabrina thanked her for helping and waved from the window as Emma struggled with her large weekend bag towards the car parked in the yard. She turned sadly towards the empty apartment and the boxes in the hallway. There were no more traces left of Elina. The walls were bare, and the furniture had been removed the previous afternoon. Gustav had taken care of that part. Most of it had probably gone to the landfill. They didn't want any of the "old crap" as Carola had called it. In a cardboard box in the hallway, Sabrina had collected her keepsakes from Elina. Emma's car was also full of things that meant something to her. There was only the two of them to share the mementos. Elina had left no money, only a small debt, which would be paid when the estate was settled.

She sat down on the floor next to the cardboard box of old letters. Emma was right, why save letters that were twenty-five years old? She took out the first letter and read the sender's name. It was written in tight handwriting that was difficult to read. *Louise Engtoft*, it said. There was no address. She opened the envelope gently, as if it were so old that it could crumble.

May 1983

Dear Elina,

I'm writing because I would like to tell you about the improvements in Josefine due to the treatment we're currently trying. Today, she was able to come outside in the lovely spring air with my support. The fresh air was so good for her that she had the energy to sit for a while with her little girl and tell her about the sounds of the birds. I was impressed she knew so many. And even though Josefine tired quickly and had to go back to bed, it was great progress. Dr. Winther is also very optimistic and says it suggests the treatment is benefiting her. Maybe they really have found the cure for cancer. We can always hope. I just thought you should know. You seemed so despondent when you were last here. There is no reason to be. Everything will work out in the end.

Love, Louise

Sabrina's heart pounded as she folded the letter and put it back in the envelope. Louise had to have been her mother's nurse and the little girl must have been her. The tears welled at the image of the girl on her mother's lap in a sunny garden with newly sprouted leaves on the trees and happy bird voices around them. They had probably sat on the garden bench next to the granite birdbath at the very bottom of the garden with a view of the house, which she only remembered from a few pictures in the photo album. But she got a warm feeling inside when she saw them, and that must have meant she had been happy and safe in that home—right up until Carola moved in shortly after Josefine's death. They had only lived there for a few weeks afterwards, then Carola had found an expensive and flashy villa on Strandvejen. Even though she cried and did not want to move to the big house with no cosiness or memories, there was no mercy to be found, neither from her father nor Carola. That was when the fine dresses and bows in her hair had started. The children on Strandvejen had to look like . . . children from Strandvejen.

She realised she was freezing and got up to close the window. When the sun was gone, the season was more noticeable. She watched a mother pick up her baby from a stroller in the yard. The letter had torn open old wounds. She suddenly remembered little things from her childhood that she had long ago left behind—or so she had thought. The fear she experienced in the big house on dark nights, all on her own in a nursery room that otherwise did not lack for anything—other than feeling safe. Carola's critical glances at her fat stepdaughter who only got fatter and fatter from comfort eating. She had plenty of money, and the bakery was on her way to school. Again, she pictured herself as a child sitting in her pretty dresses on a large rock down by the water's edge after school, eating cakes. It had increased the serotonin in her brain and calmed her down. Today, she knew that was what had happened. She had read a lot about neurotransmitters in the brain during her training as a dietitian and knew that sweet things increase the production of serotonin, which acts as both comfort and reward; paradoxically, the same substance that is increased by exercise. But, for a child, sweets and cakes are an easier way to feel better—to get that rush of happiness not provided by life. She *was* an unhappy child. But why did only the bad memories appear? Had she just been too little to remember the good ones? She sat down by the cardboard box again and took out the next letter. It was from the same year, but a month later.

June 1983

Dear Elina,

Thank you for your letter and your visit the other day. Josefine was very happy to see you. She often talks about you and misses you. Gustav is not home so much—he often works until late in the evening, so I stay a little longer with her and usually help to put the little one to bed. But she is so easy, she almost always falls asleep right away and without much nonsense. I know you are right when you say that I shouldn't get too attached to Josefine and the child, but how can I not? My own son is getting big now, so it's nice to play with the little girl. Things are still progressing. Dr. Winther is quite optimistic. Although some doctors have said there is no hope, we mustn't give up.

Love, Louise

As soon as the letter was folded and back in the envelope, she took the next one. Her hands trembled slightly as she took it out of the envelope.

November 1983

Dear Elina,

I didn't get to talk to you the last time you were here. But I heard you arguing with Gustav. Trying to talk him out of it won't do any good. I have tried, too. I don't know what happened between him and Dr. Winther, but it must have been serious. I'll visit you next week when I'm finished here so we can talk about what we can do.

Love, Louise

The letter was not put back in the envelope this time until she took the next one. All the letters were from this Louise Engtoft; she recognised the handwriting. Why had Elina never told her about Louise?

Why hadn't she said anything about those letters that told her so much about her mother? The knowledge she had always sought. Something told her reading them might not be good for her, but the urge to learn more drove that thought away quickly. She would find the truth in this box. She was convinced of it.

12

Horsens Fjord lay still in the autumn sunshine. You could just make out the water from the window. Kamilla clenched a mug of coffee between both hands, staring into the light, lost in her own thoughts, and bit into the cup's plastic edge out of nervousness. A doctor had offered her a bed so she could sleep in the ward with her mother, but it didn't take more than an hour to drive from Egå to Horsens Hospital, so she chose to drive home every night and come back the next day. Now she was afraid of not being able to react as was expected of her. The doctor had looked at her strangely after he'd informed her of her mother's critical condition and that they had to operate. He could apparently see that she felt nothing. How could she tell him, without seeming like an emotionally cold daughter, that she rarely saw her mother? He didn't know about their lives. It was a mutual unspoken agreement that they should have as little as possible to do with each other. Over the last few years, it had boiled down to a couple of obligatory phone calls every now and then that didn't benefit either of them. There had never been love between them, nor did she quite know what it was she was feeling right now.

The nurses left the single ward again. One laid a hand on Kamilla's arm and gave it a small squeeze as she walked past her. She went in and threw the plastic cup into the rubbish bin under the sink before sitting down on the chair next to the bed. Her mother was still lying with her eyes closed. A morphine drip sent painkilling fluid into her veins. Kamilla looked at the face that seemed so foreign to her on the white pillow. The woman in the bed was almost unrecognisable, and it wasn't just because of the bandage around her head and the blue and purple bruises on her face after the fall. She was only skin and bones, and if Kamilla hadn't known better, she would have refused to believe it was her mother lying there. She seemed completely out of place in the big bed. She couldn't remember ever having seen her mother lying sick in bed. The silence surrounding her wasn't right, either. Usually, her mother preached constantly about the family curse: that they would all die a painful death as punishment for the actions in her youth when she had left her inner missionary home on Jutland's west coast to live a life of "sin" with the man who became Kamilla's father. After regret set in for what she had done, she made their lives a living hell and began seeing everything as a punishment from God because she'd betrayed her faith. It took off in earnest when Kamilla's father died, which only had served to confirm the curse.

She took the hand that lay on top of the duvet. It was sinewy and limp. She searched inwardly for fond memories and experiences she had had with her mother. But none came to mind. Had she been too harsh? Should she have stayed with her instead of fleeing? She herself had experienced tragedies that overshadowed everything else. But wasn't it wrong to just deal with your own heartbreak? Maybe her mother was right. Maybe there really was a curse on their family. Was not her whole life proof of it? The divorce from Jan. Rasmus being killed by a drunk driver. Her infatuation with Danny, who she thought was to become the man of her life. She hated him, would not love him. But the feelings had become too deep for her to just let go. Now he was with Majken. Majken, who had always been her closest and most trusted friend—a sister almost. If all that wasn't a curse, then what was it?

She kissed her mother's hand. Not even its scent evoked memories. The medicine they pumped into her could be smelled through the skin. She placed her cheek against the almost transparent skin and closed her eyes. When she heard the door open, she quickly straightened up and looked at the doctor coming towards her. He smiled reassuringly, but there was a shadow behind the smile that said something completely different. It was a new doctor.

"Kamilla Holm?"

She nodded.

"I'd like to talk to you for a moment," he said softly, as if her mother could hear them but shouldn't. "Will you come to my office?"

She got up and followed him silently down the long corridor. She had always had great respect for authorities in lab coats and uniforms.

The office was bright and friendly with soft afternoon light from a large window facing the fjord. She sat down in the chair she was shown. Her heart pounded, and her mouth became dry. The feeling of terrible news trembled in the air. She didn't know how she should react.

The doctor introduced himself as Karsten Berthelsen, despite it being superfluous. It was on his nameplate: DR. KARSTEN BERTHELSEN, CONSULTANT.

"Coffee?" He pointed to an insulated coffee pot.

She shook her head.

"It's not from a machine," he said a little too cheerfully.

"I just had some, so—no, thank you."

She folded her hands in her lap, moistened her dry lips, and tried to look him in the eyes. He sat down opposite her and became serious. "Unfortunately, your mother was seriously injured in the fall," he began. "But it's not the worst. As you were probably told, the fall was due to a sudden brain haemorrhage. It's very concerning that she hasn't woken up yet—a full week after the operation. There is no reaction at all," he continued softly and leaned back in his chair.

She had to ask—what were the chances? Was there hope? Would she become paralysed and helpless, and who would take care of her in that case? Or would she become a vegetable to be kept alive by a machine? But she did not dare. Was as afraid of the answers as she was of asking the questions.

"So, what can you do for her now?"

Dr. Berthelsen looked in the file in front of him and shook his head in despair. "The only thing we can do for your mother now is palliative care— keep her pain-free with morphine."

Kamilla nodded.

"But there is a risk that your mother doesn't have the strength to tolerate the dose we have to give her."

She looked at him incomprehensibly. "Does that mean she could . . . ?"

He nodded. "I have to ask your opinion. Are there any other relatives?"

She shook her head. She could call Jan—she was after all his former mother-in-law, even though they had never been able to tolerate each other. Right now, she just wanted to have someone there with her, so she could squeeze their hand and cling to them, so she wasn't—as ever—doing and coping with everything on her own. Who it was almost didn't matter—even if it was Jan. But he would not come, even if she asked him to. Neither he nor Nina had ever forgiven her for having an affair with Rasmus's killer, even though she hadn't known who he was then and hadn't seen Danny anymore. She couldn't forgive herself, either. And they had their little boy to take care of, too. He was barely two years old. She had heard they had called him Rasmus after Jan's first son. It had cut her deep—a knife turned in a wound—when she'd heard. "My opinion?" She looked stiffly down at the table not knowing what she thought. "Are there no other options . . . ?"

The doctor shook his head and flipped through the medical file.

"I can see that your mother is only fifty-six years old, which is, of course, a young age. But what life does she have to go back to—if she goes back?"

Kamilla felt his eyes on her. She looked down at her hands, which were shaking and icy cold. *Fifty-six years.* She had never thought about her mother's age; she had always looked old. But she had only been nineteen years old when Kamilla had come into the world.

"I can only repeat that the best thing we can do for her is to keep her pain-free."

"You know best what to do," she muttered, just wanting to get out of the office as quickly as possible. Out of the hospital.

The consultant got up and put the pen in his breast pocket.

"You are, of course, welcome to stay, but unfortunately, there likely will be no improvement. We can ring when . . ." He let the sentence die out.

She stood up and accepted his outstretched hand; it was soft and warm, but the handshake was weak, and he quickly pulled his hand back, as if he didn't want to be infected with anything. He followed her to the door.

"I'm very sorry we couldn't do more," he said to her as she began to walk down the hospital corridor. The heels of her boots against the floor resonated against the bare walls.

She went back to her mother's single room. Her mother lay in the same way as when she'd left her. Her breathing was calm and regular, as if she were sleeping. Kamilla put on her coat, bent over the bed, and kissed her on her warm forehead. The morphine ran slowly in a tube next to her.

The tears came on the way home in the car, but she didn't know why. It didn't feel like grief, more like hopelessness.

* * *

It was nice to be greeted by the familiar scent in the house as she unlocked the door and stepped into the warmth. The aroma of her own home and not the hospital's mixed stenches of who knew what. She shrugged off her coat and threw it on the coat-rack. In the fridge, she found some leftovers from the day before, which she ate cold while listening to the answering machine and tidying up the breakfast things. The feeling of hopelessness had taken hold like a stink-bug.

She hadn't been in there for a long time, but she opened the door to Rasmus's room and went in carefully without turning on the light, as if he were lying in his bed sleeping and she didn't want to wake him. The door creaked lightly, as it had back then. She could always hear whenever he slipped out to go to the toilet or fetch a glass of water from the kitchen at night. The room was cleared now. Majken had helped her with it. She was actually the one who had said it was time. The only thing left was a football trophy that was dull with dust and a silver frame with the last picture taken of him. She became afraid of her reflection in the windowpane—it was as though she was a different person falling apart in the cold and dark all on their own. All alone—like *her*. Her mother was to die now, too? If she did, there was no one left, even though she had never really been there physically. There was family somewhere, of course. Lots of family members. But she didn't know them, had never heard of them. Grandmas, grandpas, aunts, uncles—and whoever else there might be. *Bloody well take her and her selfishness*, she thought. She really needed them now. She wiped the dust off the trophy with her sleeve. The date came to light: 7 August 2003. She saw Rasmus before her—seven years old in his striped football shirt and oversized shorts, eager to play a real match and eager to win. She had driven him and his teammate Jonas to the match. They had sounded like Brian and Michael Laudrup in the back seat. She had kept an eye on them in the rear-view mirror with a little smile. And they had performed like professionals on the field: writhed in the grass in feigned pain when kicked in the shin and quarrelled among themselves over injustices just like they had seen on TV. And of course, their excitement had no end when they'd won the trophy. The only thing that had taken away some of the joy for Rasmus was that his father hadn't turned up. He'd called that evening, but it wasn't the same. Rasmus had missed him that day. That day, too, yet again. She put the trophy back on the shelf and closed the door behind her.

Tarzan lay sleeping on the bedspread in the bedroom. She lay down next to him and sniffed at his warm fur that had the faint fragrance of her own perfume. Immediately, his little purring engine started. He stretched in pleasure and turned his head in a position to be petted, with his nose and whiskers straight up in the air. She didn't bother to scooch him off the bed but scratched him on the tummy while she listened to the soothing purr and stared out into the darkness.

She must have fallen asleep. She woke up sensing the cat was gone. Her warm pillow had disappeared, and she was freezing. She had enlisted the help of a neighbour to install a cat flap in the door of the utility room, so Tarzan could come and go as he pleased. A crepuscular animal was, naturally, active now. Betrayed for a mouse hunt.

Slowly, she got into her nightgown, having no energy for a shower, and sleep cast itself upon her as soon as she laid her head on the pillow.

The news came as a phone call that woke her early the next morning after a heavy and dreamless sleep.

"Unfortunately, your mother passed away in her sleep during the night."

Stomach cramps took her breath away. She ran out to the bathroom and vomited into the toilet.

13

A nne got her backpack ready and looked at the clock.

"Where the hell are they?" she said slightly annoyed.

Mads Dam looked up from his keyboard and leaned back in his chair with a small, joyful smile as he looked at her.

"Why don't you just head off? You don't want to take him with you anyway, do you?"

"God, no! But my photographer *has* to come with me."

"Kamilla! Didn't her mother die last night? She probably won't be coming to work after . . ."

He did not manage to say any more. The door opened and Kamilla stepped in, breathless, with the large camera bag over her shoulder. "Sorry I'm late. I wasn't feeling well this morning. I collected Nicolaj on the way."

Nicolaj, his hair windblown, squeezed past Kamilla. "My bike was punctured, piece of shit, I should have . . ."

Anne, who had no interest in hearing what else Nicolaj was going to do with his bike, interrupted him and gave Kamilla a concerned look. "I was sorry to hear about your mother, Kamilla. Why don't you stay home today? Everyone will understand."

"Don't worry about it. I'd rather do something instead of just sitting at home. That much I have learned. Where's Britt? Is Thygesen still off sick?"

Anne nodded and explained that Britt was in town for a meeting on Thygesen's behalf. She looked uneasily at Mads, who stood up and held out his hand to Kamilla. He was clearly hungover when he came into work, so you never knew what he might come out with.

"I was sorry to hear about your mother, too," he said. "I don't have my parents anymore, either. It's shitty when you become the next person on the list . . ."

He smiled shyly and quickly sat down again.

Kamilla thanked him and hitched up the bag.

"Shouldn't we get going?"

Anne's car was in the garage. It would be about a week before it was ready to drive again after a minor accident—someone had reversed into her in a crowded car park in the city centre. Therefore, Kamilla had to be chauffeur. She had acquired a four-wheel drive. A black Suzuki Grand Vitara, so she had room for all her photo equipment and could drive in impassable terrain if needed. She loved driving out into nature in her spare time and taking photos, and since her old Ford Ka had got stuck in mud and soft grass several times, needing help to get it free, she saw no other choice. The bank had grown friendlier towards her after she had got a job and a good steady income, so they had voluntarily given her a loan. As a freelance photographer, income was always hard to count on, and even her overdraft had often been overdrawn.

Nicolaj sat on the back seat along with the camera bag. Anne sat in the passenger seat next to Kamilla.

"Oh, I need a cigarette. Can I smoke in here?"

Kamilla nodded. "Okay, but roll down the window, so the rest of us don't suffocate."

Friday traffic was building up. It was as if people were fleeing the city in panic to get home for the weekend. On Viborgvej, the cars snaked in long queues. Only when she turned off on Gammel Viborgvej could she speed up a bit. "What's the address again?" she asked.

"We drove past it." Anne smiled gloomily.

"So, what the hell are we doing here?" Kamilla stepped on the brake, ready to make a quick U-turn.

"I just want to take a look at the bog, where the body lay hidden for all those years," said Anne, which triggered a loud *coooollll* from the back seat.

"Just turn here and drive straight ahead."

Nicolaj was the first out of the car when they stopped. He stared in awe at the trees around the bog, looking like an excited child on Christmas morning.

"Relax. It's just a bog," said Anne with a crooked smile, giving him a friendly pat on the shoulder.

"Yes, but a bog that has hidden a secret for so long! It's so cool!"

They trotted in between the trees and down to the bog.

"They found her here," said Anne, waving Kamilla to her.

The area around the waterfront showed signs of activity from heavy vehicles whose tyre prints were cast in the ground along with several different shoe prints, not all of which could be from police and technicians. How many people had passed by here just to look? The human urge to see accident sites was an attempt to face death. Kamilla imagined the dark morning with strong floodlights beaming on police officers working both in and over the water to get the body up in as good a condition as possible. She shuddered. Not everyone could choose their own funeral in advance. The woman had likely never wanted to be buried in this bog. If it was up to her, her mother would be cremated, but the thought of her fury at Rasmus's funeral changed that opinion. According to her mother's strict inner missionary faith, which sat deep within her, you should follow the Christian dogma of death—bodies should lie unharmed in the earth in as whole a state as possible for the purpose of resurrection, and though she didn't know what was happening to her body, Kamilla dared not do anything but follow her mother's belief. It was the final consideration she could show.

"Isn't it a little late to take a photo of the site?" she asked, concentrating on getting the camera ready.

"Yeah, we're late in getting to it," Anne admitted. "But a photo of the site might add a little spice to an article." She looked around for Nicolaj, who had disappeared. "He's not in the fucking bog now, is he?" she mumbled with a small smile.

Kamilla took some snaps; suddenly, she saw Nicolaj in the image section of the viewfinder and lowered the camera. "Hey, come back, you!" she yelled.

He made a deliberately comedic jump out of the camera shot and walked over to Anne.

"There is a garden centre back here. Maybe they saw something—back then," he said in a voice that trembled with excitement.

"We don't even know if they were there twenty-five years ago—my God, you weren't even born then!" Anne immediately regretted her tone, but Nicolaj seemed too busy to have noticed it. It was, after all, a good thing that he was so interested.

"So, who are we to talk to in Mundelstrup?"

She looked at him in a conciliatory manner. "There's an old woman who lives in Mundelstrup. She's supposed to know everything about everyone and has an amazing memory. She apparently knows about an episode from back then, which I would like to hear a little more about." She tapped the ashes off her lit cigarette with an outstretched arm while looking at Kamilla, who kept taking pictures. *If he says* cooooollll *one more time, I'm going to strangle him*, she thought. But Nicolaj contented himself with nodding.

"How are you supposed to find such a woman?" He looked at her quizzically with his light eyebrows drawn together and a speculative frown in the middle of his forehead. In the sun, his hair shone carrot-orange, matching the autumn leaves.

"Sometimes it happens by chance, but this time I actually rang the hairdresser's," Anne replied. After all, she was his mentor.

"The hairdresser's?"

"There are always two places where you can find out everything in a small town—the local shop and the hairdresser. Most people gossip at the hairdresser's, so I tried different salons . . . and bingo—one of them knew Agnes Isager."

Nicolaj smiled crookedly as he shook his head and looked up at the blue sky. When Kamilla was finished, they drove back to Gammel Viborgvej.

Agnes Isager's house faced open fields on the isolated outskirts of Mundelstrup. It wasn't well maintained, but that could hardly be demanded of a nearly eighty-year-old woman who lived and breathed making homemade elves and Christmas decorations. Autumn was her busiest period, and the entire dining table was cluttered with small white cotton balls (on which she painted faces), branches, cones, straw wreaths, tiny Santa hats in red felt, and mini clogs carved in wood.

Agnes didn't get up to let them in. When they knocked, she shouted a loud "Come in!" She was one of those rare old people who didn't listen to the news about the elderly being assaulted in their own homes, living in fear and shutting themselves in with chains and locked doors. She wouldn't be able to put up much resistance if she got that kind of visit anyway. Her arms were almost as thin as the elves' red pipe-cleaner arms, and her back was a little humped from being bent over her work for most of the day. Her eyes were lively and happy and full of curiosity. There was no doubt she was someone who loved to talk. She put down the brush and a cotton ball with a half-finished elf face. Anne and Kamilla sat down at the table. Nicolaj was preoccupied with the elves and was studying the details of an elf girl hanging on a ladder made of branches.

"Sorry to disturb you in the middle of your busy period," Anne said, glancing admiringly at all the Christmas knick-knacks. Some of the finished elves were standing in a row on a wall shelf, looking like little impatient creatures waiting only for December to come around.

"Not at all; I make elves all year round, so I can have everything made in good time before Christmas," she said with a laugh in her voice.

"Do you sell your elves—or is it just a hobby?" Kamilla asked.

Agnes explained that all her children and grandchildren were drowning in elves and that her daughter had made a website on the "indernet," as she put it, and that she sold a lot that way. The daughter took care of it because modern technology was not for her, she said firmly.

"But you wanted to talk about what happened in the town twenty-five years ago, didn't you?" She set about painting the Christmas elf face again with an astonishingly steady hand.

"Yes, I heard you can remember a lot from back then, and as I said on the phone, we need some information for an article about the macabre find in the bog."

Agnes nodded without showing any particular interest or fear as she calmly painted on. "Yes, it's a terrible story. I remember quite a lot from the old days; it's just about putting the right year on it. But 1983 I clearly remember—that was the year Volmer and I celebrated our silver wedding anniversary. I also remember clearly how they were searching for that woman from Silkeborg. The woman they found in the bog."

Nicolaj sat down on a chair at the table, his attention finally caught.

"Did something happen that year, and can you remember what it was?" Anne had her attentive journalist face on as she placed the voice recorder on the table. "It's okay with you that we record this, isn't it?" She smiled.

Agnes glanced briefly at the thing and shook her head.

"Something did indeed happen around the time of our silver wedding anniversary. Something that we talked about and that I later thought about a lot when I heard that they'd never found the woman. She was a nursing assistant for a family here in the town. A poor family. They moved shortly afterwards, which made us a little suspicious." She finished another elf head and laid it on the table, then she found several tiny red felt Santa hats that she glued to the round heads. Kamilla began setting up the camera, but Agnes was quite definitive about her picture not appearing in the newspaper.

"Do you remember the name of the family?" Nicolaj asked impatiently. He was taking notes on a small pad—Anne was starting to find him very helpful. He might fill in some of the gaps she missed.

"Unfortunately not. It was so long ago—and they moved. But it was the nursing assistant who was with them who disappeared. She was so kind and always smiled whenever I passed her on her bike. She cared for the wife, who was very ill. She died that year. Isn't it strange that they moved away so quickly?"

"Maybe because of the memories?" suggested Anne.

"Do you know where they moved to?" asked Nicolaj.

Agnes shook her head.

"And you're sure it was her?" Anne broke in before Nicolaj could say more.

"I don't know her name. But she was a nursing assistant and she disappeared in 1983."

"Did you tell the police any of this?" asked Nicolaj.

Agnes looked at him in astonishment. "No, why should I? It's their job to find that out!"

14

They were barking again. Annoyed, he got up from the leather chair and looked intently out the window. It was dark and hazy out there, but he could sense the kennels by the barn wall on the other side of the yard. The dogs barked loudly and threw themselves against the wire fence. He turned his gaze to the forest edge. It was probably that bloody fox again. He could only see a short distance across the fields in the light from the lamp in the yard and inside the window, then the forest disappeared in fog and darkness. There was no sign of life on the bit of field he could see. "Fucking mongrels!" he mumbled, not meaning it. The three short-haired Old Danish Pointers followed him faithfully on the hunt, which had become his passion since he retired last year. They were to leave early in the morning, so he couldn't waste time sitting here, staring at the goggle-box, either. Stag hunting season had just started.

The usual bloody Friday movie had begun, but he wasn't interested in watching it; it was, of course, also a re-run. And he had seen enough blood in his life as a surgeon and then as a GP. Patients who came howling just because they'd cut their finger and were bleeding a little. People who were *oh, so sick*, but much of it was often self-inflicted or pure whining. Obese people who couldn't understand how they had back and knee pain. *Think about how much weight that back and those knees are carrying around!* he wanted to shout in their faces. Still, he sent them further in the system for X-rays and scans—taking up space for those who genuinely needed help and didn't just need to lose thirty kilos—and he did it to be free of seeing them in his waiting room week after week. Small complaints that in the past patients would take an aspirin for, were now to be treated immediately with antibiotics, which was worse. A bad day, feeling low, or not living the perfect life that everyone demanded nowadays required happy pills. Young people couldn't even sit an exam without first having a prescription for their nerves. And he issued them gladly, the prescriptions. He had prescribed many in his life to the great delight of the pharmaceutical companies he had contracts with. An industry that benefited the Danish economy. What was there to say? Doctors were under pressure and were burned out prematurely. It was high time he retired. Ironically, he was sick and tired of being a doctor. No one could have made him stay one moment longer in the job, despite the complaints about the lack of doctors.

He turned off the television and looked out the window again. The dogs were growing more frenzied. It wasn't good—they'd be exhausted tomorrow.

"What's up with the dogs, Helge?" Victoria appeared in her nightgown in the doorway to the bedroom, looking sleepy. Her grey hair was standing on end. She wasn't the type of woman to dye it. When he saw her now without make-up, she seemed old, but she still radiated the same elegance he had fallen for. She was a little younger than him and they were always told they made a lovely couple. He had stayed masculine and slim with a healthy complexion from much time spent outdoors on the hunt and on the golf course. His hair was grey like hers, but it suited them both. Some wore silver hair with splendour and dignity. They were to leave together early the next morning: he for the hunt and she to the chemists, where she worked in the pharmacy. She had gone to bed early to be refreshed for the day ahead. The pressure at work was great these days because people were so sick and doctors were writing so many prescriptions. So, ironically, in the past, he'd been one of the reasons for her overtime. But she was due to retire too in three years. Then they were going to buy their dream house in Spain and move there to enjoy their twilight years. Many of his old colleagues lived down there. One of them even still practised on the Costa del Sol, though he probably shouldn't after the patient complaints he'd fled from here at home. The Danish authorities weren't so harsh when it came to that kind of thing. But he shouldn't complain. When working with people, a lot can go wrong—doctors are only people, too. People who can make mistakes. If they weren't looked upon with mitigating eyes by the authorities, who would dare to be a doctor?

"I think it's that bloody fox again. I'll go out and look. You just go to bed again, dear," he replied with a little smile, watching her as she obediently walked back into the bedroom with the white satin nightgown fluttering around her bare feet. She resembled a fairy disappearing into the dark.

On the way to the gun cabinet, he noticed the dogs' barking had ceased. He stood for a while listening, then went to the bar instead and poured a cognac. He took a mouthful of it as he stared out into the darkness, scouting for the fox. If it came back, he would . . .

A quick movement out there made him pick up the shotgun anyway. He was standing guard in the window, ready to run out into the yard, but inside, in the hazy light from the lamp, he saw it was just a hare. He took another sip of cognac and enjoyed the pleasant burn on his tongue. It was a good cognac. It had been a birthday present from his son. He decided to put it in the hunting bag for tomorrow, so the other boys could taste it, too.

It suddenly dawned on him something was not right. He set the glass down on the windowsill. The hare was running around wildly in the light from the lamp in the yard. The kennels were dark; he saw no movements or bright eyes. Heard no barking. Carefully, he took the shotgun in his hand and went out into the hall. He stuck his feet in a pair of wellies and stepped out into the yard.

They'd bought the country property many years before as a little homestead farm. It had been thoroughly restored, and the thatched roof was brand new. A few years ago, it had burned to the ground, and they'd had it rebuilt exactly as they wanted. The previous summer, they had painted all the lattice windows white to preserve the original appearance of the farm. Victoria had always loved horses, and her brown mare was standing in the stable—a new extension. The kennels were built up against the stable wall with a hatch into the stable so the dogs could enter the horse boxes that were set up for them. Victoria didn't want the dogs indoors. *Maybe they're just in the barn*, he reassured himself, but a strange feeling told him something was completely wrong.

At the kennels, the lamp shone so brightly that he could see inside. The first thing he noticed was the male dog, Pax. He lay there, his body distorted. Further on, lay Dax, and next to him, Max, lying in a puddle of vomit. Helge put his hand on his throat. A strange sound rumbled in it. A shout that didn't come out. As a doctor, he knew with certainty that the dogs had been poisoned. He was so preoccupied with the sight and his despair that he didn't hear the footsteps in the gravel behind him. The first strike was only a sting that felt cold and unreal. He put his hand on his back and only then did he feel the pain and the stickiness on his fingers. He gasped for breath, taking in the blood on his hand. He turned. The next blow hit him in the chest. He didn't have time to react, despite being much more masculine and in better physical shape than his opponent. The shotgun fell with a scraping sound into the gravel. The dark figure in front of him raised the knife again. It was beautiful. A hunting knife. He was a collector and had many hunting knives in his bag, but he'd never seen that type before. He stared at it. The shiny blade flashed in the light from the lamp in the yard. He felt the next stab. The cold steel slid in between his ribs. Horrified, he looked at the dark face hidden under the hood of a black sweatshirt.

"Which one of my . . . patients are . . . you?" he groaned faintly.

The figure stood motionless for a moment, then pulled the hood away from his face; the eyes stared directly into Helge's as he lifted the knife again. The doctor's eyes widened, perplexed, before he keeled over next to the kennels and his shotgun.

Victoria woke with a start and sat up in bed. The dogs were quiet now, but an eerie feeling had woken her. A dream? Or was it a sound? She got up from the warm bed and walked barefoot across the cool wooden floor to the window. It was dark out. It took a while before her eyes spotted the bundle lying by the kennel. "Helge!" she screamed. She tore open the front door and ran out onto the cold gravel that cut into her feet, ignoring the pain. A horrible scream that sounded like a wounded animal filled the dark, hazy night as she threw herself onto her knees next to her husband's bloody body.

15

———————

He hated this kind of Saturday.

It had started so well. He had lifted Irene's hair and kissed her neck as she did the washing-up after their late breakfast, and he had felt the slight tremble in her body at the touch of his stubble. Then he'd driven through the autumn forest down to Ballehage Sea Baths with a towel on the front seat next to him. It wasn't real winter bathing season yet. The sun was shining like it can only do on a beautiful autumn morning, glistening on the water's surface. After years as an active winter bather, the water felt downright warm even though it was only about twelve degrees. When he had taken a few dips, he sat down on a large rock in the sun, which was astonishingly hot. He never took his phone with him when he bathed here. It was a firm rule, even though it was not well liked at the station. Kurt Olsen had pointed this out previously, but it was the one thing Roland wouldn't change. He should be allowed to have one point in his life completely to himself. So, he had no idea what awaited him when he returned, with wet tousled hair, to the house.

"The station rang!" Irene shouted from inside their bedroom, where she was making the bed. She was still in her light blue dressing gown, as was custom on Saturdays. They could both go until almost noon before putting on clothes. The colour suited her tanned skin. She hadn't done her hair yet, so it was hanging down softly over her face as she bent over to pull the bedspread into place at the foot of the bed. Roland stood looking at her. As she moved, her robe slid aside enabling him to enjoy the hint of one breast. Enough to arouse his desire. He smiled, ran in, and toppled her onto the bed. She tried to push him away but laughed loudly as he kissed her neck. "Oh no! I'd just finished! What is it with you Italians!" she howled but embraced and kissed him. The phone chimed on the table in the kitchen, but he shook his head and pushed her gently back onto the bed as she started to get up to answer it. They made love. That was the good part of Saturday morning.

He was buttoning his trousers when there was a loud hammering on the front door as the doorbell rang aggressively. Irene opened it. Kurt Olsen tumbled into the hallway, looking like an inflated frog. "Where the hell have you been? I've been trying to get hold of you all morning! Did you not tell him to call?" he said to Irene in such an angry tone that Roland's hackles rose immediately.

"What do you mean by bursting into our home and speaking to us like that? What's happened? It's Saturday, for God's sake!" He snarled in response, pulling a black T-shirt over his head.

"Yes, if only murderers would take that into account, too. But they never say, *We can't commit murder on a Friday night, because the police need to have a lie-in on Saturday morning,* do they?" Olsen calmed his voice a little, but it trembled slightly, which disturbed Roland.

"Are you saying there's been another murder?" Roland gasped.

"Henry Leander is out there with Forensics now. Helge Vangberg, sixty-eight years old, retired doctor." Kurt Olsen wiped the sweat off his forehead with a handkerchief.

"Any connection to the other case?"

"A doctor and a nursing assistant! It damn well smells fishy! That's one of the first things you do—find out whether they knew each other!"

Roland stroked his neck to remove the sensation of small creeping ants. He put on a jacket and sent an apologetic smile to Irene, who only raised an eyebrow in irritation.

The house was located next to the forest, about five kilometres outside of Skåde, so it wasn't far from Roland's home in Højbjerg. When he got out of the car, he stood for a moment admiring the property and the location. If they had not bought Irene's childhood home when they moved from Copenhagen to Aarhus, this place would have been ideal, although he doubted that the combined salaries of an inspector and a social worker would cover it.

A flock of people had gathered at the kennels in the yard. Roland ducked under the red-and-white barrier tape and walked over. He was immediately handed a white lab suit. As he pulled it over his clothes, he noticed fleetingly how well maintained the buildings were. The masonry reminded him of the beautiful Montegiove Castle midway between Rome and Florence, where he had stayed with Irene one summer, enjoying the wonderful wine and extra-virgin olive oil.

"Who's the man in the cage?" he asked Leander, nodding at a young man squatting inside the kennel.

"Oh, good morning, Benito." Leander turned off the Dictaphone he'd been talking into while describing the condition of the body. "The vet. He believes the dogs were poisoned."

"By what?"

"That's what he's hoping to find out—it might give us a lead."

He squatted down next to Leander and looked at the victim. Helge Vangberg had been a handsome man for his age. Tanned with thick white hair. It was not easy to tell if he was wearing a red shirt or if it was completely blood-stained.

"One stab wound in the back, twelve in the chest," Leander said.

"So, it's personal!"

Roland looked up at the sound of the woman's voice, which he recognised at once. He hadn't noticed her at all.

"Stop it—has the Special Operations Unit been called in already?" he said a little sourly and greeted Julie Hermansen, who was an expert in criminal profiling and had helped them in the investigation of the Gitte murder.

"No, we were on our way out hunting," Henry Leander replied.

"Together?" exclaimed Roland, and his gaze involuntarily went to Julie's right hand, which she might have deliberately hidden behind her back.

"Yes, and with him here," Leander continued, pointing to Helge Vangberg's body.

"You knew him?"

"Not personally. He started hunting about a year ago, so I ran into him at some gatherings. In his younger days, he was a surgeon at Rigshospital—I met him there a couple of times, too."

"Surgeon! How is a surgeon from Rigshospital suddenly demoted to a GP in Jutland?"

Leander glanced at Roland and shrugged.

Roland got up. "Who found him?"

"Victoria Vangberg, his wife." It was Chief Superintendent Olsen who answered. He, too, was in a white suit. He had just returned from talking to the vet who was about to leave with the dead dogs.

"And where is she now?"

"Hospitalised for shock. Finding her husband like that really took its toll. She found him last night, but she only got herself together this morning to call the police. Judging by her state, she was sitting with him all night, out here in the cold, wearing only a thin nightgown."

No one said anything for a long time.

"What else do we have?" Roland looked down at Leander's bent back.

"The corpse stain is dried. That is, he's been dead for about eight to ten hours. And he's lying on his back. Therefore, we can assume that he was probably standing with his back to the murderer, and that the first stab wound was between the shoulder blades. He turned around and got the rest in his chest. One directly in the heart. As it turns out, he was stabbed several times, even after death had long since occurred."

Julie nodded eagerly. "Personal!" she repeated.

"The knife blade is ten to twelve centimetres long and about two centimetres wide. Rigor mortis is widespread throughout the body, so we can be fairly certain of about eight hours," Leander continued.

"Does it fit with the spouse's explanation?" Roland asked Olsen.

He shook his head tentatively, preoccupied with something going on behind the tape. The press grapevine had been set in motion, and the first photographers were trying to break through the tape. Some not-so-random passers-by took pictures with their phones, and more cars were arriving.

"Stay out there!" shouted Kurt Olsen angrily at the reporters, before addressing Roland again with desperation in his eyes. "We don't know much; she was incoherent. She says she was asleep and woke up suddenly. From her confused state, it sounds like it was around two this morning when she found him. But he may have been dead for a while by then. We have to talk to her when she's calmed down more. She's in Skejby Hospital. I'll call in there later."

His attention returned to what was going on outside the barricade. He went over and was immediately surrounded by journalists with microphones, which they stuck right up into his face. Roland caught a glimpse of Anne Larsen and looked the other way. How were they there so fast—and on a Saturday!

"I can't give you anything more precise now," Leander said defensively when Roland looked at him again, as if expecting all the answers.

"We're talking about a body that's been lying outside in fluctuating temperatures. This is what happens here in our time of global warming— we can have temperatures that are high for the season during the day and down below freezing at night, so there's a variation of about six hours, which means I can't just calculate the difference between the body temperature and the environment. If he had been lying inside, his body temperature would have been . . ."

"But he's not inside!" interrupted Roland impatiently. He had never relied much on the calculations from variations of six hours.

"And there are no maggots or other insects?" asked Kurt Olsen—who had sent the press away, whatever the cost—and he smiled a little inappropriately. Henry Leander had studied insects, which he used as an excuse for the large insect collection in his basement. But other police districts had realised his expertise in the field and often summoned him when insects were to be used to indicate a time of death.

"When I take a closer look at him at the lab, I can give you something more precise," said Henry Leander, looking annoyed.

His insects were always made fun of. He pulled off his latex gloves. "I'm done here."

"You believe it's personal?" asked Roland, who happened to be walking with Julie Hermansen back to the cars parked on the gravel road outside the farm. An ambulance with tinted windows drove into the yard to retrieve the body. Forensics would be on-site a little longer. Some steadfast journalists, who Kurt Olsen hadn't managed to scare away, remained. To his annoyance, Roland saw that one of them was, of course, Anne Larsen. He pretended to be very preoccupied with his conversation with Julie Hermansen.

"It's clear. The killer got close to the victim, and the stab wounds demonstrate hard, decisive force. It wouldn't surprise me if they already knew each other. The shotgun was lying next to the victim. Why didn't he defend himself?" Julie pushed her hair behind her ears. She had changed since he last saw her. Back then, they had called her Angela Merkel because she reminded them of the German chancellor. She didn't anymore. Her hair was longer, and she had lost a lot of weight. *That's what love does to you.* He glanced at the forensic pathologist who was waiting for her by his black Volvo. Roland had never found out from his old friend whether anything was going on between the two of them, but he had no doubt that they had seen a lot of each other since the Gitte murder. It was just that she was still wearing the wedding ring as far as he knew. And she wasn't a widow. That much he had found out, despite it being no concern of his. Her husband was a conference interpreter at the European Parliament in Brussels, so he probably wasn't home in Solrød that much. Despite being Italian, and it was generally thought that Italians looked lightly on that kind of thing, infidelity was unacceptable to Roland. If he ever found out that Irene had been unfaithful to him, he would never forgive her.

Henry Leander was now dressed in army green hunting clothes—he'd probably been wearing them under the sterile overalls.

"Were you really going hunting?" Roland said sympathetically when they reached him. "What hunting season is it? Deer?"

"Stags," Leander replied, opening the car door for Julie. "But they're not going anywhere while our stabber is on the loose. I'll notify you as soon as I have Helge Vangberg on my table."

Roland nodded and, to his annoyance, saw Anne Larsen approaching them.

"I hope this isn't the journalist's prediction starting to come true—if so, I'll have to get more steel tables." Leander slammed the car door and started the old Volvo. It coughed a few times before getting going. Roland looked at the car, pretending to be very busy.

"Is he right?" asked Anne Larsen. Her voice sounded quite cheerful. Kamilla was taking pictures of the ambulance from out on the road. Helge Vangberg's body was being carried into it on a stretcher in the yard.

"Is who right?" He pretended not to understand what she was alluding to.

"My contact. The anonymous man."

"Nobody is saying there's a connection," he muttered.

"A doctor and a nursing assistant—no connection? Oh, come on, of course there's a connection. The guy on the phone was right. There are more murders to come."

He rummaged in his pocket for a packet of cigarettes and grabbed the pack of Nicotinell again. He shook a few pieces out onto his hand and popped them into his mouth.

Anne Larsen was so close he could smell her shampoo. She smiled at him.

"'Lose the smoke—keep the fire,'" she said sarcastically.

"What?"

"It's an ad—you don't watch television?"

"Rarely," he admitted, and began walking towards his car.

"The chief superintendent promised us an exclusive press conference on Monday if we went home now. Does he mean it?" she shouted after him.

He nodded. "If Kurt Olsen said it, yep." To his relief, he saw her getting into a black Suzuki four-wheel drive with the photographer and driving away.

He was startled when Kurt Olsen laid a heavy hand on his shoulder. "Thank you for the vote of confidence. By the way, did you see her article on the front page of the *Daily News*?"

"No." He had not had time to look at the paper given the busy morning.

"She found an old woman in Mundelstrup who remembers the family that the nursing assistant worked for in 1983 before she disappeared." Kurt Olsen lit his pipe as they both watched the ambulance driving away with Helge Vangberg's body.

"Oh, that. An intern from the newspaper called and told me about it late yesterday. I've put DS Ansager on the case. He was still in the process of finding families who moved from Mundelstrup at that time, but it's bloody difficult going back twenty-five years. Not much was stored in databases like today. But Ansager will continue to search for the family on Monday. It's strange they haven't come forward."

"Very strange. Maybe you should talk to the journalist—or the intern— they might have found out something."

Roland stared at him without answering.

"But this time, we have a fairly fresh corpse." Olsen sighed, watching Roland through the pipe smoke.

Roland turned towards the house. The new thatched roof looked well trimmed in the sunlight. The straw lay side by side, so that from the road, it was reminiscent of soft, brown velvet. Undoubtedly, an impressively skilled roofer had done the work. The roof ridge was elegantly decorated with wooden pieces placed in a cross shape. A couple of crows had settled and were following the white suits down in the yard.

"Get yourself home to Irene for the weekend. We can't do much until we have the results from Forensics," Kurt Olsen interrupted Roland's thoughts, followed by another thump on the shoulder. "It looks like it's going to be a busy week from Monday."

Roland nodded and cast one last admiring glance at Helge Vangberg's lovely property before driving back towards Højbjerg. *It'll probably be put up for sale now*, he thought.

16

———————

She was pushed back into the seat as the plane took off. She loved this part of the flight most. With her eyes closed, she felt almost weightless as the wheels slipped off the runway and the plane rose further and further upwards. It was a nice feeling. As though being carried away from the troubles of the world and up where the sky was always blue and the sun was always shining. An adorable, dark stewardess in Alitalia's green coat and tight s-blue skirt had performed the safety demonstration in Danish, English, and Italian and with signs and gestures, though it was unlikely anyone had listened. Everyone assumed that nothing was going to happen on this particular trip. She looked out of the oval window and saw the runway disappear under the plane and the landscape open like a patchwork of small golden and brown squares of autumn forests and ploughed fields. Then the clouds came like a white mist, obscuring her view as the plane steadily rose upwards. She closed her eyes again until the movement of the plane told her that it had flattened out on course for Milan. When she looked out again, it was like looking into a fairy tale. The clouds lay far below the plane like an uneven white cotton-wool landscape illuminated in warm shades by the sun shining down on them from a clear blue sky. She took one of the magazines from the pocket on the seat in front of her and heard seat belts being unbuckled around the plane. She always kept hers on during the entire flight. The magazine pages were filled with ads for spirits, perfumes, creams, and make-up. She put it back and tried to concentrate on the movie starting on the small screen above the seats. The video screen was too close, and she could only hear the movie if she used a pair of headphones, so she wasn't interested in the film, either.

Elina's letters were in her hand luggage. Reading and learning about her mother was exciting. She'd never have been able to get that kind of knowledge from others—neither her father nor Elina. Sabrina now understood that Josefine had truly loved her and had tried to be a mother to her despite her illness—that she had been a happy and normal child whose father was rarely home. The suspicion that he might have been preoccupied with Carola, even then, had begun to simmer. Perhaps the answers lay in the last few letters. She'd hoped to be able to read them on the flight, but she had the window seat and didn't want to disturb people by stepping out into the aisle to find them in her bag in the overhead storage.

In the seat next to her sat a young woman with a girl of about two on her lap. The girl hadn't made a sound when the plane had taken off from Copenhagen. The pressure on the ears could often trigger the worst wails in the children on board, but this little girl sat on her mother's lap, playing with a yellow teddy bear. Occasionally, she looked inquisitively at Sabrina with almost jet-black eyes under equally jet-black lashes and eyebrows. Sabrina smiled. The girl hid her face in the teddy bear, giggled, and shyly turned her head towards her mother's chest. They were both Italian. She wondered what they had done in Copenhagen without an Italian father. Visited a Danish one maybe.

She laid her hands on her stomach over the buckle on the seat belt, which she had made sure not to tighten too tightly. It was time to tell Peter about the baby. She hadn't completely trusted the test she had used in Milan a few months earlier. Helpless, she had stood in the pharmacy and tried to explain what she needed. In Peter's Danish-Italian dictionary, she had found out that *pregnant* was called *incinta* and *test* was *prova*, but she probably pronounced the phrase incorrectly, because no one at the pharmacy had understood her. Saying *pregnancy test* in English hadn't helped, either; perhaps she'd pronounced that wrong, too. She had never been good at languages. Eventually, another customer in the queue, who apparently had a better grasp of English than she had come to her rescue, and the pharmacist had lit up with a big smile. "*Ohhh, un test di gravidanza!*" she'd exclaimed, so loudly that everyone in the pharmacy had heard it. They'd smiled and nodded. Italians love children. How were you supposed to know that when *pregnant* is *incinta?* They would probably have better understood her if she had said it in Danish. She'd never learn Italian.

She smiled at the thought of that day and of the result. The joy had bubbled up inside her when the test was positive. She'd immediately decided to tell Peter that evening, but he'd come home late; she had gone to bed and hadn't heard him come in. The next morning, he'd been busy and was not in the mood to have such news served at breakfast. And so, one day had passed after the other. Now she had been examined by her own doctor in Aarhus. She'd got an appointment since she had been home for a few days anyway. *It's true*, he had said. *You're three and a half months along.* Soon it would look like more than a bloated stomach, and how would Peter react that she hadn't said anything before?

She was torn out of her reverie when the young woman with the child said something to her in Italian. "*Scusa, non capisco,*" Sabrina stammered. Three useful words Peter had taught her so she could explain to the Italians she didn't understand anything. Due to her almost black hair, tanned skin, and brown eyes, she often received inquiries she didn't understand; those three words, which she could now pronounce almost without a Danish accent, had been a huge help. The Italian mother smiled understandingly and pointed to the teddy bear that had fallen and was lying between Sabrina's feet. She hadn't noticed at all. She picked it up and handed it to the girl, who now smiled trustingly at her and accepted her teddy bear, which she hugged tightly. Shortly afterwards, she fell asleep on her mother, who was reading a book in Italian. Sabrina closed her eyes, trying to get some sleep, too. There were almost forty-five minutes until the plane landed in Milan. She had just slipped into a dreamy doze when a touch made her open her eyes. The little girl's hand was resting on her arm while she slept soundly. The child's warm hand evoked a feeling she had never felt before. *Being a mother?* she asked, smiling to herself.

Linate Airport was, as always, full of activity. Businesspeople and tourists tried to outrun each other to get to the baggage claim first. She always thought of the accident with horror when she was here: 181 people killed in 2001 when an SAS plane, heading for Copenhagen in dense fog, crashed shortly after take-off. But those kinds of accidents didn't stop people from flying, just like 9/11 and terrorist threats no longer did. *Life must go on—* and it did. Fortunately.

She lined up at the luggage belt and felt the same panicked eagerness to grab her suitcases as everyone else. They pushed and crowded. It was just like a department store sale. After half an hour of struggling, she managed to grab both suitcases. She walked towards a sign that read *USCITA—EXIT*.

With a bag in each hand, Sabrina stood waiting in front of the airport, where Peter had agreed to collect her. It was raining gently in Milan, but the air was warm. She spotted his yellow Fiat Punto and walked over. As soon as he saw her, he jumped out, helped her throw the bags in the boot, and kissed her. "Was it a good trip?" he asked, smiling.

"I suppose; if you can call a funeral good?"

Peter started the car and looked back over his shoulder before reversing. She glanced at his profile and inhaled his familiar aftershave. He had begun to adopt the habits of the Italian men who had good taste in clothes and fragrances, but none of it mattered to her. His smile was both boyish and embarrassed when he looked at her again. "No, of course; I didn't mean it like that."

Caught in Milan's rush-hour traffic, he put a hand on her knee and gave it a squeeze. "It's good you're home for the weekend. I've really missed you!"

"Have you really? Seriously?" She smiled happily and followed the traffic. Should she tell him now?

"Yes, seriously! You should have been at the dinner at Hotel Galles."

"Did you go—on your own?"

"Of course. It was great, there was dancing afterwards. It went on until early morning. Except for the poor suckers with children who had to go home after dinner. That's how Italians are—their children always come first." He looked in the rear-view mirror and tousled up the dark hair that had got wet in the rain.

Her pulse began to rise.

"And that's not how Danes are?"

"Danes are just smarter. They wait to have children until they are ready for it and have experienced life—without children." He winked at her, took her hand up to his lips, and kissed it. "But we can have sex anyway," he whispered, and the tip of his tongue tickled her palm.

She pulled her hand away with a jerk.

He laughed and changed gears. "Don't be so prudish, Sabrina. I really *did* miss you."

"Only for that? Maybe that wasn't on offer at dinner?" She immediately regretted what she had said. Peter looked hurt, but she couldn't tell if it was just acting.

"You're not mad, are you—that I went to dinner without you?"

"Of course not. I expected you to. It was *only* my grandmother who died!"

"It sounds hard. I take it that it didn't go so well at home. Did you meet your dad—and Carola?"

She nodded, not wanting to talk about it. She'd persuaded herself to pay them a brief visit before returning to Milan. Gustav was, after all, her father, and she meant to tell him about Elina's letters, but something had stopped her. Carola had been present the entire time, chatting about everything and anything irrelevant, and it had dawned on her that Peter and Carola had had several private conversations that she didn't know about.

"Why are you talking to her about our personal relationship, Peter?"

"To Carola?" He suddenly braked hard behind a long queue at the traffic lights. He looked at her, but she had a hard time holding that gaze. She'd often wondered whether their child would get his strong blue—or her brown—eyes.

"For fuck's sake. Carola is my mother-in-law; can I not talk to her now?"

"Carola is *not* my mother."

"No, I know your mother is dead. But Carola is nice, Sabrina. She does what she can to be a mother to you!"

"Does she? Is that what she does!" Sabrina wasn't normally so easy to get fired up. It had to be the hormones, because she was shaking inside with rage. "You have no idea what my childhood was like with her. Because you've never been interested in it. She might have been in a relationship with Dad while my mum was still alive."

The traffic started moving again, and Peter changed gears with an angry jerk. "Why the hell are we arguing about that now? It's in the past. You dwell too much on the past. Do you not think it was hard for Carola, too—having to take care of someone else's kid?"

"Are you calling me *someone else's kid?* It sounds like you love children as much as Carola does!" The tears were on their way, making her voice shake.

They drove on in silence. Peter again took her hand and held it tight when she tried to pull it back. He looked at her while keeping an eye on the traffic at the same time. "Sabrina, I know it's been hard for you—going home for your grandmother's funeral. But where is all this anger coming from? Did something happen that you should tell me about?"

She couldn't answer. He released her hand as he turned into the round-about and continued along Foro Buonaparte. They drove for five minutes and were soon at home in the apartment on Corso Magenta. "I'm just tired," she said, feeling truly exhausted. She put her arms protectively around her stomach and looked out at the rain, which was a blessing after the oppressive heat before she'd travelled to Denmark three days earlier.

"We're home; let's get something nice for lunch and a glass of red wine. Then you can tell me about the funeral. And—no more talk about children, okay?" said Peter encouragingly.

17

—————

It was his birthday. The cake with seven candles and chocolate pretzel decorations stood in front of him, smelling sweetly of raspberries and whipped cream. His mum smiled and said he should blow out the candles. He took a deep breath and blew, but only the front three candles went out in an oozing stink of wax.

"Sissy!"

The African sat across from him with his tattooed arm around his mother's neck and his hand down her blouse. He got halfway up and blew out the rest of the candles. His breath stank of beer. He laughed triumphantly and sat back down.

"Honey! The birthday boy is supposed to do it!" scolded his mother, but she laughed and didn't resist when he kissed her in that disgusting way. His tongue slid far into her open mouth.

It was a shitty birthday. The cake felt sickly and sticky inside his mouth. The whipped cream tasted of cigarette smoke, and it was hard to swallow. The red lemonade was a little okay.

"Are you not going to see what your present is, Basse?" asked Mum, struggling free of the hand groping one of her breasts under her blouse. She always called him Basse. It sounded good when she said it, but when the African did it, it always sounded derogatory. He started opening his gifts. It was his day after all. The day they usually celebrated by being together and laughing and joking. Going for walks in the autumn forest and down by the lake. Now she only had *eyes for the African, and they did things in front of him that he didn't like. Part of him wanted to run out into the garden and hide in the secret plastic cave he'd made between the bushes, but he wouldn't want to hurt Mum.*

The first present was a fire truck. Red and sparkling with a crane and an indicator and everything. He couldn't hide his joy and smiled. It was from Mum. He put it down on the carpet and started playing.

"Hey, hey! There are more presents, you!" The voice sounded drunk and rough. He obediently sat back on the chair and took the next parcel. It was large, oval, and heavy and wrapped in exotic paper that had a strange musty smell. He gently pulled off the black ribbon.

"Open it now!" said the African annoyed, and he was again preoccupied with his mother. He had his hand on her thigh up under her skirt. In the package was a face. At least that's what it looked like, and he jumped back a little with fright.

"What is it, darling?" said Mum, pulling herself free to see the present.

"Oh, how beautiful! It's a mask!" She looked surprised at the giver of the gift, who took a sip of the beer bottle and nodded.

"Well done, babe! But what kind of mask?"

Mum giggled and shook her head. "I don't know. Is it from your last trip?"

"It's a hand-carved mask of happiness from Ghana. It brings courage, protection, and happiness to the one who wears it. It's also called a Bundu mask." His eyes were half closed and red because of the smoke from the cigarette in his mouth. The glow tipped up and down as he spoke, sprinkling ashes down on his mother's white tablecloth, which she had laid on the coffee table to make his day more festive.

"See how beautifully carved and decorated it is!" He pointed eagerly to the mask. But it was brown, ugly, and eerie with crooked holes for eyes and thick, almost triangular, lips.

"See. Come here!" He took the mask and waved him over.

"Go on, darling. Go into your room," Mum whispered as she began to clear the table. He reluctantly followed, glancing longingly at the red fire truck on the floor.

He had hung the mask up on the wall above the bed.

"There you go, kid. You need a little courage, don't you?" He laughed and coughed before taking another puff of the cigarette. "It's lovely, isn't it? See the fine pattern they painted in gold on the dark wood. That's fucking art!"

"Do they wear it in war dances?" he asked to seem interested.

"No, it's not a war mask, is it? I told you that it brings courage and happiness, didn't I!" The voice was harsh and reprimanding. It also didn't seem loving as he pinched his cheek before walking out. It hurt and left a red mark. The boy was left alone in his room, staring at the ugly African mask now hanging over his bed where he had to sleep. The crooked holes for eyes stared straight down at the pillow. He heard them calling from the living room and went in. Mum was lying on the couch with her head in the African's lap. His hand lay on her thigh and had pulled the skirt very far up so that the edge of her knickers was visible. He had a fresh beer in his hand, which he supported on his knee. His foot rested on the edge of the coffee table. His mother usually scolded him for that kind of thing, but she didn't say anything now. She just smiled. They had turned on the television. It was football. He hated football.

"Come here, kid. It's your birthday; that has to be celebrated with a little footy." They waved him over, Mum smiled and patted the pillows next to them as if he were a dog that must obey.

"I'm going out for a little while," he said, putting on his boots in the hall.

"Does he not even watch football? He's not a normal kid!" he heard him say, but he didn't hear her answer.

It had started to rain. Inside the cave, he could hear it drum on the plastic. Soon the leaves on the bushes would be completely gone, so you'd be able to see the black plastic from the house. Then it would no longer be a secret cave. But for now, it was still hidden by the coloured leaves of autumn. He had made a sort of beanbag chair out of a black bin bag filled with old newspapers, so he didn't feel the moisture from the cold earth. He sat down and dug in the ground, took a handful, and let it sieve between his fingers. The soil smelled a bit like the muck in the woods, where they used to tumble and fight and play chase. Mum was his best friend. There was no one at school he wanted to celebrate his birthday with, no classmates nor friends. Only Mum. A rotten apple had rolled into the cave from the apple tree in the middle of the lawn. He poked it with a stick and scowled at the window, which he could just make out between the leaves. Now that he was gone, they were probably screwing in there. That's what the big boys at school said she did. He knew well what it meant. It made him feel sick. He threw up in the bushes in front of the cave. His whole birthday. Cake and red lemonade. He began to cry. It stung his eyes when he wiped them with his dirty hands. "I hate him, I hate him!" It hissed out between his teeth. Fuming, he hurled the apple out of the cave so it smashed into the ground. He closed his eyes and imagined the mask really did give him courage. Courage to go back in. Courage to take the cake knife and plunge it into his chest. To keep going and going until he couldn't hear his laughter and hoarse breathing anymore. The sight became so vivid that he suddenly found himself in the situation. He saw his mother's face and heard her scream, she screamed so loud that he dropped the bloody knife with a thump on the floor.

He sat up in the chair, startled. The phone he had placed on the armrest of the chair had fallen on the floor making the noise, and the scream hadn't been his mother's but his own. He must have dozed off. The sun shone in through the window and dazzled him as he looked out. Yes, it was his birthday. He left and threw a coat over his shoulder. On the way out, he stopped in the doorway into the bedroom and looked at the mask hanging over his bed, as it had been back then. It used to give him nightmares, but that had changed over time. Maybe it was the only good thing the man had ever done for him after all. He could feel how the mask gave him strength and courage. He'd go out for something to eat tonight and have some fun— go to a nightclub. He knew exactly which one.

18

Cheers! And congratulations on our first anniversary!"

Majken smiled happily, smelling like a blossoming lilac. A heavy piece of gold jewellery hung down her plunging neckline. Her hair shone red in the glow of the candle.

"Cheers. And congratulations to you, too!" he said, trying the red wine. "But I feel like I've known you much longer," he added with a smile, as he put the glass down.

"You have! We've actually known each other for over two years now."

They sat in silence for a while, eating their food.

"It's turned out well, down by the river. Almost like Nyhavn in Copenhagen. We did some photo shoots here the other day; they could easily have been taken at a café in the Mediterranean," he said to steer the conversation in another direction.

Majken finished chewing. "Oh yeah, the fashion catalogue, right?"

"Mm-hmm, the shoot turned out really well." He had a mouth full of pasta salad and smiled shyly.

"I'm very impressed with the way you've set up your advertising agency, Danny. You've really made the most of the space. The only thing I do mind is that you have moved into the premises upstairs. I told you—you can live with me."

He wiped his mouth with the serviette and shook his head. "It's often late by the time I'm finished, so it's handier to just to be able to go upstairs and fall into bed."

"Hmm, how long does it take to drive to Risskov? About twenty minutes?"

"An hour on Grenåvej," he interrupted with a twinkle in his eye.

"Yeah, okay. There is heavy traffic, but still. That *is* a bad excuse." She looked inquisitively at him and turned her glass. "Do you still think it's too early to move in together now that we've known each other for so long?"

"It's not that." He leaned back, annoyed that they were now going to discuss the topic again. Soon he'd have no more excuses left for delaying a more committed relationship. And why should he? The decision was made. He felt his pocket discreetly. The little box made his heart race, and an inkling of doubt gnawed. He looked at her and saw only something he liked. She was a vision, sitting there in the orange blouse that suited her reddish hair perfectly. Her eyes were happy and radiant. And she had forgiven him. Forgiven him for something he couldn't even forgive himself for.

"Haven't you settled in, in Aarhus? I really hope you intend to stay?"

"Yes, of course. I love Aarhus. I'm going to stay." But he often missed Zealand and, not least, his hometown Klampenborg. It was a pleasure to visit headquarters over there, and he still felt very honoured that Tonny Langdahl had offered him the chance to run their Jutland branch in Aarhus. Bureau-Step2 had been inaugurated in Badstuegade last autumn. Danny had hired a small group of staff who met the requirements for the type of assignments the agency handled in Jutland.

"Who was the photographer?" asked Majken, studying his thoughtful face.

"What?"

"The photos for the catalogue, I mean. Who was the photographer?"

"Someone local, a photographer here in Aarhus who had time for an urgent job. Our top model from Sweden could only do one day, so we had to bring the already tight deadline forward."

"So, you didn't ask Kamilla?"

He took a deep breath. "It wouldn't have mattered. She'll never work with me."

Majken couldn't hide her relief. He saw it in her eyes and shoulders, which suddenly relaxed. She leaned over the table, took his face between her hands, and kissed him warmly on the mouth. "She'll forgive you, Danny. Forgive *us*. With time. But she's dealing with a lot of other things right now. The job at the paper—and the new "old" murder. It's terrifying that a corpse can lie in a bog for so long without anyone noticing it!"

He tasted her lipstick and tried to pull himself together. The past couldn't be changed, but something could be done about the future. He had to get used to it; his future was with Majken and not with Kamilla. Demanding that she forgive him was impossible. "Yes, that's the worst thing about Aarhus. All the murders," he replied, trying to sound cheerful.

"Oh, there's not that many. You've just been unlucky enough to be here for a run. First, the Gitte murder—and now the woman in the bog."

"Yes, and the doctor last night."

"Who? I didn't hear about that."

"I heard it briefly on the news this morning. The wife found him stabbed in the yard by their house outside Skåde. His three hunting dogs were killed, too."

Majken pushed the half-empty plate away. "That's gruesome! Was he a doctor? What was his name?"

"I didn't catch it. But we'll probably hear all about it on the news. Do you think you knew him?"

"I hope not. As long as it's not some psychopath who is going around killing all the doctors and nurses in Aarhus. The woman in the bog was a nurse, wasn't she?" Majken bit her lower lip nervously.

"She was, apparently, a nursing assistant—but what's the difference?"

"You mean *I* can finally teach *you* something?" She laughed, settling herself. "To be a nursing assistant, you have to take a one-year diploma. It was abolished in 1991, and the social and health care assistant course was introduced instead. To be a nurse, you do a degree in nursing that usually takes about three and a half years. But imagine if it really is a sick man who has it in for doctors and nurses."

He took her hand and smiled. "Or a sick woman! Let's leave that train of thought there. The two murders don't have to have anything to do with each other."

"No, but still. People have gone mad. They beat each other to death from road rage, shoot people on the street in Copenhagen with automatic weapons, stab each other to death in broad daylight, and mistreat and kill innocent animals, so who knows?"

"Remember—we're out celebrating our first anniversary. Would you like a romantic dessert? A coffee? Or another glass of red wine?"

"I have to drive home."

"You can stay with me. You could actually walk from here to Badstuegade in a drunken stupor, may I remind you. I can easily make up the couch," he teased.

Majken tilted her head and looked at him. "If you knew how much it meant to me—that I met you, Danny," she said seriously.

"I know. But there is something I don't quite understand . . ." He called a waiter over to their table and asked for the dessert menu. "I haven't met your family yet," he continued when the waiter had left. It was about time he detached himself from the past and moved on. They flipped through the menu. "Are you afraid that your posh family won't approve of a simple advertising man like me?"

"No, it's not that," she said quickly, pausing, as if she didn't know what more she should say. "It's my sister."

"Your sister? Is your sister not allowed to meet me?" He joked but could tell from Majken that it wasn't funny.

"I'm afraid you'll choose her instead of me and leave me."

He almost dropped the menu. "What? I would never do that. Is your sister beautiful—is that it?" He tried to sound uninterested in the answer but, judging by Majken's eyes, had failed in his quest.

"There! You see. You're already interested!"

"Stop it, sweetheart. It was just for fun."

"It's not a laughing matter. Yes, my sister is a beauty, and"—she quickly drank from her glass—"she's done it before." Majken hesitantly told him about when she had found her little sister in bed with her then husband. Danny looked at her flabbergasted.

"They're married now and have a little girl together. She must be about two or three now." Majken looked down at the table sadly and fidgeted nervously with her necklace.

"Must be? Does that mean you've never met your niece?" He took her hand; it shook a little. "That's not good, Majken. I understand well, but you have to forgive them—for your own sake."

Majken looked at him with dark eyes. "That kind of thing can't be forgiven," she mumbled.

"Rubbish! It was years ago, and you've moved on in your life. You have me now. You were able to forgive me." He said the latter very carefully.

Majken shook her head. "I just can't. You were easy to forgive because I love you. I loved Kamilla's Rasmus, too—but I love you more."

He looked away, afraid his eyes would reveal him. If Kamilla thought like that, his life would be perfect, but, naturally, she loved her son more. She hated him, and that fact tormented him as much as the guilt. He got up with his wallet in his hand. "I'm going to go over and order two desserts and two coffees that I am then going to serve with a little surprise. You sit here in the meantime and think about when we should drive to Holbæk to visit your family." He kissed her on her hair and went up to the counter. Majken watched him go as if she already missed him.

19

The streetlights had gone out on one side of the road. She kept to the illuminated side as she tottered along in high heels. She usually brought a change of clothes and shoes at this time of year and would change before going home or taking a taxi. A car wasn't something she could afford anymore. But tonight, she had chosen to walk; it had been so unseasonably warm, and she was not quite feeling herself.

The uneven distribution of light cast her shadow in front of her every time she passed under a lamp-post, and each time, she shuddered and then laughed hoarsely that yet again she was afraid of her own shadow. Walking home at this time of night wasn't good. You heard so many creepy stories.

She stopped under the next streetlamp and lit a cigarette. "I'm too bloody old for this," she said in a hoarse voice. All the second-hand smoke she had inhaled in her life had destroyed the mucous membranes in her throat. Not to mention all the cigarettes she herself had smoked. She took a long, greedy puff as soon as the cigarette lit up. Standing still while wearing only a thin coat, short skirt, and nylon stockings was making her cold, so she quickly walked on with the cigarette in her hand. She smoked it now and then, puffing the fumes into the darkness. There wasn't a soul on the street. The dark windows of the properties she walked past told her that most people were sleeping. Soon, it would be Sunday morning, when fresh bread rolls would be purchased. She envied them. But she had chosen the life she lived for herself. Or had she? The pay was sort of okay. But it had been more fun when she was young and reasonably pretty. Customers used to whistle at her and pat her bum in the little skin-tight skirt. That was back when it had been little. Now she saw how young people were treated in the same way without, however, finding themselves in exactly the same situation as she had been at that age. She felt unwelcome and a laughingstock. No one whistled, and she wasn't patted on the bum anymore, despite it becoming somewhat easier to hit over the years. Everything had been different then. She hadn't felt so alone and excluded. It had all changed the day the terrible secret had settled like a clammy hand around her, then Kit's accident, and all that followed. She took a heavy puff of the cigarette and coughed. But tonight had been different. She smiled at the thought and shook her head incomprehensibly. Maybe she wasn't as old and ugly as she thought.

She had spotted him at the bar. He sat with a drink and looked devilishly handsome. He winked charmingly at her. But he was too young. What would he want with a fifty-two-year-old woman? She immediately turned around to see what young bird was standing behind her to avoid an embarrassing situation. But no one was standing there. He winked again and signalled for her to come over to him. She carried over a tray of empty beer and spirit glasses. He probably just wanted to order another drink.

"Hello, beautiful. When time do you get off?" His voice was soft and masculine; it sent little shocks of pleasure through her. She was embarrassed to feel like that. Felt ugly, with too much make-up when he looked closer at her face in the spotlight over the bar.

"Do you mean *me*?" Even though she tried to make her voice young and light, it still sounded hoarse and rusty.

"Of course I mean you. What's your name?"

"Annemette."

"What time do you get off?" he asked again.

She was flustered and confused. It'd been a hundred years since someone had asked her that, but she shouldn't be too easy, either. "Why do you want to know that?" she asked sceptically, almost unable to wait for the answer due to a customer demanding her attention. In his drunkenness, he had knocked his beer over another customer, whose ensuing fury had resulted in fisticuffs. Several of the waitstaff had attempted to separate them.

But he sat at the bar all evening, smiling at her. She kept an eye on him when young, beautiful girls passed by, but he didn't deign them a glance. She had read about how some young men preferred older, mature women. But had she really just run into such a wonder? She smiled back as she caught his gaze between patrons. His eyes were constantly resting on her. He was still sitting there late into the night. She tried to avoid him, fearing she couldn't live up to his demands. Fear that this wonderful sense of self-worth and excitement would disappear, like when a spell is broken. It's how Cinderella must have felt.

After last orders, she was sorting the till at the bar. Her final job before going home to sleep. She felt him behind her and, shortly after, his warm breath against her neck. She tensed pleasantly, turned halfway around, and looked into his eyes. There was something about his eyes that made her feel like she had known him all her life. Her heart was pounding, and as he leaned in towards her to whisper something in her ear, she felt his heartbeat just as violently. He really was one of those wonders.

"So, are you finished now? Should I walk you home?" he whispered.

"I'd rather see to getting myself home. I also think you should leave now," she whispered back, not meaning it. His skin smelled masculine. It had been so long since she had smelled a man.

Then she was gone. Afraid he was making fun of her and just wanted to humiliate her. It had happened before—and with much older men. They'd been drunk, of course, but it didn't make their words hurt any less. Since those episodes, she had kept a low profile and did her work. Did what she was best at. But he didn't seem drunk at all. Only the faint scent of Amarula cream liqueur, which she'd thought unusual when he'd ordered it, could be smelled on his breath. Customers so rarely asked for that liqueur. Maybe he travelled a lot. He was tanned. Wonderfully tanned.

She took another puff of her cigarette and felt warm and alive. Even though nothing more had happened, it was an indescribable feeling. Better to keep it inside than be mocked or perhaps learn that she couldn't live up to such a young man's demands and suffer humiliation. My God, he could be her son! The wind blew up, making it a little colder. A thin fake leopardskin coat from Bilka supermarket was her only outerwear. She began to regret not getting a taxi. The Botanical Gardens lay like an obstacle ahead. The many rapes in the gardens made her go another way, despite it being a shortcut. And what could *really* happen to her? She was too old to be raped. Who would touch her? But, then again, she reflected, rape was a crime of hatred and power. Rapists didn't set age limits.

Footsteps behind her scared her into picking up her pace. The steps behind her now did the same. She ran, wobbling in the high heels several times. Then she heard him shout and recognised the voice. She turned around. There he stood. She started laughing nervously. He walked towards her with a smooth gait like a panther and put his arm around her.

"You're freezing!" He took off his coat and put it around her shoulders. "Why are you running? Why did you just disappear like that? I've been looking for you. Come here, let me drive you home."

She snuggled against his chest under his coat and followed him to the car. She hadn't heard him at all, preoccupied as she had been with her fantasies. But now he was here, holding her and making her feel safe.

"Where do you live?" Gallantly, he opened the car door for her.

Her body trembled when she answered, "Fuglebakkevej." Inside the car, she warmed up and straightened her hair. It was frizzy and dyed black, but she had put it up nicely—the hairclip was still in the right place. As he walked around the car, she pulled out a few locks of hair around her neck. It looked a little sexier. He sat down behind the wheel and winked at her again.

"Why me?" she asked as they began to drive.

He put a hand on her thigh and smiled warmly.

"Because it's my birthday," he replied.

20

Unsurprisingly, the autopsy showed that the cause of death was a stab wound to the heart and that the doctor had been stabbed several times post-mortem. The time of death was set between ten and eleven o'clock on Friday night, so that took them one step further than the first murder case. Leander had again, using his long tweezers, pulled an object triumphantly out of the corpse with the words that a body always retains evidence for the benefit of the investigation. It was a piece of the murder weapon that had been left behind. The violent knife wounds in Helge Vangberg's chest had caused the tip of the knife to break off in the sternum. An approximately two-centimetre-long tip of steel was placed in a bag and sent to the lab for further examination. The steel had to be analysed, as it might be possible to identify what type of knife was used. There was nothing else to report apart from the doctor's penchant for cognac, attested to by his liver.

Roland was back at the police station and had briefed his staff who, thus motivated, started their assigned tasks immediately. At the end of the day, Kurt Olsen held the exclusive press conference he'd promised the journalists on Saturday morning, allowing him to divulge as much of his knowledge to the hungry flock of vultures as he wanted. Roland had other things to see to. He smiled kindly as Isabella Munch knocked on the open door and cautiously entered his office.

"Come in and sit down, Isabella. Close the door."

Her blond hair was pinned up on her head loosely with a silver hairclip today. She wore only discreet make-up, a little colour on her lashes and a neutral lip balm that made her lips shine in the light from the window. It looked like it had just been freshened up. Her skin was like a peach.

He cleared his throat. "You've found something, it seems," he said, nodding at the folder she was carrying in her arms.

"Yes, it's about the first murder, not Helge Vangberg. I followed a lead."

Her teeth were chalk-white and straight. She pulled out the chair and sat down across from him. To his great wonder, he recognised her scent. It was Irene's favourite—Estée Lauder's Beyond Paradise. He was about to comment on it but then deemed it inappropriate.

She smacked open the folder and flipped through it a little. "I spoke to an employee from Silkeborg Hospital who was brave enough to investigate the case and go back through old papers. They have no record of her. She didn't work as a nursing assistant in Silkeborg. I dug some more and found out something else. She didn't even live in Silkeborg."

He raised an eyebrow, giving Isabella a look that said he didn't follow. She immediately explained.

"She moved. She moved in with her boyfriend in Aarhus when she started studying but didn't change her address, otherwise, she wouldn't have been entitled to the lone parent allowance or housing support from Silkeborg municipality anymore."

"So, she committed benefit fraud?"

"Yep!" Isabella cast her head slightly, making her blond hair fall out of the hairclip and hang down over her cheek.

"But they must have noticed that when she disappeared!"

Isabella shrugged. "It wasn't that easy given that she was actually still renting a house in Silkeborg. It doesn't take long to pop from Aarhus to Silkeborg to get your post—and cheques. That's probably how she could afford the car."

He nodded. *Female intuition again.* "Nice job, Isabella."

His hand lay close to hers next to the folder. His pulse rose as their skin touched when she probably innocently moved her hand slightly.

She looked at him with interest. "Is it Southern Italy you come from?"

He nodded with a lump in his throat. "How did you guess that?"

"Your skin is so dark, and your eyes are almost black. My family has travelled to Italy a lot. Especially to southern Italy and Sicily. I studied

Italian for a semester; it's such a beautiful language—but difficult. I love Italy."

He was flattered by her words and tried to imagine the beautiful blond girl among his countrymen, who followed blond hair like bulls followed red capes. They probably had fun with her name with its *-bella* suffix. *Italy probably loves you, too, my friend.*

"Have you been to Naples?" he asked, and the image of his father's grave was the first thing that came to mind. Then the dirt and rubbish piled up in the streets. Suddenly, he hoped she would say that she had never been there.

"Once. I felt sorry for the city. It is so beautiful, but as long as the Camorra are profiting from the rubbish and hold the power, its beauty won't come into its own."

He breathed a sigh of relief. She had obviously investigated the situation and didn't just believe—like so many others—that it was the Neapolitans who were dirty pigs.

"Your name isn't Roland, is it? It's not a particularly Italian name. If I were to guess, I'd say your name is Rolando?"

He nodded in surprise.

"May I call you that?"

"It would probably be a little strange. Everyone here calls me Roland." Only Irene and the family called him Rolando. It would be too familiar to be called it at work, too. It inexplicably divided him into the two people he was. Rolando in his spare time was one person; Roland during his working hours was another. To his relief, she nodded understandingly.

"Okay."

"My father was in the Carabinieri," he said, wondering why he was revealing all this. There weren't many people he had opened up to—not even his closest colleagues had been initiated into his past.

"You say *was?*"

"Yes, he's dead now." He cleared his throat, hoping to avoid the conversation, but he had already said too much.

"Did the Camorra kill him?" she asked.

He nodded, wanting to pull his hand away but couldn't. Her skin emitted a magical magnetic force.

"Was that why you came to Denmark?"

"My mother fled here. My aunt was married to a Dane and lived here. I was too young to remember. I was only a little boy. But that's how I ended up in Denmark."

"And thank God for that!"

He looked at her in astonishment and thought she was blushing a little.

"Is your wife Italian, too?" she asked quickly.

He glanced at his wedding ring, which must have given him away. Given how acquainted she was with all things Italian, she'd probably also heard that Italian men often lived at home with their mothers until they were well into adulthood.

"No, Irene is Danish. I met her at the station in Copenhagen. She was a police secretary at the time."

Isabella didn't seem to be making a pass at him. She was probably just a loving and compassionate person showing some interest in her boss. Yet he suddenly realised how wrong this was. He pulled his hand away and took a piece of chewing gum.

"'Lose the smoke—keep the fire,'" he said cheerfully, popping it in his mouth.

"Ads," she said, laughing.

He nodded. "Was there more on the nursing assistant? What about the boyfriend in Aarhus—do we have anything on him?"

"Not much; he moved abroad. But this is where it gets interesting." She imitated Anne Larsen's masterful artistic pause before continuing. "He moved to Africa."

Roland chewed. "Bloody hell. Why did Sebastian not tell us about his stepfather?"

"My guess is that he broke off contact with him when his mother disappeared—or maybe the stepfather disappeared as well."

"Can we follow up on that?"

"I've already done it. Sebastian lived with another family from January 1984 until he turned eighteen, when he moved away from home and began his apprenticeship as a mechanic, which suggests his stepfather wasn't the one looking after him. All traces of him disappear here. We don't know where Knud moved to in Africa—it's a huge continent."

He tried to look away, but even her eyes were magnetic. He had never seen eyes that colour before, and he wondered whether it was coloured lenses. Such a thing was widely used among young people nowadays. You never knew what was real. But he didn't dare ask her.

"Maybe to a place where you can buy souvenirs carved in black ebony," he muttered instead.

"You're thinking of the murder weapon? Do you think her husband was the killer?"

"I think there's a pattern here. Maybe he was committing benefit fraud, too. Maybe he actually lives here in Denmark." Isabella got up quickly, her eyes glowing with zeal. "I'll go exploring in Africa!" she said.

"We need to talk to the family that Sebastian lived with, too. They have to be able to give us some information."

Isabella nodded eagerly and walked towards the door with the file in her arms.

"By the way, does he have a name, the stepfather?" he asked her back.

"Of course. His name is Knud Engtoft." She was on her way out the door, and he involuntarily looked at her round buttocks in her tight jeans. It was sheer luck that the Criminal Investigation Department didn't wear police uniforms with baggy trouser bottoms. She suddenly turned around, and he didn't know whether he'd looked away in time.

She smiled.

"By the way, I nearly forgot. The nursing assistant went by several names. Before she got married, her name was Bente Louise Juhl; when she got married, she called herself . . ."

"Bente Louise Engtoft I take it," he interrupted her with a teasing smile.

"Not quite. She dropped her first name and used only her middle name— maybe something to do with the scam. She went by Louise Engtoft."

21

December 1983

Dear Elina

I don't know what to do. I couldn't get out to Josefine yesterday because we were snowed in. Today, when I arrived, I found her very debilitated. Josefine has not been well since the new doctor took over. He doesn't think the treatment she received benefited her. There were too many side effects, he says. Oh, if only doctors could agree on that sort of thing. I've been thinking about becoming a doctor, so I can have an opinion as well. Gustav is seldom home. I would have liked to have talked to him about it. Josefine says she doesn't like the new doctor. She doesn't trust him. What should I do? According to Josefine, Gustav is supposed to come home this evening, so I'll go out there and talk to him. I wish you could come.

Love, Louise

PS! If you had a phone, I could call you. I still don't understand how you can do without one. What if you get sick and your neighbour isn't home?

She folded the letter. That was the last letter. December 1983 was when her mother had died. What had happened? She became restless and looked at her watch. It would be a while before Peter was home, if he came home for dinner at all. She never knew. She read the letter again and became even more uneasy. Normally, she only felt nauseated in the morning, but now she suddenly had to run to the toilet and lie in front of the bowl. She placed a protective hand on her stomach to shield the baby from the involuntary convulsions that were forcing the contents of her stomach into the toilet, keeping her hair away from her face with the other.

Peter still didn't know. The opportunity had never arisen. Or else she didn't dare tell him. Maybe it would be best if she had an abortion and never said anything to him about it at all. She immediately regretted the thought and flushed the toilet. She sat down on the floor with both hands on her stomach.

"I'm sorry, little one. I didn't mean it," she whispered.

Noise in the living room made her get up and look in the mirror. Was Peter home already? She brushed her teeth, put on lipstick, and made herself a little presentable.

"Hey, babe! That's where you were hiding!" Peter took off his jacket and gave her a quick kiss. "I stopped at The Long S on the way home. The bag is on the kitchen table."

In their own language, Esselunga supermarket had become *The Long S*. It was Peter's idea because she couldn't pronounce the Italian name. "You're home early today," she said as she unpacked the goods. It took about twenty minutes, depending on the traffic, to drive from Grundfos on Via Gran Sasso to home.

"Yeah, there was not much to do—and I missed you." He put his arms around her stomach and pressed her hard against him while she put items in the fridge. She could feel him and knew what he wanted.

"Don't do that, Peter!" she said so harshly that he immediately let her go.

"What's wrong? Can I not kiss my wife on the neck anymore?" he said indignantly, angrily taking over the unpacking of the shopping.

"I'm sorry, Peter. I'm just not feeling well, and when you press on my stomach, it . . ."

"Oh, is it *that* time? Couldn't you just take the pill all the time, then you wouldn't feel so bad?" He meant it jokingly, smiling. "Maybe I'll just take a *cold* shower before dinner instead!"

* * *

He came out of the bathroom with only a towel around his waist and helped her finish the food. He was a good cook and often made food—when he was at home to do it.

She sliced lettuce as she watched him. His muscles clearly showed the results of his gym workouts. But it was not too much; she couldn't stand men with bulging muscles like Schwarzenegger clones. He had dark hair on his chest and was what she called *a real man*. He was just the right size all over and more than the right size in a certain place. He smelled of shampoo and Giorgio Armani aftershave. She wanted him, but when she thought of the child, the desire evaporated.

"Did you hit yourself?" she asked worriedly as she spotted the mark on his neck.

"Where?" he asked.

"There!" She went closer and put a finger on the mark, but now she could see it wasn't from a blow.

"I don't remember hitting myself." He searched with his hand on his neck to find the place. "It's not sore," he muttered.

Behind him, tears sprang into her eyes, but she said nothing as she set plates on the table.

Peter got dressed and took the roast out of the oven. They sat down at the table. It was romantically set with candles, a bottle of red wine, and lovely food. But the mood didn't match. They ate in silence. The noise from the traffic on Corso Magenta mingled with the clinks of the cutlery against porcelain.

"Who is she, Peter?"

"Who?" He looked up from his plate and she could see in his eyes that he knew well what she was referring to.

"Who, for God's sake!" he said again when she didn't answer. "The only thing you ever bloody well do is accuse me of everything!"

"Who is she?" she said calmly again and carried on eating. "The one who gave you that love bite."

"No, now stop!" He slammed down the knife and fork.

"Did it happen at the dinner? When you danced until early morning? And what else did you do? Is she Italian?"

Peter turned pale and poured another glass of wine for himself. "I remember now what happened. I ran into a pipe. It hurt like hell."

"Stop, Peter. I know a hickey when I see one. Her lips are practically cast in the bruise. Was I supposed to find out in this childish way?"

She tried to keep her voice calm even though everything was swirling inside like a hurricane.

"Sabrina. I love you. But a man has needs, you know, and you've been so . . . lately . . . weeks can pass between . . . when we . . ."

Well, we did it at least three and a half months ago! She nearly shouted, but instead, she finished eating and said no more.

He got dessert, but she didn't feel like it. She contented herself with drinking from her glass of water. She had managed to stay away from the wine without him commenting on it.

"I'm going back to Denmark, Peter." She made the decision suddenly and found the courage to say it.

"I knew it! I knew you'd never fit in here!" He finished his dessert and pushed the plate away.

"That's not why, Peter. I'm actually starting to like Milan and Italy. I realised that when we were landing yesterday, and I saw the view of the city from the plane. I'm coming back again—there's just something I have to see to at home."

Peter examined her suspiciously. "Does it have anything to do with the funeral?"

"It has something to do with Dad," she admitted.

"So, it's not because of me?" He sounded relieved. "That woman didn't mean anything, babe. I was just sad that you'd gone back to Denmark. I was drunk and . . . you know."

It was probably the closest thing to a confession that she'd ever get, even though she didn't want it at all. She would rather have believed the story about the pipe.

They helped each other fill the dishwasher. In the middle of it all, a colleague from Grundfos—or someone—called. Peter locked himself in his study for half an hour, while she cleaned up the kitchen and fought the urge to listen at the door. He came out and said Normann said hello—he was an operations technician at Grundfos. She thanked him and went out to the bathroom after he'd brushed his teeth and gone into the bedroom. As soon as she was alone, the reaction came. She leaned over the sink and sobbed silently.

22

Anne poured coffee into Kamilla's mug. Mads Dam was immersed in an article about AGF Aarhus's latest defeat on the pitch. Only four of the editorial staff were in. Britt had called in sick, claiming that Thygesen had probably infected her. She didn't sound nearly as ill as he did when she rang, except for some small awkward coughs that didn't sound very genuine.

"I don't understand how Thygesen is still sick. It's been a whole week now. Do we know what's wrong with him?" Kamilla asked, adding milk to her coffee. She didn't normally use it, but the coffee had been brewing in the machine since noon. "I spoke to him this morning. He'd heard about the new murder—of course. I don't know what's wrong with him, but he *must* be really sick; otherwise, he wouldn't be able to stay away from here with two murders on the agenda."

"It must be the flu," Mads Dam announced without looking up from his keyboard.

Anne smiled. She couldn't imagine Thygesen lying in bed with a thermometer in his mouth—or in the other end for that matter—but she hoped it wasn't serious. If it was just the normal flu, he would probably be fine.

"Anyway, as I said, I'm pretty sure the nursing assistant and the doctor knew each other, and I have a strong hunch that it has to do with the family who moved from Mundelstrup in 1983," Anne said.

Anne was perched on the edge of Kamilla's desk, while she was in the middle of choosing photos from the press conference where—to their annoyance—Roland Benito hadn't appeared, but the chief superintendent had again been very generous with the information in both murder cases.

"Where is Nicolaj *now?*" exclaimed Anne.

"I sent him down to the shop on the corner for ice cream—told him I wanted a *scoop* of something tasty." Mads grinned.

It reminded Anne of her own internship at the newspaper in Copenhagen. That kind of thing—and worse—was to be expected. A kind of ritual for being included in the journalist clan. She'd been told to find a good *spin* class as an intern, but *scoops* was new to her, and she doubted Nicolaj had fallen for it.

"If he actually comes back here with a mountain of ice cream, I'm going to make you eat it all," she asserted, unable to hide a joyful smile when she saw Mads Dam's facial expression. He looked very nervous when Nicolaj suddenly stepped in the door with a bag, which he set on the corner of the printer, while he took his coat off outside the cloakroom and shook the rain off of it. Anne took the wet bag out into the kitchen. It wasn't ice cream—too early for that. She sliced the raspberry jam Swiss roll. Mads breathed a sigh of relief.

"The weather! Summer is now finally over!" exclaimed Nicolaj, walking behind Mads's chair. "Unfortunately, I couldn't get a *scoop* this early, but they promised that if you go back tomorrow afternoon, they'll have something for you then," he said to Mads's neck as he patted him lightly on the shoulder before sitting down in his chair. Anne smiled. She was getting more and more fond of the lad.

Mads was left alone in the office with a cup of coffee and a slice of raspberry roll and told to answer the phones while she, Nicolaj, and Kamilla were in the meeting room.

"It wasn't that hard to find that family. They weren't the only ones who moved from Mundelstrup in 1983, but there was only one family where the lady of the house had passed away shortly before. Her husband's name is Gustav Hjort, and he is now married to Carola Hjort." Anne broke off a piece of the raspberry roll and took a bite.

"Hold on, are they the ones who have the Maritime Merman business with exclusive pleasure boats down by the harbour?" asked Nicolaj with his mouth full.

"Exactly. Do you know it?"

"Yeah. I have often admired the yachts in the harbour. Buuuut, my wallet can't stretch that far—yet."

"If you want one of those, you need to start looking for another job," she said dryly.

"Have you talked to them? Were they the family the nursing assistant was with?" Kamilla took a sip of the coffee and added more milk.

"No, I haven't spoken to them, I think we just pop by. They're probably all at home in the house on Strandvejen at this time."

"Did you talk to the police about it? Do they know about the Hjort family, too—they weren't mentioned at the press conference." Nicolaj had raspberry jam at the corner of his mouth but noticed it himself and licked it away with his tongue and a little help from his index finger.

"The police can track that family as easily as we can, so they probably know about them—unless they've put this old murder case on hold while they concentrate on the dead doctor. But they'd be making a mistake," she said.

"So, you're convinced there's a connection between the two murders?" Kamilla said.

"Absolutely! And Gustav Hjort can probably give us a lead."

"And you haven't heard from the anonymous tipper who called—now that another corpse has appeared. He hasn't rung about that or anything?" asked Nicolaj. His green eyes shone brightly, and she thought for a moment that they could use a man like him in the police. After the police reform, the department had become so apathetic that people began to do private security patrols against burglaries and the many arson cases. Maybe he was supposed to be a detective and not a journalist. Even though it was almost the same.

"Not a sound. It's like he's fallen off the face of the Earth." She looked cautiously at Kamilla and Nicolaj, who didn't comment, but were probably both thinking the same thing—maybe more bodies were going to show up. The anonymous person had to know something that the killer didn't want to be brought to light—unless the anonymous caller was indeed the murderer. She got up and threw the empty plastic cups in the bin. "Are you ready?"

The house was a neoclassical villa located in the first row facing the sea. There was no doubt that the residents were well-off. The garden was nice and well maintained—probably by a gardener—and there was a blue swimming pool in the middle of the lawn. The view from the first floor had to be of the memorial park. The façade was painted in a faint pastel blue colour, and on the balcony were exotic-looking plants.

"I'd never live here," she whispered to Kamilla as they got out of the car.

"Why not?" Kamilla's mouth was almost hanging open as she looked up towards the villa.

"To get to the sea, you have to cross Strandvejen—the traffic there is always crazy—and to get to the woods, you have to cross Oddervej! I would feel like I was imprisoned."

Kamilla laughed and lifted the heavy camera bag from the back seat. Nicolaj slammed the back door and looked at the house with awe followed by muttering the inevitable *coool.*

The doorbell rang in a large hall. Anne didn't feel comfortable having to ring the bell—not to mention having to enter such a nice home. Kamilla nervously pulled the strap of the camera bag up onto her shoulder. After a few minutes, the door was opened by a woman wearing what she herself would probably call *casual wear*—not Anne's interpretation of it, which was tracksuit bottoms and a pre-washed T-shirt—a maritime white cotton jumper with an embroidered emblem on the chest and navy-blue stripes on the sleeves and waist over navy-blue trousers that fell lightly around her slender body. She was tanned and her hair was lightened by the sun and the grey of age. She looked at them in surprise. They looked just as surprised at not being greeted by a housekeeper in a black-and-white uniform.

"We're from the *Daily News.* May we come in? We just have a few questions," Anne said as politely as she could.

Carola Hjort straightened her hair. "Have you already heard about the new yacht? I thought Gustav was sending out the press release tomorrow. But come in," she said warmly and opened the door and led them into a hall with royal blue walls and white window frames and panels. The stairs up to the first floor were lined with a patterned blue carpet; the banisters were in neoclassical style, too. A man wearing a light-knit casual sweater, white trousers, and boating shoes came running silently down the stairs.

"Gustav! I didn't think the press was supposed to know anything until tomorrow," Carola said reproachfully when he reached them in the hall.

"We're not here about a yacht," Anne hurried to say to spare the handsome gentleman's discomfort. Carola Hjort seemed annoyed; she had been so quick to let them in.

"Gustav Hjort." The man introduced himself, gesturing to a double glass door at the end of the hall. "Well, shall we go in and sit down?" He asked his wife to get Johanne to serve the coffee in the conservatory. They took off their shoes and followed him into a dining room with a light wooden floor and a ceiling with a beautiful simple stucco pattern. He opened a four-panel folding glass door, and they entered a southwest-facing bright conservatory with a fireplace and palm trees in large pots. She held back a small gasp, waiting to hear a *coool* from Nicolaj, but for once he was speechless. They sat down in deep sofas of coloured suede by a table with a vase holding a bouquet of fresh flowers. Shortly afterwards, Johanne came with the coffee. She didn't look like a maid and wore neither a white apron nor a cap on her head. In fact, she looked more like a teenager living in the house.

"Thank you, Johanne," Gustav said, making room on the sofa for Carola, right on the heels of Johanne, who disappeared again without a word.

"May we hear what it is about then?" asked Carola with a slightly haughty mouth and a voice that sounded as if she'd better take over now.

On the way in the car, Anne had told them that it was Carola Hjort who had the money—all the wealth was a legacy from her family. The family-owned factory in Fåborg had specialised in manufacturing exclusive—and expensive—sailboats and yachts, which were mainly sold abroad, in particular, the south of France, where the family also owned a holiday home in Cannes. After her father's death, Carola inherited the entire fortune as the only child. Gustav was quickly appointed CEO of the factory, which they later sold to live off the money. When the boredom kicked in, they launched the Maritime Merman ApS business at the Port of Aarhus with a few exclusive yachts, which they sold—for a healthy profit—to wealthy Danes, who continued to grow in number—according to them. Before Gustav Hjort met Carola, he was an ordinary clerk in the accounting department at Toyota with a terminally ill wife at home. Anne had read about it in an article from an online business supplement. But even if she hadn't read it, she would still be in no doubt as to who wore the trousers in this couple.

"You've probably read and heard about the woman who was found dead in the bog at Mundelstrup?" Anne said. She was still the only one who dared say anything. She had never seen rich people for anything other than what they were—people.

"Yes, it's awful. But what does that have to do with us?" Carola didn't seem nervous as she poured coffee from a shiny silver pot.

"Maybe you don't know that the murder victim has been identified?"

No reaction.

"It's Bente Louise Juhl."

All three kept an eye on Gustav's and Carola's facial expressions, but there were no changes.

"Is that someone you know?" Carola asked disoriented.

"No." Gustav drank his coffee and looked at Anne with a neutral face.

"She was your wife's nursing assistant during her illness back in 1983. Is that not correct?" she asked.

"It must be a misunderstanding—that wasn't the nursing assistant's name," Gustav replied, smiling with relief.

"No, you're right. Back then she was married and maybe used her other name—Louise Engtoft—does that sound more familiar?"

Anne tasted the coffee. It had been made with a French press and the beans really came into their own. It was the best coffee she'd ever had. Even the new coffee shops with award-winning baristas in the city couldn't compare to this.

Carola and Gustav stared at her. Neither of them said anything.

"Essentially, Bente Louise Juhl—alias Louise Engtoft—was committing benefit fraud. She had an address in Silkeborg but lived with her boyfriend in Aarhus. But, of course, you were not aware of that, were you?" She spoke only to Gustav, who had turned pale under his tanned skin. His hand shook as he took his phone, which suddenly played a classical tune, out of his trouser pocket. He looked at the phone display, looked at her, and glanced at Carola before getting up, confused. "It's my daughter. I have to take it," he said, and judging by the expression in his eyes, it wasn't an occurrence he was used to. He walked out of the conservatory and closed the four-panel door behind him. Through the glass, Anne watched him as he turned his back to the door and spoke.

"Of course we didn't know that. She'd never have been hired if we did!" Carola Hjort took the lead again.

"*We?* Would that mean you knew Gustav Hjort even then?" She stared in genuine surprise at Carola, who had started to busy herself with the flowers in the vase.

"No, of course not. I'm just so used to saying *we*. I mean that Gustav would never have hired her."

Nicolaj sat like a petrified statue that belonged in the conservatory and hadn't even touched his coffee. His eyes wandered around the room, as though photographing everything, and he had no energy for anything else.

"Is it your daughter your husband is talking to?" Kamilla worked up the courage to ask.

Carola looked at Kamilla for the first time. "No, she's only Gustav's daughter," she replied, a *thank God* implied in her tone.

He returned to the conservatory after the conversation, his cheeks red. "Sabrina is in Denmark again. She's just landed in Copenhagen," he said happily to Carola, who clearly didn't share his enthusiasm.

"What is she doing here again?"

Gustav looked at them apologetically and openly tried to explain his wife's hostile attitude towards his daughter. "Sabrina lives in Italy with her husband. She was just home for her grandmother's funeral a few days ago, so it seems strange that she's coming back already." He looked at Carola again. "She wants to talk to me about something important, so I've agreed to meet her tomorrow morning. She's taking the night train to Aarhus." Carola contented herself with nodding, but it was clear from her eyes that there would certainly be more talk about it once the journalists were gone.

"But what does Louise Engtoft have to do with us?" asked Gustav, remembering where he'd left the conversation.

"She disappeared in 1983 and wasn't found until last week—murdered and thrown into the bog only about a minute's drive from where you lived at the time . . ."

Gustav looked at her with a fixed gaze. "She always walked down to Gammel Viborgvej on her own and took the bus or was collected by her boyfriend or husband, or whatever he was. Any of the psychos out there—even back then—could have taken her to the bog."

She nodded.

"Was she going anywhere else that night?" Finally, Nicolaj took the floor, and Carola and Gustav Hjort looked at him in astonishment as if they'd only now noticed him.

"She didn't talk about that kind of thing."

"You've probably also heard about the murdered doctor, Helge Vangberg. He wasn't by any chance your wife's doctor, was he?"

Gustav Hjort shook his head a little too eagerly. "Josefine's doctor was a Dr. Winther," he stammered.

"A first name?" asked Anne.

"We knew him only as Dr. Winther."

Kamilla opened the camera bag, but when Carola saw it, she held both hands up in front of her with outstretched fingers. "No photographs here!" she said sharply, getting up and smoothing her trouser legs. "I'll follow you out!"

They realised their audience was over.

Kamilla took some pictures outside the house anyway. One never knew if they would come in handy one day, in some celebrity scandal. Anne lit a cigarette while Kamilla photographed. She wasn't used to such upper-class people. "There's something fishy here," she said to Nicolaj, who enjoyed her confiding in him.

"I sense that, too. What do we do now?"

She stubbed the ashes of the cigarette into the white gravel of the courtyard and opened the car door for Kamilla so she could get the camera bag into the back seat. "It could be exciting to find this Dr. Winther. I thought the nursing assistant was working with Dr. Vangberg. And I also think it's worth taking a closer look at the nursing assistant's boyfriend or husband, who used to collect her up on Gammel Viborgvej."

"What about the daughter suddenly returning home from Italy to talk to her father about something important—about what? And the nursing assistant's son?"

She shook her head. "Maybe, Nicolaj, but what could they know? They were only children when all this happened," she replied thoughtfully.

23

———

Wasn't he the estate agent from Home?" Niels Nyborg asked, pointing to the hallway before closing the door behind him.

"Do you know him?"

"Yeah, he sold our apartment when we bought the house."

Roland hid the sales brochure in a drawer, but Niels spotted it anyway.

"What the hell! You're not selling Irene's childhood home, are you?"

He scratched his neck and smiled awkwardly, feeling caught red-handed. "No, I'm just curious to know what the house is worth nowadays," he said.

"You're not thinking about moving from this wonderful place, are you?" Niels pulled a chair in front of his desk.

"No, no. No plans to do that," he replied evasively. But in the drawer was a brochure for Helge Vangberg's property and a valuation for their house in Højbjerg, and to his surprise, being able to afford the Vangberg property wasn't an impossible dream—if they could get what the real estate agent reckoned for their house. A little top-up loan would do the rest.

"Well, what do you have for me?" Roland deliberately changed the subject.

Niels Nyborg loosened his shirt collar and cleared his throat. "While you were in that *important* meeting, I received an answer from Forensics. The steel from the tip of the knife in the doctor's sternum has been analysed. We have to go back to Africa." Niels sat down on the chair opposite Roland with his legs spread and his elbows resting on his knees. He turned his wedding ring. He reminded Roland of the old men sitting in the shade on the streets of Naples, turning a Catholic rosary. But Niels Nyborg wasn't that old. They were the same age.

"And how are we going to 'go back to Africa'? It almost sounds like a Karen Blixen title." He was in a good mood after the meeting with the estate agent. One of his great dreams was suddenly within reach.

"Gert Schmidt will fax a report, but what he said briefly was that it's a certain kind of steel. He called it carbon steel."

"That's not much to go on. Lots of knife blades are made of carbon steel now. Does he think it's African steel since we are going back to Africa?"

"He thinks it's very *old* African steel. Maybe even from a knife that could be a museum artefact. The steel is made the way a tribe from Tanzania has forged it for about two thousand years. The Haya people, he called them."

Roland suddenly felt guilty about spending a few hours in the afternoon talking to the estate agent. He should have been trying to find this Knud Engtoft, given that all the leads were gradually pointing to him. Kim and Isabella were tirelessly combing for clues in both Africa and Denmark.

"Have any museums reported a theft?"

"Not in Denmark at least."

"But we still don't know exactly what type of knife it is," he said, a little annoyed.

"No, maybe not. But if we find it, then we'll definitely have found the murder weapon. It would have been worse if it'd turned out to be one of the knives that all kids use today."

"Let's not go there," Roland muttered. There had been too many stab-bings lately. Young people said they carried knives to defend themselves against other young people carrying knives, but that was exactly what was escalating the situation. When a young lad drew a knife, the others had to as well, and then everything could go wrong. Especially when under the influence of spirits and various substances. On top of that, gangs of young girls had now begun to commit crimes, but they hadn't yet brought knives into the picture. They contented themselves with humiliating each other by cutting off hair and peeing or vomiting on the victim—which was bad enough. Fortunately, Aarhus had been spared that kind of thing until now. He caught himself slipping away from the topic at hand. "Did Gert not say anything about the time of death—in the bog case, I mean? Or have they given up trying to find out?"

"It's hopeless trying to get an exact time of death after so many years. But we do know that she disappeared on 19 December 1983, and that no one has seen her since. We probably won't get closer than that."

Roland mumbled, tossed the chewing gum in the bin, and poured a cup of coffee for himself. "Take a cup, Niels," he urged, nodding to the stack of white plastic cups by the printer.

"I see you have a real mug from home," teased Niels, getting a cup for himself.

Roland leaned towards him. "Irene thinks it might make the coffee taste better, but . . ." He sent Niels a look that said she was not right. "In any case, it would be nice to have a time of death to be able to check on people. No alibi? Okay, we may need to bring you in for further questioning. What the hell do you do when it was so long ago? Can you even remember what you were doing twenty-five years ago?" He drank from the cup and looked defiantly at Niels Nyborg.

"We were thirty years old then, Roland. Do you not think we were doing something a little more fun than this?"

"I got married when I was thirty," he recalled, heading back in time for a split second, but returned quickly. "Mikkel has gone out to Gustav Hjort, for whom she worked as a nursing assistant. He must know when she left their home that night—if he can remember. He's a big shot these days, after marrying Carola Krondahl. You probably remember the Krondahl dynasty in Fåborg, don't you?"

"Yes, very well! So, that's who he wound up with?" Niels whistled slowly.

"It does Mikkel good to get out on his own. He just wanted to get a little taste and see what they know. If he suspects something, we bring them in."

Niels nodded. "Is Mikkel still striving to get higher up in the hierarchy?"

Roland smiled at the fox. "Mikkel goes straight for one of the high posts. Salary grade 37 is probably the least of his goals!"

"Wasn't that your plan?"

"Me! Nooo! I'm shamefully well satisfied. I may well stay here for the next twelve years. What do you get out of giving yourself more responsibility?" He answered the question himself. "More problems—that's what you get."

"Ah, think about it now, Roland. You'd make a much better chief than Mikkel Jensen. Besides, you'd get there faster than he would." He emptied the cup in one mouthful and smiled encouragingly before standing to his full height, which was not so little. He was two heads taller than Roland.

"By the way, the vet finished the autopsy of the dogs." Niels pulled a piece of paper out of his pocket. "I had to write this down," he said, reading from the crumpled handwritten note. "The dogs were anesthetised with M99—etorphine hydrochloride." He could barely pronounce the words; his language skills had never been good, and he was tongue-tied. "It is an anaesthetic used for elephants. The vet explained it's related to morphine. He traced a milligram in each dog, which is the dose administered per ton to an elephant, so three little doggies could hardly survive it."

"Where do you get that stuff?" Roland rubbed his neck, annoyed.

"M99 can only be used legally by registered veterinarians under strict requirements. They have to apply for a permit from the Danish Medicines Agency, and it's only granted after a proper application. The perp had to be a vet. Of course, it could have been stolen . . ."

"How the hell was it administered to three strong hunting dogs. Food?

"The vet says darts. Tranquiliser darts shot with great precision from a weapon. But the darts weren't in the dogs, so they must be in the kennels somewhere."

"Unless our cunning killer removed them before disappearing. He could have left fingerprints on them."

"Should I drive out to the property and walk around the kennels?" Niels Nyborg asked willingly, as he opened the door.

"No!" Roland exclaimed a little too firmly. "I'll do it."

"Why use a knife when you have tranquiliser darts that can stun an elephant? Helge Vangberg wouldn't have survived a shot of one milligram of M99, either." Niels shook his head incomprehensibly.

"An arrow was probably thought too easy a death. The intention was for the doctor to suffer. I'm inclined to believe Julie Hermansen—it is personal."

The rain hit the driver's window as he drove home early that evening. They'd held a little status meeting to assess what the day's work had brought them before deciding to go for a drink. Unfortunately, it wasn't much. The image of the tip of the knife was hung on the board next to the piece of ebony. The pictures of the doctor's bloody corpse, focusing on the many stab wounds to the chest, hung on the same board. There was now no doubt about the cases being connected and the murderer having some relation to Africa. Would they be that hard to find? Many Danes travelled to Africa. Travelling to South Africa was almost no more expensive than travelling to southern Spain. Knud Engtoft was an obvious suspect. Kim and Isabella were working overtime in their search. They had tracked him down to 1983, when he, too, had disappeared into thin air. Probably on a plane to Africa, or maybe they'd find him mummified somewhere. Gustav Hjort couldn't remember exactly when the nursing assistant had left that night. Understandable, after so many years. Mikkel didn't think the couple had anything to do with her disappearance, but Roland was afraid the high-class surroundings had affected his judgement. Jensen talked about the house as though he had wandered into Marselisborg Castle.

He sighed and braked for a red light on Oddervej. Speaking of houses. He still had not come to terms with the fact that the estate agent estimated that they could probably sell the old villa in Højbjerg for around 5 million Danish kroner, even though it was becoming more difficult to sell than it had been. Only now did it dawn on him how cheap they had got it from Irene's parents when Dagny and Carl Ernst moved into the apartment in Aarhus after they retired. But he probably shouldn't tell them—his mother-in-law would quickly find a way to be reimbursed. But persuading Irene to sell would be difficult.

The large copper beech in the driveway, which stood with dark, wet leaves in the rain, and the spicy autumn scent of the garden that greeted him as he got out of the car, made him doubt his intentions. Would he be able to do without this lovely spot on Earth with all the memories? Helge Vangberg's well-kept property appeared in his mind's eye, and the sight made his heart beat lustfully. It was something he really wanted to own—whatever the cost. Niels Nyborg's words also rang beautifully in his ears. Promotion? It had never been his goal to rise the ranks, but things would be tight in the new home. A salary increase would be nice, and he wouldn't get it unless he started playing with the top-notchers. Kurt Olsen was heading for retirement soon.

There was no smell of food in the hallway. The only one who greeted him eagerly when he opened the door was a little black-and-cognac-coloured German Shepherd puppy, for whom they had not yet found a name. It had been Irene's idea. She had got it the other day when it was old enough. Having a watchdog in the house made her more comfortable, and he could train it as a police dog. Her eyes had beamed when she suggested it, and, as always, he'd had a hard time resisting her impulsive ideas. He hung his coat on the coat-rack and squatted down in front of the puppy, which had sat down straight on its rump and looked up at him with one ear attentively lifted and the other at a charming angle. "Hello, little friend. What are we going to call you?" He patted the dog awkwardly on the head. He wasn't used to animals, and he didn't really know what to do. Irene was better at it; she had grown up in the country. The puppy licked him on the hand and wagged its tail eagerly. It would be a while before it was a guard dog. "Where is Mum? What should we have to eat?" It followed him into the kitchen. Was it one of those evenings where she waited until he got home so they could cook together? She did that sometimes when he worked on a case, so she didn't have to wait with the food. But he always called if he worked overtime. That much consideration had to be taken. Or maybe she'd made something cold. She was on a new craze—eating according to your blood type. They were both blood type O, so that, at least, was easy, but there was a lot they weren't allowed to eat with that blood type, and he had such a hard time remembering what—and Irene wasn't there to ask. But why should it also be so hard to eat? He had asked her about it when she'd suggested the new diet. *What did the Stone Age people do?* he had asked to emphasise that they had eaten what they could find without thinking about calories, cancer, and blood types. *They died*, was Irene's answer, and he couldn't come up with a counterargument. They would die no matter what was in their stomachs. The good news was that blood type O should eat a lot of meat, and that suited him just fine. The dog's food was different. He poured food into the empty bowl, and the puppy immediately began chomping and crunching.

He found Irene in the conservatory. She was standing on a ladder, painting the wooden frame over the windows—which had long been in need of attention. She'd donned one of his discarded checked shirts. It was far too big for her, and it was covered in splashes of white paint. Her hair was tied up in a multicoloured scarf to keep it away from her face. It wasn't exactly one of her usual well-put-together outfits. He stood in the doorway watching her with a warm feeling in his stomach. When she spotted him, she almost fell off the ladder.

"God, Rolando, you scared me. I didn't hear you, and Bend didn't bark. What time is it? I took off my watch so as not to get paint on it."

He lifted her down from the ladder and kissed her. "Bend? Is that what you're calling the puppy?"

"Yep, that's his name. The way his ear has that cute fold. That's why!"

"Hmm, Bend . . . The angle of his ear. Good idea. But what about your uncle Ben."

"Oh yeah—I hadn't thought of that. He'll be annoyed about that." She took off the stained painting gloves and blew away a tuft of hair that had strayed out from under the scarf onto her face. "What's *angle* in Italian?"

"Angolo."

"Well then, let's call him Angolo!"

Roland nodded. It didn't matter to him. "So, why are you painting all of a sudden?" he asked instead, looking at her work. She had come a long way and had probably been painting for most of the afternoon.

"I just felt like it when I got home. Are you hungry? There's some lasagne we can microwave."

He nodded. Lasagne suited him just fine. He lit some candles and set the table while she took care of the rest. It was now that he used to light a cigarette, but he tried to still the urge. Angolo lay in the dog basket with his head on his forepaws, watching all their movements.

"What about red wine? We can drink that, can't we?" he asked before going over to the wine rack.

"Yes, we can."

He smiled. This blood type diet was better than the other ones Irene had subjected him to.

"Have you had a good day otherwise?" he asked as they sat down at the table. He poured a large glass of wine for her.

"The usual. And not. Birthe was assaulted by a client who was dissatisfied with the government's new policy on unemployment benefits."

"What? It's not her fault!"

"No, but we're the ones that people on the receiving end take their frustration out on."

He finished chewing and toasted with her. She hadn't taken the scarf off her head; it suited her. An item of clothing that had stirred quite a bit of debate. But wearing it didn't make Irene neither oppressed nor a terrorist.

"Promise me, my love, that if anyone ever lifts a finger to hurt you, you'll call me!"

Irene nodded, but he knew she would never do it. She wasn't the type to take advantage of being married to a police officer.

"What about your cases. Have you made any progress?"

"A few leads have come up. We'll have to see what tomorrow brings." He looked at her while she ate, then he cleared his throat. "Irene, I'm thinking of going for promotion. It won't be long before Kurt retires."

She looked at him in surprise. "You've never mentioned that before."

"I've only just started thinking about it. Niels said it to me this evening. It would mean a better salary, and . . ."

"And more work, Rolando. We're doing fine. We have plenty of money."

"There's somewhere we have to go this weekend, Irene. I have a little surprise for you."

She smiled uncertainly. "Where?"

"We're going to look at a property that I've fallen in love with. It's a great place for—Angolo," he hurried to add as she frowned. "When you see it, you'll feel the same as I do and—we can afford it. I let an estate agent in this morning. He was here to assess the house."

He always knew when Irene was angry. A vein began to throb in her right temple, and her cheeks flushed.

"Did you let an estate agent assess our home—my childhood home— without asking me first?"

The tears were a new addition to the way she expressed her anger. His heart sank. He had really hurt her. He hadn't thought it through. "I'm sorry, Irene. But you just have to see the property. It's what we've both always dreamed of."

"Tell me . . ." Irene looked at him sharply. "Isn't that where the murdered doctor lived? One man's poison is another man's meat."

"No, no," he averted, turning his face away from her in disgust at it being put so bluntly. "Though it is only up for sale because Helge Vangberg was murdered, but . . ."

Irene got up from the table with a snort and a crumpled napkin in one hand, which she clenched so hard her knuckles turned white. She hadn't finished her food and had only drunk half her wine. "If you think I want to leave my childhood home to live in a house where a doctor was brutally murdered, in the middle of a forest, where I'd be on my own most long, dark evenings, then you'd better think again! If you get a promotion, you'll be home even less than you are now."

"Oh, Irene. I don't come home that late. And it will be some time before I get a promotion—if I do at all. And you have Angolo as a guard dog."

Irene's eyes flashed. "So, choose—that house or me!"

It was the first time he'd heard her slam a door. The crumpled napkin she'd abandoned on the table slowly began to unfold as if it were alive and intending to throw itself at him. Angolo looked up at him and turned his head away. Roland poured another glass of wine and looked through the kitchen window, where the rain had turned to sleet out in the dark. Small ice crystals hit the pane and ran down it as they melted. He got lost in the sight and jumped when his phone rang.

"Sorry, I'm disturbing you," Isabella's voice said. "I just think you should know that Knud Engtoft is here in Denmark. I had a hunch he was the one who called the journalist—from a phone booth at the airport—last Wednesday. I checked both the arrivals and departures around the time she was contacted. It wasn't easy to know whether he was going in or out of the country. A British Airways plane from London Heathrow actually landed at Kastrup Airport around that time. The plane came from Abuja, Nigeria. I got a copy of the passenger list, and who should be on it but . . . ?"

Roland hated the guessing games that everyone played these days thanks to all the quizzes they were bombarded with on television; soon there would be no other form of entertainment. But this one wasn't hard to guess. "Knud Engtoft," he said emphatically.

"Precisely. But he disappears again here. He didn't travel on to Jutland the same day, I checked all flights and passenger lists, nor did he take the train. I'll keep looking. At some point, he leaves Djævleøen in Greenland— I'm sure of that. And it wouldn't surprise me if he was here in Jutland on Friday night when Helge Vangberg was murdered."

24

Even in rain, the view of the wet roofs of Aarhus from above was breathtaking. From this distance, the façade of Bruuns Galleri peeped out at the height of the City Hall Clock Tower, which had almost disappeared in the misty rain and Arbejdernes Landsbank's sign was read back-to-front. She sat with her elbows firmly planted on the windowsill with her chin resting against clasped hands as she enjoyed the view. A cup of fragrant, freshly brewed coffee stood on the windowsill next to her. She felt more relaxed than she had been in a long time.

"Help yourself to more coffee." Pernille came out of the bathroom rubbing her short, wet hair so it bristled all over the place. She was wearing only a skimpy thong. Her breasts were small and pert like a teenager's, despite her being the same age as Sabrina and having given birth to a child. They'd gone to high school and played sports together, so walking around half-naked in front of her friend didn't bother Pernille. Sabrina had slept in a guest bed in the living room. Pernille and Tobias's apartment on Jægergårdsgade wasn't very big, but it was Pernille herself who had offered her a place to stay.

They'd gone to bed late because they'd been drinking green tea and talking about the old days. They hadn't seen each other or talked together in the six months she'd lived in Italy, so there was a lot to catch up on. Tobias had gone to bed before them. He was an IT administrator at Aarhus Technical School and needed to go to bed early. He probably didn't want to listen to their girl talk, either. Adam was only a year and a half, so he had long since been put to bed.

"I'm so sorry I have to go to work. I can easily skip it," said Pernille with a toothbrush in her mouth. She was a clerk in Magasin's perfume department.

"No, don't. You have to go to work," Sabrina said firmly, sounding like a mother. She looked down at her stomach. And she was. She hadn't told Pernille and Tobias, and they hadn't heard her throwing up that morning. Pernille had never cared for Peter, so sharing her good news wouldn't be well received.

"Okay. But it's good I finish early today." Now dressed, Pernille poured some coffee into a mug. She sat down next to her and set her mug on the windowsill, too.

"You have such a beautiful view," Sabrina said excitedly, having hardly taken her eyes off it since she had sat down.

"Well, when you have it every day, you don't see it. But you have a nice view from your apartment on Dalgas Avenue, too."

"Mm-hmm, but it'll be another six months before I can see it again."

"Come home! Let Peter stay in Italy! Leave him to his own devices with his Italian mistress. He's asking for it."

"I don't know if she's Italian. And he said it was a mistake."

"Yeah, that's what they always say! Throw him out. He might be good-looking but looks aren't everything."

Sabrina wanted to tell her about the baby, but she was afraid of being told to have an abortion. She had considered it, but abortion meant taking another life, and could she take the life of something she—and Peter—had created? Did she have the right to decide over life or death?

"It's tempting, but I love him, Pernille. You know, I always have."

Pernille nodded incomprehensibly and got up. She drank the last of her coffee and put the mug in the sink.

"I have to go now. Will you do the dishes—not!" she teased.

"Ha ha!"

Pernille rummaged out in the hall.

"And it's okay that my father comes here, isn't it?" shouted Sabrina. Pernille stuck her head in through the doorway to the kitchen and looked at her, almost losing her balance as she was putting on boots at the same time. "Yeah, of course. If he can settle for my humble abode.

Why don't you just visit him in his royal palace? Is it because of the evil stepmother?"

"You could say that." She smiled at the comparison. "I can't talk to Dad properly when Carola is there."

Discomfort crept up. She had no idea how to start the conversation with her dad.

"If you get bored, there are some old newspapers on the bench in the kitchen to entertain yourself with and get a little updated on what's been happening here in Aarhus while you've been away. Have you heard about the two gruesome murders?" Pernille fastened the last button of her coat and waved to her through the doorway. "I'm leaving now. Say hi to your lovely father," she shouted without hearing Sabrina's answer. The door slammed shut, and the apartment fell into silence.

Gruesome murders in Aarhus—sounded like an interesting read. She had always been interested in anything related to death. The newspapers lay in a neat stack on the corner of the bench. The latest ones were on top, and she read first about the doctor who had been found murdered in the yard in front of his property, a little outside Skåde, with his three dead hunting dogs. She picked up the next paper. A picture of a bog made her study it more closely. It was the bog at Mundelstrup. The town in which she'd spent the best time of her life, even though she didn't remember much of it. The article reported the discovery by two boys of a body that had lain in a bog for twenty-five years. There was something from a press conference at the police station. They'd identified the body—it turned out it was a nursing assistant who'd disappeared from Silkeborg in 1983. There were photos of where she was found. Unnerving that a dead woman was lying in *that* particular bog for twenty-five years. There was an interview with an elderly woman who made Christmas elves and remembered something about a family in Mundelstrup, who the nursing assistant had been working for when she disappeared. She took the next newspaper and discovered it was a more recent publication. Apparently, Pernille hadn't sorted the newspapers by date. "Murder victim committed benefit fraud" was the headline on the front-page story. She was about to put down the paper—typical that any and all dirt had been dug up, despite it having no use anymore; but that's what people couldn't get enough of— but then a name in the article caught her attention. *Louise Engtoft.* Pieces were beginning to fall into place. A family who moved from Mundelstrup in 1983. The letters to Elina from the nursing assistant Louise Engtoft. The last letter was dated December 1983—the month Louise had disappeared.

She dropped the paper on the floor when the doorbell rang. It sounded like the bells of Westminster. Flustered, she looked at her watch. Her dad was ten minutes late. She felt nauseated again and got up slowly to open the door.

Gustav Hjort entered the narrow hall that could hardly fit two people and pulled off his wet wool coat. "You get soaked just getting out of the car and crossing the road." He took her face between his cold hands and kissed her on the forehead. "Hi, my little darling. It's so good to see you again—but you're very pale. Does the sun not shine in Italy?" He sounded in great form, but she was too shaken to let it rub off on her.

"Would you like some coffee, Dad?"

He nodded and rubbed his hands together to warm them while looking at the view of the wet roofs. But he didn't comment on it. It couldn't be compared to his view from Strandvejen.

"Why did you move in with your friend instead of staying with your old dad? We have plenty of room," he said, a little offended, and sat down at the table where she'd put the two cups of coffee.

"You know why, Dad. Carola and I . . ."

"Well, my girl, Carola is harmless—surely you've realised that by now. She never wanted to be your mother . . ."

"No, exactly!" she interrupted, not wanting to talk about Carola anymore. It was always her—whether she was talking to her dad or to Peter.

"But it's a good thing. Carola knew she could never be your mum. Josefine was your mum, and she always will be."

"It's actually *Mum* who I want to talk to you about—without Carola interfering."

Resigned, Gustav pulled down the sleeves of his cotton jumper and looked sadly at her. "I told you everything I can about your mother. Josefine was a wonderful woman—and mother. You look a lot like her. We both loved her very much. But sometimes fate is cruel—you know that well from your job—some people get so sick they can't be helped back to life." His eyes were full of sorrow, and she had no doubt at all that he had truly loved her mother.

"That's not what I want to ask you about. I want to know about the woman who nursed Mum. Who was she?"

He didn't look at her. "Why in the world would you want to know that—now?"

"Because I found some interesting old letters in Gran's drawer. They're from the nurse."

Gustav stalled. "Well then, you know who she was." He drank some coffee and set his face in an unreadable expression. "What else did the letters say?"

"Who was Mum's doctor?" She struggled with feelings of both anger and pity. He had kept too much hidden from her for far too long. Was it only to spare her?

"It was Dr. Winther," he replied angrily, as if the question annoyed him.

"According to the letters, you found another doctor, even though Mum felt safe with Dr. Winther and was recovering with his treatment. Why?"

Gustav winced on the chair. His back, which was usually proud and straight, sank, and he sat half bent over the table. He grabbed her hands and held them so tightly that she clenched her teeth in pain.

"You have to understand, Sabrina, that when you're faced with someone as sick as your mother was, you try everything. I went to another doctor to hear what he had to say about the treatment she was receiving. A second opinion, you know. And even if it helped her, it would have destroyed her in the end. The other doctor said that the treatment had such severe side effects that Josefine—given how weak she was—wouldn't have survived it."

"But, Dad. She didn't survive. Who was the other doctor?"

He let go of her hands and waved into the air. "I don't remember. Does it even matter now, Sabrina?" he pleaded, looking at her with eyes that would make anyone pity him.

"Yes, Dad. It does matter. Especially now. The dead woman they found in the bog was Mum's nursing assistant who disappeared in 1983. I just read about it in the paper. That's the same year and the same month that Mum died. Did she disappear after she'd been with us in Mundelstrup?"

"I don't know. She went missing shortly afterwards, but I didn't realise it was her. She went by another name back then, and God only knows how many others she had."

"But the letters indicate she was a really good nurse who took good care of both Mum and me. She wanted to be a doctor—if she'd had the chance—did you know that?"

She felt a stab of pain in her chest when Gustav looked at her. His lower lip trembled like a sad little boy's.

"We had nothing to do with that woman's disappearance," he said, choking on tears.

"*We?*" she said accusingly with a raised eyebrow. He'd pre-empted her next question about Carola.

"Yes. The two of us, I mean." He dodged, but she could see something else in his eyes.

"Was it Carola who kept you away from Mum and me night after night? I read in the letters that there were nights when you didn't come home at all and left Mum and me all on our own. How could you when Mum was so sick? I was only four years old!"

Gustav's facial expression changed. She'd never seen him with such an angry and distorted face. It made him completely unrecognisable. "She was a lying witch! I never left you on your own at night. But that was the picture she painted for Elina to put me in a bad light. Now you know why your grandmother hated me! Wasn't that what you wanted to know?" He snorted and drank furiously from the cup.

She shouldn't say any more and respect her dad's anger because she'd rarely experienced it and because it always occurred only when there was good reason for it.

They sat in silence. She looked down at the table and felt his eyes, full of guilt, rest on her. Suddenly, he took her hands again. When she looked up at him, he had tears in his eyes. That, too, was a rare sight.

"I have nothing to do with the murder of that woman! You have to believe that. You *have* to believe it! But she wasn't a good person—you must have read that in the paper, too. Benefit fraud! But it was probably her terrible husband who got her into it. I don't think she was smart enough to come up with a scam at two addresses—and names."

"Do you know her husband?"

"No—thankfully. I've only seen him once, and that was enough. A lump with an earring and tattoos on his upper arms. A real smart-ass!"

She couldn't help but smile despite the seriousness. She knew how he felt about those types. In her teenage years, she'd thought of finding just that type of man to get back at both him and Carola. Or find a man of another ethnic origin than Danish—give Carola a heart attack.

"What did he do?"

"Nothing, I think. He was probably a drug addict, too. We never understood how he could afford all those trips to Africa, until . . ." He suddenly stopped and drained his cup.

"Until what, Dad?"

He got up, looked at his watch, and took his coat, which he'd hung to dry over the back of the chair.

"Carola is waiting for me. There're some journalists coming today about the new yacht. I really hope the rain stops before then." The familiar boyish smile was back as he put on his coat. "Come home to us, Sabrina. You shouldn't be staying in these poor conditions when you have a family with a nice big house!" he said, looking at her with his hands in his pockets, as though waiting for her to start packing and come with him.

She didn't get up to follow him out. When she heard the door slam, she sat back with a feeling that there was still a lot he hadn't told her. She picked up her phone and called Information. Now she just had to find this Dr. Winther—if he was still alive.

25

Sebastian Juhl wasn't at all how she had imagined. Expressive, unnaturally blue eyes looked inquisitively at the person who had rung the doorbell uninvited. When she finally spoke, she sounded confused and was sure both Kamilla and Nicolaj could hear it, which made her blush.

"Uh . . . we're from the *Daily News*—we're doing an article on your mother, who . . ." She cleared her throat. "We know you weren't very old then, but maybe you can help us present a more accurate picture of your mother . . . as a person, I mean."

He pushed back the slightly too long fringe on his forehead and sat down. "Well, yeah, the paper. I wondered where you were," he said with slightly understated irony.

"And, of course, we were very sorry to hear about your mother . . . I forgot to say," she added, feeling silly.

Sebastian contented himself with nodding.

They sat down at the table and Nicolaj took out his notebook. He'd made a note of the questions he wanted to ask, and when Anne suddenly seemed slightly incapacitated, he took the chance to begin the interview. "You were eight years old when your mother disappeared; isn't that right?"

Sebastian nodded. "Yeah. And I'd like to help present a different picture of her. You only write the shitty stuff, like she was committing benefit fraud and that sort of thing. She wasn't like that."

"We just write what the police tell us." Anne defended herself. "We know you couldn't have known what your mother was doing at the time." It was supposed to sound like a consolation, but Sebastian didn't seem comforted.

"She wasn't like that, I said!" He snarled and looked sharply at her. She swallowed a few times. She had never seen such distinctive and piercing eyes before; they captivated and frightened at once.

"If it's true that she was living a double life, it's his fault!" he continued in a more controlled voice.

"Who? Your stepfather?"

"Don't call him that!"

"But you're talking about the man your mother married, right?" she continued.

He nodded.

"Did your mother talk about the family she was working for before she disappeared?" Nicolaj asked, getting Sebastian's attention again.

"No, or, at least, I can't remember if she did. Do you know who the family is?" His eyes sparkled with interest.

"Not for sure," Anne quickly lied, afraid that Nicolaj would start revealing too much. If Sebastian thought the Hjort family was behind his mother's murder, it could lead to him taking the law into his own hands, and that would only aggravate the situation. It also annoyed her that Nicolaj was taking the lead and had emerged as the one in charge.

"Tell me everything you remember from the day your mother disappeared. You were in school but what happened when you got home?"

Sebastian narrowed his eyes, forming a deep frown.

"I remember that day. Of course I remember that day; it's the tragic things in childhood that you remember best. They're the ones that really stick in the subconscious, aren't they?" He looked directly at her as if she should confirm that theory, which she very well could. Suddenly, he looked away and seemed to disappear into the past but quickly returned to the present again. "Only after three days did the police start searching for her, and after a few months they gave up and said she'd probably just run away with her husband." He flung out his arms. "That's the only thing I remember."

"So, the police thought she'd run away?"

He nodded. "They thought she'd gone to Africa with him. He'd lived most of his life there and came home with these gross souvenirs that I don't think Mum was too fond of. She gave them away sometimes, so I think she hated them, too." He shuddered demonstratively.

"Where can we find your stepf—"

"I only know he travelled to Africa at the time, as the police said. I was placed with a family I didn't know. But they were good to me," he hurried to add.

"So, he's in Africa now?" exclaimed Nicolaj, probably seeing a chance for a trip to the hot continent.

Sebastian nodded without looking at him.

"You loved your mother very much, didn't you? And it was—*he* was the one who got her into the fraud?"

"She was the sweetest person in the world. In fact, I don't think she even knows—knew—that she was committing benefit fraud and doing something illegal."

Nicolaj and Kamilla exchanged telling glances behind his back.

Anne ignored them.

"Do you know anything about a doctor your mother worked with?"

"No. Well, he used to visit a lot because Mum was really good friends with him. She wanted to be a doctor herself, so they talked a lot about that." He smiled distantly.

"Can you remember his name at all?"

Sebastian thought again. "Yes, I can actually, because we teased him about it—especially in the summer. His name was Winther. A nice man. I called him King Winther because he looked like an old king with a white beard."

"Can you remember his first name, too?"

"Yep. Ole. I've never forgotten that. But he must be a very old man today. He was old back then." He stood up. "But I thought you wanted to write something nice about my mother? Would you like to see her?" He went into the bedroom. When he returned, he had a picture of a pretty, fair-haired woman with whom he shared certain similarities. The photo was in a black heart-shaped frame.

"Is it okay if I take some pictures?" Kamilla asked. She'd been no use as a photographer since photographing Helge Vangberg in a body bag strapped to a stretcher.

"Of course," Sebastian replied generously, sitting back down at the table with his mother's picture next to him. He looked directly into the camera. Kamilla photographed from several angles and thanked him afterwards.

"Okay, but you can only use those photos on one condition!"

He said it so threateningly that Anne looked at him nervously, but then he smiled.

"That you write something nice about my mother!"

She only relaxed when they were sitting in the car again on their way back to the office.

"Mysterious guy," Nicolaj said from the back seat.

"Exciting man," corrected Anne.

"Oh yeah, you girls like that type." Nicolaj met Kamilla's eyes in the rear-view mirror.

"I think Anne liked him," she said, winking at him.

"Yes. I wouldn't run fast if he was after me."

"You wouldn't? With a killer on your heels!"

"What do you mean by that? An eight-year-old boy can't be a murderer!" she replied with a slight snort, turning to face him. Nicolaj withdrew a little and placed an arm on Kamilla's big camera bag. "But you have heard of that sort of thing happening before, haven't you?" he side-stepped.

"And tell me how exactly a little boy got her body down to the bog!" She slapped her forehead to indicate how ridiculous he was.

"With the help of his stepfather or King Winther," Nicolaj replied defiantly, giving the finger before she turned around.

"He may well have murdered the doctor when he grew up. You can't rule him out as the killer."

"For what reason—tell me why! But speaking of the other doctor. I'd like to talk to him if he is still alive."

She called from her mobile and gave Mads Dam a set of instructions and a message to find a doctor named Ole Winther. He rang back shortly afterwards, and Anne directed Kamilla out of Aarhus Centrum.

"We might as well talk to him now," she said excitedly.

26

Gustav Hjort couldn't hide his joy at the press's interest and enthusiasm for the new yacht. TV 2 East Jutland had volunteered to do a report, too. They were so excited. Seldom had a yacht been seen that could reach sixty knots in calm seas. The result had been created through close collaboration with one of Italy's large boat builders. The hull of the yacht was made of carbon fibre and equipped with gas turbines like those used on warships. The exhaust was made of titanium, partly due to its weight and partly to cope with the high temperatures from the gas turbines. His son-in-law had helped them find the right supplier. Peter was getting well established in the Italian business world, which Carola took full advantage of.

He poured a glass of champagne for both of them. Luckily, the horde of reporters hadn't slurped it all for themselves. It pleased him, despite him not buying the most expensive champagne for the occasion. He had longed to be left alone with her; the day had been so crowded he hadn't been able to get her by herself to talk. She was standing on the deck, saying goodbye to the last journalist. Luckily, the rain had stopped a little past noon, and the sun had broken forth from an almost cloudless sky. Gustav looked at her. He'd never met a woman like her. The sun made her hair shine. Her up-do had come a little undone in the wind on the high-speed test sail with the journalists. Her hair had been done by the city's best hairdresser before the press conference. She was so photogenic. Dark sunglasses shielded her beautiful green eyes. For the day ahead, she'd dressed in a white maritime blouse embroidered with an anchor and a rudder on the chest, white sailor trousers, and sailing shoes. At sixty-five—three years younger than himself—she still dressed youthfully, and she could because of her slender, well-trained figure. She smiled her most captivating smile at the journalist, who shook her hand and alighted the yacht. He went out to her and handed her the champagne. She pushed the sunglasses up into her hair, smiled, and accepted the glass.

"Thanks, my love. That's just what I need." She took an eager sip, as if it were juice.

"It went well! Shall we sit down and relax a bit?" He pulled a deck chair towards her, and she sat down with a grateful sigh.

"Thank you, my love. It went well, yes. We better enjoy *The Whirr of Wings* while we have her. I'm sure she's going to be sold soon."

She'd always been good at coming up with names for the yachts. *Vingesus* was a good name for this one. When it sailed, it was like flying over the waves. But according to Carola, Danish names didn't work. They had to be translated into English so that most nationalities could understand them. Foreigners were their biggest customers, though a fair share were Danes, too.

"What a day! And it's just the prototype. Imagine what it's going to be like when we get it put into production." She leaned back and closed her eyes with a well-satisfied smile. Her lipstick had worn off during the busy day, and she hadn't had the opportunity to touch it up in the yacht's otherwise superb bathroom. But he liked her the way she was now. Fresh and natural. Josefine had never used make-up. She had a natural beauty that Sabrina had inherited. He dismissed the thought and resented the fact that Josefine was again occupying his thoughts. He leaned back in his chair and listened to the calm laps of the waves against the bow, soothed by the sound and the rocking motion of the sea. He'd always loved the sea. He'd no idea where the interest had come from. But it was that interest that had brought him and Carola together. His father had worked in a factory, but not in as high a position as he had reached. His father had always been a *man on the floor*, as he'd said himself. One of the men they had kept on the payroll for years when they had the boat factory in Fåborg. He'd often thought of his father back then. Wished his father could see how far his son had come. The man who'd always scornfully predicted that his only son would never amount to anything. That he would end up like his father, working like a dog for someone else for a paltry wage. He'd shown the old man when he'd passed his exams and become an accountant, but that had become another problem. Office work was for women. Real manly work needed effort and strength. You were supposed to work yourself to the bone, so you deserved your wage. He'd also blamed him for Josefine's illness. He'd never met Carola, even though he could have if only he'd dared to admit that his son's second wife wasn't *a sick weakling of a wife* as he'd previously described Josefine. He had no interest in his grandchild, despite Sabrina being Gustav's greatest life accomplishment. But, of course, she should have been a boy. His mother had watched in silence. She never said no to her husband, but he could see in her eyes that she was on her son's side and would have liked to have backed him up. She just died far too soon. She didn't even get to see him graduate. The many years on his own with his father had almost driven him insane. Then, fortunately, he'd died of a blood clot in his heart and could no longer criticise his son's life. But that had meant he hadn't had time to see what his son could do, either. How far he could go.

He gasped for breath and discovered that Carola was lying down and looking at him. She sat up with the glass resting on one knee.

"I haven't had a chance to speak to you at all today, my love. How did the chat with Sabrina go? What did she want?" she asked worriedly.

He sat up, too, looked out at the water, and watched an ice cream wrapper floating around. "Yeah, how did it go? She'd found some old letters in Elina's drawer. She was full of criticism."

"What letters? Criticism of what?"

"I don't know. But apparently, the woman who nursed her wrote the letters—back then." He looked directly at her and saw the change in her face.

"Who nursed her? Her . . . ?"

He reached over and squeezed her arm. "It was so long ago. It doesn't make any difference today. Those letters are twenty-five years old," he reassured Carola. The pain returned to his chest. The memory of the past and Josefine cut him more than ever recently. Ever since the body had been found in the bog.

"What was in the letters, Gustav?"

He waved his hand and smiled. "Nothing of importance. Elina was very upset about Josefine's illness. The nursing assistant was probably just telling her how things were going."

"But what did Sabrina say? What did she want from you?"

Carola's voice sounded worried, and he regretted dragging her into it. "Nothing, my darling. Let's leave it. As I said, it makes no difference now." He clinked his glass against hers and winked at her. "Let's enjoy the success of our golden years. The two of us were a hit today."

Carola smiled uncertainly; he could see something was gnawing at her. Josefine's name—and Sabrina's—had always caused her unease. They'd never managed to develop a good relationship. It tormented him. It was bad for Sabrina. She'd had a hard time getting used to a new mother so soon after Josefine's death, but . . . his stomach cramp came back. He dropped the glass as he doubled over in pain. Carola put her arm around his back and leaned in towards him. She kissed him on the cheek.

"Is it your stomach again, my love? Don't you think you should see the doctor? You've been . . . lately."

She fell silent when he looked into her eyes. "You're scared," she said. "You're afraid of what will happen next."

27

———

That was the day everything changed. The day the world began to fall away from under him.

It was the summer holidays, and he was enjoying not having to go to school. Mum was sitting out in the sun, in the garden, reading a woman's magazine. He could see her from the window of his room, and he thought she was so beautiful with the sun on her face. Her hair lit up like a halo around her head. She looked like one of those angels on the altarpiece in the church. It was nearly time for coffee, so she'd soon get up and go in to make a drink for herself and pour some juice for him. He knew her routines, and it made him feel safe that every day had the same calm and monotonous pace. He watched her put her sunglasses on the garden table and go into the kitchen; he got up and went out there to help her set the table in the garden. It was a lovely, hot summer day.

It was when they were sitting in the garden that she brought it up. The first bit was not so bad.

"Something strange happened last night at work. I didn't get to tell you at all."

"Mmmmm, what happened, Mum," he asked, his mouth full of cake.

"It was a little creepy. A man fell over. He wasn't breathing. At first, we thought he was drunk, but . . ."

"Did he die?" he asked curiously, taking a sip of the juice.

"No, honey-bunch. He didn't—Mum saved him!" Her eyes shone with pride, and he knew by instinct that he should praise her now.

"Wow, Mum. What did you do?"

She ruffled her sun-bleached hair and laughed, embarrassed. "I don't actually know. I shook him and shook him, and suddenly he woke up, gasping for breath." She lit a cigarette. Her smoking was no longer a secret. The African smoked a lot, too, but he was travelling, which was one of the reasons why it was a lovely summer holiday.

"Did an ambulance come?" he asked, daring to take another piece of cake now that Mum was so occupied.

"It did indeed!" She blew out the cigarette smoke in rings. It looked cool when she did it, and he followed the rings with his eyes until they dissolved in the warm summer air. The stink of the cigarette reached him, stinging his nose.

"And the paramedics praised me. They said I saved the man's life. That I'd given him a heart massage just by shaking him so hard. It was an absolutely fantastic feeling—it's almost impossible to describe to you." The cigarette stuck out between two slender fingers, and she leaned in across the table towards him, so their eyes were directly opposite each other. "So, I've decided to become a nursing assistant!"

He had looked at her and smiled happily. "Aren't you going to work in Aarhus at night anymore?"

She shook her head and smiled.

"Nope!"

"You won't come home smelling of old cigars and drink anymore?"

"Nope!"

Mum's joy and the prospect of a new life made him run out onto the lawn and perform a kind of war dance. Up on the decking, his mum laughed. "Come here, Little Basse. I have more good news."

He sat down at the table again, obediently, and looked intently at her.

"I'm going to start studying after the summer holidays, but it means we have to move."

His enthusiasm waned. He loved this place—it wasn't far to the sea or the woods—but then a new joy sprouted. "Does that mean I'm not going to school anymore?"

His mum laughed and waved the cigarette eagerly. "Not to the school you're in now. But a new school with new friends and teachers."

"Woohoo!" was the only thing he could think of shouting. This summer holiday was the best ever! He wanted to do another war dance on the lawn but stopped. "So where are we moving to?"

"To Aarhus. We're going to live near the new building that's in the paper—Musikhuset. We'll be able to see lots of performances there together. It opens next summer."

"Are we going there together—just the two of us?" he asked expectantly.

She didn't respond until she had sent new smoke rings up against the blue sky. "Maybe not completely alone—just the two of us. I have some more news for you to hear." She paused as she flicked the ashes off towards the edge of the ashtray.

His heart was about to leap out of his chest from excitement. It was going to be the best year of his life.

"You're going to have a new dad. Not your real dad. A stepdad. He proposed to me, and I said yes!"

The icy chill that filled him inside didn't match the hot summer day around him. He couldn't arrange his face in a suitable expression. He didn't want to make Mum sad; she was so happy. He tried to smile. She reached out for him, grabbed his arm, and pulled him hard into her. It hurt his arm. She smelled of sunscreen, cigarette smoke, and sweaty skin that also smelled burned by the sun. And when she kissed him, it was with a mixture of cigarettes and coffee on her breath.

"I know you don't like him, Basse. But he loves me. He loves us both, and he'll take good care of us. We can live with him in Aarhus. He has a nice apartment there." He was paralysed in her arms. Paralysed by her scent and the idea that they were going to live with the African—forever.

28

I t has to be the next left!" Anne directed her out onto Marselis Boule-vard; she moved into the lane to turn left and drove onto Kongsvang Allé. "There, Kamilla! It's there!" Anne shouted and pointed eagerly as they were driving. The neighbourhood was all beautiful houses. Kamilla parked behind another car in front of the house that Anne had pointed out.

"I thought everyone out here drove a Mercedes," Nicolaj said, staring at the car in front, which was an old, rusty Toyota Corolla with a long-expired NO TO THE EU sticker on the rear window. It was a little frayed around the edges. They all fell silent when a woman in her late twenties came out of the house and got into the car. She had shoulder-length dark hair and was wearing a pink raincoat.

"Probably a daughter," Anne said after the Toyota had driven off.

The doctor lived as one would expect a doctor to live. Kamilla thought of Majken, who was the exception. Okay so she lived in the second row from the water in Risskov, but her home wasn't characterised by luxury. Had they still been friends, she could have asked her for advice. Maybe she knew both the murdered doctor and Dr. Winther—they were colleagues after all. Thoughts of Majken were followed by thoughts of Danny. She hurried to focus her attention on the woman who opened the door when Anne banged on the heavy oak door with the cast-iron lion's head door-knocker. The names ODA & OLE WINTHER were engraved on a newly polished brass sign. "Yes?" said the woman, raising an eyebrow, which was very dark compared to the rest of her face. Both eyebrows were drawn on heavily with an overly dark eyebrow pencil; they didn't suit the woman's grey hair and lightly wrinkled skin.

"We're here from the *Daily News*. May we come in for a moment?" Anne asked.

"From the paper? Is it about Ole again?" asked the woman, letting them in. The gold bracelet rattled as she opened the door, and a little dog, which needed only a broom handle in its back to resemble a mop, jumped up to meet them and began barking. "Now, now, Little Dote," said the woman, picking up the dog in her arms. It breathed with its tongue hanging out of its mouth and tried to lick its owner's face.

Kamilla smiled. Amazing what people called their pets. Mind you, she'd called her cat Tarzan—was that any better?

"Yes, actually it's Ole Winther we'd like to talk to. Was it your daughter who just left?" asked Anne.

"No, no. We don't have any children. It was a young woman who wanted to know about my husband. Very mysterious. It's almost a year now since he passed. Would you like a cup of coffee? There's still some in the pot."

"Is your husband dead? But we found him in the White Pages," said Anne, nodding in affirmation to the coffee offer.

Kamilla looked at her watch. She could do without the coffee, but she was no longer a freelancer, so it was Anne who set the pace. She'd taken tomorrow off for the funeral, so she dared not say anything to Anne, despite her getting the feeling that neither she nor her camera was needed this time, either.

"Yes, the young lady who was here before said that, too. She had found us via Information. But that's just because I didn't get around to telling the authorities that Ole is dead. To me, he's still alive." Oda Winther set cups on the coffee table and got the pot from the kitchen. "Actually, I thought they deleted people automatically when they died, but obviously not," she said, sitting down in an armchair. Little Dote immediately jumped up to her, tail wagging.

The house wasn't as impressive inside. It was sparsely furnished, and what furniture was left was old and worn. The three of them sat down on the sofa opposite Oda Winther, who, as though reading their thoughts, began to explain that she had sold a lot of furniture when her husband died and that she could only afford to stay in the house because it was almost paid for after all the years they'd been living here. She had only her pension and the money her husband had left her to live on, which wasn't a little sum by any means, so she'd manage, she assured them.

"Ole reached eighty-five, so I'll probably be leaving here soon, too," she concluded, sounding quite relieved at the thought.

"Did your husband tell you anything about his work? In 1983, a nursing assistant he worked with disappeared—do you remember anything about that?" asked Anne. Nicolaj sat with the notebook and pen ready.

"Yes, I remember the woman disappearing. They talked about it every single day on the radio. Ole was very concerned about it. And now they've found her in a bog all these years later. It's so awful." With a slightly shaking hand, Oda Winther raised a cup to her wrinkled mouth, which she pursed long before the rim reached her lips and drank with a loud slurp.

All three of them smiled and glanced at each other, but they managed to keep their laughter in.

"Do you know if your husband was working with her the night she disappeared?" Nicolaj's voice held a touch of laughter when he asked, but Oda Winther didn't seem to notice. She put the cup down again just as slowly and looked at him.

"No, he certainly wasn't. He was ordered to cease his treatment," she replied indignantly.

"By whom?"

Oda Winther looked at Anna again. "Him, the sick woman's husband. I don't remember his name. They lived in Mundelstrup."

"Why did he do that?"

Oda shrugged and scratched the dog behind its ear. "I think it was something to do with a falling out about the side effects of the treatment. A new doctor took over. I don't remember who."

"Have you heard the name Helge Vangberg before? He was a doctor like your husband. Maybe you knew him?"

"No, I don't know him." Oda Winther showed no signs of recognition, so she had apparently not heard or read about the murder, either.

"Not to worry," Anne said, smiling encouragingly. "You wouldn't have anything left from your husband's work from back then, would you? Letters, files . . . ?"

Kamilla looked at her with a frown. It was a good job Roland Benito wasn't here to witness this. The police should know if that kind of thing existed. Anne had crossed the line between journalistic and police work before, and Kamilla didn't want to be dragged into it again.

"The young lady who was just here asked the same thing. I gave her what I had lying around, so she took it with her. I have no use for it."

"Did you just hand it over to a random stranger!" said Anne indignantly.

Oda Winther shook her head. "Maybe you'd better talk to her . . ." She got up slowly from the sofa and went out into the kitchen. When she returned, she had a note in her hand. "She gave me this number in case I thought of anything else." She handed Anne the note. "Ole was her mother's doctor, so it must have been her father who asked him to stop the treatment. Though she wasn't very old at the time. She told me she found some old letters that belonged to her deceased grandmother. My husband was mentioned in the letters—that's why she came."

They thanked her for coffee and quickly left. Oda Winther followed them to the door with the dog in her arms.

"So, it was Gustav Hjort's daughter in the Toyota. She was due to come home from Italy to talk to her dad. What the hell is going on!" said Nicolaj, who was again placed on the back seat along with the camera bag, which would soon be collecting nothing but dust.

Kamilla looked at the clock in the car; it was well past time for a drink after work. "Do we have more to do today?" she asked gently. "I have a funeral to go to tomorrow, so . . ."

"Oh, I forgot—your mum's funeral is tomorrow. I'm so sorry, Kamilla— why didn't you say something?"

"Oh, I'll get through it." She smiled weakly. "I doubt anyone will turn up," she added sadly. And it really was sad to think of her mother's life that had now ended so abruptly. This morning she had laid fresh flowers on Rasmus's grave, dreading the new grave. Despite her not having anywhere near the same feelings as she'd had for her son, losing her mother like that had been tragic. There was so much she hadn't managed to ask her or to say.

"Would you like us to come and be with you?" asked Nicolaj, one arm hanging on the back of the front passenger seat and the other on the driver's seat, so his head was between them.

She glanced at him. His freckles were very evident from this close. She could smell his deodorant and smiled. He was very thoughtful considering his young age, but she didn't want to drag them into her miserable private life.

"No, it's okay, Nicolaj. But thanks for offering."

They drove the rest of the way without talking to each other. Anne and Nicolaj were dropped off at the paper where their bicycles were. Anne's car was still in the garage, and she and Nicolaj could easily cycle—they didn't live far. But Kamilla had to drive home along the busy Grenåvej to Egå, deep in thought.

29

He hadn't slept that night. Or maybe he had, because the clock's annoying chime had woken him.

Irene was asleep when he went to bed after sitting in the dark room, listening loudly to the music of the late Luciano Pavarotti in his headphones. He'd raised the Danish flag to half-mast when he'd heard about the death in the news that September morning, and tears ran down his cheeks as he watched the report on television. It was like losing a family member. He had always loved his countryman and his music dearly, now it had become melancholy to hear *Nessun Dorma*—"Let No One Sleep"—because that was exactly what he was doing now, his great idol. Asleep forever.

Irene had been lying motionless with her back to him all night and still had been when he got up. She didn't get up with him. That wasn't so strange—she seldom did on Tuesdays, as she started work later that day. But she used to turn around and give him a good morning kiss. Even in her sleep, she'd always done it. That morning he had the feeling she was pretending to be asleep. Angolo, on the other hand, wasn't asleep. The slobbery lick on his face when he bent down to put on his socks gave Roland quite a fright. He had to get used to the dog. He patted it on the head, and it followed on his heels out into the kitchen.

The dog was also the one who discovered the letter on the floor under the letterbox as Roland was on his way out after strengthening himself with an espresso. He went without breakfast; rolls from the canteen would be served at the briefing. The envelope was thoroughly sniffed, Roland picked it up and recognised Zia Giovanna's scrolling handwriting and the Italian stamp. Aunt Giovanna usually rang. Unease rushed into his stomach. There was no time to read it now; he put it in the dresser drawer, gently pushed the puppy back onto the mat as it tried to go out with him, and closed the door. When he heard it whine pitifully, he thought it might not just be because it wanted to go out with him. He could let Irene clean it up, but . . . he cast a glance at the clock, sighed, and went back in. A short walk around the garden—there was no time for anything else.

After the morning briefing, most of Roland's team had been sent out on assignments. With two murders under investigation, he could well use a few more people. Several times he wondered whether proceeding with the investigation of the murder from the bog twenty-five years ago was hopeless and whether it would be better to put all their efforts into solving the murder of the doctor on Friday night, where they still had fresh leads. Given that there wasn't enough staff resources, he had to prioritise one over the other. Would they find the nursing assistant's killer by solving the murder of the doctor? That was the question, because it meant this was where they should place their focus. Either way, he'd put both Kim and Mikkel on the Vangberg murder, and he was going to concentrate on that today, too. Victoria Vangberg was still hospitalised. He'd talked to her, but she couldn't tell him any more than she'd already told Kurt Olsen. She was being discharged the following afternoon and was moving in with her son and daughter-in-law in Skanderborg until the country property was sold. She could never return to it, she had asserted with horror in her voice. Some people never get over a shock like the one she'd had.

Isabella interrupted his pondering when she knocked on the doorframe. Kim had left the door open when he'd left the office half an hour earlier, and Roland hadn't bothered to get up and close it again. "Come in, Isabella. Any news on Knud Engtoft?"

"Mind-reader." She smiled, and he thought briefly that he wished he was. She looked at him flatteringly.

"Knud Engtoft flew from Copenhagen Kastrup to Aarhus Airport on Friday afternoon. He was here in Jutland when Helge Vangberg was murdered."

Isabella leaned against the doorframe. The light from the window fell obliquely on her face, making her blond hair shimmer in a variety of shades.

"Great, Isabella! Then we only need an address . . ."

"I'm working on it, but he didn't check into a hotel. If he's staying with friends, it could take a long time to find him unless we send out an APB. He hasn't used his credit card or mobile phone." She sighed.

Thank God for anti-terror laws that enabled the government to make changes to the Danish Administration of Justice Act, so they now had new means of surveillance available. He looked at the young female officer and an idea struck him.

"It would be best if we had more evidence before we issue an APB for Knud Engtoft. If he is guilty and hears that we are after him, he'll disappear like dew in the sun—the African sun. But maybe we can find the evidence to hold him. I was just on my way out to the doctor's property to search for the missing tranquiliser darts in the kennels. If his fingerprints are on them, we have him." He paused for a moment to reconsider his idea, but then decided. "Do you want to come with me?"

Isabella looked at him in surprise. "Do you want me to come on such an important mission?"

"Of course; we're leaving in ten minutes."

After the rain and sleet of the night, the ploughed fields looked more autumnal with the almost black soil. The trees' wet leaves displayed warm colours, and they could smell the forest when they got out of the car in the yard. Isabella inhaled loudly and looked around in awe. "Oh wow!" she exclaimed.

"Do you like it?" He looked lovingly at the farmhouse. The thatched roof seemed darker when wet.

"The property? Yes, absolutely. It's beautiful!" She walked to the end of the yard where there was a view of fields and woods. He heard her voice through the wind and saw her standing with her back to him, her hair fluttering about her in the wind like a golden cornfield. She hadn't put her hair up today like he was used to seeing it. He had to control himself not to enter the property and look around—it wasn't why he was here, and a FOR SALE sign had yet to be erected. It pleased him, as it meant he might be the only one who knew the country property was to be sold. But the thought of Irene curbed his joy. How on Earth was he going to persuade her. She just needed to see the place, he convinced himself, then she would be just as excited as Isabella.

"Was this where the doctor was murdered?"

He took his dreamy eyes from the farmhouse and looked at her. She was standing at the exact spot where Victoria Vangberg had found her husband's body. The reason they were here slowly dawned on Roland like an unpleasant cold. "Yes, that was where his wife found him. And the kennels are there," he said unnecessarily. They went in and started searching the ground to find the darts. In reality, they didn't know what they were looking for, but he had a hunch they would know when they found it. The kennels weren't large, so it wouldn't take the two of them long to walk around it.

"There seems to have been a struggle here. Poor dogs," Isabella said quietly.

"Yeah, there was definitely a fight to the death, so maybe the evidence is under something. We probably have to *get our hands dirty*. He handed her a pair of latex gloves."

"Do you remember where the dogs were found?" she asked as she pulled them on, looking resigned.

"One was about there, the other there, and the third around here." He pointed to where he remembered the dogs lying.

When they found an area that looked suspicious, the two officers very carefully examined the ground. They were about to give up when Isabella spotted large empty water and food bowls by the door. She squatted down by them. "I've found something!" she shouted after moving the water bowl.

Roland went over to her.

"How far can a tranquiliser dart fly in the air in the heat of a fight?" she asked with a twinkle in her eye, picking up a little needle from the ground with her thumb and index finger.

"Be careful with that! A few milligrams can fell an entire elephant, and ten milligrams kills a hundred people." He'd had the opportunity to read the vet's report and was amazed at the impact of M99. It was eerie to think that a man like Knud Engtoft had maybe owned it.

She got up and held out the needle so he could see it.

"So, that's what they look like." He smiled.

"But where are the other two? They're not very big, so maybe we missed them." She put the dart into the small bag Roland held open for her.

"Knud Engtoft seems to be a sly fox. He gave himself time to find them and take them with him. He probably just couldn't find this one because it ended up behind the food bowls when one of them nudged it off. Or he may have been interrupted. But one is all we need. If we find his fingerprints on this, we won't need the others."

Isabella nodded. "But why haven't Forensics been looking for them?" she asked as they walked out of the kennels. He held the gate for her.

"They had plenty to do with the doctor. A vet saw to the dogs, but we'd no idea they were killed with darts. The first assumption was that they'd eaten poisoned food."

Isabella nodded again and went into the barn building. The door stood open. He followed and enjoyed the sight of the well-kept building; even in the barn, everything was newly renovated.

"It smells of horse in here. And one seems to have stood here," she said, looking into a horse box with Swedish-red woodwork and a freshly painted black bolt.

"Yes, the doctor's wife has a horse. She told me this morning when I spoke to her. Her daughter-in-law who lives in the country is taking care of it."

"I love horses! She can't afford to live here on her own, can she?"

"No. The property will be put up for sale," he revealed with a treacherous and selfish joy at that fact.

"Wow! Too bad I'm not a millionaire!" Isabella exclaimed, running over to the farmhouse. She peered in through a window, screening her eyes with both hands to better see inside.

"Would you like to live here?" he asked cautiously from behind her.

"*Would* I!" She turned towards him abruptly. He was standing so close behind her that she turned right into his arms. Terrified, he took a step back.

"Doesn't it bother you at all that a man was brutally murdered in the yard?" he asked quickly, realising he was using Irene's words.

"No, not at all. It only makes it even more exciting," she said, lightly tapping his chest with a relaxed hand. "We're police, aren't we?" She started walking back to the car. He followed. Maybe that's why. They were officers of the law; Irene wasn't.

They didn't talk to each other in the car until they reached the city centre rush-hour traffic of Aarhus. It started to rain.

"I can't wait to see whether they find Knud Engtoft's fingerprints on the dart. I'd better work on finding where he is, so we can get him immediately if . . ."

He nodded and looked out into the traffic. "I'm sure we have him. Both murders solved in one fell swoop."

Isabella smiled proudly. "Rolando . . ." she began but fell silent when he looked at her reproachfully.

"Don't call me that!" he said, thinking it was a little too loud when the words came out.

"Why can't I call you by your real name?" she replied defiantly.

He shook his head as he kept an eye on the car in front that was starting to brake for a red light. "Because . . . because it's inappropriate."

"But I'd really like to speak Italian," she continued stubbornly.

"*Ma, non mi piace, signorina,*" he replied, glancing at her to see if she had understood what he was saying at all. But she smiled and nodded.

"I know you don't like it, Signor Inspector," she replied, and he realised she knew more Italian than he expected. He laughed and parked the car in the station's car park.

"Up you go to find Knud Engtoft—and thank you for your help today," he hurried to add, slamming the car door.

She looked at him mischievously over the roof of the car.

"Thank you very much—Roland."

30

The rain turned to sleet; the snowflakes piled up by the windshield wipers, which couldn't keep the window clear at all. He turned off at Nørregade and continued down the busy street, where city buses struggled for space along with eager cyclists winding their way in and out of traffic, trucks, cars, and people unexpectedly crossing the road—even where there were no pedestrian crossings. But he had no problem driving in Aarhus. The streets were built so that they were all somehow connected. Were it not for all the bloody one-way streets, it would be rather straightforward to find your way around.

The car bumped over the cobblestones as he drove in through the gate and into the yard in front of the advertising agency on Badstuegade, a small cosy salmon-coloured building with black half-timbering that only came into view when you entered through the gate. He always thought the atmosphere was right out of Den Gamle By.

It was late afternoon, but as usual, a couple of desktop publishers were still there working. No wonder there were so many divorces in the graphics industry. It was difficult for partners to understand that you couldn't just go home when a newspaper or a printing company was waiting for material and the deadline had long since passed due to technical problems or late proofreading from customers. He thought of Majken and how he repeatedly neglected her in favour of work. He hung his wet coat in the wardrobe and opened the door to the "drawing room," as the desktop publishing room was still called, even though not much was actually *drawn* in that sense anymore. The smell of new wooden floors, computers, printers, and coffee struck him—as well as the heat. Now that the weather had suddenly turned abruptly autumnal, the radiators in the old leaky building had been turned up. On the new computer desks, which could be raised and lowered, were flat screens with rotating screensavers; others were off. He could clearly see which of them was neat and tidy. Torben's desk was overflowing with manuscripts, advertisements, a leftover banana, a box of Ga-Jol liquorice, and various DVDs. Tine's was nicely cleared, and her assignments lay in their trays. Only her rinsed coffee mug remained on the desk to testify that she had been at work. Danny was doing well at work and in Aarhus, although not everything had turned out as he'd hoped when he'd moved here. Here, he had his own employees who didn't know of his past, and so they weren't as reproachful towards him as his old colleagues; those same colleagues who had also driven home drunk from the reception that March evening that changed his life.

He stopped behind Martin, who had probably heard him come in and didn't move his eyes from the screen for that reason. He looked at how the desktop publisher placed an image in a document and deftly moved the text to fit.

"Still doing the housing catalogue?"

"Yep. Just the last corrections before I get it ready for printing."

"It's due early tomorrow," Danny reminded him. He was generally rarely nervous about deadlines; he trusted his employees and knew they would stay at work until the job was done.

"Yes, eight o'clock said the last message. But I also had to do the brochure for the new customer, and there was a problem with the printer again." Martin looked up for the first time at his boss, who was also in charge of the equipment.

"That bloody printer; I'll look at it again. But could Sara not have done the brochure?"

"Yes, if I hadn't been delayed with the shoe ad. I was waiting for a picture to come via email from a supplier, but I didn't get it until I'd sent them a hundred reminders," Sara defended herself behind her screen. She was still working, too.

"Yeah, but you didn't need to spend an hour trying to fix the paper jam yourself, you know—we need everyone on the job, don't we?" teased Martin.

Sara's tanned face surrounded by curly black hair and dark eyes appeared over the edge of the computer screen, and Martin felt a piece of crumpled paper hit the nape of his neck.

"Okay, you two!" Danny smiled indulgently, picking up the ball of paper from the floor and tossing it onto the fragrant orange peels in the bin under Martin's desk. It was good they had fun together. Joy, freedom, and self-determination gave more creativity, he had read.

"Can I help with anything?" he asked, feeling bad that they were still working while he had "only" been at meetings for most of the day, drinking litres of coffee, and talking about marketing and finance. Without the desktop publishers behind the scenes, his work wouldn't be worth much.

"Only with the printer—paper jams are happening all the time." Martin nodded at the printer without looking away from the screen.

"Do we need to get a professional, do you think? We can call a technician from Canon tomorrow." He looked up at the clock hanging just over the printer. "You need to get home, too—do we have time to do the rest early tomorrow?"

"I'll be just another hour," muttered Martin, and Sara opened a bag from the føtex supermarket bakery and choose a carrot bun.

"Me, too," she announced.

"Okay. Would you like anything? Shall I bring you some food?" He looked worriedly at Sara's carrot bun and Martin's apple lying on their desks. They couldn't live on that, but they didn't want anything else. On the way out the door, he snatched the copy of an ad for proofreading from Torben's desk. Living above the shop was ideal—there was the large apartment above the premises that had been converted into the advertising agency, even though Majken had pestered him to move in with her in Risskov. Living so close to work had its advantages, but, naturally, it had its disadvantages, too. He looked at the ad copy on the way up the stairs. There wasn't much to correct. No spelling mistakes, and it was well designed. But the customer would no doubt find something to fix anyway. Whenever clients received the final proof, they always thought they had to find a mistake; otherwise, they somehow felt the agency wasn't doing a good enough job. Proofreading meant finding errors after all. He threw himself on the couch and turned on the television.

Majken had talked about the murdered doctor almost all the way to Holbæk. She knew a little about him. He had been a surgeon at the

Rigshospital, but rumours had swirled in the medical circles—something about taking morphine at work, she'd heard. It was a big problem in the sector—doctors becoming addicts by having such easy access to drugs, combined with their stressful everyday lives. Vangberg had come in to receive treatment for his addiction but had then disappeared for a few years; no one heard anything from him. Later, he reappeared in Jutland, married, and worked as a GP until retirement.

There was no more coverage about the murder on the news. He turned it off again. Majken had asked him to come over, but he didn't want to. He hadn't shaken off their quarrel yet. Knew well he was probably being unsympathetic, but he had a hard time accepting her bitterness towards her family and her intense jealousy. She had been happy when he'd picked her up that morning, looking forward to the trip and to telling her parents the big news. She told him about their beautiful home with a view of Holbæk Fjord. But the closer they drove, the quieter she became, and when she saw her sister's car in front of her parents' house and the pram parked on the garden terrace, she'd asked him to turn around. She was angry and beside herself, which was when they'd quarrelled. Accusations had flown, and he'd been left doubting whether he could live with a woman who possessed so much jealousy and hatred inside. He'd been through it before with Sanne. It wasn't the time he had spent driving to Zealand or the petrol that had made him angry. It was Majken's hatred and, most of all, her distrust of him. She kept saying how he'd probably choose her sister at some point—or some other woman—and drop her, or that he wasn't over Kamilla; something had to be wrong. He had done what he could to show it was *her* he wanted. Had even proposed to her. It had been the surprise in the romantic dessert when they'd celebrated their first anniversary. Majken had thrown herself over him in joy and shouted *Yes, yes, yes!* so loudly that everyone in the restaurant had turned to them and smiled. What else could he do to show her he'd chosen her and no one else? Maybe she could sense, on some level, that the deeper feelings were absent. If he couldn't lie to himself, what about her?

On his way home from the last meeting in Hornslet, he'd stopped at Egå Cemetery again and had laid a bouquet on Rasmus's grave. It was the only way he could communicate with Kamilla. He could do no more. The punishment of the justice system had been bad, but hers overshadowed everything else. If only he had been honest so she'd heard it from him, then things might have been different. He could choose to live on his own, but you had to have someone to share your life with. He'd experienced enough loneliness in his life. His mother was now so senile that she no longer remembered him. She had chosen to live alone as a martyr after his father died, even though she'd had many suitors. That's not how his life was going to end.

31

Kent read the description of the site on www.geocaching.dk again and entered the specified coordinates into his GPS. He was getting ready to embark on the adventure. There was a new treasure, or *cache* as it was technically called, to be found. He had waited a long time for something exciting to appear. The geocoin he'd been lucky enough to find on his last geocaching tour in Hobro Østerskov lay ready on the table. It was about time he put it in another cache. He'd cheered when he found it, and as soon as he got home, he'd logged in to the coin's tracking number online and followed its long journey, which he would now carry on. It was nicely designed with a compass-like engraving in the middle, and it confusingly resembled an old gold coin. It had come all the way from Sweden, migrating to Skagen and down through North Jutland from cache to cache. It was tempting to keep it. Some people did keep caches as collectibles, even though it wasn't allowed. According to the rules, a found geocoin should always be put back in a new cache so its journey wasn't interrupted, and it should be logged online so that other people could follow its progress. Some geocoins had managed to travel around the world. Ready on the table was also his own signature item, which he always left as an exchange in the caches he found. It was a white golf ball with his initials KGB signed in waterproof red felt-tip pen. He'd always loved his initials. Before he became interested in geocaching, he'd painted graffiti on boring house walls and train carriages on the railway—he needed some excitement in his life—he used the same signature on the golf balls as he'd used for his graffiti. It was no accident that it was a golf ball. They were easy to get hold of through his father, who was fond of a few rounds on the golf course with the guys from work. Not that any of them were particularly wealthy, but they probably felt they were when they walked on the grass in their fine golf shoes—right up until they had to pay club dues or buy new golf clubs; he smiled at the thought.

The expectant excitement and adventurousness tingled in his stomach as he put on his raincoat. It was dark and cold and raining. Had to be around midnight. A thunderstorm would have been optimal, but, unfortunately, the season for that had passed. Darkness was important. Night geocaching intensified the excitement. Plus, there was a greater chance of locating an FFC—First Finder Certificate—which was the greatest triumph. Being the first to find a cache was great, especially when a new cache was listed as a *mystery cache*—that meant there would also be tasks to be solved along the way, making it an even greater challenge. As long as it wasn't that stupid Sudoku or some other maths equation, then he'd leave it. But this cache owner seemed to be one of the most inventive. Just following a few simple coordinates on a GPS and going from one Tupperware box or tin to another with all sorts of loot—usually a lot of useless plastic gadgets—gradually became too monotonous and trivial. That was ideal for families with children, but he demanded more now. That's why this geocoin was a scoop. But this was even greater. Much greater. This cache was to be found in Marselisborg Forest. It was about a three-kilometre bike ride out there, and it was worth it. He printed the instructions from the website. It was creatively called "Marselisborg Murder Mystery," which boded well. The final cache was the crime scene, but it had to be found first. The tasks consisted of gathering evidence in different places. Five locations were given with coordinates. Each location had a clue in an independent cache. Once he'd gathered all the evidence, he could, by combining it, arrive at the final coordinate, which would then reveal the location of the crime scene. In other words, he was going to play detective, and that was right up his street. He smiled; he had been waiting a long time for this. This would enable him to prove his worth as a geocacher. He put on his backpack and a headlamp, which he had learned was very useful when practising the sport in the dark.

* * *

The forest was exceptionally dark and wet that night. Heavy drops fell around him, and he could hear only the drops of water hitting the withered leaves, his breathing, and the sound of his hiking boots snapping little twigs on the forest floor. It smelled wet and musty. Loving the forest at night, he inhaled the scent of autumn and filled his lungs. It was cool, so he zipped his raincoat up to the neck and pulled the hood well out over his forehead so that only the light and his eyes were free. Many of the leaves on the trees had fallen off, so there wasn't much shelter from the rain.

He quickly found the first waypoint and was able to move on in the hunt. The geocoin was placed in the first cache he found. The next one who found it would further its journey if it didn't end up in the clutches of a collector.

Four caches with evidence and coordinates were found after a good hour of hiking around the damp forest. It pleased him; they looked untouched. An FFC lay ahead. He was ready for the fifth location, which would allow him to find the final coordinate for the end goal. He had to, even if it took him until dawn. He wasn't going to give up. He had never given up on a geocaching trip—only if he came across a Sudoku task. Fortunately, no cache had yet been *muggled*, geocaching jargon for when a cache was destroyed or stolen. Such a thing stopped any hunt, as it meant a lack of information to move on. Right now, unlike the Muggles in the Harry Potter series, he felt he had magical abilities and control over life. That feeling had made this sport his. He was in his element on his own out in nature. Here he could think without being disturbed.

Thoughts stopped abruptly when he found the fifth location. The excitement increased, and his breathing was loud, intensified from hiking in the uneven and muddy terrain. He wasn't exactly in top physical form. He rummaged in the leaves where the next cache should be located. He'd soon be able to find the crime scene. A raindrop hit his neck; the raincoat's rubber amplified the sound inside the hood, so it sounded like a gunshot. He quickly turned around and laughed nervously when he realised it was only a raindrop that had hit him. His nerves were on edge. Looking for a random cache of plastic animals was one thing; solving a murder mystery on a dark night was something else entirely. It took a while before he spotted it in the light from the headlamp. An animal fled and rustled the withered leaves. A hedgehog looked away from the light. He retrieved the fifth and decisive clue from a bush with prickly thorns. He cursed quietly; he'd forgotten to bring gloves with him. He read the note in the plastic box and smiled proudly as he wrote himself into the logbook and took an item from the cache with the same value as his golf ball in exchange, even though he thought his KGB signature was worth much more than all the junk that lay here. Now he actually knew where the crime scene had to be. He checked the coordinates in the geochecker and was close to having a *geogasm*, as he called the sensation, when they turned out to be correct.

He advanced slowly according to the calculated coordinates. The GPS pointed the way to a large old tree that had probably fallen over in the storm of January 2005, its roots sticking out in the dark like long tentacles. Now it was almost rotten, and it stank terribly, too. Kent knelt and fumbled with his hand underneath the tree trunk. The moisture from the forest floor penetrated his trousers, making his knees wet and cold, but he was too eager to find his cache to feel it. He hoped he was the first and would be awarded a well-deserved FFC. But his hand didn't find the box or tin it was looking for, rather it grabbed rotten leaves and moist soil. After he'd clenched several disgusting soft mushrooms, hard squirming beetles, and writhing earthworms between his fingers, and the unbearable smell was about to make him vomit, he got up, annoyed, and brushed the soil off his knees. "For fuck's sake!" He snarled between his teeth. If it was all a big joke, and there was nothing to be found, he'd be furious. He'd just spent all night on it. He bent over the tree to see if he had the strength to push it away in case the cache had slipped far below it, but the head-lamp caught something sticking out from under the tree trunk. A moth had been attracted to the light from the lamp and flapped in his face. He straightened up and waved the creature away with a fiery "Get lost!" Was the cache owner so inventive as to place a mannequin under the tree trunk to increase the tension? He squatted down and looked at the hand more closely. It wasn't made of plastic. One of the long red nails was broken, and the nail varnish was peeling off the two fingers bent forward in the light. The earth around it was alive with teeming ants and beetles. The skin had a strange greenish tinge, and suddenly the stench was so noticeable that he had no doubt that something nearby was rotting. A human!

He got up quickly and staggered backwards as he looked around the woods, which suddenly seemed even darker, as if the tree trunks had moved closer together around him. It had stopped raining, and the moon shone its special white light down on the trees. The wind blew up, rustling the withered leaves in the treetops, and shadows danced on the forest floor. He set off at a run without having any idea in which direction to head. The light of the headlamp flickered on the foliage in front of him, and he stumbled on branches and holes in the forest floor a few times. Someone was after him. The smell was stuck in his nose. He tried to throw up without stopping and without succeeding. He heard his own panicked cry between the sound of the wilted leaves and branches cracking beneath him. His nose was streaming, and he was sobbing loudly when it dawned on him that he was lost and hadn't only forgotten his gloves but extra batteries for his GPS, too. He desperately tried to call from his phone, but there was no signal here in the middle of Marselisborg Forest.

32

It didn't take long for him to reach the forest by car, and with so many dead people being found not far from his residence, he was beginning to worry. He prayed that this time it was a tragic accident; a mountain biker who hit something or a runner who had fallen. Still, given the circumstances, he'd chosen to drive out when he got the call.

Last night had been a late one, and Irene was already in bed when he got home. However, she'd left out food that just had to be heated in the oven for him, so he wasn't completely in the doghouse. As he ate, he read the letter from Giovanna. The food had grown cold because he'd completely forgotten to eat and because it took him a long time to read it. Firstly, thanks to his aunt's illegible handwriting and secondly, thanks to the language. "I'm forgetting my bloody mother tongue, too," he mumbled. Another weight on his already heavy conscience. He had a hard time blocking out the contents of the letter from his mind as he drove.

Zia Giovanna was almost middle-aged and had come into the world a year before her brother's death. In Naples, most families had many children at that time, and there had been nine siblings. Giovanna was the last of them. She had a little antiques boutique on a side street off Via Chiaia in Naples. But neither a side street nor a shop La Camorra ignored. She still fought valiantly in the spirit of her brother, whose memory had been kept alive in the family in the manner of a martyr. Roland's feeling was that the family had looked down on his mother because she'd fled with only him and a few bags. The rest of the family had continued fighting the hopeless battle. The battle against the mafia. Giovanna refused to pay them protection money. She was even part of a group that had set up a website against the mafia, where they collected signatures in protest. They supported each other in resisting the mafia—*the system*—despite their lives being the potential cost. Roland shook his head and changed gears. He was worried about her safety, but that wasn't even the worst. What the hell could *he* do? Why was she involving him in it now? He didn't have time to feel sadness at the thought because he'd arrived at the forest.

Henry Leander and a team of forensic technicians, reminiscent of ghosts in their white suits in the twilight, stood waiting for him with the lost and still shocked treasure hunter who had called 112 as soon as he'd found his way out of the woods and had mobile coverage again. His name was Kent Gert Berggren. He gave a technician the coordinates of the site so they could find it using GPS, too. Then he was sent to a crisis psychologist. He looked like he was about to lose consciousness. It must have been a hard night.

It was a long and impassable hike, and Roland lagged, but he was able to keep a constant eye on the forensic team's white suits ahead of him even though he was the last person to reach the site. He crawled under the barrier tape, wading through a mixture of withered and rotten leaves and brown needles from the conifers. Henry Leander was already at work. Roland could see the top of the suit's white hood sticking up behind a fallen tree trunk with long thick roots protruding. Nature was marvellous. It completely surpassed man's ability and sense. How could a storm topple so huge a tree?

"He's here now," he heard one of the technicians say to Leander, who was apparently in better shape than he was and could keep up with the young forensic technicians. Roland had feared getting lost in the vast Marselisborg Forest, especially considering the five more or less contiguous small forests that had originally belonged to the Marselisborg estate. He tried to conceal how breathless he was. It was a cool morning, and the haze that lay between the tree trunks after the night's rain made the air even damper. And the smell, which now reached his nostrils, made him gag a few times.

A technician shook a Tupperware-like plastic box, causing it to rattle. "I found the cache," he shouted, laughing, though Roland didn't think there was much to laugh about that morning.

"What?" he mumbled tiredly, walking a little closer, where he abruptly stopped.

"The lucky finder is a geocacher. He just didn't find the treasure and unfortunately for him, it's an FFC."

"A what?"

"It's a certificate awarded to the person who finds the treasure first. It brings prestige to the geocacher who finds it."

"But certainly not to whoever finds a corpse," Roland muttered inaudibly.

The talkative technician continued: "My son is an active geocacher. I've been out with him a few times. Coming across this in the middle of the night in a dark forest would definitely give you quite a fright." Roland just nodded gloomily.

"I'm sorry, Benito," Leander shouted, sticking his head out from behind the tree trunk.

Roland realised with horror that they were facing a new murder victim. They had knocked the tree trunk away, so the woman was now lying free. She was curled up in the hollow that the roots had left behind when they'd been ripped up from the ground during the storm. Roland's initial thought was that she must have frozen in her thin black tights and short skirt. He noticed she didn't have any shoes. No one could have pushed the large tree trunk aside on their own to place her there. It would have taken four strong men to move it. The murderer must have stuffed her down there, thinking she'd never be found. Or perhaps there was more than one perp. Or maybe the murderer was a huge giant. Roland avoided taking a closer look at the woman after that. He'd had enough of corpses lately, so he contented himself with the smell and listening to Leander's voice describing the condition of the body. When he was done, he got up so Forensics could get in. The area was illuminated by strong floodlights, despite the morning light of dawn breaking.

Henry Leander walked over to Roland, who was still standing at an appropriate distance. "The body is in the decaying phase," he said.

That fact didn't surprise him.

"The greenish skin colour indicates that death occurred several days ago. Maybe three or four. She was stabbed to death in the same brutal manner as the doctor. But not here. There'd be a lot more blood if she'd been stabbed here. The body was moved here."

"Bloody hell, another crime scene to dig up." Roland snorted. The cold air made his nose run, but with the inhalation came the stench, which he'd been trying to keep out by not breathing at the same pace as usual. He took out his handkerchief.

Leander stuffed a small plastic box into his pocket.

"Have you found one to—um, treasure?" Roland asked sarcastically.

Leander's smile was hidden behind his face mask, but Roland could see the last ripple of it under his dishevelled white moustache as he pulled the mask down under his chin. He took the small plastic box out of his pocket again and held it up to the spotlight so Roland could see the bustling life at the bottom of the box, where Leander had laid some leaves so the insects inside had something to hide in and could make themselves at home. A couple of large maggots lay writhing in there like pale belly dancers.

"No, I collected a few little helpers. Ants, beetles, and larvae. All the maggots and eggs at this stage attract insects that feed on other insects, including beetles, ants, and wasps. But there are not many wasps anymore. There are so many maggots in the body that the temperature has increased by almost fifteen degrees," Leander explained in the same tone as when he said he'd eaten soft-boiled eggs that morning. "Only when I know what type of fly laid the eggs will I be able to tell how long the body has been lying here from the larval stage. Given that so many days have passed, it's not only blowflies that have laid eggs in the cadaver. The common housefly does it, too, so think about it the next time a fly lands on your pâté." He paused and looked knowingly at Roland. "Out of the fly's seven stages, these seem to be in the third larval stage, so they would have been laid forty to forty-eight hours ago."

"Did you learn that during your stay at The Body Farm?" Roland asked, shaking excessively. He still had a hard time imagining that such a place existed, but it really did, in a remote wooded area of Knoxville, Tennessee, at the foot of the Smoky Mountains, where Dr. William Bass had received one hectare of land so that he and his assistants could research how dead human bodies decay in the open air. Henry Leander had stayed there for a few months to gain more forensic knowledge.

He looked lovingly at the insects in the plastic box. "Nature can teach us everything, Roland. It was here before us, and if we don't learn from it, we'll be none the wiser. We should be thankful scientists like Bass exist and that humans are willing to donate their dead bodies to research so the importance of insects at every single stage of the process can be mapped."

Roland stepped from one foot to the other and put his hands in his pockets. "But who are they? The deceased. The ones who donate their bodies?"

Leander looked at him. The light was about to reach down to them, and Leander's cheeks were flushed with enthusiasm. Julie was probably the only one who wanted to hear about his insects.

"Some of the dead are homeless, others are people who've donated their bodies to science—organ donors, in fact. Other people sign up voluntarily and want to rest in peace at The Body Farm, happy to help the police catch criminals. And then, of course, some people just want to save on funeral costs."

"Come here!" shouted a technician, very conveniently interrupting the conversation. Not that the time of death didn't interest Roland, but he could do without the other talk, especially now that his breakfast was pressing against his uvula.

Leander trudged back and disappeared behind the tree trunk. Roland reluctantly followed, trying to catch a glimpse of the morning sky. The sun seemed to want to peek out today. He held his handkerchief up in front of his nose.

The woman was laid on the stretcher. Roland couldn't take his eyes off the grave beneath the roots, where ants and beetles teemed crazily in the beam from the floodlights, confused that their livelihood had been taken from them.

"Have you noticed the strange fibres in her mouth? They're in her throat, too," the technician told Leander, wiping his forehead with the back of his white-gloved hand as if he were sweating, even though it was cold and he didn't have a lot of meat on him. Some of his less sensitive colleagues called him "Bones" because he was so thin. Many of those who worked closely with death every day had a bizarre, dark sense of humour. A survival mechanism. The less morbid ones called him "The Stick."

Leander leaned forward and observed the phenomenon that Roland didn't want to look at. He kept his eyes on the ground. The insects were gone—as if by magic—in search of a new meal on the forest floor.

"It could be hair, but how the hell did she get it into her mouth? We'll take a closer look at them back at the morgue—they might be important," said Leander.

The Stick took a series of pictures before picking some of the fibres out of the woman's mouth with tweezers and putting them in a bag.

"Have you seen her shoes?" asked Roland. He had examined the entire illuminated area attentively.

"No, there's not much more to find here. But we'll expand the area and start to move outwards—that might give us something," replied another technician as he closed the zipper of the body bag.

Roland waved to the talkative one who'd found the plastic box. "That geo—uh, treasure hunt—could the murderer have arranged to leave the treasure here so the body would be found?"

The forensic scientist was a little weed with crooked teeth, bright curls, and big glasses. He didn't look at all like the beautiful specimens of his kind from the *CSI* series that Roland had stumbled upon the previous night. (He had been zapping between TV stations to find something interesting to unwind to before going to bed.) Angolo had lain with his head in his lap, following his moves. Even the dead resembled supermodels in that series, but maybe that was life in Miami. He'd heard that many young people had become interested in the subject due to the series, which was actually a strangely distorted view of an industry where death and misery were the raw realities of everyday life and only the tough coped with the hardships. A dead person wasn't always beautiful. The scene in the middle of the forest, where daylight had now begun to reveal all the details, was clear proof of that.

"I strongly doubt that." The technician answered his question, still with a smile. "Cache owners tend to be honest people. It's more likely that the body ending up here in the same place as the cache—which was probably here for a while first—is a complete coincidence. But you never know. We'll take the cache in for technical examination, too," he added, going back to the others to help get the body ready for transport. Roland was relieved he didn't have to carry it all the way back to the waiting hearse.

Leander and Roland walked back to their cars together. They were parked on the outskirts of Storskov by Skovmøllevej, not far from where Helge Vangberg's body had been found in the yard. Was the location of the woman's body deliberate?

It took them a while to find their way out on one of the many trails that had been trampled by walkers, runners, and mountain bikers. Roland cursed whenever his trouser legs got stuck in branches or his shoes sank into an anthill, despite both men being sensible enough to don suitable footwear. In different circumstances, it would have been a beautiful hike. They walked for a moment near the Giber Å River and could hear the water trickling, as if nothing had ever disturbed the peace of this lovely spot of nature.

Roland brushed off his clothes when they reached the light again. The sun had risen and was shining on the wet leaves and dewdrops in the grass. They stood in silence, breathing heavily as if they needed to get clean air into their lungs.

"Have you thought about how close we are to the doctor's desirable property?" Henry Leander asked, almost in response to Roland's gloomy thoughts both about the close location of the deceased and his dream property. Not physically close in each case, but his dream of owning the farmhouse was beginning to fade. Irene refused to move from Højbjerg. As soon as she got wind of the new murder—and that it was a woman—so close by, the project would be doomed. It wouldn't be long before the press knew, though strangely enough they were excelling in their absence currently. Even Anne Larsen from the *Daily News* hadn't heard about the find yet. It amazed him; she was always the first one on-site, as if she had been listening in on police radio.

"Yes, I have thought of it," he mumbled, opening his car door as he watched the forensic pathologist carefully place the plastic box of insects on the passenger seat. Roland almost expected him to put the seat belt around it. He smiled grimly at the idea.

"Has Julie Hermansen been taken back to Djævleøen?" he asked as the insects reminded him that she, too, had a penchant for creepy crawlies, which was probably one of the things that had brought her and Henry together. It probably wasn't so easy to find women with that interest.

"No, she's still here," Leander admitted, looking at him appreciatively. "Didn't you hear that Olsen asked her to help with these cases?"

Roland felt excluded, but let it go. "We haven't had a chance to talk about it yet, but it's a good idea. Corpses are popping up in bogs and forests, so we're undoubtedly talking about a fairly psychopathic serial killer—that is, if there is a connection between the murders."

"I'll start on the autopsy as soon as I get the deceased back to the morgue. Then we may be able to clear up whether an antique African knife was the murder weapon here, too."

Roland nodded as he popped a piece of chewing gum in his mouth. He longed for a cigarette to take away the ugly taste in his mouth. Given how things were turning out, he wondered whether his willpower would hold or if he'd end up buying a packet of Cecil cigarettes. He began sweating at the thought.

"Right, well. I'll see you later. Say hi to Julie," he said, getting in behind the wheel. Leander's brief nod without comment reinforced Roland's suspicion that she was staying with him this time and not at the hotel.

33

The organ sounded slightly out of tune, and the woman next to her on the bench wasn't exactly hitting all the vocal notes. The coffin was decorated with white roses and lilies, which she found pure and beautiful. She didn't know what her mother liked. She had just listened to the pastor's few words about her. What could he say when the woman's only daughter could contribute nothing? She had a nagging feeling in her chest, but it wasn't sadness; she knew that feeling well. This was more like a guilty conscience, shame, or something indefinable. As the congregation sang and the vicar stood on the altar with his back to them, she let her gaze run around the few in attendance. There were probably no more than usual on an ordinary morning in Vor Frelsers Church. The funeral of an unknown woman was unlikely to draw a crowd. She refocused her attention on Hymn 729 in the hymnal. It was impossible to sing along with the church singer's high soprano voice, so she just read the lyrics and thought about the words.

And when at the command of the Lord
our hourglass runs out,
an eternal summer with our God
in Paradise we will find.

She had chosen the hymn "Now Fades the Forest" by Grundtvig because she'd always loved it and it suited the season. She glanced at the coffin, hoping her mother would find the paradise of the verse, despite her believing that the curse she had brought upon the family had deprived her of the right to a place among God's chosen. Kamilla had not been to a funeral—not even in a church—since Rasmus was buried. The grief of losing him intensified. She fought back the tears, but they broke through her defences anyway and rolled down her cheeks. Her guilty conscience grew bigger.

Now she was sitting here, at her mother's funeral, crying—over her son. The bellowing of the organ put an end to the song as the last verse was sung. She took a deep breath to gain control of herself. Slowly, people began to leave the church.

There was only her, a married couple who had to have been her mother's neighbours and had probably felt obligated to show up, and a woman she didn't know by the grave when the coffin was lowered in by four strangers whom the priest had helped her find, as there were no other options for pallbearers. It was all terribly sad, and she felt so sorry for her mother that it hurt her physically. To be laid to rest without anyone to remember you and miss you. At the same time, she realised that she would have to change her own life soon to avoid ending up like her mother.

She stood graveside with her head empty of thoughts when the ceremony was over, and she suddenly noticed that the unknown woman had remained, too. She met her gaze and recognised something in her features. Had one of her family members really travelled from the west coast of Jutland to Horsens? Her theory was confirmed when the woman, who was dressed in a worn grey coat and a blue scarf, which had been wrapped around her hair and tucked down by the coat's collar, came towards her and looked at her with dull grey eyes.

"Are you Gloria's daughter?" she asked in a dialect that Kamilla immediately recognised as West Jutlandic.

She nodded. The sound of her mother's name, Gloria, which she herself had never called her, evoked old memories: her father faintly calling *Gloria* from inside the bedroom when he was ill, and her answering sharply back from the kitchen without going in to see him; or when he tried to appease her by repeating *Gloria, sweet Gloria* so many times that it became embarrassing, and she didn't so much as look at him. How could such a cold person have such a beautiful name?

The woman held out her hand, which was dry and cracked from hard work, towards her. "You must be my niece," she said, and Kamilla assumed it was a smile she saw on the woman's colourless lips. She hesitantly reciprocated the handshake. There was a little resemblance to her mother. The same pale eyes that had a flushing expression of fear. Perhaps she, too, had broken out of Inner Mission and was afraid of the punishment from God.

"Thank you for coming. It's a long journey," Kamilla replied, hoping it was enough, but the woman remained standing as if she wanted more.

"I had to make sure that Gloria was properly buried and laid to rest," replied the woman, who hadn't introduced herself. She probably assumed Gloria's daughter knew who she was. Kamilla didn't respond to that comment but was glad she hadn't opted for cremation, which had been her initial thought. When the woman followed her out of the graveyard, she found it too cold not to say something more to her. Her age was hard to judge because she was so grey and hunched, but she guessed early fifties, so she had to be her mother's little sister.

"Would you like a cup of coffee?" she heard herself ask, immediately regretting it when the woman nodded without a smile or a polite thank-you. She remembered that there were a few cafés on Nørregade. They walked on in silence, Kamilla regretting her offer more and more. She chose the first café they came across and opened the door for her aunt. There weren't many patrons, which suited her just fine. She ordered two coffees. They sat down at a table next to a window facing the street.

"How did you get here?" was the only thing she could think to ask while they waited for the coffee. Perhaps, most of all, because she feared having to offer accommodation, too.

"I have a little car, so it was no problem. It only took about three hours to drive here from Agger, where we still live. It was a beautiful journey down around Nissum Bredning." For the first time, the woman smiled, and it suited her. She loosened the scarf and let it hang loosely around her neck. Her hair was grey, but its nuances revealed she had once been blond, like her sister—and Kamilla herself.

"Are you not hungry after the long journey?"

Her aunt shook her head. Once she'd had some of the coffee, her eyes filled with a little more life. There were small spider veins on her cheeks. She looked exactly like what she was—a fisherwoman from windswept West Jutland.

"Yes, so you are Gloria's daughter," she said quietly, assessing her. "How old are you now? Thirty-six?" she guessed.

"Thirty-seven," corrected Kamilla. She had just turned a year older in July.

"I hardly know anything about you. But I suppose your mother told you about your aunt Astrid?"

She shook her head regretfully and had to confess that she hadn't seen much of her mother over the last few years.

"No, I suppose not. We didn't talk to her either after she broke off contact," Astrid said quietly, sipping her coffee again.

"Broke off contact? I was under the impression *you* were the one who broke off contact because Mum wasn't living according to your—norms," she exclaimed, feeling a little more refreshed from the caffeine.

Astrid looked a tad prim, but then she straightened her coffee cup and looked directly at her. "Yes, Mother and Father—your grandmother and grandfather—were very religious. They refused to accept Gloria anymore after *that*. But Bjarne and I"—Astrid lifted her hand with a wedding ring displayed, so Kamilla figured Bjarne had to be Astrid's husband and her uncle—"we still wanted to have contact with her, but she didn't want that. *If you must break your ties, it has to be with everyone*, she once said to me," Astrid continued with a sigh, her eyes shining at Kamilla.

Kamilla grew curious. Something didn't add up. Could an entire family really break apart just because a daughter chose a different way of life than what was the norm in the family? What about love and family ties? Growing up in a Christian home couldn't have been that bad. Wasn't Christianity all about love and tolerance?

"What really happened? Why did my mother suddenly move to Horsens?" she asked gently.

Astrid writhed nervously on the chair as if it were a topic she didn't want to talk about. "Did Gloria never tell you?"

Kamilla shook her head.

"They are all gone now. Your grandfather and grandmother died a long time ago, and now Gloria is gone, too, so I don't suppose anything will come of me telling you." She hesitated, then continued in a theatrical whisper as though fearing others were listening. "As a child and young woman, your mother was very . . ." She considered the word for a long time. "Rebellious. Mother was strict in her parenting; it was what she herself had been raised with. She interpreted the Bible orthodoxly like her mother—your great-grandmother—had done. It was ban on ban. We weren't allowed to dance, to drink, to play cards, to dress up for Fastelavn, or to listen to the same music as our peers did back then. And associating with boys and later young men was unheard of. Gloria couldn't fit in. She did what she wanted—and it had fatal consequences." Astrid's forehead formed worry lines.

"What about you, Astrid. Did you just go along with it?"

She shook her head slowly. "I was lucky enough to meet Bjarne. He's from the Inner Mission, too, so Mother and Father approved of him immediately. But he's not as orthodox as your grandmother and grandfather were—they're called fundamentalists nowadays. You have to understand, Kamilla, there are many degrees of faith with us; not everyone believes in the same way as everyone else. Bjarne and I are believers, but our children were raised as conventional Christians, where love and forgiveness are higher values than condemnation and punishment."

Condemnation and *punishment* were precisely what had defined most of Kamilla's childhood. But how did that fit in with her mother fleeing from those beliefs? She poured some more coffee for Astrid and herself. Astrid sat for a long time, staring out the window, lost in her thoughts.

"So, I have cousins, then," Kamilla said to get her to continue.

Astrid woke from her thoughts and smiled faintly. "Yes, you have. And they are long grown up. Kristina lives in London and Mathias in Copenhagen—he's studying to be a priest. He's a good boy," she added proudly.

Kamilla smiled. It was strange to get confirmation that there *was* close family out there, even though she'd had the feeling there was. Her mother hadn't been an only child—that much she did know. "But I don't understand why Mum didn't want to see you anymore?"

Astrid's eyes were distant again. "Something happened that separated us. It was just as much my fault, because for years I believed in Mother's version of events and not in Gloria's. I regret that now, and now it's too late. Maybe that's why I needed to be here today."

Kamilla saw the pain in her eyes. The pain that came from carrying guilt that can't be forgiven. She had seen it somewhere before.

"Are you sure you want to know what happened?" asked Astrid in earnest. Kamilla sensed the air almost trembling around the little grey woman. She needed to get what she knew out in the open so she might be able to obtain the forgiveness she obviously hadn't received from her God.

"Sometimes uncertainty is better than the truth," her aunt continued warningly.

Kamilla knew all about that. If she hadn't found out the truth about Danny, she would be with him now and not Majken. She contented herself with nodding.

"Our brother was almost seven years old at the time. A real 'afterthought' and the apple of Father and Mother's eyes. Gloria must have been around eighteen . . ."

"Your brother? Do I have an uncle, too?" she blurted, immediately regretting it when Astrid sent her a sharp look, as if she were a disobedient child interrupting an adult.

"Are you sure I should tell you this?" she asked again. "You have to realise that knowing the truth will change your life." There was a threatening tone in her voice now.

She was too curious to ask Astrid to stop her story. She wanted a change in her life, despite being afraid that the change Astrid was alluding to probably wasn't exactly what she had in mind.

She nodded again gently.

34

Do you need to borrow the car again today?" asked Pernille, buttering a slice of bread and topping it off with a thick layer of strawberry jam.

"No, but thanks. I'm going to keep reading the papers I got from the doctor's wife yesterday, so I'll stay here. Besides, don't you need the car today?" Sabrina was beginning to feel at home with her friend. She sat on the kitchen counter with her back to the wall, her legs pulled up as she warmed her fingers on a mug of coffee that was placed on one knee. She was still in her pyjamas even though it was the middle of the morning. Pernille was due at work later, so they'd enjoyed a leisurely breakfast, which Sabrina had prepared, as she had to get up anyway because of the morning sickness. Tobias had hugged her as a thank-you for the food and had slipped out to the crèche with Adam before Pernille got up. Adam was a great little kid, and Sabrina hadn't been able to take her eyes off him while he ate his porridge. She couldn't wait for it to be her turn to say *Here comes the aeroplane*. But she couldn't picture Peter in that role.

"Yeah, but if you needed it, we could figure something out." Pernille smiled. "What do you get out of reading those papers anyway?" she continued. "It can't change the fact that your mother is dead."

Sabrina knew well that Pernille didn't understand. Sometimes she didn't either, but finding out what had happened back then had become an obsession. She had asked herself if she was just doing it to have an excuse to come home to Denmark and be away from Peter, but she wasn't sure. After reading about the murder of the nursing assistant, her investigation had taken on an entirely different meaning, and if she found out the whole thing wasn't just a coincidence, then she would go to the police with what she knew. That's why she hadn't told Pernille everything, either. "It gives me a chance to get to know my mother in a new way. I was only four years old when she died, so I never really knew her, you know?"

Pernille nodded, her mouth full of bread, and finished chewing before answering. "Yeah, but doesn't that make it all much worse—getting to know her, I mean?"

"I don't think so. So far, I've learned that I was once a beloved child, and it *was* Carola and not my mother who made me an unhappy, fat little girl." She tried to smile, but she knew that the slim, sporty, and toned Pernille believed you were always in control of your own body—even as a child. It was a topic they had often discussed. But Sabrina didn't believe it to be the case. Children couldn't take responsibility for whether they became over-weight. Parents had to guide them to eat healthily and exercise and make sure that they were not so unhappy that they would comfort themselves by overeating, as she had. Maybe it was easy to say. She looked down at her stomach. Soon she would have the chance to give a child all that she herself had not received.

"Okay, okay. What do I know about it? Luckily, I still have my parents. Maybe I'd be doing the same if I were in your shoes," Pernille capitulated, clearing the table.

"I'll do the dishes, so off you go," Sabrina said, stretching her legs out on the bench.

Pernille blew her a kiss from out in the hall. "Be careful we don't become dependent on you," she warned, slamming the door behind her with a smile.

She was alone again. As alone as she'd always felt in the apartment in Milan as soon as Peter went to work. Only she didn't feel nearly as lonely here because those she heard passing out on the stairs and down on the street spoke a language she could understand, and she knew she could communicate with them if she needed to.

She had a shower and got dressed. Then she did the dishes and went back to the papers she'd received from Oda Winther the day before. She had read many of them last night before her eyelids had grown heavy, but there were still some left. As with the letters Louise Engtoft had written, Ole Winther's notes also told of great improvements being made regarding Josefine's illness. She couldn't understand everything that was written because of Latin names and terms that she didn't know. And the doctor's handwriting wasn't always legible. She got another cup of coffee and sat down on the bench. She was hoping to find out why her father had asked Dr. Winther to cease treatment, but the doctor seemed to have taken it with ease. The last thing he had written was a brief note that he was giving up treatment and another doctor was taking over. There wasn't much more. She sat back, feeling deeply disappointed. The only thing she had got out of those papers was that Louise Engtoft had told the truth. Ole Winther had repeatedly referred to her as a skilled and competent nursing assistant. Who had wanted to murder her, and how much progress had the police made in their investigation? She knew they had talked to Gustav and Carola, and given that she had only been four years old at the time, it was unlikely they could use what she had to say. Or could they? Could she really help the police if she told them what she knew?

She jumped when her phone rang. "Sabrina," she said briefly without looking at the number, as she figured it was someone she knew. Maybe Peter—she had left him several voice messages after numerous futile attempts to reach him.

"Is that Sabrina Dahl?"

She confirmed that it was and listened without being particularly surprised by the inquiry. It was one of the journalists she'd been waiting a long time to contact her. It was only a matter of time before they found out she belonged to the family that Louise had worked for shortly before her death. The reporters probably didn't care that she didn't know anything. They were just looking for a sensational story. Still, she agreed that the journalist could come and talk to her. Maybe the reporter could give her more information and guide her in what she should do. Because soon Sabrina wouldn't know where she stood with it all.

"Anne Larsen," the journalist introduced herself as soon as she entered the hall where footwear, coats, and jackets took up so much room that she could barely open the door. It hadn't taken her long to get there from the paper.

They sat down at the kitchen table, and Anne accepted a cup of coffee. She opened the conversation. "We almost bumped into each other at Oda and Ole Winther's—the doctor."

"We did? I didn't realise that." Sabrina wondered what the press had been doing there.

"You were driving off as we arrived. A nice car with a NO TO THE EU sticker on the rear window. That was my feeling at the time, too."

Anne Larsen drank from the cup and sent Sabrina a sisterly look that made her feel a little trapped. She'd never had an opinion on politics. It bored her, so Peter dealt with that kind of thing. He was, as far as she knew, strongly in favour of the EU. In her opinion, it didn't matter who was in power and whether Denmark was in the EU or not; it didn't affect her everyday life except when they started tinkering with something that made the conditions for the sick and dying worse.

"It's my friend's car. I borrow it," she parried.

"Oh yeah. You live in Italy, don't you?" asked the journalist, obviously already in the know.

"Yes. My husband works in Italy; I chose to take leave and go with him. We'll be moving back to Denmark in six months."

"Italy is beautiful, isn't it?" the reporter kept the conversation going.

"Yes. Especially southern Italy," she replied.

"The inspector who is investigating the murders comes from southern Italy. Have you talked to him?"

Sabrina realised it was a clever tactic to get her to reveal something, but she could honestly say she hadn't spoken to the police. It seemed to please the journalist; she had got to Sabrina first.

"Oda Winther told me she gave you some papers written by her husband—the doctor. Do you still have them?" Anne Larsen smiled kindly, but her eyes shone with greed.

"Those papers are about my mother's illness and are neither for the police nor the press," she replied, hearing how direct and unfriendly she sounded. The reporter responded with a hurt expression, but then her face grew quite serious instead.

"Everything that pertains to the murdered nursing assistant comes under the remit of what both the police and the press should know. We— the paper—would like to pay you to see those papers," she said, looking directly at her. "And aren't there also some letters the nursing assistant wrote to your grandmother?"

"Those letters are also only about my mother's illness and are private," Sabrina replied with the same serious tone of voice as Anne's, trying to calm her anger.

Annoyed, the reporter leaned back in her chair and seemed to be carefully considering how to explain the seriousness of the cases. Then she leaned in across the table towards her. "The police are investigating two murder cases here—or rather three. They found a woman's body in Marselisborg Forest this morning. You probably didn't hear that on the radio," she concluded. "They are in the process of carrying out the autopsy at this very moment, and if it turns out to be the same murderer, then we're talking about a serial killer. Not something we like here in Denmark, is it?"

Sabrina moved uneasily on the kitchen bench, lowering her gaze. Another murder? What was going on, and could it really be related to the murder of her mother's carer? Her belief that she could handle this on her own began to waver, but she answered as comprehensively as she could. "I still don't see what my mother's illness has to do with it. It's just a coincidence that the nursing assistant was with us before she disappeared. Nobody knows if she had planned to go somewhere else afterwards, and that kind of tragedy happens where you least expect it. The wrong place at the wrong time." She knew how weak it sounded, but she just wanted the journalist to leave. What business was it of hers to come here, sniffing around her mother's illness and even trying to bribe her?

Furious, Anne Larsen stood up. "Naturally, I can't force you to hand over the papers, but the police can when they find out. They'll come with a search warrant, and you won't be able to do anything about that."

Sabrina took it as a threat, even though there was nothing but concern in the reporter's eyes. She looked sad, the way one eyebrow hung a little. It looked like a scar. She briefly regretted being so dismissive. It hadn't been her intention to show her reluctance so clearly. The journalist was only doing her job. But it was too late to smooth things over now. To her relief, the phone in the reporter's backpack rang. Anne picked it up with an annoyed expression. She listened, all the while maintaining eye contact with Sabrina.

"I'll be right there," she said briefly into the phone, hanging up. "Unfortunately, I have to go. Press conference at the police station about the new murder. They've probably identified the woman and learned that the murders are connected." Suddenly, she leaned in towards Sabrina with both hands resting on the edge of the table. Their faces were awfully close to each other. Sabrina could feel the journalist's breath on her face, and Anne's voice had a slightly threatening tone. "I am certain the murders have something to do with your mother. Her nursing assistant was murdered, and a doctor, who the police have not yet been able to tie to the nursing assistant, was also murdered—and now another woman." She straightened up again and put on her backpack. "If the police discover that the murdered doctor, Helge Vangberg, and the new murder are also linked to your family, I can promise you, you will be handing over those papers."

Silently, Sabrina followed Anne Larsen out into the hall. At the door, Anne turned and looked at her intently. "I think you should cooperate, Sabrina. Have you thought about the fact that you, too, may be in danger due to what you know?"

Sabrina slammed the door after her. She stood for a long time with her back to the closed door, listening to the footsteps disappearing quickly down the stairs. When everything was quiet again, she began to shake. *Helge Vangberg*, the journalist had said. She went to the kitchen counter and started rummaging through the newspapers. She found the one that mentioned the doctor's name again. She hadn't noticed when she'd first read the article. She picked up Ole Winther's notes and read the last line again.

I have ceased treatment at the request of next of kin. Treatment has been handed over to Dr. Helge Vangberg as of 1 December 1983.

35

───────────

Isabella was on a high when she entered his office and revealed that they had found Knud Engtoft. He'd used his credit card in the mini-market at the Blommehaven campsite—not a smart move if you didn't want to be found.

"Not so far from the site of the murder and where the body was found," Roland stated gloomily. He was relieved that yet another press conference was successfully done and dusted. Chief Superintendent Kurt Olsen had insisted he attend after the autopsy. It had been worse than the others. The ventilation hadn't been able to keep up at all. Roland still felt nauseated. Once you were acquainted with that smell, you never forgot it. Sweet and rotten, it stuck to clothes, to hair—to everything—and rose without warning in your nose when you least expected it. The woman had been identified as Annemette Knudsen, a fifty-two-year-old waitress at the NightCap nightclub, one of the finer nightclubs on Thorvaldsensgade. There was no immediate connection to the doctor or the nursing assistant except that the murder weapon might have been the same one that Helge Vangberg had been killed with. The condition of the body made it difficult for Henry Leander to determine exactly, but the murder method seemed to be the same. Several aggressive stabs in the chest with a knife. It had hit a rib, and the imprint it had left showed it could be a knife with a broken tip. But it could easily be a completely different type of knife. There was no trace of semen or signs she had been raped. *Then again*, Leander had sighed, *there's a lot we can't uncover on a nearly four-day-old corpse. The strange fibres found in her mouth were in her lungs, too. It looks like hair. Animal hair. I have sent them for analysis so we can determine the kind of animal. They could be from her own dog or cat—if she had pets, that is.* The time of death was set for the night between Saturday and Sunday; Leander didn't dare come any closer. DS Niels Nyborg had gone out to the nightclub owner, who was going to gather the staff so they could establish exactly when the waitress had gone home from work and whether she had left on her own.

"I feel we have the killer now. Apparently, he lives in a caravan when he's not in Africa. Strange he doesn't just put it in a forest or somewhere where he'd be more anonymous," commented Isabella.

He looked at her softly. "It is forbidden to camp in picnic areas, on streets, in forests, and on beaches. He'd have to go deep inside a dense forest not to be noticed—and he wouldn't be able to get the caravan in there. If he really wants to hide, a crowded campsite is actually not the worst place."

Isabella nodded understandingly. "Were there any fingerprints on the cannula?"

"We haven't heard anything yet. And no other needles were found. Kurt sent Forensics out to search the area further. It's dangerous to leave something like that lying around."

"Does he not trust us?" Isabella played the injured party.

"It seems not. But then it was determined they had been removed. Perhaps by Knud Engtoft. Time to have a chat with him."

She seemed ready to move out to bring in Engtoft right away, but Roland didn't want her to accompany him. They'd no way of knowing what awaited them in the caravan, and he wanted to spare her from that kind of thing for a little while yet. He had to give her another assignment and get hold of Jensen.

"I'd like you to, with DS Ansager, look into Helge Vangberg's, Bente Louise Engtoft's, and"—he looked up the autopsy report to refresh himself on the last name—"Annemette Knudsen's pasts for any connections. Were they both patients of the doctor? Anything you can dig up. Everything is of interest. And will you send Jensen in to see me?"

He avoided her eyes so as not to see her disappointment, but he still heard it in her voice when she answered "Okay" and left without closing the door.

* * *

If you were into camping, Blommehaven wasn't the worst place to choose, he had to admit as they approached the campsite, which was beautifully located in the autumn forest on both sides of Ørneredevej, with one section leading all the way down to the sea with its own strand and jetty. Only five kilometres from the centre of Aarhus in Denmark's most beautiful forested and nature area—Aarhusians themselves say—and with lots of facilities. Roland's in-laws camped there every summer, which gave them a nice excuse to visit their daughter and their old house in Højbjerg when it suited and when it didn't. When they came, they always behaved like they still lived there. His thoughts wandered to the beautiful property in Skåde again. If he and Irene got their own place, he'd be free of all that drama, too. He couldn't hold back a deep sigh.

"It is *so* beautiful, isn't it?" said Mikkel Jensen, misunderstanding the sound. He seemed quite captivated as he looked out the passenger window. Roland nodded. He hoped he didn't bump into Dagny and Carl Ernst. Fortunately, their camping season had ended in early October despite the summer still hanging on. When they got out of the car, the smell from the sea, from the forest, and from the campsite, where someone was grilling food, hit them immediately. The information office kindly told them that Knud Engtoft's permanent plot was number 300A. She pointed in the direction of the sea.

It took a while before they found where the older Wilk caravan with blue speed stripes was parked. The logo was on the back next to the dealer's name. A crooked TV antenna sat on the roof. The curtains were drawn, and it looked uninhabited. Roland knocked on the door and listened; there was silence for a long time, but then they heard a noise coming from inside and, a moment later, a hoarse sleepy voice asked who it was.

"CID," Roland replied, listening again. Mikkel Jensen stood behind him and explored the terrain. The door opened slowly, and something resembling a wild creature stuck his head out without opening the door all the way.

"Can I see some ID?" he asked as his gaze wandered nervously around them and stopped abruptly at Jensen. Roland politely introduced them both, wondering what such a highly trained man could be afraid of out here. They showed their badges. Knud Engtoft let them in.

It was even more cramped and stuffy than in Roland's office. Bad air followed every breath. They sat down on a kind of corner sofa in gaudy velvet with convoluted patterns of flowers and leaves in shades of brown. There was a cushion in the corner that didn't match. He had to pull his stomach well in to be able to fit between the folding table and the back of the sofa. On the table, which was covered with a stained oilcloth—also in brown—lay a pack of Dunhill Lights cigarettes in a metallic blue and silver box that had certainly been purchased in Africa. Roland looked longingly at the cigarettes sticking out and chewed more energetically on his gum. Knud Engtoft laughed, and his blue eyes shone the way they do only on a true adventurer. "Ah, someone recently gave up smoking," he said with laughter in his voice, as he took a cigarette out of the pack. He lit it provocatively with exaggerated movements and inhaled deeply. Then he offered the package temptingly to Roland and Mikkel, who both politely declined. Unhindered, he slowly blew the smoke into their faces as he sat down on a small folding stool that looked like it was about to collapse underneath him. Tattoos wound around his upper arms. It was difficult to decipher the motifs, which looked more like bruises on his very tanned skin. Roland guessed they continued on his back. His hair was thin and grey and gathered in a short ponytail at the nape of his neck. He had handsome features, and Roland thought how they must have made a lovely couple when they were young—he and Bente Louise.

"Do you know," Knud began, tapping the packet of cigarettes so one rolled out onto the table, "that the tobacco industry has now begun to take hold in the Third World because you've all stopped smoking here in the West?" He looked at them accusingly. "They seek out children and hand out free cigarettes to them to get them addicted. They are deliberately choosing countries with weak legislation." He snorted so the smoke came out through his nostrils. "And the major tobacco companies have actually doubled their profits by doing that, instead of—as you would think—taking a cut in their earnings. That's the result when you quit smoking." He took another puff of the cigarette and looked Roland straight in the eye as he let the smoke seep out between his lips.

Those eyes were full of life wisdom. There was no doubt they had witnessed a little of everything. But had they also watched Bente Louise die and her body sink into the water of the bog twenty-five years ago?

"But anyway, what does CID want with me? Does it have something to do with Louise?" he asked unexpectedly.

Roland sat tensely on the narrow sofa. His leg was cramping, and he almost felt guilty for being to blame for the tobacco industry now selling cigarettes to children in developing nations. At the same time, he was reminded why he hated camping holidays. But Knud's direct question had affected him. This man was either completely unscrupulous or a psychopath without a conscience.

"Yes, it is your wife we would like to talk to you about," he replied calmly, fleetingly noticing that Knud Engtoft was no longer wearing a wedding ring. Bente Louise hadn't been, either. It had probably disappeared in the bog.

Knud got up to get an ashtray, while Roland looked around the caravan, which Mikkel had already done and had turned pale as a result. The entire end wall was covered with shelves full of African souvenirs. Masks, wild animals carved in wood, jewellery, antlers from antelopes and other African bucks. Jensen discreetly elbowed him in the side and nodded towards a corner to the right of Knud, who was emptying the used ashtray into the rubbish bin. Roland caught sight of the black ebony rhino horn standing on the shelf that Jensen was alluding to.

"If you're looking to find out who left her in that swamp, don't ask me. I don't know." He sat down again on the small stool and placed the ashtray in the middle of the table so the smell reached Roland's nostrils. "I tried to warn you through the press. Now you see, I was telling the truth?" He didn't look guilty; in fact, he looked like a man who didn't have anything to hide, but Roland doubted it.

"So, you were the one who called the *Daily News*?" Mikkel asked.

"Yes, I bloody well was. I wanted to warn you and tell you to be vigilant."

If he hadn't smiled triumphantly when he said it, it might have sounded like a kind gesture, but Roland's face grew serious. "So, you wanted to warn and tell us to be vigilant—do you fear the same *danger*?"

Knud's eyes flickered briefly, but then he smiled again. "Me? There's not much I'm afraid of—a lion in the bush and the angry trumpeting of an elephant," he replied confidently.

"And who was it that you were warning us about? Wouldn't a more detailed description have been appropriate?" Mikkel's voice had taken on a furious undertone that always made Roland wary.

"I thought the police would work it out. Louise was murdered, there's no doubt about that. I figured the murderer wouldn't be happy that what had been hidden had come to light. I'm sure he's feeling safe and thinks everything is fine and forgotten after so many years—the perfect crime, you know? But suddenly, he needs to be on his guard again. Someone has to know something, and I'm sure he wants them dead before they say too much." Knud shook his head and shrugged afterwards. He leaned back against the fridge and looked at them. "Sometimes it's better to let the past and the dead rest in peace," he said.

"Are you someone who knows something? Are you afraid of the murderer?" teased Roland.

Knud got up again and opened the mini-fridge. He seemed restless. There were only cans of beer in it. "Do you want one?" he asked, slamming the door hard as they both declined. He opened a beer, spraying it everywhere, but didn't answer Roland's questions.

"Why did you come back to Denmark? Was it just to warn us?" Jensen asked sarcastically.

"I also have things here in Denmark to see to. I'm not a South African citizen; Denmark is my home country, though I love Africa just as much. So many people need help down there." He took a sip from the can and wiped his mouth.

"What exactly do you do in Africa?"

"Argh, a bit of everything. Safari mostly. I'm a tour guide for tourists looking for adventure and who need the excitement of getting close to wildlife."

"Does it pay well?"

"I get by."

"Do you run big game hunts? Do you tranquilise wild animals?" Jensen asked.

"I've been on plenty of big game hunts, yes. But anesthetise animals? No, we don't do that. We shoot them. Keeps the herds down." He tossed the cigarette butt into the ashtray with more force than was necessary. "Where are you going with these questions? I've helped you as best I can. It's up to you now."

Roland considered the many African objects with a mixture of both admiration and disgust in his eyes. Some of them were truly beautiful works of art; others were downright creepy. The masks for example.

"Do you have knives in your collection, too?" he asked.

Knud nodded eagerly. "Lots! Hunting knives, daggers, machetes— whatever. Why do you ask?"

Roland was confused. Either Knud Engtoft was a sly fox who could even pass a lie detector test, or he was as thick as two planks. Or he was taking the piss out of them.

"The rhino horn up there. Do you have any more of them?" He nodded up at it.

"Unfortunately, I don't sell my things," Knud replied, as if misunderstanding the question.

"It looks very robust. I guess it doesn't break easily—you'd need strength to break it, wouldn't you?" Mikkel was getting impatient for answers.

"Ebony is a sturdy wood as long as it hasn't got brittle heart—then it can crack."

Either Knud Engtoft had no idea why the questions were being asked or he was just pretending.

"What's brittle heart?" asked Mikkel Jensen, beating Roland to the same question. There were so many foreign terms in the Danish language.

"You probably know it more as ring shake or star-shake. It can be caused by fungal damage to the tree."

Roland shook his head. He knew nothing about diseases in trees—about trees in general. Gardening was Irene's department, and the copper beech in the driveway had never been sick.

"Unfortunately, veins in the wood can also make it less robust; its strength depends on the direction of the fibres. I bought a couple of wooden figures that had that defect, but if they're just decorative, it doesn't matter. An old craftsman in a poor little village in the mountains makes them. He knows a lot about wood—he's the one who told me about it. I usually buy a few pieces at a time, that way there's money for food for the family again," Knud continued, looking pious.

"I see you only have one copy. Where are the others?"

"I give a lot away. Louise got a few." He looked down at the table and fiddled with a bump in the oilcloth.

"The night your wife disappeared, what happened?"

Roland pushed himself back on the bench to ease the cramp in his leg.

"That was years ago. I was supposed to have collected her." His voice was indistinct and hoarse. "I always collected her when she worked evenings. I never saw her again." He sniffed and dried the skin under his nose with the palm of his hand. His eyes had turned red.

"Do you have an alibi for last Friday night and for Saturday, too?" asked Roland.

"That was when the new murders were committed. I read about them in the paper." The fear returned to his eyes. "I haven't done anything. Friday night I flew into Tirstrup and took the airport bus to the train station. From there, I took a taxi to here. I'm sure the driver and the information office can confirm this." He thought about it. "I slept on Saturday—I was tired after the trip. Saturday night I went to a pub."

"A pub? It wasn't a nightclub, was it?"

"No, I don't go to nightclubs in Denmark; they're boring. It was a pub—on Nørregade. I can't remember exactly which one."

Roland nodded. "We will, of course, be verifying that information, but if it can't be corroborated, I hope we can find you here!" His voice made it a clear command.

As soon as they were out of the caravan, they heard Knud Engtoft lock the door.

"Should we have brought him in?" Mikkel asked.

"On what grounds? Because he owns a black ebony rhino horn?"

"Because he has African knives and committed benefit fraud," Mikkel said reproachfully. Roland didn't appreciate the tone. DS Jensen probably thought he had already been promoted.

"His wife committed benefit fraud. And it's not illegal to collect African souvenirs and knives as long as he doesn't walk around with them."

"But maybe he did do that on Friday and Saturday," Jensen said again.

They got into the car. Roland fastened his seat belt.

"What about the safari thing? Are safari guides paid so much that he can afford all those trips to Africa and back again several times a year? If the Danes want to get up close and personal to wild animals, why on Earth don't they just go to Ree Park Safari in Ebeltoft?"

The question hung in the air unanswered.

"I bet you a pint we won't find a taxi driver or anyone in the information office who can confirm his story!" Mikkel put on his seat belt with an angry jerk.

"Then we'll bring him in," Roland stated, reversing from plot 300A.

The curtains in the caravan lifted slightly. Knud's eyes peered over at the forest.

"He's scared of something," Roland muttered. "What the hell is he afraid of?"

"Lions in the bushes and the angry trumpeting of an elephant," Jensen replied sourly, looking sharply out the passenger window.

36

F ortunately, not all corpses that ended up on his table were the victims of a crime. Other bodies came to the Institute of Forensic Medicine for him to identify the cause of death. Most often, the person had just dropped dead, and, in many cases, it was a cardiac arrest. The majority of autopsies showed natural causes. Last year, only 25 out of 478 autopsies had revealed homicide and violence as the cause of death. But the same thought flew through his head every time: *Always be ready for death; it will come when you least expect it.*

He stuck the needle through the tough skin and pulled the thread. It might seem unnecessary to sew the dead up when the body was to be either buried or cremated, but it was for ethical and religious reasons that the work had to be done. Everyone had the right to leave the Institute with as much dignity as possible.

He had just finished a routine autopsy. A regimen he carried out without thinking about much else other than doing his job correctly. First, he made a Y-incision in the body. He examined the ribs for injuries and cut the sternum away so he could examine the heart and lungs. He took a blood sample from the heart that would be tested for alcohol, drugs, and other toxins. In this case, the man was known, and there was no crime involved, so the blood wasn't for DNA analysis as identification or evidence, as it would be in a murder case. He removed all the organs and weighed and examined them carefully. He'd also examined the man's head. The ears for bleeding. Teeth for blows. The eyes for subconjunctival haemorrhaging, which could indicate asphyxiation. The scalp was examined hair by hair, after which he had pulled the skin off the skull and cut it open with a saw to examine the brain. As he stood now, looking at the man on the steel table, it was hard to tell that he'd been examined inside and out at all. The head and face were without seams—they were in the neck. Only the Y-incision stitches, which stretched from the groin almost up to the collarbone of the dead body, revealed that Leander had put the knife in him. Another one for the statistics on the Danes' unhealthy lifestyle, despite the deceased not being remarkably overweight. But inside, he showed no signs of health.

Along the wall of white tiles was a long steel table with a sink and water faucet. The taps were extended clear pipes for further reach when pathologists had to rinse something. The steel table was under a series of windows that allowed good light into the room. It hadn't been difficult to settle into the new premises in building 18B at Skejby University Hospital, despite the initial chaos before the moving boxes were unpacked and the last of the tradespeople had finished their work. It was completely different from the old, cramped Institute, where the lack of space meant they'd had to use the Institute's two portable cabins when they had to do office work, hold meetings, or eat. The Forensic Chemistry Department had also moved to the country; they had been three kilometres away in a lab at the Psychiatric Hospital in Risskov, which had made working together quite difficult. Now they were divided into two departments—Forensic Chemistry on the first floor and Forensic Pathology and Clinical Forensic Medicine on the ground floor and basement, which allowed access to the autopsy rooms and for ambulance transport. The closer proximity meant better opportunities— and in research, too.

He rinsed the instruments, then pulled off his gloves and stretched his back. Standing bent over the examination table was not a position his body was particularly fond of anymore. If he didn't take his long walks in the woods on his hunts and do the Five Tibetan Rites every morning with the same predictability as brushing his teeth, he had no doubt he would already have succumbed to arthritis. The thought of hunting reminded him of the doctor, Helge Vangberg; they were supposed to have met him last Saturday. Something had piqued his interest when he'd received the result of the tissue samples he'd sent for further examination. He had mentioned it to Julie as they ate breakfast, and she'd agreed with him that it might be important for the case. He smiled at the thought of Julie and looked at his watch. They were having lunch together, and he was already looking forward to it. She was a breath of fresh air in his life, even though he had never dreamed any woman could replace Mary. The only thing that bothered him was the thought of Julie's husband. Infidelity was very much against his values. Leander could sense that Roland Benito was suspicious. Naturally, he knew about Julie's marriage. But she'd always said she was going to file for divorce. That their marriage had ended several years ago. Her husband was never at home anyway, so leaving him wouldn't make much of a difference. *I want* you, *Henry*, she had said. *I'll talk to Asger soon.* But it never happened. Now they had known each other for a long time, so if nothing happened soon, he would have to act. Sharing his life and interests with Julie—hunting, insects, solving murder mysteries, and much more—had become the goal for his future. As soon as she was divorced, he was going to propose to her. He looked forward to introducing her as his wife. To being able to call her Mrs. Leander. A name he had begun to get used to never having to say again. He made plans for what he thought would surprise her as much as possible. As he wasn't that romantic, it was a huge challenge. It would have been great to be able to get advice from Roland. Italians were so romantic after all, so he probably had an idea for how to sweep her off her feet. But Henry couldn't involve him. Not yet. He was a man of honour and morals, and marriage was sacred to him. That was one of the reasons he hadn't told his old friend about the affair with Julie. Roland couldn't know until the divorce was final.

Before he'd finished cleaning up after himself, Julie knocked on the door and stuck her head in. She wasn't allowed to enter—it required different clothing from her beige autumn coat and black fashion boots.

"I'll be finished soon, darling. Two minutes!" he shouted at her. She smiled and nodded before closing the door. He just managed to notice how good she looked.

He had intended to contact Roland about the result of the tissue test. He was sure it had a bearing on the murderer's knowledge of his victim. Julie's theory that the motive was personal couldn't be ruled out, but he wanted to have lunch with her first.

37

Was she really such a bitch?" asked Nicolaj, not without amusement in his green eyes, as he took a giant bite of pizza.

Anne nodded her head a little. She hadn't fully recovered from her encounter with Sabrina Dahl and her hostile attitude.

"I just don't think she's realised the seriousness of the situation—yet. I'd hoped the press conference would announce a connection between the doctor, the nursing assistant, and the waitress. It shook her, but the police haven't found a link yet." She sighed and wiped her mouth with a napkin.

They had ordered pizza from Just-Eat.dk. None of them had time to pick up anything. Thygesen's illness had begun to worry them. They'd had a whip-round for a Get Well Soon bouquet to send to him at home. As there weren't that many of them, the bouquet wasn't that big, but "it's the thought that counts." Kamilla was quiet—it couldn't be just because of Thygesen's illness. She hadn't said much since the funeral; she seemed to be in another world. Her mother's funeral had obviously been traumatic. For a split second, Anne thought of her own mother. Anne hadn't seen her in years. She didn't even know whether she was still alive, but it didn't worry her. She started gathering up the empty pizza boxes. Mads was out, so they also had to cover the phones. Yet again, no one knew where he was. The door to the editorial office was open, but not many called. There was a kind of doomsday atmosphere—as if Thygesen's illness was putting everything on hold.

"I don't know what the hell is going on. First, a twenty-five-year-old corpse in a bog that turns out to be a murdered nursing assistant. Then a brutally murdered doctor. And now a waitress who seems to have suffered the same fate as the doctor. Police suspect the same knife was used for the last two murders. What is the motive? *Is* it really a serial killer?" She angrily stuffed the pizza boxes, which she had squashed to almost nothing, into a bin bag. This was the result of life in an apartment with a waste chute. You learned to fold rubbish down to an absolute minimum.

"A serial killer?" Finally, Kamilla woke up with a startled expression in her eyes.

"Do you think it's a serial killer?" Nicolaj looked at her, excited. He had chosen to be an intern at the *Daily News* at the right time.

"Somehow, it seems we've—fortunately—been spared that here in Denmark." Anne took his paper cup of cola, even though it wasn't finished.

"Have there ever been any here at all?" Kamilla asked, hurrying to save the last slice of pizza before Anne grabbed the napkin she'd put it on.

"We've had at least two: Dagmar Overbye, who was convicted of nine child murders in the early 1900s, and an Iranian refugee who was active in 1994, and who resides in the high-security psychiatric institution in Nykøbing Sjælland indefinitely. We may have a third one with this case— or do we need to go all the way back to 1983?" Resigned, Anne sat down on a chair.

"How do we move forward?" Nicolaj asked gently.

"I don't know. I wish Thygesen was here!" Nicolaj and Kamilla looked at Anne in surprise. Anne knew how incredible those words sounded coming from her mouth, but she had no idea how to cover this story. Had she actually asked Thygesen for more advice on other stories than she realised?

"Is medicine or illness the common denominator? A nursing assistant and a doctor?" suggested Nicolaj.

"And what the hell does a waitress have to do with medicine or illness?" she asked, annoyed.

"Perhaps Africa is the link," Kamilla said, mostly so as not to seem completely uninterested.

"You might be onto something. Let's try to find out if the waitress had anything to do with Africa. The nursing assistant did, through her husband. I've tried to get hold of him, but no luck. We don't know whether the doctor was ever in Africa—maybe he worked there? We need to check that."

"I'll do that," Nicolaj volunteered.

"Okay, so we'll go out to talk to the waitress's colleagues," Anne said, looking at Kamilla. "I got the name of someone who apparently knew Annemette Knudsen a little." Anne suddenly brightened up completely. Only Kamilla's worried face put a damper on her excitement.

"Is it something to do with the case here? You seem so—strange. Or is it the funeral?" asked Anne when they were sitting in the Suzuki. It had been a long time since they had been together without Nicolaj, who had practically become Anne's shadow. Kamilla didn't look at her. But Anne had struck a nerve. Kamilla did feel strange. Like a completely different person, which she was, so to speak, after Aunt Astrid's surprising account of her mother. But she had decided it wasn't going to affect her life; she had believed that her inner turmoil had stayed camouflaged. But it was obviously noticeable on the outside, too.

"The funeral was dreadful. I'm only now realising how lonely my mother was."

"I'm sorry," Anne replied uneasily. They drove for a long time in silence, thoughts racing through Kamilla's head. It was a relief when Anne turned on the car radio and the song "My Secret Lover" broke the silence.

When they arrived at the address on Søndervangs Allé, she turned into the car park in front of the apartment block and parked as close to the entrance as possible.

No one opened the door when Anne rang the doorbell. She knocked with her fist, but there was still no response. DITTE AND ANDERS it said on the nameplate. They were about to turn around and leave when they heard fumbling at the door.

"Who is it?" asked a drowsy voice.

Kamilla looked at her watch. Only people who worked nights slept at this time of the day.

"We're from the *Daily News*. Do you have time to talk to us?" Anne asked through the letterbox. The door was opened by Ditte, who had wrapped a purple dressing gown around her. She had a pair of men's socks on her feet—probably belonging to Anders.

"Is it about Annemette?" she asked, squinting at the light from the stairwell's skylight. Anne nodded. They were invited into a dark hallway and out into a cluttered kitchen displaying several days' worth of dishes. Tired,

Ditte sat on a chair and pushed her hair away from her forehead. They looked like genuine red curls surrounding her round head. She was heavily built, with a large bosom, and did nothing to hide it when the dressing gown slid slightly aside as she lit a cigarette.

"Do you want one?" She handed the packet of Prince cigarettes to them, and Anne hurried to accept it. Ditte lit the cigarette for her with her lighter.

Kamilla wondered about the apparent indifference to the death of her colleague, but the explanation came quickly. "I didn't know Annemette very well. None of us did. She was much older than the rest of us. Over thirty years older, in fact. And I don't understand why she wanted to keep doing that shitty job."

"As a waitress, you mean?"

"Yeah. It was laughable; she wore microskirts at her age. But that's a requirement at NightCap."

"Were you at work on Saturday night, too?"

"Yeah, but I left before Annemette. She had to count the receipts on Saturday." Ditte looked at the glow of the cigarette, then suddenly at them with an expression of horror in her eyes. "Oh my God!" she exclaimed. "It could have been me!" That fact seemed to have just hit her.

"Did you talk to her before you left?"

"No. The police talked to all of us, but like I said, not many people knew her. I just know she lived alone in an apartment near the Botanical Gardens. I do know she was divorced or separated. At least, I heard rumours she had a daughter." She tapped the ashes of the cigarette into a used coffee cup.

"How old is the daughter?" asked Anne.

Ditte shrugged. "I heard she's in a home for the disabled."

"Do you know where?"

She shook her head indifferently.

"Did you see if she went home on her own on Saturday night?"

"She probably did. At her age, I mean." For a moment, her eyes shone with triumph at still being young. She was probably in her early twenties.

"So, you didn't notice anything unusual?"

Ditte sat for a long time, turning the cigarette as if it fascinated her. "There was a fight between some guys at the bar. That doesn't happen that often. It's kind of a nice place. Annemette helped to separate them." She smiled as if it had been a fun experience.

"Did Annemette know anyone from Africa?" Anne stuck out the cigarette with its long ash to show she needed an ashtray. Ditte understood the sign and got one from the living room. It belonged to the nightclub—the NightCap logo was printed on the bottom in gold letters.

"No, not that I know of." She thought about it. "Though, there was a weird guy," she said, keeping an eye on Kamilla, who was getting the camera out of her bag. "No!" She waved her cigarette in the air. "You're not taking any pictures of me with bed hair and in a dressing gown! No way. I'm drawing a line there."

Kamilla put the camera back in the bag. She was starting to feel superfluous, and the job was beginning to get on her nerves. She was unhappy with her life on the whole at the moment. She needed to be alone and try to find herself. Astrid's words were still ringing in her head, paralysing her brain. They were the only thing she could concentrate on.

Ditte looked at Anne again and waved the cigarette up and down between two thick fingers with red nail varnish on artificial nails.

"The guy was weird. He only drank African liqueur. And he seemed to fancy Annemette. We—the other girls and I—made fun of it a little. She was all flustered and embarrassed. It was really weird. He looked really good, even though he was old?"

"How old? Grandad or great-grandad?" asked Anne.

"Eh, dad old." Ditte smiled at the phrase.

"So, how old is your dad roughly?"

She shrugged and the dressing gown slid even further to the side as she reached out to tap the ash off the cigarette in the ashtray next to Anne. Kamilla couldn't help but stare. Ditte had to be popular with a chest like that.

"Did you get his name?"

"No. We don't ask customers their names. I figured he was an acquaintance of one of her old friends. I heard she was married to a half-African."

"Do you have her friend's name?"

Ditte shook her head again and blew smoke out of the corner of her mouth. "No. I just know from Annemette that she had worked at Night-Cap once—before the nightclub was rebuilt and modernised. But it was years ago. Long before I was born."

"Did Annemette tell you anything else? Where the friend lived, for example?" Anne's voice trembled. She stubbed the cigarette out in the ashtray even though she hadn't smoked it down to the filter.

"No. I only remember Annemette saying her friend's husband travelled a lot in Africa and gave away some of the ugliest souvenirs he brought home. Annemette kept some on display just to be nice. I forgot to ask if you'd like a cup of coffee. Anders probably left some."

She seemed to be waking up and got an insulated coffee pot from the kitchen counter. The coffee wasn't entirely fresh, having been brewed that morning. It wasn't hot, either.

"But I do remember a great story Annemette told about that friend," Ditte continued when she had sat down again. "On a night shift, the friend saw a man fall over, and at first she thought he was shit-faced. She shook him violently and brought him back to life. When the ambulance arrived, it turned out the man had had a cardiac arrest and she had actually saved his life!" Ditte laughed and shook her head, so the red curls danced around her. "And do you know what she did then?"

She waited for them to draw the obvious conclusion, and after an artful pause and a sip of coffee, she continued.

"She started studying to be a nursing assistant."

38

D S Dan Vang was the only one they were waiting for. Roland drummed his fingers impatiently on the table.

The board in the briefing room was gradually becoming a variegated image gallery of more or less unappetising images, ranging from a brown mummy to a liquefied corpse. Maybe that was why no one had helped themselves to a bread roll or pastry.

"Have you found a name for the puppy?" asked Niels Nyborg to fill in the time.

"Yeah, Angolo," Roland replied a little reluctantly; he didn't want to bring his private life to work. Those two things needed to be kept separate. Rolando and Roland.

"As in *angle* in Italian. Isn't that what it means?" Isabella asked quickly, reaching for the coffee pot first.

"Yes, that is what it means. One ear sits at an angle—it's a little bent— but the other stands straight up."

"Aww," resounded around the table, like when women see an adorable baby. Roland pictured the little dog's head and had to give it to them. Angolo was an exceptionally adorable puppy.

"I've spoken to Bjarne Lund from the Canine Unit. He'd like to look at Angolo before he's twelve months old. He might make a good guard dog."

"Do you want to advance to being a dog handler, Roland?" asked Kurt Olsen, giving him a teasing smile. "The dog kennel costs are tax-deductible," he added.

"Yes, yes. Very funny. Irene mentioned that, too." He looked at the clock and decided to start the morning briefing without Dan. His participation didn't make much difference, even though Roland had a few small assignments for him.

"We'd better get started. The positive development . . ." he began and was interrupted when Dan came in quickly and sneaked over to a chair as close to the door as possible. His cheeks were red, and Roland hoped it was due to shame. He mumbled an almost inaudible apology and looked intently at Roland, who sent him a reproachful look, but he didn't say anything in response. So much had been said to Dan Vang already.

"The positive development in the case of the waitress is that we have a crime scene," he continued. "Late yesterday afternoon, Forensics identified an area on the forest floor where there were signs of a struggle. The leaves were clustered unusually.

"It could have been an animal—a fox for example, that had attacked some prey—but analysis of the blood between the leaves shows that it's the deceased's. It has rained a lot in the days since Annemette Knudsen's murder, so Forensics are sure there was much more blood than they found. Much of it was washed away. But they are certain that's where she was stabbed. When they expanded the search area, they found one of her shoes a hundred metres from the crime scene and the other one half a kilometre away. There are indications she managed to escape from the perp, but that he caught up with her in the woods."

It was very quiet at the table. Roland watched their eyes shine with horror as the scenario unfolded in their minds. He hurried on. "Unfortunately, we have to face the fact that the perp is cunning and far more dangerous than we first assumed. Even if we find the murder weapon, there'll probably be no hope of fingerprints."

"Have we really not found any at all? Not on the needle from the kennel, either?" DS Mikkel Jensen asked.

"No one touches M99 without gloves. So, no prints were found on the needle. Neither was anything of significance found at either the site of the crime or where the bodies were found."

"What did you get out of the waitress's colleagues, Niels?"

"Not much. No one knew her privately, and she doesn't seem to have been the most talkative person. It looks like she left the nightclub alone. But a few people did notice a man flirting with her at the bar, which, by all accounts, was a rarity."

"And we know the man's name, of course?"

"Unfortunately, no. No one had seen him before, and he paid cash. His description could fit anyone. The only thing all the girls agree on is that he seemed like a gentleman. He wasn't drunk and drank only a few small glasses of liqueur."

"No video surveillance in the nightclub?"

"There's surveillance of the street area at the entrance. I got the tape and am going to review it with the young women who saw him. But the nightclub was full last Saturday, so if someone can recognise him a week later, it'll be sheer luck," said DS Nyborg.

"Try anyway," Roland said encouragingly. "Does no one want a bread roll today?"

Most of them took half a roll. Nyborg passed the plate to Roland. He accepted it as he poured a cup of coffee for himself.

"One of the waitresses heard that Annemette Knudsen has a disabled daughter. I've been told she lives at Haslevænget—a home for the disabled," continued Niels.

"How old is she?"

"She just turned twenty last week."

"Was she born disabled?"

"The woman I spoke to at the home didn't want to say much, so she referred me to a grandmother. Annemette's mother, that is."

"What about the father?"

"Spanish, I think, but I can't find out whether he lives here in Denmark or not."

Roland sighed and took a bite of the roll. There was silence around the table while everyone chewed and watched him intently. "My feeling is that we should consider the three murders as one and the same case. The murders of Helge Vangberg and Annemette Knudsen may be a chain reaction to the fact that Bente Louise Engtoft's body was found in the bog."

"So, you mean whoever murdered the nursing assistant twenty-five years ago kept quiet for that long but is now starting to murder again?" muttered Kurt Olsen sceptically.

"Something along those lines. As long as the body was hidden in the bog, the perp felt safe and thought he had gotten away with the crime. But now he may have to silence those who know or saw something that could reveal his identity." Roland shuddered at the thought of how easily that murder could have become one of the dreaded unsolved cold cases in the statistics. If the two boys hadn't . . .

"What did you find out from the cold case from 1983?" asked Olsen.

"It's a dead end. Arne Svendsen handed everything over to us. We reviewed the file and evidence from back then, and even though Forensics have advanced, there are no leads. No usable DNA—and old shoe prints aren't relevant. It's unlikely anyone has shoes from twenty-five years ago. We re-questioned the witnesses who are still alive, but no one had any new info to contribute. Most of them had almost forgotten about it."

Roland saw the discouragement in the eyes of his staff and felt his own. "The next breakthrough is that there may be a connection between Dr. Helge Vangberg and his murderer." He nodded at forensic pathologist Henry Leander, who was sitting with Julie at the end of the table. He'd asked them both to attend.

"As you all probably remember from the autopsy report," Leander began, "Helge Vangberg had cirrhosis." He paused as Julie poured coffee for him and passed the pot on. "Cirrhosis of the liver can be caused by many circumstances, such as alcohol—the doctor liked his tipple—disease of the immune system, bile ducts, metabolism or too much fat in the liver, chemicals, some types of medicine, and so on. However, the results of the tissue test showed the hepatitis virus. He had chronic hepatitis B. It'll all be in the final autopsy report. It takes an average of about fifteen years to develop cirrhosis of the liver from the time of infection."

"But wouldn't that mean he was terminally ill?" asked Isabella, looking very serious.

"Not necessarily. Chronic hepatitis can progress without any symptoms."

"Why is this relevant?" asked Niels Nyborg, who had black poppy seeds from the roll between his front teeth.

"Because it's proof that Helge Vangberg lived in an area where hepatitis B is widespread—Africa, for example," Roland replied.

"You can get hepatitis in other ways," protested Mikkel Jensen taking a custard Danish.

"Yes, you can. The disease can be transmitted through blood from an infected person or through sexual contact. In Denmark, the disease is most prevalent among drug addicts and homosexuals."

"But Helge Vangberg had actually been stationed in Africa by Médecins Sans Frontières some years ago," Roland interrupted. "I spoke to Victoria Vangberg again, but she didn't know her husband worked for the organisation, so it must have been before he had met her. Did you get to talk to them, Kim?" Roland looked at him expectantly. He had just taken a bite of his bread roll with cheese and quickly finished chewing before answering.

"Yes. I spoke to a communications officer, but there wasn't much they could tell me. Helge Vangberg was fired, but I was sworn to secrecy."

"Do we know why?"

"Yeah, but I'm none the wiser. It was according to point three of the Chantilly Principles. They would not say more." Kim sighed.

"The principles were adopted in 1995 in the town of Chantilly, which is forty kilometres north of Paris. The fourteen principles cover the working of the organisation. Ten rules for emergency aid and four for how the organisation should be run. In 2006, it was expanded with the La Mancha agreement," Leander explained.

"Do you know what point three is?" interrupted Kim.

"As far as I can remember, it's about respecting medical ethics and has something to do with the Hippocratic oath," Leander said.

Julie Hermansen watched him admiringly as he spoke, but quickly concentrated on her coffee cup when Roland called on her.

"How far are you with the profiling, Julie?"

She cleared her throat. "The profile resembles a serial killer, but his victims don't seem to be randomly selected. He doesn't leave any clues at crime scenes, so he's a man of order, which reveals something about his personality in each case. Serial offenders are driven by their imagination, which is often reflected in a particular pattern—a signature—which recurs from time to time. It's the signature that can give us a picture of the perp. That's why what's going on in his head is so important to know in order to find him or calculate his next move."

Now it was Henry Leander who looked admiringly at Julie. Roland suppressed a little smile. "But what is going on in his head? I'm having a bit of a hard time seeing a signature," he admitted.

"His aggressive behaviour towards his victims reveals something about him. I'm still sure it's personally driven and the murders are being carried out in anger. Maybe long pent-up anger. The victims are to suffer. The first stab wasn't what killed them"—she looked at Leander, who gave a quick nod in affirmation—"which tells me that the perp wants his victims to see that he is the one taking their lives. The victims probably know why when they see him."

"But the signature?" Jensen asked impatiently.

"The signature is his brutality, the violence with which he stabs his victims several times in the chest, even after death has occurred. That makes me think it's not the same murderer from twenty-five years ago. Blunt force and stabbing indicate different behavioural patterns. If we are really dealing with a serial killer, it's also unusual that he has been at rest for so long and then suddenly returns with a completely different murder method."

"What about the African murder weapons—isn't that a kind of signature?" asked Isabella.

Julie hesitated briefly. "Yes, that's something that confuses me. Apparently, the murder weapons in all three murders are of African origin. There may be some connection, but I still doubt it's the same perp."

"We can't ignore the connection to Africa. I managed to get the result of the analysis of the animal hair we found in the murdered woman's mouth, neck, and lungs before I left for the briefing. They're from a leopard. A genuine leopard," Leander interjected, wiping breadcrumbs from his white handlebar moustache. Julie had discreetly made him aware of them.

"Leopard hairs! What the hell is going on? They can't be from her fur—it was fake—so we have to find a leopard somewhere. I doubt there's anyone around who keeps leopards as pets—which is illegal anyway—so, we have to assume we're looking for a leopard skin." Roland drank his coffee and continued. "It could be a taxidermized animal or even a rug." He fell silent as he vaguely recalled something that he just couldn't put his finger on. He didn't have time to think because Dan, who had otherwise been very quiet, offered his suggestion for the leopard.

"What about the zoo?"

"Excellent idea, if we had a zoo in Aarhus, which we don't, Dan," said Roland patiently.

"Ree Park Safari?" Dan tried again.

"They don't have leopards. They're cheetahs," Mikkel said, annoyed. "And anyway, you can't make it from Ebeltoft and back again in the time it took from when Annemette Knudsen left the nightclub until we think she was murdered. And definitely not to Aalborg or Copenhagen!" The look Mikkel gave Dan implied *idiot*. Dan remained silent and looked down at the table.

"Do you have anything on him . . . the treasure hunter, Jensen?" asked Roland to draw attention away from Dan. Sometimes he felt sorry for him. He was so young.

"The cache owner is a young man from Skovby. The cache was laid under the tree nine days ago, so it seems random that the waitress was left there. He didn't sound like a psychopathic killer on the phone, but we should take a closer look at him."

"Yes, of course, you can take Vang with you to Skovby."

Mikkel didn't seem enthusiastic about his assigned partner. It would almost certainly end badly.

"First, we need to investigate whether our treasure hunter has any connection to Africa."

"Did you see the article about the son in the paper? Have you ruled him out completely?" asked Leander.

"We haven't spent much time on Sebastian Juhl. He was so young that the case hardly affects him," Roland replied, looking at Isabella and Mikkel, who were sitting next to each other. "Did you find his foster family?"

They both nodded and Isabella answered. "Sebastian was placed with a family in Sabro when his mother disappeared and Knud Engtoft fled to Africa. They would like to talk to us."

Roland nodded. "We need to talk to them; I'll take it." He considered sparing Mikkel and bringing him along but changed his mind when Isabella smiled at him. Her intuition was certainly better to have than Jensen's. "Is there any news on the tranquiliser that killed the three hunting dogs?" he continued.

"I contacted the Danish Medicines Agency and reviewed the list of the few veterinarians who are licensed to use M99. No one reported a theft, everyone had an alibi for Friday night, and none of them had a relationship with the doctor. I was told that it's used in Africa to stun large animals, such as rhinos and elephants. We have to assume it was smuggled here—maybe by the perp," Kim suggested.

"From Africa—by plane—with the war on terror and strict controls? Would it even be possible!" Kurt Olsen sounded slightly scornful.

Roland cleared his throat sharply. He sensed a quarrel brewing when DS Kim Ansager began turning red in the face over doubts being cast on his assessment.

"So, Africa is a common denominator—we need to find the African connection to Annemette Knudsen. Forensics found some African souvenirs in her apartment—including a black ebony rhino horn. They took them for further investigation to find out if the piece of wood from the murder weapon may have originated from one of them. The stabs could have broken a horn. We'll hear from them when they know more. It was similar to what was in Knud Engtoft's caravan, so maybe we have the connection here."

DS Niels Nyborg held up a ballpoint pen like a school student. "Remember—the unknown man was drinking African liqueur at the bar." He looked down at his notes. "Amarula."

"That doesn't necessarily mean anything. He may just know the drink from travelling around Africa. Maybe he was the one who gave her the souvenirs."

Ansager pulled some papers out from a little pile in front of him. "As for Knud Engtoft's finances, there's something fishy going on there, too," he said. "I checked his account. All his income goes to travelling and paying for the caravan in Blommehaven. Safaris bring in a little, but that's not the only place he has money from. Every quarter, a sum of money is deposited." He handed Roland the papers—bank statements. Kim had put a red dot by a fixed amount logged into the account on the first of the month every quarter. "The money comes from a secret account in Switzerland."

Roland quickly skimmed through the figures. The last transfer was a week ago when the amount doubled. The first payment was transferred in early 1984.

39

Death was always difficult to understand and especially for a child. She could see it in his eyes, despite him no longer being a child. It was as if it lay in his gaze and gave his eyes a bottomless expression. Reading what was hidden in those depths was hard, but you couldn't direct your anger at a concept like death. Something more tangible was needed. Sabrina put down the newspaper. It was Anne Larsen who had written the article. Her name and email address were under the headline "Sebastian misses his mother." She did, too. Both her mother and father; death had taken *her*, and Carola had taken *him*. Sebastian Juhl was Louise Engtoft's son. Judging by his age, he must have been about eight years old at the time. He remembered his mother better than she did. But was that an advantage? Did he remember hers, too? Louise had mentioned a son in her letters to Elina; had he been in their home? Did he perhaps know what had happened back then?

Unease began to tingle inside her. She grew restless and got up from the chair where she had been sitting with her legs up on the coffee table while reading the paper. It might seem rude when Tobias and Pernille weren't home, but they both did it themselves. For them, it was the norm that you did what you found most comfortable. And Sabrina was enjoying it. It was the complete opposite to the rigid behaviour she had to adopt in her father and Carola's stylish home.

She sat down by the window. The sun shone its sharp light into the kitchen, but dark clouds were forming on the horizon. From the movement of the trees down on the street, she could see it was starting to get windy. What was the weather like in Italy right now? Once again, she tried to call Peter; she needed to hear his voice and his opinion on all this. He would definitely ask her to forget it all and come home. Home to Italy. Maybe that would be best for everyone. Again, the answering machine clicked in; she heard her own voice saying they couldn't come to the phone but that a message could be left after the tone. She did it again and then tried his mobile. What was he doing? Was he not listening to the messages? Had something happened? No, she would have been told, wouldn't she? Was he with *her*? This last thought was relentless, linked to a fit of gnawing jealousy. Would he have been unfaithful to her if he knew about their child? She laid both hands on her stomach. She could feel a small bump, and a smile pulled at the corners of her mouth. Peter would have to be told soon. It would make him happy. If he loved her, it would.

The sun was shining on the wet roofs. A pigeon sat polishing its feathers on a gutter while another one kept watch. A window banged open, and a woman shook a blanket so dust particles danced around her. Further away, another woman hung dangerously out of a dormer window to clean the glass. So much happened over the city that people on the street never noticed because they walked around in their own little worlds and didn't look up or ahead. How much had happened near her that she didn't know about?

The article about the murder of the waitress didn't mention anything about her being connected to Louise and the doctor. Maybe the journalist had just tried to scare her. And she had succeeded. If there was a serial killer out there, her knowledge might well put her in danger. But who knew about her? No one. She tried to shake off the unease. No one knew anything about the letters. Only Oda Winther, the journalist, and her dad. He'd almost certainly told Carola, too. She had smiled superciliously at her from a large photo in the newspaper taken on their new yacht and with sun and wind in her hair. Sabrina had skimmed the article so as not to be caught completely unawares should anyone start talking to her about her family's amazing news.

She looked at the picture of Sebastian again. Did they have a shared past that they each knew something about? Doubt raged in her, making the restlessness unbearable. She had to do something, but was it to call the police, talk to her dad again, talk to the journalist—or speak to Sebastian Juhl?

On the desk, Pernille's laptop was turned on. It always was, and occasionally an email came in with a muffled pinging sound. She sat down at the laptop and opened Internet Explorer. Shortly afterwards, she was on the White Pages website and typing in his name. *Sebastian Juhl, Aarhus.* The information came immediately; he lived on Klostergade. There was only a mobile number. Did he know anything, and did she even want to know what he might know? After much deliberation, she took her mobile and dialled his number. After all, no harm would come from talking to him.

Wherever he was, it was very windy. It whistled, and the connection dropped a few times before the sound came back as if he were turning and trying to find a sheltered area to get a better signal. His voice was pleasant and as deep and unfathomable as the eyes in the picture in the paper.

"Sebastian."

"Sebastian Juhl?"

"Yes," he replied expectantly.

"It's Sabrina Dahl. I'd like to talk to you about your mother. I'm sorry . . ."

"Another journalist?" His voice was hostile.

"No! I'm Josefine Hjort's daughter. She's dead now. Your mother nursed her years ago."

There was a long, deep silence. She heard only the wind and another sound, which she recognised as waves. He was by the sea, she realised. The voice had taken on a new sound when he answered. "Oh, the little girl. What do you want?"

"I think we probably have a lot to talk about, so . . ."

"Not on the phone!" The voice disappeared again and returned shortly afterwards. Now it sounded like he had found a covered area. "I'm in a summer house; it would be better to meet here." He gave her the address. She grabbed a pen from Pernille's collection and scribbled it down on the newspaper next to his picture.

40

That morning felt different. She noticed it when she walked through the door to the paper. A coffee aroma hung in the air, mingled with another smell, which she immediately recognised. Thygesen's aftershave. Bread rolls and mugs stood on the conference table, waiting impatiently for them. He was in his office behind the glass window, reading the newspaper, as if he'd never been away. But he didn't look like himself. He was thinner; it suited him. His eyes were dull as he looked up at the sound of Anne and Mads, who were now squabbling. Nicolaj arrived shortly afterwards, looking very sleepy. They were all almost a quarter of an hour late. Anne and Mads immediately fell silent when they spotted Ivan Thygesen. Anne smiled and shook off her backpack. "Welcome back. Are you better?"

Thygesen got up and seemed shy. "Thank you, yes—my doctor says so. And thank you for the flowers. Just as well they didn't land on my grave." He always used dark humour in both suitable and unsuitable situations.

"But you've lost weight," Kamilla said worriedly. Not that his shedding a few kilos was a bad thing, but it showed how sick he had been.

He looked down at himself and gathered the tweed jacket closer around him; it was at least three sizes too large, and the shoulders hung off him.

"My clothes are certainly too big now. Well, let's get to it. It seems we're busy. There's coffee and rolls for everyone." He looked around. "Where the bloody hell is Britt? She's usually bright-eyed and bushy-tailed in the morning."

"Britt's sick. You must have infected her," said Nicolaj. Thygesen looked at him, at first angrily, then he smiled. "So, you must be Nicolaj, the new intern. Welcome. Has she been good to you?" He nodded at Anne, and Nicolaj blushed as he stammered that she had. Anne sent him a crooked smile and a feigned threatening look.

"What's wrong with Britt? I hope I didn't infect her because she wouldn't survive what I've just been through." He laughed cheerfully and started to cough. It took a while before it was over. He turned beetroot red in the face, picked up a serviette, and blew his nose loudly. They each sat down and silently took a roll from the plate he sent around—no doubt seasoned with his bacteria.

"Did *you* make coffee?" Anne sounded a little too surprised, and Thygesen looked offended when he replied.

"You've earned it—you all have." He looked around at the small crowd of slightly blushing staff. "I'm very impressed with all you did while I was absent. I've been following the *Daily News*."

Kamilla wondered whether he was entirely well again. Maybe he still had a little fever. It was extremely rare for him to give words of praise.

"But something is missing." He spread a thick layer of butter on a poppy-seed roll. It probably wouldn't be long before he brought the usual plain rolls back.

"What's missing?" Anne was immediately on the offensive.

"Well, what does the nursing assistant's husband think about all this? Why didn't you find him in Africa? He seems like a prime suspect to me."

"At the press conference, we were told that the police have already questioned him. He's currently living in a caravan in Blommehaven. They aren't able to connect him to the murder of his wife of twenty-five years ago—or the other murders, by the way." She sank her teeth into her roll.

"Bloody hell, Anne, you know how the police work. The fact that they leaked it to the press probably means that they *do have* him under suspicion. They are probably just afraid he'll catch wind of it and run away again."

Anne swallowed quickly and looked at him angrily. "The police pretty much share everything in these cases. It's their new tactic. Maybe it's part of the police reform," she said with a small smile that quickly disappeared.

"It's not a new tactic at all! It's ancient! It's called cheating the press. And you were fooled. You were bloody well fooled!" Thygesen drank furiously from the coffee and seemed to burn himself, or else he discovered it was as strong as tar. Kamilla had a hard time getting it down even though she had poured lots of milk into it. But no one said anything. That he had put a filter in the funnel and added beans was an achievement. She was sure everyone was thinking the same thing—that it was good that Britt usually made the coffee.

"Well, we'll talk to him today. The dead doctor's wife?" continued Thygesen.

"She has been hospitalised for shock, and the press isn't allowed to speak to her." Anne's voice was submissive. Thygesen just shook his head, annoyed.

"The other doctor's wife—the one the family threw out. Wonder why?"

"Nothing there, either." Now it was Nicolaj who answered. "I visited her again yesterday. She doesn't know any more than she's already told us, and she doesn't know why Gustav Hjort asked her husband to stop Josephine's treatment, either. Neither does Ole Winther have anything to do with Africa. But Helge Vangberg does. He actually worked down there."

"When?" Anne asked angrily. That was one piece of information she would have liked to have had before this meeting.

"No idea. It could just be a rumour. Médecins Sans Frontières wouldn't confirm it, at least."

"What about Hjort—the wealthy couple on Strandvejen?"

Everyone looked down at the table. Only Mads Dam looked pious. He'd spent the time at a couple of football matches and pubs to measure the effect of the smoking ban—whatever that had to do with the sports section.

"The nursing assistant's son?" Thygesen continued. The usual grim expression was back on his face. His eyes were narrow and shooting daggers.

"He was only eight years old, was in school that day, and only remembers that his mother disappeared. Didn't you read the article?"

"Yes, I did read your article. 'Sebastian misses his mother,'" he muttered. "So saccharine!"

Anne wanted to say something but got the impression it was probably best to keep quiet.

"Perhaps your efforts aren't so impressive after all," Thygesen teased them again. "There's a lot we need to get to grips with today. You start with

Knud Engtoft." He looked abruptly at Anne. "And take Kamilla with you. We need some useful images before they lock him up."

"Shit!" Anne snorted as they jogged down the stairs.

It was raining; the first major storm of autumn was causing withered leaves to swirl on the pavement along with empty cardboard McDonald's cups, flyers, crumpled newspapers, and other street rubbish that had adorned Aarhus with the prestigious title of one of the dirtiest cities in Scandinavia. They passed one of the few rubbish bins that had long since been filled up and went through the gate into the yard where the cars were parked.

"You've got your car back," Kamilla exclaimed when she spotted Anne's yellow Lada. She was looking forward to the return to the normality of no longer being Anne's chauffeur and instead being called in when the journalists had finished their interviews—if she was needed. In the days without both Thygesen and Anne's car, Kamilla had wasted far too much time where neither she nor her camera had been needed anyway. Consequently, she hadn't been able to assist Britt with the local news and Mads Dam with sport in the same effective way that she usually did.

"Yep, that's why I was late today. I had to pick it up from the mechanic this morning. And you?"

"I don't really have a valid excuse. Just slept awfully last night." She had tossed and turned in bed with one nightmare after another. Nightmares about boats that capsized. Children drowning. Shouts and screams and hatred. Unwanted children.

"I know those nights well." Anne sighed, lighting a cigarette. "Let's take your car."

After they'd been driving for a while without talking to each other, Anne asked, "Is it because of your mother's funeral that you can't sleep? Do you feel like a significant bond was broken when your mum died?" The last part of the sentence was drowned out by the noise of the traffic and the water on the road as she wound down the passenger window slightly to let the cigarette smoke out. Her short black hair flew around her face. Kamilla's hair fluttered madly, too, and she asked Anne to close the window again. She obeyed and stubbed out the cigarette into the car's ashtray.

Kamilla nodded in answer to the question and looked out into the rain and traffic. The tail-lights on the cars ahead resembled a sea of blazing red lights flickering in the rain. Wet leaves splashed against the windscreen where the wipers were swiping hard. A leaf got stuck and was pulled back and forth until it finally released its hold and disappeared in a strong gust of wind. *More than that*, she thought. *Much more than that.* But she didn't want to mention Astrid's revelation of what had happened in her mother's youth or that it had turned her own life upside down, leaving a lot of questions she would never get answers to now.

The caravan in plot 300A looked abandoned. All the caravans did. Many plots were empty. People had finally admitted that summer was over. Anne knocked hard on the door and windows and tried to look inside, but the curtains were drawn and there was no sound from the caravan to indicate that there was life inside.

"He's been taken in," said a woman with a half-smoked cigarette between narrow, colourless lips. She'd stepped out of a caravan nearby and was pouring a bucket of soapy water onto the ground. "By the police," she added, looking at them curiously. "Do you know what he did? We've been neighbours here summer after summer; I bloody well hope he's not a serial killer!" She laughed out loud at her joke.

"Are you sure it was the police who took him in?"

The woman nodded and knocked the ashes of the cigarette down the wooden steps of the caravan. "It was a police car, at least, but there were no flashing lights, so it probably wasn't that serious. A speeding ticket that wasn't paid or something. He drives like a madman." She laughed again.

"Do you know him well—given that you've camped so close to each other year after year?"

She was clad in far too tight jeans and something resembling the top of a blue tracksuit with a zipper and hood and speed stripes on the sleeves.

"He travels a lot, so other people stay in the caravan when he's away. But he's a nice guy. Sometimes, he shares a crate of beer with us and tells us about his dramatic adventures. He once shot a lion! It was him or the cat, he said. And then he has a lot of unusual drinks in there." She threw her head towards the abandoned caravan. "I think that's what attracts Henrik— my husband—the most. African liqueur and beer. Mongozo—the beer—it tastes like coconut. Henrik thinks it's filthy, but I like it. Are you family?"

Anne shook her head. "I'm a reporter, Anne Larsen. This is my photographer, Kamilla Holm."

Kamilla nodded in greeting. The woman closed her eyes.

"From the paper. Oh my God! Are you going to write what I just said?" She straightened her messy mousy-brown hair as if she were counting on her photo being taken.

"It was Knud Engtoft we wanted to talk to. Do you know who borrows his caravan when he's not here himself?"

"Yeah, it's mostly people who've been on safari with him and who would like to spend a few days in the Nordics. You need to have a taste for Africa to endure living in that caravan." She threw out her hand so the ashes sprinkled from the cigarette, which would soon have smoked itself. She tossed it into the bucket. It hissed before the embers were extinguished in the splash of soapy water that was left. "It's full of creepy junk that he bought down there," she continued, interrupted by a phone ringing. "It's probably Henrik—I have to collect him from the city. We're going home tonight. I hope they haven't put Knud in jail." She laughed again and disappeared into the caravan. They could hear her talking loudly on the phone.

Anne slammed the door as she got into the car. "Damn it! Thygesen was right. They've been taking us for idiots this entire time!"

"There'll probably be another press conference soon," replied Kamilla, who couldn't see any problems anywhere other than in her own life.

"I doubt it. I had planned to tell Benito about the waitress's acquaintance with the nursing assistant, but if that's how they want to play it, then so be it!"

"Wouldn't they have found out for themselves by now?"

"It wouldn't surprise me. They leaked so much at the beginning to make us think they were being informative, but it was only to fool us and keep their knowledge to themselves." She snorted the words out.

Kamilla pulled the seat belt across herself and fastened it. This day was definitely different.

41

Roland's day wasn't ordinary, either. He looked at Isabella's profile but was careful not to stare too much. The traffic was heavy at this time of the morning, and the storm tore at the car as it drove out into the open terrain.

She was wearing a light coat that matched her hair, and the blue scarf around her neck was the same colour as the eyes following the traffic, as if she were behind the wheel. He smiled, feeling a chemistry he hadn't experienced since meeting Irene. He'd always regarded older men as naïve when they thought they might interest a young woman in her twenties. Maybe it wasn't so naïve after all? Maybe it could really happen? He glanced at himself in the rear-view mirror. He wasn't so bad to look at. The southern Italian sun had refreshed his colour, he had shaved that morning and had used just a splash of the expensive aftershave—only so Irene didn't grow suspicious. Not to mention he'd been to the barber and had a little discreet colour added to his grey temples. The salon was just around the corner from the police station, so he could quickly pop in during his lunch break. It didn't usually take too long, but it had that day. If she used natural hair colour, then no one would be able to tell it was dyed, the hairdresser had said. No one had said anything at the morning briefing. Maybe they'd never noticed the grey hairs to begin with, so he'd wasted his money. Not entirely. Irene had said he looked good when she fixed his tie before leaving. She was thawing and had agreed to going to Skåde and looking at the property. He knew well she was saying it to keep the peace and would probably find fault with everything. But he felt calm about that. There were none, and when she saw it, well . . . He hadn't told her about the letter from Giovanna yet, there was no reason to upset her.

An electric shock ran through him when Isabella put her hand on his as he changed gears. "I think this is where we need to turn right," she said without looking at him. But the touch was enough. They drove past Sabro Church, and he told her it was there that his granddaughter, Marianna, had been baptised. An attempt to remind her—or himself—that he was an old married man and far more Danish than Italian; there was none of the Mediterranean romantic about him. He'd even betrayed his Catholic faith. He was a traitor to Naples, where there was far worse crime to fight as a police officer than in Aarhus. He was a traitor to his Italian family, to Italy, and he was also about to become one to Irene. He still felt the heat from Isabella's hand even though she had moved it and was now pointing out the window. "Turn there," she commanded. Shortly afterwards, they drove on to Ristrupvej and looked for the house number.

"Have you thought about how close we are to the bog now?" she asked, looking at him for the first time during the entire drive to Sabro. He nodded; he had thought about it as soon as he'd learned the address of Sebastian's foster parents. It was a charming old house in a country setting. Roland guessed it was from the beginning of the twentieth century, but it was immaculately maintained. The tiled roof looked new, and the mortar-washed wall was painted white. There was the carport, too, consisting of only six wooden poles and an end wall of wood that held up a sloping roof. It looked homemade but nice. In the garage was an old yellow Morris Mascot. It wasn't often that you saw that model. Roland smiled, as it reminded him of Mr. Bean. Sebastian's foster parents were retired now. Anton Kjærsgaard answered the door. His wife, Ellen, rattled cups in the kitchen. She greeted them with a tray in her hand on her way into the living room.

"I hope you like coffee," Ellen said, setting the tray on the dining table before shaking hands.

The living room was white, too. The wooden ceiling had once been dark wood, but it was now painted white, which made the room bright. The curtains were white, but the furniture was dark, and the high-backed armchairs and a three-seater sofa in black leather looked new or were just well kept. Ellen and Anton only took their seats at the table when Roland took his. They both looked as if they hadn't been up long. He spotted an unmade double bed in the bedroom a little further down the hall. Pensioners could probably sleep until after nine, but it was useful to talk to them before they questioned Knud Engtoft, who had been brought in for an interrogation, and which he had to attend when they returned to the police station.

"Sorry, we're here so early," he began.

Isabella sat down next to him and looked at a picture of Sebastian as a teenager, which stood on a sideboard alongside many pictures in beautiful frames. Roland had also glanced at it. He hadn't forgotten those eyes. Ellen Kjærsgaard must have noticed their interest in the picture.

"He's always been a good boy," she said lovingly.

"Despite how hard fate has been on him," Anton added.

"Yes, and now this—that his mother was murdered back then," Ellen continued.

Roland took a mouthful of the coffee she had poured. "We would like to know as much as possible about Sebastian. You knew him best."

They looked at him proudly. It was clear that they loved their foster son, and Roland was sure they were good parents. They were wearing glasses with matching frames. They resembled each other so much it was comical. Like Mr. Bean's car in the garage. Ellen had short grey hair like her husband, whose was a little thinner on top. They both wore almost identical T-shirts. Anton had once worked at the railway and had probably been quite muscular then. Now the muscles hung on the thin forearms. Ellen had worked in a shop her whole life and had maintained her slim figure.

"Haven't you talked to Sebastian?" she asked, giving Isabella a look that said she didn't realise there were female officers.

"Yes, we've talked to him. But he doesn't remember much from that time. We hope you can contribute something."

Ellen looked at Anton, and they both smiled at the memory of Sebastian's arrival into their lives.

"Sebastian was eight years old when he came here. It was after the blizzard; do you remember, Anton?"

He nodded. "We had two other boys in care; they were somewhat older than Sebastian, so they moved on a few years later . . ."

"And Sebastian became an only child," Ellen concluded.

"Has he ever talked about his mother and stepfather?"

"He didn't want to talk about his stepfather; he said he hated him. But children say so much they don't mean. Especially when they feel let down."

"You don't think he meant it?" asked Isabella, convincing Roland he had been right to take her with him. Turning a comment into a counter-question was always a good tactic.

"Well, he embraced his stepfather's passion. Would he do that if he hated him?" Apparently, Anton Kjærsgaard knew the tactic as well.

"His passion for Africa, you mean?"

They both nodded. "He was barely twenty before he started travelling there. He learned Swahili—whatever he's going to use it for," said Ellen with an uncomprehending shake of the head as she smoothed the table-cloth around the saucer with both hands.

"Did he meet his stepfather on his travels?"

They shrugged simultaneously, looking like twins. Is that what happened after decades of marriage? He saw himself and Irene sitting in the gazebo in Skåde with the same hair, glasses, and movements. The thought made him shudder.

"I'm pretty sure they didn't meet," Anton said firmly to Ellen. "His stepfather travels mostly to South Africa; Sebastian goes to East Africa. Tanzania is his favourite. He's always bringing home horrible souvenirs." He frowned.

"Well, some of them are very nice," reprimanded Ellen, and they followed her gaze to a large, dark wooden figure representing a warrior with a spear and shield, standing in the living room halfway hidden behind a palm tree that seemed to set it in the right environment.

"Do you think that's nice?" protested Anton. "And what about the ugly mask that always hung right over his bed? I never understand how he didn't get nightmares from it. His stepfather had given it to him as a birthday present. What kind of a present is that for a little kid?" He snorted and wiped his nose when something came out. Everyone was suffering from some kind of cold after the abrupt change in the weather.

"It gave him courage; you know that! Lots of children have those kinds of talismans or invisible friends. You probably had some yourself!" Ellen handed him a tissue.

Isabella looked at Roland and smiled. They weren't getting to ask a whole lot of questions, but at least something useful was coming out of listening to their quarrel.

"How does Sebastian afford to travel? Did his stepfather give him money?"

"Not a penny, as far as we know. As soon as the wife disappeared, he fled to Africa. He probably still lives there." Anton said it as an implied question, but Roland didn't respond. Again, he was glad that it was Isabella who was with him. Mikkel certainly wouldn't have been able to keep his mouth shut. Isabella drank her coffee and smiled at him with her eyes over the edge of the cup.

"But Sebastian made his own money. He has always been a hard worker. We've never had a lot of money."

"How did he make money?"

"As a boy, he had a newspaper route every morning regardless of the weather. And in the afternoon, he delivered shop brochures. But still, he did his homework and always got reasonably good grades. As he got older, he also sometimes worked in restaurants in Aarhus."

"Like where, for example?"

Again, they performed a symmetrical movement when they shrugged. "But then he got an apprenticeship as a mechanic in Hasselager, and he moved to Klostergade. What about the mask—did he take it with him, or did you throw it out?" Anton asked Ellen.

"No, I didn't. I wasn't allowed to touch it. Not even to dust it. I remember once when I . . ." She let the sentence die out. "It's probably still hanging over his bed," she continued with horror in her voice.

"Those poor girls he undoubtedly brings home." Anton laughed and promptly received an elbow in the side from Ellen.

"Maybe he *has* a girlfriend. We don't see him that often anymore. He takes care of himself now. But he still travels to Africa and always remembers to send us a postcard." They smiled at each other. "Oh, yes, he was also a developing country volunteer for the Red Cross. His Swahili skills came in very useful there." Ellen drank from her cup.

"But he never told you about the day his mother disappeared?" asked Isabella, who seemed to want to return to the police station soon and move on in the investigation. Roland had the same wish. And now the discussion began again.

"No, he never talked about it. Actually, he didn't speak for six months. Not a peep. A psychologist said it was a natural reaction to a child experiencing something traumatic. They encapsulate it in silence. You see it in child refugees, too."

Anton interrupted immediately. "If he did see something, he's repressed it. But who knows if it will all surface one day?"

"Oh, I hope not, the poor thing."

"It might help the police." Anton looked at Roland for confirmation. Roland got up and thanked them for the coffee; Isabella followed his example. Knud Engtoft had probably arrived for interrogation by now, and he didn't want to miss it. Ellen Kjærsgaard got up too and started putting the cups on the tray while she continued the conversation with her husband.

"But to think that they found him in his mother's car all alone and abandoned on a dark country road that cold winter night. What he must have experienced—and repressed . . ."

42

He lived here almost more than in the apartment on Klostergade. From the living room window, there was a view of the sea that was getting more and more aggressive. The wind picked up; soon it would be a hurricane. Most people would probably say it wasn't the weather for staying in the summer cottage, but he enjoyed it. The special thing about Denmark in relation to Africa was how the changeable weather reminded him so much of his own mind. Bright and friendly one moment—dark and threatening the next.

It was not a flashy summer house like many of the others at Skæring Strand. They were more akin to luxury villas. It was mainly a wooden shed with a small living room, kitchen, and bedroom. But the location was perfect. Slightly secluded and yet close to the beach. No one knew he had bought it with his first few weeks' wages as a mechanic's apprentice while still living for free with Ellen and Anton.

He listened to the storm twisting around the corner by the window; the howling sound reminded him of the time the voices had been drowned in the same sound from the blizzard that had ravaged the countryside that December.

But he'd caught most of the words up on the top step of the stairs to his room, which he had never really got used to. Not the house, the school, the new classmates, the stepfather, and everything else he'd been dragged into.

But she seemed happy. That was the only thing that mattered. It was her voice he remembered best. Mum's gentle voice. The other woman's voice was hoarse. Her friend from the old job at the nightclub. She'd often come to visit, so he knew her well. He had sat and listened to both the blizzard and the voices, wearing only pyjamas, his bare feet freezing on the cold step.

"But you have to report it, Louise. It's murder!" said the hoarse voice, agitated.

He hadn't understood the meaning of much of the conversation before he grew older, but he had never forgotten it. It had been replayed repeatedly in his head as he grew up and slowly began to comprehend what it meant.

"It's not murder in that sense, Annemette. It's called mercy killing. But I didn't want to be part of it; Josefine was improving with Dr. Winther's treatment. She could have survived, I'm sure of it. I was just paralysed, I . . ." Mum started crying. He got up, half ready to run down and comfort her, but he quickly sat down again.

"The Nazis in Germany called it euthanasia in 1939. It allowed them to kill thousands of physically and mentally disabled people who they believed were a burden on society." The African's voice chimed in. It gave him such a fright he almost fell down the stairs. He didn't know he was in the house, too. He must have returned from the long trip he'd been on even though the snowstorm had closed the country. No one else was allowed to drive unless it was essential; they had said on the radio. That was also why Mum's friend was still there. She wasn't allowed to drive home and had to spend the night.

"Rich pigs! I'm sure they did what the Nazis did and got rid of a burden. They probably bribed the doctor to do it. Could that be why this Dr. Winther was sent away? He probably wouldn't be part of it, either. You should have refused to participate, Louise!" His voice reached the top step of the stairwell because he was so wound up and shouting.

"It was . . . going to . . . but I couldn't . . . believe . . . that they would really do . . . and I didn't . . . dare . . ." Mum's voice broke with tears and then fully cracked.

"Why did they do it, though, if she wasn't dying?" asked the hoarse voice.

"If they didn't, he couldn't get the bitch and all her money. Isn't that what you're saying, babe? That he could only leave his sick wife if she died, and that if he married the rich bitch, then he'd become the owner of a huge company that makes billions?"

He could hear that the African had started walking back and forth. Mum didn't answer, or maybe she'd nodded. Perhaps he just didn't hear the answer as a snowdrift slid noisily down from the roof at the same time. He tiptoed silently down the steps and stood behind the half-closed door. He didn't dare look inside the room. Mum and her friend were probably sitting at the dining table, so they'd easily be able to see him. The African's footsteps stopped abruptly; he snapped his fingers like he always did when he thought he had a brilliant idea.

"I've got it," he said so softly that he wouldn't have heard it if he hadn't sneaked down.

"What do you mean?"

"They're rich, babe. They'll bloody well pay anything for this not to get out. Euthanasia is against the law in Denmark."

"Do you mean blackmail?" The hoarse voice sounded shocked.

"Shit! They can afford it. We'll be millionaires!"

"I don't want any part of that. I think we should go to the police." The voice had become more hoarse than usual.

"And what use would that be? Louise is, so to speak, complicit because she participated in the ordeal. How much do you want to keep your bloody mouth shut?" His voice made a sound that got everyone to shut up and obey. "Would half a million help? You can give up your shitty job in that nightclub."

Mum's friend no doubt nodded reluctantly, but he wasn't sure, and he didn't dare take a peek.

"I'll contact them tonight and make our demands. You pick up the money tomorrow. I'll drive you out there, babe."

"What if *they* contact the police?" Mum's friend sounded very scared.

"They wouldn't dare! They'd be reporting themselves. They're the ones who broke the law!" the African replied scornfully.

"Quiet. Basse can hear us." Mum's voice was clearer here behind the door, but he froze when he heard her push the chair back over the wooden floor. "I'll just go up and check on him."

"He's asleep." A match was struck, and a little later came the smell of the cigarettes that only filled the house when he was home. The heavy, sweet smell of his African cigarettes. Mum had stopped smoking after she trained as a nursing assistant. She'd tried to persuade the African to stop, too.

His first thought was to run up to his room, but he quickly realised it would be impossible to reach the stairs in time. He made it to the second last step and turned towards the door, just as she opened it.

"Basse! How long have you been standing here, my little man?" Her voice trembled a little. She stroked his hair. He could see she was crying.

"I'm . . . I'm thirsty."

"Are you having nightmares again?" She took his hand, and he went out into the kitchen with her, where she filled a glass with cold water from the tap and followed him up the stairs. She squeezed his hand a little too hard. Halfway up, she spilled some of the water. Her hand was shaking. She tucked him under the duvet and kissed him on the forehead. For the last time. The next day was the nineteenth of December.

He tasted something salty on his lips. The sound of a car engine drowning out the breeze made him look out the window as he wiped his eyes.

She was here.

43

How would people live if they knew they could have another chance—that everything could be done again in another life? But is that not how we live anyway?

Kamilla reflected on the thought as she looked out at the sea that was growing more and more restless, as if it sensed danger approaching. The abandoned sailboats followed the furious pace of the waves. Some were knocked out of tack by a violent wave and took water in. She spotted a woman with her raincoat pulled all the way down over her face, her wet hands clenched around it as the wind tried to peel it off in vicious blasts. The woman was standing close to the harbour basin, staring out at the troubled sea, where the horizon was a grey mass trying to form a wall between the danger lurking out there and the vulnerable people on land. The woman was trying to keep her balance in the strong gusts of wind. As small and slender as she was, she could easily have been blown into the harbour basin. Kamilla watched a yachtsman suddenly break through the grey wall and noticed the change in posture of the woman in the raincoat. She let go of the hood, which was immediately whipped back, and her blond hair swirled around her face. She waved and shouted something that drowned in the roar of the sea. She ran to the harbour bridge, where the sailboat was trying to dock in the difficult waves. She defied the wind and the foaming water that reached up to the jetty, trying to catch her legs and pull her out. Her husband or boyfriend? Either way, it was someone who was close to her. They embraced each other in the rain of seawater.

That was one of those things that could never be changed; if he had sailed out and never returned. Like Rasmus, who cycled to the sports hall to play football and never came home again. Like her mother, who . . . That's how it was back then, years ago. The boat had returned to Agger Strand, with one missing. It couldn't be changed. They had sailed out—her mother, the forbidden boyfriend, and the little boy, Johannes, who could have become her uncle. He'd never been found. The strong current in the North Sea had taken him. When Aunt Astrid had talked about it, she'd had tears in her eyes. Eyes that couldn't hide the contempt for the sister's irresponsible deeds. But Kamilla also understood what her mother must have felt. She had been responsible for her little brother, like Kamilla herself had been for her son. They had both failed in their responsibilities. Why had she never told her about it and the resulting consequences? Especially given what had happened in her own life.

The waiter was there again, looking at her with interest.

"I'm still waiting." She looked at the clock demonstratively. "He should be here soon."

The waiter smiled and left again.

Was this the right thing to do? It had felt right when she'd made the decision, but now she was in doubt. She heard herself say the same words that had made her decide again. "But what happened wasn't Mum's fault. It was an accident. She didn't pay attention for a moment. Don't you think losing her brother and feeling that it was her fault was punishment enough? How could you blame her and turn your back on her?" But she understood what had happened. She had reacted in the same way, except in her case it wasn't too late to change things.

Astrid's voice sounded again along with a gust of wind that blew withered leaves and salt water against the window and instinctively made her pull away a little. "She was forgiven. Mother's consolation to Gloria was that God called Johannes home early. It wasn't that."

She didn't hear him coming. It was the cold he brought with him that made her look up. He smiled, but the smile was uncertain. He sat down cautiously, as though he wasn't sure if he should. He'd barely sat down before the waiter was there again, telling them what the day's lunch menu consisted of.

"Is it okay if we wait? Can we have some water?" she asked. The waiter nodded with an annoyed expression on his face.

"Kamilla. I'm glad you want to talk to me. But I have to admit, I was somewhat surprised by your message. And then, here at Restaurant Egå Marina, I . . ."

"We have to, Danny. So much has happened . . ." She caught sight of the ring on his finger. The waiter returned and set a jug of water on the table so she could no longer see Danny's hands. She doubted what she had seen. She looked out the window again so as not to look him in the eye. The harbour was empty of people now. Only restless boats, bobbing at their moorings to escape. Like herself.

"What do you want from me, Kamilla?"

She looked at him, wishing she'd never contacted him. "I can never, ever forgive you, but . . ."

"I understand. That's why I have to move on," he interrupted. There was impatience in his voice, as if he didn't want this conversation, either.

"To Majken, you mean?"

He nodded. "Majken is dealing with a lot, too, Kamilla. Maybe you should talk to her."

"I'm not the one who stopped talking to her."

"No, I know that it's because of me and the brief relationship we had. But that's over now." A sort of *Isn't it?* was left hanging in the air. He poured water into her glass and then into his own. "Majken needs someone to talk to. She . . ." When he put the jug down, she could see his hand again—and the ring.

"I didn't want to talk to you about your fiancée," she interrupted. The words had an unintentional nasty tone.

"Then what do you want, Kamilla? I had to cancel a meeting and drive out in a storm to meet you in the belief that . . ."

"What did you think, Danny? Did you think I'd forgiven you? But you've already decided!" As she took her coat under her arm and ran towards the door, she realised how unfair she was being. What had she been hoping for?

The wind tore at her clothes and took her breath away. The cold from the sea cut through to the marrow. She hurried to the car as she put on her coat, shaking so much that she couldn't get the key in the ignition. The waves crashed up from the harbour as if trying to reach her and drag her into the depths. But she was already there. She sank further and further into a deep abyss where she didn't know who she was. She hadn't thought about how important it was to know her roots. But the truth about her mother had changed everything and made her understand a few things. Now she knew exactly why she'd never been loved by her parents—and that it hadn't been her imagination. They had both left her without any explanations or answers. "Fuck you!" she said aloud, meaning her mother. It was as if the hatred had grown bigger, like a big sponge that filled her completely and absorbed everything. Why had her mother never talked to her about what had happened? She was her daughter, and she had a right to know.

Danny came running out of the restaurant, pulling his coat closer around him and pushing through the wind to his car nearby. His face was contorted and grim. A cold hand grabbed her heart and squeezed. He didn't see her. It wasn't the same car as the one he'd been driving when he killed Rasmus. The navy-blue Opel Vectra had been replaced by a silver-grey Saab. It disappeared too quickly towards Grenåvej. She couldn't pull herself together to start her car and follow him. Her aunt's voice kept ringing in her head like an unwanted song that she couldn't get rid of. *The consequences made Mother and Father wash their hands of Gloria, so she fled from Agger—she got pregnant by the man she had sailed away with. She was pregnant with you when she packed her suitcase and disappeared. We—her siblings—were told that our sister had killed our little brother in lust, and hence we could see what fornication leads to.*

Kamilla pulled herself together and turned the key. Even though her vehicle was a heavy four-wheel drive, the storm still tried to push it off the road. She shouldn't have come out. Warnings on the radio advised against all journeys and warned of fallen trees and falling roof tiles. There weren't many cars on the road, either; fortunately, it wasn't far to Mejlbyvej. The music filled the car with soothing classical tones, but the gloomy melody of Astrid's slightly drawling voice didn't disappear in her head. *Meeting a fishing worker who loved her so much that he adopted you as his daughter was what saved Gloria.* Only when Astrid had driven back to Agger and Kamilla was sitting in the car on the way to Egå that day, did the truth of those words dawn on her. She had a biological father somewhere. A man who had been to blame for her mother not keeping an eye on her brother so that he had disappeared into the sea. Was that when she had been conceived?

As she turned into the courtyard amidst swirling withered leaves and fallen branches, she knew what she had to do. She had to find him.

44

———————

It wasn't the most beautiful summer cottage Sabrina had ever seen. As the storm had picked up, she'd regretted having driven out there. But it was too late to leave now—he'd spotted her from the window.

The smile seemed genuine when he opened the door, but there was no joy in his eyes. She recognised something in them from her own eyes.

"So, you're 'the little girl.'" He didn't offer his hand but showed her into a living room where there was a table, two chairs, and a sofa.

"And you're Louise's son, Sebastian?"

He nodded. "Would you like something to drink?"

"No, thank you; I won't stay long. I need to get home before the hurricane really hits." She sat down on the very edge of a chair. From here, there was a view to another room with a bed. The door was ajar, and she was able to glimpse an eerie mask with crooked eyes hanging over the bed.

Sebastian threw himself on the couch and stared at her.

"What is it you wanted to tell me?" she asked meekly.

"Oh, well, weren't you the one who wanted to tell me something?"

"You said I should drive out here because we couldn't talk on the phone."

"You wanted to know something about my mother, right?" He swung his legs up onto one of the armrests of the sofa and folded his arms behind his head on the other, but he didn't take his eyes off her.

"Yes, and about *mine*. Josefine Hjort. Do you remember her?"

Sebastian looked up at the ceiling in an overly speculative way that offended her. If he was only going to make fun of her, she'd be livid after driving out here in this weather.

"Yes, I faintly remember your mother. You look a lot like her. Back then, you were just a little unruly kid."

"Unruly?"

"Yeah, you cried quite a lot. I went to collect Mum from your house sometimes when it was late. But your mother was very sick and your father a real bastard."

"My father is not a . . . !"

"He was always with *her*—his mistress. Mum tried to help you as best she could, and then . . ."

"And then, what?"

"So, you don't know anything?"

"I read some letters your mum wrote to my grandmother at that time. The correspondence stopped in December 1983. Do you know what happened?"

He sat up quickly and leaned forward towards her with narrowed eyes. "Yeah, I do. My mum disappeared. She was murdered for fuck's sake—don't you read the papers?"

Sabrina stood up. His voice was so unexpectedly harsh, and something about his appearance frightened her. She had an unnerving feeling that the mask's crooked eyes were following her from the bedroom through the crack in the door.

"Sit down. Sorry!" He stood up with his hands raised in front of him in a disarming manner. "We both seem to be suffering from the death of our mothers and trying to find answers. Trying to understand what happened, right?"

Sabrina could only nod.

"I might actually know something. Come on." He opened the front door. The gust of wind that blew through the hall slammed the bedroom door shut with a bang and sent the rug whizzing across the floor.

"Go out! In that weather! What are we going out for?"

He put on a raincoat and headed out into the storm; she followed hesitantly, pulling the hood of her coat up over her head. Further ahead, between the trees, she spotted a small shed. Maybe that was where he was hiding whatever she needed to see, though most of all it looked like an old-fashioned outhouse with a carved heart in the door.

He turned around up on the slope. "Stay close. There could be adders here!" he shouted through the wind.

It was hard to walk in the wet sand. There was a bit of shelter when she reached the trees on the slope around the house. The sea thundered, the leaves rustled, and the wind howled so much that she could barely hear his voice, but she had heard the word *adders*. Didn't they hibernate at this time of year, and would they even come out in a storm? "What are we going to do?" she shouted, holding her hair tightly with her hands. The hood had long since been blown off, and she had given up trying to hold it.

He stopped and waited for her. "Hurry up; it's over here!"

She obeyed without knowing why and looked back. She could see the house from the back and the perilously high foamy waves of the sea on the horizon. The shed was an outhouse. But another building behind it had to be a tool-shed.

He came towards her with an outstretched hand to help her up the slope. "Be careful!" he yelled. "There's no cover on . . ."

Sabrina spotted it, just as she took a step and couldn't feel anything under her foot.

"The septic tank."

She heard the words and saw him reach out, but it was too late. Only her upper arms prevented her from falling through, but they slid slowly into the sand. The fabric of her coat rubbed against her like sandpaper. She instinctively grabbed the edge as she'd slipped so far down that her elbows no longer supported her. Her legs kicked out into nothing. How far was she going to fall? What was on the bottom? Her fingers slipped in the sand and some pebbles fell under her. When they landed, she heard a plop in the water.

"Septic tank?" She looked up at him in horror. He just had to reach down and pull her up before she fell. He had the strength for it. But when she saw the change in his face above her, she knew he wasn't going to help. Her fingers slipped some more, her hand was cut, and a nail was broken. The pain spread up her entire arm. "Help me!"

He smiled as he put his foot on her bleeding hand with the broken nail.

The hard soles of his shoes drilled into her skin, but he didn't put his full weight on it. Helping to hasten the inevitable was also unnecessary. The power in her arms began to fail. They shook.

"You have to help me, Sebastian. I'm pregnant!" The words became a sob.

He lifted his foot, just as her hands gave, and the fall into the unknown began.

She landed on her back. The hard blow sent a shooting pain through her lower back, and she screamed. The water was dark and reached up to the middle of her hips. She tried to sit up, but the stab of pain forced her to stay in the same position. There wasn't much room for anything else. The only light in the tank came from the opening where the cover had been. But now his face blocked the light. He squatted up there and peered down at her. His voice echoed around the empty tank, where the sound of the sea and the storm didn't reach.

"Fortunately for you, the septic tank hasn't been in use for a while. But the water penetrates by the cover. Sometimes, when it rains a lot, it reaches the edge." He looked up at the sky, and even though she couldn't see his face clearly, she sensed his satisfied expression as he pulled the raincoat over his head and looked down at her again. "And it's raining a lot today. It's bloody lashing. The water's like a little tidal wave down the slope around here." He disappeared.

She tried to orient herself in the dim light. She had fallen a little over two metres. Above her, she saw two pipes that probably drained into the tank. They were brown with rust and dried faeces. The stench was nauseating and stuffy. She gasped for breath and tried to quell the claustrophobic panic. The pain in her stomach returned with a violent shock. His face was blocking the light again.

"Do you know what the word *septic* in septic tank means?" He made a funnel around one ear with his hand and tilted his head as if he were listening. She didn't answer. "It comes from the Greek word *septicos* and means rotten or rotting. Do you think twenty-five years will pass before they find you here like a brown mummy?" His voice was hoarse and didn't sound like it came from a human.

"Sebastian, don't do this. I have a pain in my stomach. I'm afraid it's my baby!" The echo of her voice intensified the panic and desperation.

"Did you think I'd buy that? That you're pregnant? I'll just ask your dad if he's looking forward to becoming a grandad . . ." He disappeared again. She heard him pull something through the sand.

"He doesn't know," she cried. "No one knows yet!" The words were suffocated by a scraping sound as he pushed the cover into place. Some pebbles plopped into the water around her, then it got dark and quiet. Only the noise of overly rapid breathing mixed with sobs echoed against the thick iron sides. A soft splash made her look up. The cover wasn't completely in place. He'd pushed it aside a little. Certainly not to give her air or the streak of light that slipped through.

The rainwater pooled on top of the cover and cascaded down into the tank.

45

The time is twelve forty-five. Commencing interrogation of Knud Engtoft. Present are Chief Superintendent Kurt Olsen and myself, Detective Inspector Roland Benito," he said into the tape recorder and put it on the table.

Knud Engtoft reclined in the chair opposite, looking very at ease. His eyes shone with roguish adventure.

"Would you please state your name," said Kurt Olsen, sitting down on the chair next to Roland.

"Well, the inspector stated it quite correctly. Knud Engtoft. What's all this about? I gave you a watertight alibi."

"You did, yes. But we would like to hear a little more about your financial records." Roland laid the bank statements on the table so Knud Engtoft could see that they had the documentation in order. For the first time, uncertainty flashed in his eyes.

"Where the hell did you get them from?"

"It is not beyond the reach of the police to obtain such evidence," replied Kurt Olsen. "What is the transfer to your account every quarter?" He selected a printout and demonstratively took a closer look at it. "Large deposits," he added, looking at Knud Engtoft again.

"Payments from my customers, of course."

"What kinds of customers make such large deposits?"

"Some pay a lot of money for safaris. Especially if they bring something home. Animal skins, tusks, or whatever."

"Animal skins and tusks. Isn't that illegal?" Roland asked with over-played naïvety, looking at Olsen, who nodded while still staring at Knud Engtoft.

Olsen said, "Yes, it certainly is. You're not involved in poaching, are you?"

"No, of course not. I respect animals, and I teach participants that, too. That's included in the price."

"The money is transferred from an account in Switzerland. Does that ring any bells about who the payer might be?"

Knud Engtoft laughed as he scratched at the tattoo on his upper arm. He'd been wearing only a white sleeveless vest and grey dappled tracksuit bottoms when they'd brought him in, but he didn't want to wear a jacket. He was the type who never felt the cold, he had said.

"Ah yeah, I remember now. That customer wants to remain anony-mous. That's the agreement we made."

"And what is the reason for this—secrecy?" asked Roland.

"Why do you think he has an account in Switzerland? Tax benefits, right?"

"So, you're not going to give us the customer's name. Do you see how that looks a bit suspicious if it's *only* about safaris?"

"Loyalty is something I value with all my customers. And you can't trace a Swiss account." It sounded more like a question.

"He goes on safari often, your customer. The money goes in every quar-ter and has done so since March 1984. That's only a few months after your wife was murdered!"

Knud Engtoft looked at them quizzically. "Yeah, he travels a lot and has been a customer of mine for many years. I don't see anything strange in the first payment being lodged a few months after Louise disappeared."

"The amount was just doubled. Can you explain that?" Roland pointed to the last transaction on the bank statement.

"Yes. The last safari included staying in a luxury hotel and hiring an interpreter, as the customer wanted to visit a village."

Knud Engtoft always had an answer at the ready. Was he telling the truth? Roland looked at Kurt Olsen, who looked equally bewildered. This could turn into an interrogation that dragged on for days before they learned something useful. Or they would have to let him go. Roland was about to ask another question when there was a gentle rap on the door.

Isabella stuck her head in and asked them to come out for a moment. They apologised and left Knud Engtoft, who leaned back in his chair in an exaggerated waiting position.

"Forensics have finished the analysis of the rhino horn from Annemette Knudsen's apartment. They compared it to the piece from the murder weapon, and they can't rule out that it could be what killed Louise Engtoft. The search of the caravan is now complete. There was also a rhino horn carved from black ebony and we found a leopard-skin cushion. Genuine leopard. That alone violates the Washington Convention and allows us to hold him. The cushion has been sent for technical examination. If it turns out that the animal hairs are identical to those in the lungs of the victim, then we have him!" Isabella's eyes shone with zeal.

Roland remembered the cushion. He recalled thinking that it hadn't coordinated with the rest of the interior, but he hadn't dreamed it was genuine leopard skin. Modern fake furs and skins were so realistic. "How long before we know the results?"

"Tell them to look at that rhino, too. If it's the same kind that the waitress had in her apartment, then we have a connection," Kurt Olsen interjected.

Isabella nodded. "They promised to do it asap, so if you can hold him for that long, I'll let you know as soon as I do," she whispered.

Olsen nodded contentedly and went back in to Knud Engtoft.

Roland lay a hand on her arm. "Nice work," he said softly, closing the door.

Engtoft didn't look quite so confident when he saw their faces. They had a hard time hiding their triumph.

"We don't think safaris are your only livelihood," said Kurt Olsen as he sat down.

Knud turned pale and scratched nervously at the tattoo on his arm.

"We have reason to believe that illegal goods are being traded. Animal skins from endangered species, for example? Illegal trade under the Convention on International Trade in Endangered Species of Wild Fauna and Flora or the Washington Convention as it's also known."

Roland observed Engtoft and noticed an expression of relief in his posture. Was there something else? Murder perhaps? Now they just needed convincing evidence and to get him to confess. "Something might have slipped through—but that's only a fine. Just give me the payment details if you have any evidence." His upper lip stuck to his front teeth when he smiled. Roland's mouth was dry, too. He stood up.

"I'll get us something to drink. Is there anything in particular you'd like, Knud?"

"Wait—are we not finished?"

He saw on their silent faces that they were not.

"Okay, then I'd like a Coke."

When Roland returned with the drinks, they were in the middle of a talk about infectious diseases in Africa. "Only the bloody mosquitoes are dangerous. They leave parasites that can kill the strongest man. Even me! The worst is called *Plasmodium falciparum*. But you can guard against getting infected with malaria. I always sleep under a mosquito net"—he took the cola and drank from the bottle—"and I take malaria tablets, of course. Why not do it when preventative medicine is available? It'd be stupid not to."

They talked about the weather, hoping to get him to reveal something. But he didn't. He denied any knowledge of the waitress and thought she must have got the souvenir from someone else who had travelled somewhere in Africa. That was a possibility. Roland eyed the clock. If only they'd hear from Forensics soon—they could only hold Knud Engtoft for so long. At some point, he would probably ask for a solicitor. Another knock on the door raised his hopes. Roland quickly jumped up and walked out to Isabella. He closed the door behind him.

"Bingo! The hairs are from the cushion, and the ebony rhinos are the same and were made the same way—they're almost identical. We can hold him. They also found DNA on the cushion. Forensics have been fast. It's Annemette Knudsen's DNA. Saliva."

"Saliva? Did she spit on his cushion?" Then it dawned. "He tried to smother her first with the cushion . . ."

"She got away and fled into the woods, throwing off her remaining shoe to run faster, but, unfortunately, he caught up with her, and . . ." Isabella continued.

Roland was about to hug her but resisted. "Now we just have to link him to the murder of his wife and the doctor. Will you talk to Kim and Mikkel about what they've learned? And check out how far it is from Knud Engtoft's caravan to the crime scene in the forest, too."

"Of course. Niels has just returned from the nightclub. There were no results from the video surveillance outside the entrance. No one recognised any of the men who were there that night, such as the man Annemette talked to at the bar. Luckily, we have other evidence."

Roland nodded. "But let's look at them again anyway. We have to be able to see when Knud Engtoft arrived to catch his prey. We should also get a DNA sample from him. Anything else?"

"Yes, they found some medicine in the caravan. Antiviral drugs. Retrovir, Norvir, Zerit, Invirase . . ."

"HIV—AIDS?"

Isabella nodded. "He's HIV-positive."

"So, he doesn't protect himself against all dangerous diseases," he mumbled. She looked at him quizzically. He waved his hand and smiled to show it didn't matter.

She turned and was about to leave but stopped just before Roland opened the door. "By the way, Jensen and Vang spoke to Annemette Knudsen's mother. They want to talk to you when you're done here."

He nodded and opened the door. Olsen and Engtoft looked up at him.

"The time is thirteen oh five, and you are being arrested on suspicion of the murder of Annemette Knudsen," he said. At the same time, an officer came in and took Knud Engtoft's arm. He turned beetroot red in the face, the words were stammered.

"What's happening . . . ! What the hell is going on, man . . . ? I didn't do anything. I don't know a bloody thing . . . What's going on? Don't lock me up, I have . . ." He bit his lower lip, as tears welled up in his eyes.

"We know, Knud. You'll have your medicine. We'll make sure of that."

"What was all that about?" Kurt Olsen asked as Roland began to gather up the papers and remove the empty bottles.

"He's HIV-positive and needs his medication. That's what's keeping him alive."

46

Anne rang the doorbell again and then knocked hard on the penthouse door, but no one opened it.

"Shit!"

Kamilla had taken Nicolaj out on a job that Thygesen had assigned to them. She was on her own again, but not when it came to making decisions. Thygesen had taken complete control of that, and now he had decided that she was to get the letters Sabrina kept—even if she had to steal them, he'd said. She was about to walk away when a fair-haired woman with a child in one arm and a buggy under the other struggled up the stairs. She wore heavy make-up, and the perfume reached Anne before the woman was visible on the stairs. She guessed it must be the friend and the owner of the apartment and reached out for the buggy. Pernille looked up at her in surprise.

"Anne Larsen. I'm a journalist. I'd like to speak with Sabrina Dahl. But let me help." She smiled, taking the buggy.

"Thanks. Hasn't Sabrina opened the door?" Pernille hitched the boy up so he sat better on her arm as she dug the key out of an overflowing shoulder bag, which he kicked several times with his swinging feet. He gnawed on a bread roll and had crumbs all over his face and up along his arms.

"It seems that no one is home." Anne took the buggy in. Pernille threw the keys on the kitchen table, put the boy down on the floor, and pulled off her coat as she called for Sabrina. The boy was fairly steady on his feet but had the funny totter that children in nappies often do. He knew where his room and the box of toys were located. He poured the contents onto the floor, found a mottled stuffed giraffe, and handed it to Anne. She squatted down. "Ooh, how cute," she said. What else were you supposed to say to children of that age?

"She's not here. I don't think she had any plans today, but you never know with Sabrina." Pernille took off her coat. "I'm afraid I can't help you. What is this really about?"

"I've been here before to talk to Sabrina . . ."

"She didn't mention that." Pernille looked questioningly at her, as if she and Sabrina usually told each other everything.

"She has some letters that would be great to refer to in an article I'm working on. We just spoke about them."

"Oh, the letters to her grandmother? Why don't you sit down?"

Pernille sat down on a chair in the kitchen, Anne sat opposite. "Do you know anything about those letters?"

"Yeah, they were from her mother's nursing assistant to Elina, her grandmother. She has just passed away, and Sabrina found the letters in her wardrobe when they were clearing out the apartment. What interest do they hold for the press?"

"They're probably more interesting to the police. Did Sabrina not tell you that the nursing assistant who wrote the letters is the victim they found murdered in the bog?"

Pernille opened her mouth, but no sound came out. The boy made a noise with a fire truck and laughed out loud to himself. "Be quiet, Adam!" she shouted, annoyed. "I don't believe that. Sabrina would definitely have told me that."

"Well, it's true. The worst thing is that Sabrina could be in danger, too. Do you have any idea where she might be?"

"She could be with her dad, maybe. But she'd rather not go there if Carola—her stepmother—is home."

Anne nodded, understanding that very well. "I can try Gustav Hjort, but . . ."

Pernille took out her phone and found a number in its contacts. She pressed Call. "You don't have to. You've scared me; I want to know where Sabrina is—if she's in danger." She put the phone to her ear and listened. "Hey, Gustav. This is Pernille—Sabrina's friend. Is Sabrina with you?" As she listened to the voice that was so loud and animated that Anne could hear fragments of it, Pernille turned pale. When she hung up, she stared at Anne with empty eyes. "Gustav has received a call that Sabrina is no longer alive." She was too paralysed to cry, but her mouth trembled.

"From whom?"

"I don't know!"

"A man or a woman?" Anne got up and swung on her backpack by one strap.

"Gustav said *he*. A man," Pernille replied without force in her voice.

"I'm going out to Gustav Hjort. Has he called the police?"

"I don't know; he didn't mention it." Pernille looked apathetically at Adam, who had crawled up on the chair by her computer, but she didn't get up until he started throwing things down on the floor. First, the newspaper next to the computer, then the pencil holder. Pencils, felt-tip pens, and ballpoint pens rolled noisily across the parquet floor.

"I'll leave now. Thanks for the chat. Here's my business card if there's anything you'd like to talk to me about." Pernille didn't hear it. She took Adam down from the chair and began to gather up the pens. Anne slipped out the door quickly and closed it quietly. Why had Sabrina not listened to her when she said she could be in danger. Who could do something to her? It couldn't be Knud Engtoft—as far as she knew, he had just been arrested and charged with the murder of Annemette Knudsen. There was a press conference in a little over an hour, but she could just make it out to Strandvejen before it started. She had reached the main door in the stairwell when Pernille came running down the stairs with a bewildered expression in her eyes.

"I found this newspaper by the computer. There's an address next to that picture. That's Sabrina's handwriting."

Anne took the newspaper and looked at the picture. It was the one Kamilla had taken. "Sebastian," she said quietly.

47

DS Jensen looked a bit run down. He stretched his legs out under Roland's desk. "What kind of bloody weather is this? Is this the end of the world?"

DS Vang was sitting in the chair next to him, biting a hangnail on his little finger. Roland stood at the window with his back to them. The asphalt down on the car park looked alive with the aggressive rain and wind. He tried to gather his thoughts. The press conference was in half an hour, and his brain was still mulling over phrases like *dark numbers* and *killers walking around freely.*

"So, tell me," he said.

"First, we drove out to Skovby and talked to the cache owner. We can rule him out. He has an alibi for the entire week—a fishing trip in Sweden with some fellow students. Afterwards, we talked to Annemette Knudsen's mother, Sidse Knudsen. She lives on Silkeborgvej, so it was on the way."

Dan Vang scowled at Roland's neck, then cleared his throat. "Why do we have to do all this when the perp has been caught? We have him."

Roland turned and looked at him calmly. He sat down at his desk so they were at eye level. "We are always very thorough, Dan. You know that. Yes, Knud Engtoft has been arrested and charged, but he has not been convicted, and he denies it's him, so the question is how long we can keep him. We'll be lucky if he'll be remanded in custody after the hearing, but that is also the time we have to find the evidence needed to get him convicted in court. Therefore, we must continue to work on all possibilities. And, who says he committed the murders on his own—if it *is* him?"

Dan nodded, apparently understanding.

"What did Sidse Knudsen say?"

Mikkel seemed discomfited by the embarrassing interruption. "She didn't see much of her daughter, either. Annemette apparently lived a rather secluded life without many friends and acquaintances. It wasn't an easy life. Ever since school, she has only worked in nightclubs as a waitress and has never had an education. Her mother only knew that she had two jobs for years to get by. She had just started a new one as a bookkeeper; they were training her. The home for the disabled, where her daughter lives, isn't exactly the cheapest."

"So, it's not a municipal home?"

Mikkel shook his head. "Only the best was good enough for her daughter. Her mother thought it was due to a guilty conscience. On the whole, she sounded pretty bitter towards her daughter."

Dan nodded in confirmation.

"What's wrong with the girl?" Roland took a piece of chewing gum and looked at his watch. The press conference was approaching.

"She's paralysed on the left side and uses a wheelchair. When she was fourteen, she was on the back of her boyfriend's moped. He was driving too fast and drove headfirst into a car—killed on the spot. The daughter, Kit, was on a ventilator for four months; the doctors said there was nothing more to do, but Annemette wouldn't have it turned off to end her daughter's life. It sounds like Annemette's mother was against this decision, too. She still thinks it would have been best for all parties."

"And the father?"

"Spanish—she'd no love for him, either—a one-night stand during a holiday in Spain, as Sidse put it. She tried to get Annemette to have an abortion, but she wouldn't put an end to life at the foetal stage, either. The mother clearly believed that everything should have been put to an end back then; that way, they would have been spared all the suffering."

"Did she know where her daughter's African rhinoceros horn came from?"

"She didn't know anything about it."

"Did you talk to the disabled daughter, too? Kit—that was her name, wasn't it?"

Mikkel shook his head. "No, what good would it do to torment her further; her mother being dead is enough. There is no one to pay for the home now, so what's going to become of her?"

Roland nodded. He agreed. There was no reason to bother the poor girl.

"What about her grandmother; can't she pay?"

"Can't—or won't, perhaps. She retired early. But we discovered something very strange when we left." Mikkel glanced at Dan, who sent him a reproachful look. "In fact, it was Dan who discovered it. There was a large black BMW with leather upholstery in the garage. I got the reg and checked it out. It was bought in 1984. Paid for in cash—by Annemette Knudsen."

Roland clicked his pen against the tabletop a few times and looked at the clock again. Time had run out during the most exciting phase, like in some TV series. The press conference would start soon, and he'd promised Kurt Olsen to say something this time.

He got up and pulled down his sleeves. "Have Ansager examine both Annemette Knudsen's and her mother's finances back to 1983. I'm going down to the press conference."

He took the stairs. It was not so strenuous anymore after having quit cigarettes for almost a year. Maybe the quick little walks with the puppy had worked, too, even though he mainly just stood and watched. After all, bringing a dog to do its business was mostly a stationary job while the mutt sniffed its way to a suitable place to do it. Would Irene even have taken him out in that storm? The entire police station was feeling the effects of the weather situation—phone calls were non-stop when nature raged. He hoped it could keep the journalists away so it would be over quickly, but he wasn't that lucky. He sat down next to Kurt Olsen and pulled a microphone a little closer. His eyes clearly said, *Let's get this bloody thing over with.*

48

It was hard to keep the Lada on the road. Anne considered turning around. The sea was wild, but there was a little more shelter down towards the summer cottage from the large trees surrounding the area. The treetops rustled back and forth with unnatural force as if an angry troll had grabbed them and wanted to shake off the last pitiful leaf. She parked in front of the house and pulled her hood up over her head. The storm took her breath away. She turned her head away to avoid being strangled.

The house looked abandoned. It was old, and had it not been for the shelter of the slope and the tall trees, the roof would probably have long since blown off. She looked in through the window but could see only darkness. Was Sabrina in there? The door was locked. She walked around the house, peering in through the windows. There was no sign of life. She stood there for a while, bewildered, knowing the best thing to do was to go back to the car and drive home to safety, but she couldn't. Sabrina had written this address on the newspaper next to Sebastian's picture. She must have met him here. They must have spoken.

When she decided to throw a stone through the window, it was followed by the thought that a broken windowpane wouldn't look unnatural after a storm. That is, if the house was even still standing tomorrow. If the hurricane—as meteorologists warned—was going to rage all night. She put a hand in and opened the clasp. Was careful not to cut herself on the sharp glass. She opened the window and crawled inside. A withered potted plant landed on the floor, and a small table toppled over with a bang. *Bloody wind*, she thought, and couldn't help but smile.

It was an easy enough house to navigate. Probably only about sixty square metres divided into a living room, a kitchen with a gas cooker, and a bedroom. There was no electricity, and the many burned-down candles dotted everywhere had to be the only source of light on the dark evenings. Gently, she opened the door to the room with a bed. It smelled of old mattress and something weirdly exotic. She went in and then retreated again. The room was full of wooden figures. It was the wood that smelled. Some of them were beautifully carved and decorated and were, with good intention, appealing; others depicted evil spirits, fantastic animals, and warriors with dramatic spears. Over the bed hung a mask with thick triangular lips and crooked holes for eyes. Goosebumps flared on her skin, not just because the room was cold. This was a connection to Africa. Was this Knud Engtoft's place? Had Sebastian lured Sabrina out to his stepfather's cottage? Or had Engtoft? But then why did he live in a caravan? No, he'd been at the police station for most of the day.

The storm howled around the corner by the window. Violent gusts of wind made the planks of wood moan, and the remaining window sounded like it would soon give in and burst out of its frame in a shower of glass shards. Anne spotted herself in a mirror above an old dresser with three drawers. Startled, she jumped, as she hadn't seen the mirror. It was as dark as everything else in the room. She was paler than she'd realised. Her eyes were large and looked frightened. She pulled out the first drawer. There were only a few combs, a razor, and other grooming items. The second drawer was empty, but at the bottom, she found an A5-size book. The cover resembled snakeskin, and when she touched it, she did not doubt that it was genuine. She picked it up and opened it. On the first page were some words written in easily legible handwriting: *Kila lenye mwanzo halikosi kuwa na mwisho.* She turned the page. On the next page was only one word: *usaidifa.* Every page of the book was full of words. She didn't understand any of them. They were written in a language she'd never seen before. She stuffed the book in her pocket and went to a tall, narrow wardrobe. It was empty. A final inspection of the house gave her no indication of who lived here. On the whole, it was left as though no one was coming back before the next summer season. Maybe Sabrina hadn't come out here at all? Everything pointed to her instincts being wrong.

The storm attacked her as soon as she went out. It tried to whip the coat off her torso and knocked her over as she fought her way back to the car through the slushy sand. The rain was driving hard against her and hit her in the face like an axe. In no time, her clothes were soaked. She turned away from the gusts of wind and caught sight of the shed up between the trees. An outdoor toilet—she'd wondered where it was in the house. The larger shed behind had to house the shower or other sanitary ware, although someone who lived so close to nature, as the owner of this place seemed to, would probably bathe in the sea.

The tree trunks creaked as if they would soon be all out of fight. Some branches had lost the battle and lay on the ground like amputated arms. One had hit her car and was lying on the radiator. Water flowed like little tidal waves up from the slope. She had better get home. A phone call settled it.

Thygesen's voice thundered as brutally as the sea.

"Where the hell are you? The press conference is about to start. You better show up at the station in five minutes. I'm waiting for you!" She didn't get to answer that it was impossible for her to make it, nor to point out that he could bloody well manage a press conference on his own given that he was there anyway. She started the car and tried to reverse, but the rear wheels only spun round in the sand and the car didn't move from where it was stuck. If only it'd been Kamilla's four-wheel drive. She cursed. Got out. Out into the storm trying to keep her inside the car. Trying to reverse again and again wasn't going to help, the wheels would just dig themselves even further into the sand. She looked up at the shed. Just the thought of heading up there was too much, but maybe there were some tools she could use. Shovels and other useful equipment weren't something she had in the car. She'd never needed it—until now.

She gasped for breath when she made it up to the top of the slope, but there was a bit of shelter here. The shed was relatively new and looked solid. She tried the door. It was locked. There were no windows. She stood for a moment, shivering with the cold, not knowing what to do, then she set off at a run down the slope. She knelt and began digging away the water-heavy sand from around the wheels with her bare hands, which immediately stiffened from the cold.

49

Kim rushed at him when he returned from the press conference. He hadn't even made it to his office.

"I've been through the waitress's accounts. No money was withdrawn for the purchase of a BMW in 1984. Mikkel has spoken to her mother again. She claims Annemette won half a million kroner in the lottery, but didn't know which one, and I haven't been able to figure it out. Though it *was* a long time ago."

"What about the Lotto?" Roland answered absentmindedly, still a little groggy after the press conference where questions had been thrown at them like the storm throwing rain against a window. He sat down heavily at his desk.

"The Lotto wasn't an option then. It didn't exist before 1989. I remember it clearly because I won a thousand kroner on my first lottery ticket." Kim straightened up and pushed his chest forwards.

"Well done, Kim!"

"I thought it could be the Klasselotteriet—the one established by Frederick V over two hundred years ago. But that didn't yield results, either. Maybe a foreign lottery. Spanish maybe, given that she travelled there, and . . ."

"It's interesting that both Knud Engtoft and Annemette Knudsen suddenly come into big sums of money in 1984," Roland interrupted. He turned the chewing gum with his tongue and looked up at DS Ansager. He had got new glasses, he suddenly noticed.

"Maybe he paid her for something? Is it possible she sold safari trips for him? They must have known each other. Where else would she have got the rhino from?"

"The leopard fur wasn't genuine in every case."

"Maybe she provided other services? Could the money have been Knud Engtoft's motive for the murder?"

"So long afterwards? But you're right that the money could have come *from* him. He had the means to pay her for something, but for what . . . ?" Roland rubbed his chin while thinking of possibilities. "Silence," he said then. "What about paying for her silence?"

"Her silence—about what?"

"That's what we need to find out. What about the doctor?"

"He was immaculate—at least in terms of finances."

Ansager sat down on the edge of the desk. "If Annemette needed two jobs to make ends meet, that half a million must have evaporated quickly."

"She also bought a BMW for her mother, travelled to Spain, and later . . ." Roland began.

"Later, it all went on the private disability home and the daughter," Kim suggested.

"I guess that ate up the last of the money."

"Definitely. And it was actually only in 1984 that she didn't work. I contacted the nightclub owner—the one who owned it at the time—and he confirmed that she had won the lottery at some point and stopped working. But she was back again the following year. Maybe she just missed her job."

"Yes, or the money. Nice work, Kim!" Roland slammed his fingers hard against the edge of the table, a sound that indicated it was now time to move on.

Ansager knew it intimately and got up. "Did the press conference go well?"

"Like that kind of thing usually goes, but the vultures were sated a little." He smiled contentedly, and Kim left him in peace.

And peace was what he needed. It had all gone so fast; he had an ugly feeling it might all have been too easy.

He had to reconstruct the course of events in his head. Knud Engtoft killed Annemette Knudsen, but there was only weak technical evidence of that. That she had been near his leopard cushion in the caravan wasn't proof that he was the murderer. Maybe the DNA results would give more? But what were they supposed to compare them to when no DNA had been found at the crime scenes? Knud was infected with HIV—did that play a role? Was it revenge? Had the doctor let him down? Had Annemette infected him? He straightened at the thought and called Forensics. It took a while before he got Leander, but he couldn't confirm his suspicion. Annemette Knudsen hadn't been infected. Knud Engtoft had probably contracted the disease from someone in Ghana—perhaps under a protective mosquito net. What was the motive? And what was the motive for the murder of his wife and the doctor? There were far too many unanswered questions for him to consider the matter settled. Too many loose ends. Who owned the Swiss bank account? Swiss banks offering tax havens to the wealthy had been heavily scrutinised in recent years and had been accused by various governments of not only protecting tax evaders but also of helping criminals launder money, including drug dealers and terrorists. After 9/11, opposition to the system had grown. As always when it came to crime, power, and money, the mafia came to mind. Al Capone had benefited from the Swiss Banking Act of 1934—it had inspired him to buy his own bank in Switzerland to deposit money from his slot machines. It still went on today with drug money, dirty money, and everything else in between. It would take time to unravel a case with a hidden bank account in Switzerland. But it could—and would—be possible if it came this far. If they didn't break Knud Engtoft. His head had begun to throb violently. He was looking for a packet of Panadol in the drawer when she knocked and opened the door.

"We've got him!" she said, standing in the doorway.

"Maybe we'll get him, yes. Come in, Isabella." He dropped the tablets and closed the drawer. The sales listings were still in there, and he thought fleetingly of the coming weekend when Irene was to see the property. It gave him completely different butterflies in his stomach.

"What do you mean by *maybe*?"

"There isn't enough evidence to hold him. Knud Engtoft is currently only charged with reasonable suspicion. But he hasn't confessed. And there's something that doesn't make sense."

"Didn't Nyborg say that the direction from the caravan to the murder scene fits? That's the route you'd take if you were fleeing in panic into the forest in the dark; it's only about half a kilometre to the place where the shoe was found."

"No, I haven't spoken to DS Nyborg." Roland looked up at her with interest. "Did they find footprints?"

"Unfortunately, not a trace. Though it has rained a lot, and . . ."

Resigned, he threw his arms up and slammed the pen on the table. "There, you see! No proof. Only clues. It won't work; no court will accept it."

"Would he actually go to prison when he has HIV? I mean, he's sick." Isabella sat down, worried.

"According to a section of the law, an HIV-infected person can risk up to four years in prison for having unprotected sex with a healthy person. If he can be imprisoned for having sex, why not for murder?"

"You might be on to something there."

Isabella didn't say anything more for a while; she seemed embarrassed.

"Have we found a connection between the three murder victims?" he asked. They shouldn't stop just because Knud Engtoft was a possible perp.

"We don't have a connection to the waitress—she's the only odd one out. There may well be a connection between the doctor and the nursing assistant, but, unfortunately, we haven't found it yet."

"We have to find something that can give us a motive. A motive for Knud Engtoft murdering three people. Which of the five motives could it be: sex, lust, jealousy, revenge, or honour?" Roland flipped through the case file.

"Honour?" said Isabella guessing, reminding Roland that she was new.

"Honour can be linked to shame or exclusion," he explained, looking at the file again. "If we take local murder as our starting point—the perp and victims knew each other—the motive is most often desire, jealousy, honour, or revenge. If it's random murder—the victim and perp don't know each other beforehand—then the motive is most often sex, lust, or blackmail. No one kills without a motive. Without the motive, we'll never find the murderer," he continued. He realised he was mumbling, but Isabella had heard him.

"Could it have something to do with money?"

"So, blackmail? Either way, money is involved—large sums. Do you have any suggestions?"

"Extortion?"

He nodded and thought of his own suggestion to Kim—payment for silence. Blackmail. "Someone knows something that someone else is paying for to keep quiet."

"The murder of Bente Louise Engtoft?" suggested Isabella.

Roland stared at her without really seeing her, something was taking shape in his mind, and it wasn't just the headache that was intensifying. "It worked for twenty-five years, but now the amount has been doubled. What does that mean?"

"The nursing assistant being found in the bog."

Roland asked the questions, Isabella answered. For the third time that day, he wanted to take her in his arms and give her a hug. "Knud Engtoft receives money, so he must know."

"He was also the one who called and warned the journalist. He knows her murderer." Isabella had become so eager that she got up and started pacing back and forth, looking up at the ceiling, as though struggling with a difficult maths problem.

"He could have done it himself?"

"If it's him, is he getting money for the murder? Maybe he's a hitman."

She was good. "What about the waitress? Where does she fit into all this?"

Isabella sat down. She had developed red cheeks, but now she looked at him wearily. "That's what gets me. Did she get money, too?"

"Half a million kroner—said to have been won in the lottery."

She thought. Suddenly, she looked at him. "She knew something, too. Maybe she saw him murdering his wife?"

"Maybe, but what about the doctor? Why did he have to be dispensed with?" He realised he was testing her, and maybe she perceived it, too.

She threw out her arms. "I give up!"

They were interrupted by the phone. Isabella was on her way to the door when he answered it and Mikkel said there was someone who wanted to talk to him.

"Who is it?

"She says she's a friend of Sabrina Dahl and her name is Pernille Lauritzen. She's just reported Sabrina missing. She's come in with some letters that are related to the murder in the bog. Should I send her in?

"Yes, definitely. Send her in!"

50

Nicolaj had been full of argy-bargy for most of the day, so Kamilla's head felt completely woozy. The storm alone could have done it. Thygesen sent them out to do a report on overturned scaffolding on Amaliegade. The first thing Nicolaj complained about was that it wasn't about macabre deaths. But it easily could have been. The scaffolding had destroyed two cars and was very close to smashing a window in the building on the opposite pavement. The company that had set up the scaffolding was there, too, and they couldn't understand how it had happened. Nicolaj did the interview while Kamilla took the photos. When they returned to the office, windswept, Thygesen said that he'd gone to a press conference because he couldn't get hold of Anne, and that they should go home before the storm turned into a hurricane.

Kamilla made a cup of hot tea and sat down with Tarzan on the couch. He didn't deign her a look as she scratched his neck.

How do you find your biological father? If her mother had stated "father unknown" on her birth certificate or had indicated the fisherman, Henning Holm, was her father, she wouldn't have been able to get help from the parish office in Horsens, which was the first place she would contact. But had she done that? According to Astrid, she had been very happy with her boyfriend so wouldn't she have only considered abortion if she hadn't been happy? Was that how she was supposed to have ended up? Murdered as a foetus by her own mother. Maybe that's why everything had gone wrong for her—her marriage, Rasmus, Danny, her mother, her life. She wasn't supposed to have existed at all, so she wasn't entitled to anything. *Now you sound like your bloody mother,* she thought, drinking from the teacup. Swearing had been strictly forbidden in her childhood home and was met with immediate punishment. It had always sat deep inside her. She had once been locked in the closet for an entire night because of a *shit.* At only six years old. She thought they had forgotten her and she was going to stay in there forever. That's probably why she was afraid of the dark. *Don't be like her, for God's sake!* But didn't she resemble her the most? Was she the prejudiced, doomsday-forecasting, negative person that Gloria had been, or did she have some personality traits from her father? Did she look like him the most? Were there any hereditary diseases she couldn't do anything about?

She got her laptop and sat down on the sofa with it on her thighs. She typed *Horsens Parish* into Google and clicked on the website, scrolled down, and found the contact details. *Vicar(s)/Parish office.* Bingo! She clicked on the link. The name and telephone number of the church registrar stood at the top. She jotted down the phone number. Could she be so lucky that he would answer now? She looked at the clock and suddenly got cold feet. Did she really want to find her father? Who was he and what kind of life did he live? A drunkard, a criminal, a drug addict—deceased. Maybe he was no longer alive; if that was the case, would it not be better to simply get on with her life believing that her father was out there somewhere? She put her phone back on the table and looked at Tarzan. Oh, to be a cat! She poured more tea and watched a report on the storm on TV 2 News, where they warned it would turn into a hurricane during the night. She texted Anne to check whether she was safe at home. The answer came ten minutes later. *Yes, home safe now, car got stuck, but you know all about that :-) Have a lot to tell you tomorrow. Love, Anne.*

She looked out at the trees in the garden through the patio door. They moved like restless creatures trying to tear themselves free of the earth and flee to shelter. She picked up her mobile again, decided, and dialled the number to the church registrar. It took a long time before the receiver was picked up at the rectory, and she heard the well-known Horsens dialect. He explained that children born in 2003 and later are listed in the electronic church register nowadays, but when she said it was about a birth in 1971, he replied that she could come to the church office and get a transcript of the church register. She thanked him and hung up. Then the unrest returned. She doubted again whether she wanted to know him—perhaps he didn't want to know her.

51

Pernille Lauritzen looked haggard. She hurried into Roland's office and set a cardboard box on his desk. "It's the letters," she said quickly, looking at her watch. "I don't have much time, my son is with the neighbour, the weather is terrible, so . . ." She hyperventilated and was on her way to the door again.

"Sit down for a moment and tell me what happened. What are these letters, and why do you think they have something to do with the murder?"

Reluctantly, she sat down. Her eyes were large, brown, and full of anxiety under very long lashes and a significant amount of eye shadow. She smelled of expensive perfume.

"Sabrina hasn't told me anything. At least, she didn't tell me that the woman who wrote the letters is the same one who was found dead in the bog."

"Sabrina is Carola and Gustav Hjort's daughter, isn't she?"

"Only Gustav's daughter. Carola is Sabrina's stepmother, and they can't abide each other. I thought she was with them, but she's not. She's disappeared!"

Suddenly, she started crying, but quickly pulled herself together and looked at him. The mascara wasn't waterproof. The words jabbered out as he calmly listened and asked questions if there was something he didn't understand.

"Why didn't Gustav Hjort contact us if his daughter has disappeared?"

"He's probably counting on me contacting you. I know most of what's going on in Sabrina's life—she's staying with us. I called him shortly after he'd got a message that she was no longer alive."

"What message—from whom?"

"A man who called him."

"When did he get the call?"

"It must have been about three or four o'clock; I'd just come home from work. A reporter was waiting for me in the stairwell. She told me about the letters. She wanted to talk to Sabrina about them," she concluded, looking at her watch again. She got up. "I have to go! I promised the neighbour it would only take half an hour."

Roland got up, too. "What reporter?" A suspicion gave him goosebumps on his arms.

"From the *Daily News*. Anne Larsen. She came to get the letters but suddenly changed her mind. I think she forgot all about them when she saw the picture in the newspaper."

The goosebumps spread to his neck. "What picture?"

"I don't know. It was a man. Sabrina had written an address next to it. Anne Larsen said a name before she went out the door."

"Do you remember the name?"

"Unfortunately not—and now I really have to go. Promise me you'll find Sabrina!" The tears were back in her eyes when she looked pleadingly at him. Then she was gone.

Roland sat down. He was almost hyperventilating, too. So, she was back in the game, Anne Larsen. What had she uncovered and forgotten to tell the police now? He typed the editor's number into the phone but got only an answering machine that reeled off the opening hours. Workplaces were probably deserted; everyone had gone home to safety before the hurricane broke out in full force. After all, they had advised people to stay indoors. Maybe he should head home, too, and do the same. Anne Larsen could wait until tomorrow. He called Mikkel Jensen's extension instead.

"Sabrina Dahl has been reported missing, hasn't she?" Mikkel confirmed.

"I think we need to talk to Gustav Hjort. Apparently, he got a call that his daughter is no longer alive. Will you look into it?"

"*Now?*" Mikkel sounded terrified.

"Talk to him on the phone first. I know it's not the best weather to go out in. We have to hold back on the search until the storm is over anyway."

"I'll ring him," mumbled Mikkel.

Roland took the cardboard box with the letters under his arm. There was a bit of overtime to take home.

Angolo greeted him at the front door, ran around his feet so he almost fell over, and jumped up on his trouser legs.

"We need to train him. He growled at the postman today," Irene said with her back to him. She was standing at the kitchen table, and he was glad to see her even though it was only her back. The last few evenings she'd been in bed when he got home.

"Good dog," Roland said, patting it.

"Don't praise him for that!" She turned around with a plate of salmon sandwiches, which she put on the table. There were also wine glasses by the plates. She took a bottle of white wine out of the fridge. Just the homecoming he needed today. "Isn't he supposed to be a guard dog?" he asked, squatting down. Angolo immediately licked his face with a soft, hot, and wet tongue, but he didn't like it. You never knew where a dog's tongue had last been—he'd seen it often enough when they went for a walk.

"Yes, but Rolando—the postman. It's a little too stereotypical." She laughed. It had been a long time since he'd heard her laughter.

He took off his coat.

"You're home early today; I expected you to be out in that weather. The emergency services are probably busy."

"Yes, now it's their turn. Did anything special happen today?"

"No, but shouldn't we celebrate your breakthrough? I heard on local radio that you've arrested the carer's husband."

The press was faster than even he thought.

"I don't know if you can call it a breakthrough. He didn't confess, and the evidence is weak. I was thinking more about whether *you* have something to celebrate. Salmon and wine!"

He smiled broadly.

"Not exactly," she replied. "Or maybe I have? I saw the letter from Zia Giovanna on your desk. What does she want? Is it an invitation? I miss Italy!"

Oh, shit, he had forgotten to put the letter in the drawer last night. "We're practically just home from there." He sat down at the table and firmly pushed Angolo down as the pup tried to crawl up his legs.

"Yes, but still. Sun and heat are better than this weather." She looked out the window where the copper beech was fighting for its life out in the driveway. You could hear it complaining along with the storm's aggressive howl. It sounded like two creatures fighting.

Roland squeezed some lemon over his salmon and dried his fingers on a napkin. "I didn't tell you about the letter because you were so sad."

Irene sat down opposite him. "Nothing happened, did it?"

Angolo had his snout right up at his plate again. He gave it a piece of freshly smoked salmon to get some peace.

"You shouldn't teach him that. He's supposed to be a real police dog without those kinds of bad habits."

"Bjarne Lund from the Canine Unit would like to look at him; do you think we should try?"

"Of course. Would you be more at home as a dog handler?"

"Unlikely," he replied simply, as it had never come up.

"So, you don't want to tell me about the letter?"

"Yeah, yeah." He chewed and took a sip of the cold wine.

"Will you translate it for me?"

"Of course. You still want to go out and look at the property on Saturday, don't you?" He could hear how it sounded like blackmail, but Irene just nodded silently.

"I'll get it so you can read it out when you're finished eating."

"Aren't you going to have something to eat?" he asked, wanting to postpone that letter a little longer.

She went into his study. Angolo seemed to be in doubt as to whether the desire for more salmon or his curiosity would win. It was curiosity. He followed Irene. Roland smiled. Curiosity was a very important trait for a patrol dog.

The letter lay on the corner of the kitchen table while they finished eating. Angolo lay down in his basket when he learned that no more salmon was coming. Roland hoped she would forget about the letter so he could hide it while she stacked the dishwasher, but unfortunately, Irene had an excellent memory. "Here," she said, handing it to him as soon as he had emptied his plate.

Roland opened the letter again. He had read it many times to make sure he understood it all. Then he suddenly folded it, distributed the last of the white wine between their glasses, and looked at her. "I want to tell you what it says instead. You know Giovanna. She says things so . . . direct."

Irene drank from the glass and looked intently at him. It was how they usually conducted themselves. Talk to each other about everything, worries and joys. But why so hesitant on this topic? He cleared his throat. "She wrote that Salvatore got a job," he began.

"Well, that's great for him. It's not so easy to get a job in Naples. But isn't he only fourteen years old?"

"He just turned fifteen. But it's not so much that. He should be in school, but he doesn't want to go anymore."

He was silent for a long time, deep in thought. Irene waited impatiently. She ran her index finger up and down the stem of the wine glass.

"Do you remember when we rented a car and drove to the area of Giugliano and Villaricca?"

Irene's facial expression changed. She nodded.

"You remember, Giovanna called it the *land of bonfires*, because the clans make the Romani boys burn the rubbish for a fee when the landfills are full? Money that poor families desperately need."

She nodded again and drank more wine.

Roland took a sip, too, before continuing. "There are over forty landfills in that area. Several of them for disposing hazardous waste. The soil is so poisoned that it's infertile. It makes landowners sell, and who do you think are willing buyers?" He didn't wait for her answer, didn't even look at her but instead down at the empty plate. "Once the mafia buys it, they make more landfills, and so it goes on and on. The soil contains copper, arsenic, mercury, lead, nickel, and other metals—waste from the chemical industry and hospitals in northern Italy, who have paid the 'garbage' mafia to get rid of it. Why is it so clean in Tuscany?" he exclaimed indignantly.

Angolo raised his head when Roland raised his voice. Both ears stood straight up in the air for once. Roland glanced at him briefly and continued. "Those who live in the area die of cancer, women miscarry or give birth to malformed children. Seventeen years ago, an episode with a truck driver led to the first investigation of the rubbish mafia. He'd had an accident with a lid on a barrel of rubbish that had popped open. The fumes from the barrel were enough to give him swollen eyes and corrode his skin. He went blind. Today, most drivers refuse the route. Those who do take it won't empty the trailer the barrels are transported on. They want to be free from having to go near them. They leave that to others. They're not old enough to have a driving licence yet, so they get lessons while waiting for the next load of rubbish—they're only fourteen and fifteen years old."

Roland's voice had become hoarse, and water welled in his eyes when he looked at Irene. It started running down his nose. Irene took his hand, wanting to say something.

"That's the kind of work Salvatore is making money on," he continued once he'd gained control of his voice. "The children get the equivalent of a couple of thousand kroner for each trip they take with the deadly cargo, and the more they breathe the fumes, the closer they get to death."

"How did La Camorra get hold of him?"

Roland put his hand up to his face and wiped his cheeks with both hands. "Giovanna thinks they contacted him and his friends at the bar where they usually meet after school."

"Yeah, but has Giovanna not explained to Salvatore how dangerous it is? That he'll end up dying from it?"

He shook his head in hopelessness. "Of course she has, but it bounces off him. He just feels even more significant doing a dangerous job that no one else—not even adults—wants to deal with. We die somehow anyway, he had told her." Roland suddenly got up. It was all so hard to deal with sitting down. He went to the window and leaned on the kitchen table, as if he had a pain in him, and looked out into the darkness. Out into the other chaos.

Irene got up, too, put her arms around him, and laid her cheek against his back. He closed his eyes. "What the hell am I supposed to do, Irene? Giovanna wants me to help."

"You have to be able to do something," she whispered into his shirt.

He straightened up and turned to face her. "But what! What the hell can *I* do?"

"You're their family, Rolando. Soon the last of the men in the family left. Of course she's come to you. Families help each other, don't they? But why did she write—why didn't she just call like she usually does?"

"The letter was sent from a tourist hotel that takes the guests' post to the post office. It's also fourteen days late. God only knows what's happened in the meantime. She fears being bugged. The *System* has eyes and ears everywhere."

"Don't call them the System, okay!"

"They call themselves the System!"

"That's what I mean," Irene said. "How does Aunt Giovanna think you can help?"

Roland waved his arms theatrically. "Probably by coming home to finish my father's work. But I can't, Irene. I just can't!"

Angolo ran restlessly around their feet, yapping.

"She asked if we would take Salvatore for a while. Get him away from that environment. She hopes I can talk him out of it."

He knew it didn't suit Irene, and it was precisely this conversation that he hadn't looked forward to. "We can't, of course, but Giovanna asked and is waiting for an answer."

Irene squatted down next to Angolo, who jumped up on her and licked her face. "But what about school? He should be in school at his age."

"He's dropped out. What boy is going to go to school when he can earn the same as two thousand kroner to drive a single truckload. And it's fun for a lad his age, too. Think about how much he could earn in one day. Not many jobs in Naples pay that well, even if you study for years."

Irene lovingly pushed the dog down and got up again. "What does he say to it? Does he even want to come to Denmark?"

"Giovanna believes she can persuade him. She's going to try to come up with something he won't suspect. But we can't do it, Irene. We have our jobs, and we can't . . ."

"Don't you think it's about time you did something for the family, Rolando? If it can help Salvatore, then he should stay with us for a while! I have holidays that I can take whenever I want, and your murder cases have been solved, so your long workdays are over. Ring Giovanna tomorrow and tell her."

She started to clear the table and stack the dishwasher. He took the letter into his study. Angolo followed right on his heels and lay on the floor in front of his feet while he read the other letters—the letters written by Louise Engtoft. There were lots of them. It was going to be a long night while the hurricane raged.

52

By Friday morning, the wind had died down. It was completely unreal that the day before had been the great showdown by which nature had taken revenge on humans. Only rubbish that had been blown around the streets wasn't completely under control yet, but the clean-up was well underway thanks to the people in orange reflective vests. Kamilla parked in the yard and hurried up the stairs to the paper's offices.

Britt was in. So, she'd recovered conveniently enough just before the weekend. She hadn't lost any weight at all, so it probably wasn't Thygesen who had infected her. She was in the process of making morning coffee; its aroma filled the entire office.

"Good morning," Kamilla shouted as she took off her coat and scarf. "So, you're all better."

Britt looked up from behind the coffee machine and smiled. "Yeah, it took ages"—her smile faded—"but I mustn't complain. How are you? I heard about your mother . . ."

Kamilla sat down and turned on her computer. "We weren't very close, so it's not so bad," she lied.

Anne blustered in with loud sighs and apologies and hung her coat up on the rack. "Shit and shit! Sabrina Dahl has disappeared without a trace, and her friend handed over all the letters to Benito!"

"What letters?" asked Britt.

Anne stopped abruptly. "Oh, so someone found their way back to their chair. Are you all better now?"

Britt was offended by the sarcastic tone, but Anne was in the mood to quarrel, so she kept going. "If you don't do your job, you can't keep up with what's going on, and updating you will take most of the day, so you'll have to wait until the morning meeting!"

Kamilla thought Anne a little unfair, but she also knew saying something wouldn't lead to peace.

"What happened yesterday that you wanted to tell me? Where did your car get stuck?" she asked. Britt could listen along.

Anne turned on the computer and threw herself into her chair. She pulled a black knitted hat, which she almost forgot she was wearing, off her head and threw it up on the coat-rack. It stayed there, but it seemed more from luck than precision. She swooped into Thygesen's empty office and straightened her hair. "Don't tell me he's sick again?"

"He's coming in later," Britt said from behind her screen. "Something about the hurricane last night he had to look at."

"Tell me now, Anne. What happened yesterday?"

Anne told her about the visit to Pernille Lauritzen, about the newspaper where Sabrina had scribbled down an address next to the picture Kamilla had taken of Sebastian, about the cottage, the fact that she had to dig the car free of the sand—she held out her fingers, which were covered in cuts and blisters—and about the little snakeskin notebook she had found in a drawer. She laid the book on the table and had started flipping through it when Thygesen came in with a surprisingly cheerful *good morning* and *welcome back* to Britt. Shortly afterwards, Nicolaj and Mads Dam turned up. The force was united.

"We're having a morning meeting!" announced Thygesen, going into his office. That meant putting mugs on the table and pouring coffee into insulated pots. Just as well Britt was back.

The meeting started with a dressing-down for Anne for not attending the press conference at the police station. Then it was about the devastation from the hurricane—a pig truck had been overturned, killing several pigs while others were left scurrying around the area, and an overturned mast that meant Djursland was still without power. Then came a summary of the press conference. Thygesen returned to Anne's absence and wanted to know where she had been. She told it all again and took out the notebook.

"Wouldn't the police have an interest in it, if it is Knud Engtoft who owns that house?" asked Nicolaj.

"Maybe, but they have something that we should get hold of in return—the letters from the nursing assistant. Sabrina Dahl's friend handed them over to the inspector yesterday. And Sabrina herself has disappeared. There are indications that she is with the son, Sebastian," replied Anne. That got Thygesen's attention.

"What the bloody hell are you saying! Why didn't you tell me such an important thing before now! Did you get it on the front page?" He looked angrily at the day's newspaper.

Kamilla looked worriedly at Anne. She was easy to provoke today, and a serious quarrel between her and Thygesen wouldn't be a pretty sight. But Anne pulled herself together and answered ingratiatingly instead. "That sort of thing shouldn't be read about in the paper, Thygesen. We should be talking about how we're going to approach it. There's not much to write about. There was no trace of Sabrina at the cottage, so she mustn't have gone out there, and I have no idea what is in that book." She pointed to the notebook.

Thygesen flipped through it. "It's an African language, I think. Swahili, maybe."

Nicolaj leaned in over his arm to look. "It is. We had an assignment about East Africa at journalism school. I did a report on the dialects of the language." He smiled proudly.

"Maybe you can translate it then?" said Thygesen, handing him the book.

Nicolaj laughed and shook his head. "No, I only learned a few words. The funny ones and the ones that are easy to remember. Like *hujambo* means hello, *simba*—like the lion cub in Disney's *The Lion King*—means lion, and *daktari* means doctor; it's not that difficult."

Kamilla took the book and looked at it. She'd never seen Swahili before, so she couldn't make heads nor tails of it.

"What did you say *doctor* is?" Anne looked at Nicolaj, who repeated the word with a quiet shake of his head as if to imply the word wasn't that difficult to remember.

"*Daktari.*"

"It says it here and here and . . . !"

Anne tore the book out of her hands and stared at the page. "Where?"

"There!" Kamilla pointed.

"It says something about a doctor in the text. Which doctor? Dr. Winther or Dr. Vangberg!"

"Try to get a translator." Thygesen got up and looked at his watch. "I have a meeting in a little while. You're taking this, Anne. We need to know more about Sabrina Dahl, too. Take Nicolaj with you. Do you have anything on today, Mads?"

Mads Dam didn't seem fully awake yet—the hurricane probably meant he hadn't slept, as his family lived in an old house just outside Rønde. "I have a handball match I need to rewrite and some digital photos that need to be touched up, too." He looked tired to Kamilla. "Afterwards, I'm going out to NRGi Park to get a grip on the badminton league showdown and Aarhus Elite Badminton's young talents."

Thygesen nodded contentedly. "And, Britt? Do you have something to work on now that you're back after your illness?"

"Yeah, I'm going to a kindergarten to hear more about a meal plan that the parents are very opposed to. I'll finish my article about that."

"Good! Let's get started!" Thygesen put on his coat and quickly disappeared out the door. Anne and Nicolaj did the same. Mads Dam sat half asleep finishing his article. Kamilla went to the Danish National Register's website to find information on where to go when she went out to the parish office. They should be able to tell her where her father lived based on the name and address in the transcript from the church register. Mads Dam asked for the pictures for his article. Processing them took only five minutes. She sent them to his email. Shortly afterwards, he took his coat and announced he was going to NRGi Park. Kamilla nodded and assured him she'd answer the phones. As soon as he was out the door, she called the national register. It cost fifty-two kroner to get an address. There was a lot she had to get done before closing time, so there would be no overtime today.

53

Nicolaj sat flipping through the notebook eagerly. Anne reminded him authoritatively about the seat belt, which he absently put on without taking his eyes off the book. "Where can we find an translator who knows Swahili?" he mumbled.

Anne turned the key. It took a while before the engine started. She regretted not asking if she could take Kamilla's Suzuki. Was tempted to just "borrow" it, but Kamilla might have a photo assignment. Mads Dam or Thygesen might need her. "That's not our priority," she replied, reversing the car out of the yard. The car hit an overturned bin with a bang that made passers-by turn around and look at the yellow Lada. Anne pushed down the accelerator and drove out onto Frederiks Allé far too fast. Looking in the rear-view mirror, Anne spotted an elderly woman shaking her head. Anne gave her the finger in the mirror, but it was mostly for Nicolaj's sake. Fortunately, the woman didn't see it.

"So, what are you doing—a Lewis Hamilton impersonation?" he joked.

"If you don't like it, you could always get out and walk?"

"No, you're fine. It's just that, oddly enough, I don't have a death wish."

Anne sent him a menacing look but slowed down a little. "We're going to Skæring. I want to investigate something at the cottage—I didn't get to do it because of the storm. There's a shed behind the house that we have to look at."

A light immediately went on in Nicolaj's eyes. "Do you think Sabrina is being held captive there?"

Anne shook her head with certainty. "No, I don't think Sabrina went out to the cottage at all."

"Could she have gone back to her husband in Italy?"

"I strongly doubt that. But who knows?"

They drove without talking until she turned off at Skæring Havvej and continued along Strandvangsvej.

"Wow, it's beautiful here," Nicolaj exclaimed blissfully, admiring the Kalø Vig cove. Djursland was hidden in the haze on the opposite side of the water. It looked grey and cold.

"Who do you think owns the cottage?"

"I tried to find out last night but couldn't find any owner—maybe there's something in the shed that can tell us."

"Do you think the police could tell us?"

"The police!" Anne looked angrily at his profile. "Why do you always want to get the police involved in our work?"

"Because . . . because I thought crime reporters worked closely with the police. Am I wrong?"

"Definitely! The police don't tell journalists anything, and we don't tell them anything!"

"Competition, then?"

They arrived. Anne got out of the car without answering. That Roland Benito had fooled her was still a delicate subject, but if that's how he wanted to play it!

This time, having learned from experience, she hadn't driven all the way up to the house but had parked by the road. It didn't look anything like it did when she'd been there the day before. The sea was still now, and everything was peaceful. Even the birds were chirping in a playful spring-like way in the treetops.

"How far is it?" asked Nicolaj, after they'd been walking for a while.

"It's the house up there on the slope." She pointed.

"The little shack!"

The hurricane had torn some of the sheet metal off the roof and over-turned the empty bin; it lay halfway in between the trees.

"It looks completely empty. The hurricane took its toll last night. A window's broken."

"Yeah, bloody weather," mumbled Anne. "Let's go up to the shed."

The sand was wet, and it was difficult to get a foothold on the slope up to the shed. It was quite sheltered, so there wasn't much noticeable damage. Nicolaj was occupied with looking in through the windows of the cottage and came rushing after her. Suddenly, she saw him fall. She laughed at how comical it looked, but grew uneasy when she didn't see him get up again. She couldn't see him because of the slope. When she went down there, he was on all fours trying to remove a cover.

"What the hell are you doing?" She ran up to him and almost fell herself.

"I fell over this cover; it wasn't put on properly. I think there's something down there. I heard something. It sounded like a splash."

"It's probably just some stones that were dumped there. Did you hurt yourself?"

"No, no. Help me!"

They both took hold and dragged the cover away. There wasn't much light down there, but Anne had learned something from the previous night's episode. "I'll get a torch from the car," she said and was gone in a flash.

Nicolaj tried to peer down into the darkness. He thought he could see something moving. A rat, maybe. It smelled of shit, so it could be a sewer.

"Is anyone down there?" he yelled.

There was a faint splash again, and something that sounded like a tiny voice.

"Hello!" he shouted, standing up. He felt like an idiot. If anyone saw him . . . He looked around, but there wasn't a soul to be seen. The summer cottage was deserted. If Sabrina had been here, no one would have noticed. That thought brought him back to his knees. "Sabrina!" he yelled. "Is that you down there?" He heard a faint sob. That was no rat. It sounded like someone almost drowning. Where the hell was Anne with the torch!

"Sabrina! Give me a sign if it's you." He thought about what she could do if she was so weak she could not answer. "Cough, if it's you!"

Some time passed, then a faint cough came from the darkness, and a splash again. "Stay there, Sabrina. My name is Nicolaj, and I'm here to help you. Hold on, I'm going to call the police." He rummaged in his pocket for his phone and could hardly hold it as he dialled the number for the police station. He asked to speak to Detective Inspector Roland Benito.

Afterwards, he knelt down and talked to Sabrina. He didn't know whether she could hear him, but she just needed to know he was still here and that help was on the way. If only it wasn't too late. As long as it wasn't too late. She was so quiet now.

He saw Anne come running with the torch. "What are you doing— are you talking to rats?" she teased, laughing breathlessly as she handed him the light. "It could just be a cat that got blown down there," she continued.

Nicolaj tore the torch out of her hand. "It's Sabrina!" he said, visibly moved. "Hopefully she'll make it. I've called the police; I hope they will be here soon with an ambulance."

"What have you done! Why did you call the police, you idiot! Do you realise the story here, if it really is her? It's huge! Entire front-page news on every newspaper, and we'll be the first—or we could have been! Now every other reporter is going to come running, too. You idiot! You big idiot!"

Nicolaj gave her a stinging slap, and she immediately fell silent and put her hand on her cheek. It had been a long time since anyone had hit her. Not since her stepfather had . . . Tears welled in her eyes, and her anger grew, but Nicolaj's gaze made her keep quiet. She didn't know those green eyes could hold so much seriousness.

"What kind of a reporter are you? If that's how reporters work, then I don't want to be one! Is it so long since you were in journalism college? Where the fuck is your compassion?"

It wasn't so much the words as the way they were said. She sank quietly to her knees next to him. The sirens could be heard in the distance. They kept coming closer.

Nicolaj shone the torch around in the tank. At first, they saw only rust-coloured water, then they spotted something that resembled a face. Sabrina was struggling to keep her eyes, nose, and mouth above the water. A few more millimetres of rain and she wouldn't have made it. Once in a while, her face disappeared completely under the water, but the survival instinct made her nose and mouth resurface again with a convulsive jerk. Every time she moved, the water splashed up her nose. Panic shone out of her eyes that didn't look at all human.

"How long has she been fighting for her life like that?" whispered Anne, so Nicolaj could barely hear her. "Why doesn't she just sit up?"

"She probably can't."

Suddenly, the area was teeming with police and emergency responders, who brutally pulled them out of the way and set about getting the woman out of the tank.

54

When Roland got the call from the intern, he tried all morning to get hold of Anne Larsen at the newspaper's offices. At first no one answered the phone, then he got hold of the photographer who didn't know where Anne was. When he saw her now, standing with the emergency responders by a stretcher, he almost felt like shaking her vigorously. He had read all the letters during the night, and if she knew anything about them, she should be quarantined. Although the letters weren't that useful, they did show where the nursing assistant had lived before she was murdered. If that helped at all. He began to relax. Perhaps those letters weren't of any benefit to the case at all. But what did she know about Sabrina's disappearance? There was something about a newspaper and a picture. But he didn't want to make a scene here, so when he arrived, he just stared at her angrily and said nothing.

DS Mikkel Jensen had contacted Gustav Hjort, who was standing by the stretcher, squeezing his daughter's hand. So, it was her they'd found in the tank. What the hell was going on?

He showed his badge and shook hands with Gustav Hjort, whom he hadn't greeted before.

"It *is* her," he said tearfully. Roland nodded.

"Do you have any idea what she was doing out here in that weather?"

Gustav Hjort shook his head and desperately followed the paramedics' attempt to bring his daughter back to life. Roland discreetly withdrew and asked Jensen to look in the house and shed to see if there was anything that could tell them who owned it. He turned and was about to walk back when Anne approached.

"I think it's Knud Engtoft's summer cottage—or maybe his son's," she said.

"And why do you think that?"

"Because the bedroom is full of African sculptures—and I found this there. It probably requires a Swahili translator—if you can get one." She handed the notebook with the snakeskin cover to him, but when he went to take it, she withdrew it. He knew that look.

"Okay, if there's something in it, you're given the exclusive rights to the story."

She gave him the book.

Nicolaj sent her a big smile.

"So, you've been inside the house? Usually, we call that B and E," said Roland grimly as he started to walk. She followed.

"No, it's not, because the storm smashed a window."

"It's still B and E! Pernille Lauritzen told me something about a newspaper with a picture and an address. Don't you think it's time you helped us a little?"

Anne capitulated and told him the entire story as they walked back to the cottage together. It was crowded with police.

Gustav walked next to the stretcher carrying Sabrina, who was taken up to the ambulance by two paramedics. They'd managed to get her to regain consciousness and had given her an oxygen mask, but they needed to get her to the hospital urgently.

Mikkel came running back from the shed. "The door was locked, so we broke it open. There's nothing in there but old junk. A rusty bicycle, old sun loungers, garden furniture, and cardboard boxes containing letters and papers."

"Go through it all anyway."

Mikkel nodded and went into the cottage to join the others.

Roland took out the phone that was playing the James Bond 007 tune in his pocket. It was DS Kim Ansager confirming that the house was owned by Sebastian Juhl.

"And where is he now?" Roland listened with a frown.

"Send out an APB—right away!" He folded the phone and put it back in his pocket. Anne Larsen looked at him curiously, but he didn't say anything.

"Do you know where they're taking Sabrina Dahl?" she asked gently.

He stopped and turned towards her abruptly. "Now you listen here. You—" He corrected himself when he caught sight of Nicolaj just behind her. "You have to let us come first. Stay away from the hospital until I allow you to talk to her. Is that understood?" He didn't raise his voice, but his seriousness was crystal clear. His eyes were pitch black.

She entered his office immediately, as though he had summoned her. He needed to discuss the case with someone who possessed female intuition. And maybe he also needed to see her. Something about her gaze and her smile touched his vanity. He felt attractive when she looked at him the way she did now, from the door. "Come in, Isabella. Mercifully, I have received more important information from the reporter, so we have more to work with. Sit down. I'd like to hear your opinion. Coffee—water?"

"Coffee, please." She sat down and waited quietly while he poured the coffee. He also needed something hot after the trip on the cold strand.

"So, it was Sabrina Dahl who fell into the tank?"

Roland warmed his hands on the mug. "It was her, yes, but did she *fall* in? Why was the cover put back on? I think she was meant to drown there. Be found like his mother."

"His mother? You mean Sebastian Juhl's?"

"Yes, I mean Sebastian. It's his summer cottage, and according to the address Sabrina wrote on the newspaper next to his picture, they had agreed to meet there."

Isabella turned the mug between her fingers. Her nails were long and had a white border. A French manicure. He moved restlessly on the chair— the way her finger caressed the mug gave him strange sensations he didn't need right now.

"Wouldn't it be very natural for them to contact each other in the circumstances? Both of their mothers died shortly after each other in the same city. How did Sabrina's mother actually die?"

"Long-term illness. Cancer," he replied.

Luckily for Roland, she stopped caressing the mug and crossed her arms, but it made her chest lift. Roland looked away. The sun was shining, highlighting all the dirt the hurricane had blown up on the windowpane. You could hardly see out.

"Dr. Vangberg was also Josefine Hjort's doctor. There were some papers from Dr. Ole Winther in between the letters that Pernille Lauritzen brought. He noted that Helge Vangberg took over the treatment in December 1983. What does that tell you?" He looked at her again.

"That it all has something to do with the Hjort family. Is Dr. Winther dead, too?"

"Yes, though of natural causes. Old age."

"Thank God for that. But what about the waitress, Annemette Knudsen. She's the only one who doesn't fit in."

Roland smiled grimly. "Yep, she fits in as well; Anne Larsen was gracious enough to tell me how. She was the nursing assistant's old friend from the nightclub where she worked before she became a nursing assistant."

Isabella got up and stood by the window with her mug and her back to him. "So that means Sebastian Juhl must have known her, too—and maybe the doctor as well? Why didn't he mention it?"

"Maybe because we haven't talked to him as much as we should have," Roland replied. It was a huge mistake, he sensed now. They had simply not been thorough enough.

"Maybe they met in Africa—did we check that out?" She turned slowly enough for him to avert his gaze and look her in the eye.

"I have just received that information, but that is actually what I would like to ask you to investigate. We need to know when both Helge Vangberg and Sebastian Juhl were there and where they stayed. If Jensen is bored, he can help you find out who to contact. We also need to get the text in this notebook translated. It's Swahili. The journalist found it in a drawer in the cottage. Maybe it contains important information, too." He handed her the book, relieved that Anne Larsen hadn't got that far, which no doubt was her intention had they not found Sabrina.

"I hate snakes," she said, accepting it, an expression of disgust all over her face. Their hands touched in the process, and he again got the feeling that it wasn't accidental.

"The creature is dead." He smiled.

"I hope so," she replied, carrying it out between two fingers.

"And Isabella . . ." he said before she reached the door. She immediately turned around.

"Yes?"

"Will you also check up on how things are going with the search for Sebastian?"

"Of course. Anything for you." She closed the door with a small smile, and he hoped she didn't notice him blush.

When he was alone, his brain was once again able to focus on the case without distractions. He had to pull himself together. She was nearly thirty years younger than him, and he loved Irene. But what if it was possible? Just to try it once. How would it feel? Her smooth young skin and firm breasts, her hands, lips, tongue. Blood throbbed in all his limbs, and he breathed a sigh of relief when the phone rang—until he heard what Chief Superintendent Kurt Olsen had to say.

55

Anne Larsen was being reprimanded again in Ivan Thygesen's office. They could see the pair through the window but couldn't hear what was being said even though there was shouting. Thygesen was red in the face and had to stop his tirade from time to time to cough, which made him even angrier.

"What happened?" she asked, looking nervously at Nicolaj.

He smiled. "Nothing, Kamilla, other than Anne Larsen for once behaving like a proper journalist and passing on important information to the police."

Kamilla looked at the two adversaries again. Now it was Anne moving her mouth. Strangely enough, that made Thygesen close his for a moment. She focused on her screen. Just before noon, she had to go out because Mads had asked her to take photos of some young badminton talents in NRGi Park. Now they were photo-edited and cropped and ready for the sports journalist whenever he returned. There had to be time for a Friday beer before the regular pub first.

Luckily, she was soon finished so she could drive to the parish office. The decision to contact her father had been tossed back and forth throughout the day. For and against. Pros and cons. What if he didn't know of her existence or didn't want to—how would she react to that rejection?

Finally, Anne came out of the lion's den. Kamilla quickly looked up at her as she walked past, and afterwards at Thygesen, who had thrown himself into his work. She could only see his comb-over and still bright-red forehead above the computer screen. Anne winked at her, so she didn't seem upset at the reprimand. She was getting used to it, but Thygesen's anger was no joke. Nicolaj smiled at Anne and gave her a thumbs up. Anne squeezed his shoulder as she walked past him into the kitchen for coffee. Kamilla sensed that something had happened between them out in the field, but Anne certainly wouldn't confide in her.

"Good, Sabrina has been found. How is she doing?" she asked, and even Britt, who had been sulking since coming back from the kindergarten, looked up with interest from her keyboard.

"We're not to talk to her until Roland Benito contacts us. But I hope she makes it so she can tell us who threw her in that tank. What a disgusting place to end up. Amazing she survived. The water was splashing down all night. To think I was so close to her without knowing it yesterday afternoon."

"Didn't she drown?" Britt asked doubtfully.

"It was close. Wasn't it, Nicolaj?"

"Yeah, she only had a few minutes of strength left to keep her head above water. She hit her back on the fall and couldn't move very much."

"No, it was good you found her, Nicolaj. You are the hero of the day." Anne toasted him with her plastic cup.

Kamilla sent the pictures to Mads Dam's email, shut the computer down, and got up. She drank the last drop of her cold coffee and tossed the cup into the bin before putting on her coat.

"Is it *so* late!" muttered Britt, beginning to turn off her computer and pack up. Anne and Nicolaj still had a lot to do. It was food for thought that the crime reporters were the busiest at the paper.

"Have a good weekend!" Kamilla shouted, jogging down the stairs. She would have to rush to make it to the parish office in Horsens and the civil register before they closed.

A roof tile had fallen from her old house on Mejlbyvej during the night. The trees hadn't provided enough shelter despite there being many of them around the yard. She picked up the roof tile and put it in the garage. She couldn't immediately see where it came from. She would have to get a roofer out to look at it soon. If her father happened to turn out to be a roofer, then . . . She smiled at the thought, but the smile slowly died. She really needed a man in her life. Not only because of the practical things—some men weren't so handy. Jan had been one of them. He couldn't hit a nail. Danny? He had restored his old apartment in Klampenborg and had probably also done a lot himself in renovating the advertising agency on Badstuegade.

Tired, she threw herself on the sofa. The tension had been released. She was empty inside and even more in doubt about what she should do. Now she knew who her father was. Her *real* father. She had immediately looked at the copy from the church register when she received it. *Father: Mogens Arnskov Aagaard. Born 1946 in Agger* it said under *Parents* along with the name of her mother. She had breathed a sigh of relief. He wasn't registered as unknown. Addresses at the time of birth were stated for them both. The address they provided in the civil register was, to her surprise, not too far away. She had expected it to be in North or West Jutland, but he lived in Bønnerup in Djursland. He was a fisherman, which didn't surprise her. But why did he live in Djursland? She looked through the papers again. He had also lived in Horsens for a while, had moved there in the late 1970s, shortly after her mother had moved from Agger. Had he been following her? Had he given up on her when she married Henning Holm? Their romantic relationship began to take shape in her head, giving her hope and a little more courage. If that was the case, then her father had really wanted a life with her mother. Maybe he knew about his daughter and wanted to do the only right thing—marry the mother of his child. But why had he not done more about it? Probably because Gloria had rejected him, hateful as she was. But he could still have tried to contact his daughter. It had been easy enough to find him—he could just as easily have found her. It was probably best to forget him. Now, at least, she knew who he was and where he lived.

She went to the wine rack and got a bottle. Finally, she could open a "Friday wine," but was there anything to celebrate other than the weekend? As she opened it, she scowled at the papers and was again left in doubt as to whether she should contact the man who had suddenly become her father. Was it too late to have a dad? Didn't you need a father most as a child?

She had spent the previous two evenings emptying her mother's apartment. Her things had testified to the sad life she had lived for many years. A lonely cup in the kitchen sink, an almost empty refrigerator, no hidden letters, postcards, or invitations from friends, acquaintances—or family.

Kamilla had a knot in her stomach and a lump in her throat the entire time. She had to take several breaks as she looked at things that set memories in motion. Things Gloria had saved. But there wasn't anything connected to her. No shared memories. There was the cross that had always hung over her mother's bed and the Bible that had its fixed place on the bedside table under the lamp. As she flipped through it, consumed with thoughts, a black-and-white image fell to the floor. It was curled as if it had been clenched by a hand. The little boy was fair-haired and was wearing a knitted jumper. He was standing on the deck of a cutter with green fishing nets and buckets around him. He was probably about six or seven years old. Maybe the picture had been taken the year he'd disappeared into the sea. Had Gloria taken it? The boy was laughing. Kamilla felt the tears and hurried to finish the clean-up. She stuck the picture in her pocket.

She sat down on the sofa with the glass of wine. Just needed to unwind for a moment and get a handle on her emotions. She took a sip of wine and left it in her mouth until it began to sting her tongue; she swallowed. It was a strong wine that had a good aftertaste. She leaned her head against the back of the sofa and closed her eyes. This was where they had been sitting when they'd got together a few years ago. She felt Danny's hand slide behind her neck and his kiss again. That night could be tonight—she remembered it so clearly. All his movements, his touches, and his words. Even those he hadn't said. She sat up and drank again. Rasmus's eyes looked at her over the football in the picture on the bookshelf. The hatred flared up again and burned more than the wine. "Sorry, Rasmus," she mumbled. "I hate him, too. And Mum. And Majken. And the ring on his finger."

She poured more wine when the glass was empty and saw Tarzan sneak in through the cat flap. Shortly afterwards, she heard him crunching his food. *The lord of the house,* she thought with a little ironic smile. She took her mobile and stared at it for a long time. Took another sip of wine and gathered her courage. Then she dialled the number listed under the address.

It rang for a long time. Very long. She was about to hang up and felt strangely relieved, then came a voice, just as she was about to end the call.

"Alice Arnskov Aagaard," came the voice in a neutral tone. Children talked and laughed in the background.

"Hello, who is it?"

Kamilla hung up. It was a possibility she hadn't even thought of. Of course he was married and had his own family.

56

___

The fire crackled in the open fireplace. Every time he threw something in there, embers jumped towards the spark catcher. He poked the fire and threw more on. The cardboard box stood on the floor between his feet, and his movements were monotonous and indifferent. His gaze was hypnotically bound by the flames. He didn't look at the letters as he reached down into the box and threw them into the fireplace one at a time. They disappeared without a trace, absorbed by the fire. He felt rather than heard her come in and sit down next to him. He didn't even turn his head and look at her as she caressed his neck. He smelled her perfume, and his heart shrivelled even more.

"You're sure there are no more, right?"

He nodded.

"Nobody saw, did they?"

He shook his head. "No, they were all occupied in the house."

"Good, you heard about them. Have you read them?"

"No, why should I? I know what they say. You know how much Elina hated us."

"But still. Aren't you just a little curious, Gustav?" She reached down into the box, wanting to pick one up, but he grabbed her wrist hard and squeezed until she let go. For the first time since returning from the hospital, he looked her in the eye.

"Leave it, Carola. It will all be over in a little while. I have to go to the police."

"Of course you don't have to. What kind of nonsense is that? How is Sabrina?"

"It looks like *she* made it." He sat for a long time, throwing several letters into the flames without saying anything.

Finally, he said, "Did you know Sabrina was pregnant?"

"Pregnant! Good God, Peter will get a shock. He doesn't want a child now; he has his career, and . . . she can have a . . ."

"She lost it."

His voice was so full of emotion that she looked at him in surprise. She wrapped an arm around his and laid her cheek against it as she looked up at his impassive face, which had a warm glow from the flames. But they weren't the only thing making his eyes so shiny.

"It's the best thing for them," she said quietly. "You know that, too."

He nodded. The last letter. He pulled his arm from her and folded up the cardboard box, then threw it into the flames as well. The fire flared up violently, and they sat in silence, staring into it until it calmed down again.

"I asked Johanne to come in here with tea. Don't you need it?"

He kissed her hand. "Yes, darling."

"We did the right thing back then," she whispered into his ear.

"Did we, Carola? Are you sure?"

"Josefine wouldn't have survived anyway. Maybe only a few more months, but . . . We did her a favour. The greatest thing you can do for someone."

"Perhaps the treatment Ole Winther was trying would have helped. We don't know. They can cure cancer patients today—maybe with that exact treatment."

"You know what Helge Vangberg said. He was our family doctor for years. He knows—knew—what he was talking about. It was only for the good that you replaced Winther. You must never, ever doubt that."

"Well, the home c—"

"She threatened us, Gustav. It was self-defence; I couldn't do anything else. It was her or us. We should have done the same with him, so . . ."

Gustav thought it was useless to say any more and stopped her by raising his hand. She was silent for a while.

"Do you think he read the letters? The son?" she asked.

"Sebastian—without a doubt. Why else would he store them for so long? Old letters to his mother from an old crone."

"Elina was not so old, Gustav." She shook his arm teasingly.

"He tried to murder my daughter."

"Do you really think he could do that; he was just a little snot-nosed kid back then. What would he have against Sabrina?"

"Revenge, Carola. I think it's all about revenge. Sabrina was how he could get to me, to us. The past always catches up with you; you can't run from it—or keep it hidden."

He got up and put the poker back in the companion set, then straightened his back and looked her in the eye. She was beautiful, sitting there in the glow of the fire. Her hair shone like golden silver, and though wrinkles hid in her tanned skin, he didn't see them. She was the one he had done everything for. She was the one he had built his entire life around. But had he forgotten his own daughter in the process? How would she feel about him now? She would hate him. Just as much as—no, probably even more than—she hated her stepmother.

"As soon as we have drunk our tea, I'll drive to the police station. Isn't the Italian leading the investigation?"

"Stop, Gustav!" She pulled him back down on the bench in front of the fireplace. Johanne came in with tea. She set up a small table next to them and wished them a good evening and weekend. Carola had given her time off. They weren't going to be home, either. She had booked a weekend away for two in Paris, but . . .

She put both hands around his face and forced him to look her in the eyes. "Listen, my love. It's all over now. It's over. Finished. We did it! That revolting man is in prison. It won't take long before they have the son, too. Who'd believe them? Common criminals. No one can touch us now! And we haven't done anything wrong!"

He was embarrassed by the tears. It was the first time he'd revealed himself like that to her. He knew she took tears as a sign of weakness.

"Yes, but, money . . ." he began.

"I *closed* the account. It no longer exists and never did. Everything has gone exactly as it should. It only gets better from here."

He couldn't look her in the eye and hid his face in her chest like a little boy wanting to be comforted. She stroked his hair.

She was always right. So why shouldn't she be right now, too?

57

Roland hadn't said anything to anyone about the development in the case, and neither had he changed the agreed meeting at the end of the day. He didn't want his staff to work less thoroughly or maybe even give up completely for that reason. He could feel how it affected him; all the energy was evaporating out of him. That wasn't to happen to everyone. The conversation that had just ended, first with Kurt Olsen and then the commissioner of the National Danish Police hadn't re-energised him. On the contrary. He clicked his pen nervously. The window was open even though he was freezing, just so he could breathe. The pane was as filthy as the sky. The wind had died down, but bad weather was definitely on the way. Rain or snow—maybe a new storm. He hadn't heard the weather forecast in ages.

Three knocks on the door—Kim's signature—made him straighten up in his chair and look resolute.

"The translator is here with the book," Kim said softly.

"That was fast. Yes, send him in."

He closed the window. Maybe there was still hope no matter what the commissioner of the National Danish Police and Kurt Olsen said. There was something that didn't add up. That was why it was so important that he kept the pot boiling for as long as he could. It wouldn't last for long, so work would have to be done quickly.

The translator was a tall man with glasses and more stubble than Roland, but it wasn't as visible on his almost black skin. He hung his camel-coloured wool coat over the chair and presented himself as Said Hashi from southern Somalia. He had been living in Denmark since 1992 and was training as a computer scientist at Aarhus University. He spoke four languages, so he worked as a translator alongside his studies. His Danish wasn't entirely without an accent, but it was very correct in both grammar and pronunciation. He sat down and rolled up the sleeves of his chalk-white shirt. Roland felt immediate sympathy for him. He judged him to be in his late twenties. He had heard from Irene that many Somalis dropped out of school prematurely to work and send money home to their families instead—that's if they didn't end up unemployed.

"It's the skin of a *Python sebae*, also called the African rock python, and in Danish, rock python. Very beautiful, isn't it?" He slid his long fingers caressingly over the skin of the notebook. Roland nodded and offered coffee.

Said turned to the first page and read the text first in Swahili, then he translated it. "*Kila lenye mwanzo halikosi kuwa na mwisho*—everything that begins must also come to an end."

Roland looked admiringly at Said, who put his lips to the mug.

"What does that mean?"

"Not much. It's just an old Swahili saying. The next word is much more interesting." He flipped through and spoke Swahili again. "*Usaidifa*. That word makes me wonder, and the only thing I can think of is that it's made up. It's not uncommon to construct your own words in Swahili, especially by putting a *u* in front. When you do, words become concepts. An example is *dogo*, which means small. With a *u* in front—*udogo*—it means insignificance."

Roland cleared his throat impatiently. He hadn't asked for a Swahili lesson, and he didn't have much time. "So, you mean it's a concept, but what does it mean?"

Said Hashi, who was clearly used to having plenty of time, considered the word for a long time, and Roland began to fear they'd spend the day going through the whole book.

"Yes, a concept; that's the only explanation. *Saidia* means help, and *fa* means die. *Kufa* means to die, *Kifo* and *kifu* mean death." He flipped the pages of the book against his thumb as if shuffling cards. "All these words are repeated throughout the book."

"So, it's about death?" Roland asked, not really understanding the meaning.

"The correct translation of *usaidifa*—a combination of help and die—would probably be euthanasia."

"Euthanasia?" Roland scratched his neck. The ants were beginning to invade it again. "We don't have time to review the whole book, but is that what it's about? In what context?" The little puzzle inside his head that hadn't been able to form a whole picture because some pieces were missing was finally starting to take shape.

"I have read the entire book, and I don't need to translate page by page. It's little tales. Several different people from villages in Kenya who each told their story. But since it's the same handwriting throughout the book, my guess is that the stories were told in their tribal language and written down in Swahili. It's about a doctor who performs euthanasia." He drank again slowly from the mug. "You need to know a little about Africa to understand it. Euthanasia is not a concept that exists in Africa. The term *natural causes* is also non-existent. Whether a person dies in a car accident or from an illness, it is interpreted as someone being jealous and having 'dealt with' the deceased. Usually by witchcraft. Even family members are nervous about being accused of 'being behind it.' The main suspect is typically someone who recently had good luck or success in some way. This is, of course, a huge generalisation." He looked at Roland with glowing eyes.

"Are any names mentioned in the book. The doctor, for instance?"

He shook his head and quickly flipped through the book again. "No names, no. Only different diseases for each death. But if what is written is true, it's certain that a Danish doctor carried out euthanasia in those villages. Where did you get this book from? Someone who travels around Africa?"

Roland nodded. That Sebastian once worked as a volunteer in Africa for the Danish Red Cross, and Helge Vangberg was sent there by Médecins Sans Frontières were the only thoughts he homed in on. Helge Vangberg had been a doctor for Josefine Hjort until she died. Extortion, violent killings resembling revenge. Something had happened in that home that December, which was having repercussions twenty-five years later. But what? He sighed. And did it even matter now? He looked at his watch. There was only a quarter of an hour until the meeting.

"I am very interested in the stories in the book because they were told by so many people quite a few years ago. I don't suppose I could . . ." Said began.

"For the time being, it's evidence in some murder cases, so we'll keep it for a little while longer, then we'll see. If the owner wants it back, then, of course, it is his property."

If they found Sebastian, and *if* it was his.

Said got up and put on his wool coat. "Of course. I hope it can help clarify something important." He shook hands to say goodbye.

Roland sat absently flipping back and forth in the notebook. Could it all be a coincidence? Two cases mixed together. Three maybe? Or were they completely unrelated? He didn't get any further in the considerations, as Kurt Olsen stepped in without knocking. "Did you cancel the meeting?"

"Of course not. We just need to have everything. Everyone has worked so hard. You never know if something will come up." He looked imploringly at Olsen.

"Okay, but then let's get going." He left the door open as he walked out. Roland got up resignedly and went to the briefing room. Everyone was already there, sitting and waiting. Kurt stood and studied the board of pictures. Roland hoped he hadn't said anything. First, he wanted to hear what had come out of the latest investigations. Kurt sat down next to him. He smelled of pipe smoke; not an unpleasant odour, just a smell that gave Roland a sting of longing.

"There have been some developments, so as things stand, this will probably be our last meeting in the case. Isabella, did you find out when Dr. Vangberg worked for Médecins Sans Frontières and Sebastian Juhl for the Danish Red Cross? It's crucial now that the translation of the notebook from the summer cottage has been conducted."

"They were in Kenya the same year but not the same time."

"Kenya. Are you sure they were both in Kenya?"

Both Mikkel and Isabella nodded. Roland realised Mikkel had helped her find the information.

Mikkel took over. "The strange thing is that Helge Vangberg was fired from Médecins Sans Frontières after Sebastian Juhl went back to Denmark. He was fired because someone else reported him for performing euthanasia on patients with, for example, AIDS. We couldn't find the name of the informant, only that he had worked for the Danish Red Cross."

Roland frowned. You didn't have to be clever to figure it out. Even Dan Vang seemed to have caught the connection.

"So they knew each other?"

"We have to assume they did. Or that Sebastian Juhl had heard of Helge Vangberg at least, otherwise he couldn't have reported him."

Roland laid a hand on the notebook. There didn't seem to be any doubt as to which doctor it was about. He quickly shared his new theories. Helge Vangberg hadn't been a completely clean doctor.

"Euthanasia is punishable in Denmark under section 237 of the Penal Code, although no one doubts that it still happens to a certain extent," he concluded.

"Death on demand," mumbled Henry Leander. "Euthanasia in legal language—section 239," he continued. "The Frenchman Bernard Kouchner, co-founder of Médecins Sans Frontières and also the minister of foreign affairs and European affairs, has been a prominent supporter of euthanasia for many years. He even admitted to taking the lives of several of his patients as a doctor. Médecins Sans Frontières suspended any collaboration with him for good reason. It is a very ethically sensitive subject, so if anyone had some knowledge of what you are suggesting here, Roland, it would certainly be a motive for both extortion and murder."

"And revenge," Julie broke in. "If Sebastian knew his mother was killed and who did it, it may have triggered a wave of retaliation against those who were behind it or kept their knowledge secret. If he repressed the episode as a child, it may have surfaced when his mother was found in the bog. Nobody knows what the poor boy witnessed back then. But how do all the victims fit in?"

Kurt Olsen, who had been sitting silently with an elusive expression on his face, harshly interrupted the emerging debate.

"The case has been solved. There's nothing more to discuss!" He paused to gain control of his voice. "Regardless of what has happened, Knud Engtoft confessed to the murders this morning."

Roland tried to appear neutral as everyone looked at him reproachfully. *Did you know anything about this?* their eyes said.

"We might as well see if we can get conclusive evidence. There's something wrong here, and why is Knud Engtoft taking the blame for Sebastian's actions?" he countered.

"The case is closed, Roland!" Kurt Olsen's voice was firm and determined. "We can only declare the case closed!"

"What about the Swiss bank account?" Mikkel asked.

"Also closed. I tried to get the National Danish Police on the case and investigate who owned it, but they can't spend time and resources on it when we have a confession" Roland sighed, trying to hide the desperation in his voice. With a full confession and no strong evidence to contradict it, there wasn't much room for manoeuvring.

When the others had gone home for the weekend, Roland was alone with Kurt Olsen. They cleaned up and peeled the images down from the board. They were both silent. Roland was sure that Olsen was thinking the same as he was.

"Kurt?"

"Hmm."

"You said there was someone who visited Knud Engtoft just before he confessed."

"Yes." Kurt did not look at him.

"Who was it?"

"His son."

"His son? Does Knud Engtoft have a son?"

"A stepson," Kurt Olsen replied, annoyed. "Sebastian Juhl."

58

The knife slid slowly through the water. Cut through it as it rotated slowly until he could no longer see it in the brown water. He looked at the women in the colourful dresses. Only some children and women from the village were down by the river. Washing clothes and fetching water. The children played around them, not afraid of anything. The mothers didn't seem nervous either, despite the dangers lurking in the thicket and in the water. There were lazy hippos on the opposite bank. Not like Danish children. In Denmark, children and parents were afraid of everything; they didn't even dare let their children walk to school unaccompanied and drove them instead, even if they lived only a few metres from the school.

None of the women looked at him. He was as indifferent to them as the hippos and crocodiles further up the river. He lay back on the blanket and listened to the sounds he had missed for so long. He felt at peace now. The turmoil that had always filled him was suddenly gone. He had never felt so free and uplifted as he did now. The sun's rays penetrated, as only they could in Africa. His eyes closed softly, and the images began to roll. Cool pictures of the ravages of a snowstorm from a long time ago.

The snow blew down from the roofs and across the road, making it look like a white sea of turbulent waves. Large snowdrifts, taller than himself, lay on both sides of the road. He couldn't see the house and tried to gather his thoughts about the Donald Duck comic that the African had stuck in his hand. Donald

Duck was for babies, but he had nothing else to do and was beginning to freeze. What was taking so long?

He had begged to come along even though Mum kept saying no. There were only five days until Christmas Eve—maybe they were trying to buy presents for him—but when the African finally gave in, Mum gave in, too. She just had to pick up something in a house on the way, then they could drive into town and buy lots of Christmas presents, he had said, emphasising the lots. He began to look forward to it and didn't even protest when his mum pulled the knitted hat down over his head. He hated it because it was really itchy.

First, Mum had gone up to the house while the African waited with him in the car, but when almost half an hour had passed and he'd been cursing and mumbling incomprehensibly as he smoked cigarettes that made him cough painfully as he sat in the back seat, the African got out of the car and walked without saying where he was going. The African seemed to have forgotten he was there. He watched the African walk up to the house and disappear behind the snowdrift.

He looked at the clock in the car. The African had been gone a long time. Where did they go? He threw the comic aside and pulled on his gloves. It was slippery where he got out of the car, and he almost fell. When he came around the snowdrift, he saw the house. It looked cosy in the snowy landscape. There was a Christmas tree with lights in the garden, and there were lights in two of the windows. Had they forgotten about him? He went down to the house and looked inside. He couldn't see anyone. He went to the next window and the next and was suddenly in a back garden. The snow had been trampled here, it looked like children had been playing in it. He caught sight of a girl as he looked in through the next window. She wasn't very old. She was asleep in her bed. A little lamp was turned on, so he could see her face. She had dark curls. The expression on her face made him think of an angel. She was the one he had seen playing with dolls one day when he'd gone to get Mum. But he couldn't see either her or the African. He looked around the garden. If only they had a garden like this. He could make exciting hidey-holes, like in the garden in Silkeborg. They didn't live there now. But soon they would move into a nice, big house, the African had said.

He spotted something strange in the snow. It had melted in some places and was red. It seemed to be running from somewhere behind the birdbath. He slipped in the snow as he walked around. She was completely covered in snow. Only one hand protruded, but he recognised it immediately. Mum's hands were something special. Crying, he threw himself down next to her and started digging in the snow, but every time he got her face free, it was quickly covered again by new snow falling on her. The red was coming from her head. He remembered her story from the nightclub and tried to lift her up to shake her, but she was too heavy, and her body was stiff and cold. He heard shouts from the house. It was the voice of the African. He needed to know what had happened to Mum. He ran crying towards the door facing the back garden. There were small panes in so he could look inside. The African was standing in front of a man and a woman in nice clothes. He had a knife in his hand and was threatening them.

"This is going to cost you more. Much more!" he shouted so loudly that it could be heard in the garden. The woman handed him a heavy bag. "Why couldn't you just have given it to her; did you not think I was here? Didn't you think I would watch out for her? Did you think you could just get away with this!" His voice didn't sound normal.

He saw the blood on the carpet and the ugly wooden rhino the African had given to his mum, but which he knew she had given to the sick lady of the house. It was in the middle of the pool of blood, so it looked like it was bleeding. He realised that the African knew what had happened to his mum. But why wasn't he calling the police? Why wasn't he doing anything? At once, he turned around and strode towards the front door. It slammed after him. The woman and the man were alone. He hugged her and stroked her hair. He didn't know what to do. The man suddenly peered out into the darkness of the garden, and he knew instinctively he had to leave. As he came around the house as fast as he could run in the snowdrifts, he saw the lights from a large car disappear out onto the road. The garage was empty. The African had stolen their car. That was when he found the beautiful knife in the snow; he must have dropped it in his haste. He shook, cried, and threw up in the snow. It was only bile, as it had been a long time since he had eaten anything. It melted the snow and made a yellow hole. Like Mum's blood had melted the snow in the back garden and dyed it red. He didn't know where to hide or what to do, and when he fell into the snowdrift up by the car, he couldn't get up again. He just wanted to die. Die like Mum under the snow. But after a while, he froze so much that he couldn't bear it any longer and crawled shakily into the car. There was a blanket in there. He pulled it over him until the cold took hold of him, and he thought no more.

* * *

His face was splashed with water, making him sit up abruptly. The children's laughter surprised him, and when he turned, a little Samburu boy of about six was standing with a clay jar of water between his dirty hands. His legs were grey with mud up to his knees, and the gaudy clothes were too big and filthy, but his teeth were chalk-white, and his eyes shone with joy. He sat down on the blanket with the water jug in front of him and looked up at him expectantly. He was waiting for the usual—exciting things from the white man's strange land. The boy smelled of sweat, like he had done when he tumbled with his mum in the woods on his birthday. Sebastian tried to ignore the heavy feeling in his chest. He found his key ring in his pocket and handed it to the boy, who greeted him with admiration in his eyes and began to examine the keys; they clinked inspiringly. The key to the stepfather's caravan was there, too. He wiped the water off his face and looked at the drowsy hippos. He should have handed it in, but what use would the African have for it in prison? He'd probably die soon of AIDS anyway. He felt no shame or sorrow at the thought. The African got what he deserved. He would never forget his astonishment at Sebastian's unexpected visit to the prison and the fear in his eyes. Finally, their roles were reversed. The threats had worked. It was jail time no matter what he said. Or death. If the African didn't confess to all the killings, he would reveal his knowledge of the murder, of euthanasia, and of twenty-five years of blackmailing the rich couple on Strandvejen. They got what they deserved, too. She was certainly dead now, Sabrina. That was the only thing that touched him. He saw her face before him again, as he had seen it that night through the window; she looked like a little angel. She wasn't supposed to die. He only meant to show her the letters he kept in the shed, so she could see for herself what her father and stepmother had done, but as that cover hadn't been put on, one thing led to another. It had to be that way. They were to be punished, not her. Had he spared her, he couldn't have hit the Hjort family harder. Now they could feel what he had felt for so long—uncertainty, hopelessness, grief.

A strong pain through his head caused him to rub his temples, and his face twitched in spasm. The boy looked up at him and laughed. He thought he was making fun, like usual. But the violent jerks had got worse down here in the bright light. They'd started when he began to remember. When the memories slowly began to return, after the two police officers had told him about her being found in the bog. Everyone had told him she'd left him for the African. Left him to strangers who tried to make him remember what he wouldn't remember. The conversation in the kitchen that he'd heard as he sat on the stairs had surfaced again and again. Mum's friend, the waitress with the hoarse voice who had known everything but could be bought for money and, therefore, by staying silent, was guilty. She could have prevented it all back then. And she thought he was romantically interested in her. He snorted, and the boy laughed again. The keys were no longer interesting. He put them back in his pocket. The pain slowly subsided, and he tried to relax his facial muscles. They sat, watching the brown water of the river. Small waves from the undercurrent played, chasing each other. He'd played chasing in the woods this year on his birthday, too. He felt nauseated. It usually accompanied the seizures. Or maybe it was the thought of her, the waitress. The smell of blood and the sound of her screams when he caught her in the woods and stabbed her with the knife for the first time. The tough resistance until the blade slipped through. A liberating feeling of letting justice prevail. Like the punches in the school-yard. Her eyes had filled with horror in the dark. Like the doctor's had done, too, when he'd pulled off the hat and revealed his face. He knew his eyes were a faithful copy of his mother's. It was clear he hadn't forgotten them. How many had the doctor killed in the name of justice? Helpless and sick in Kenya right up until he put an end to it. And Sabrina's mother. No one questioned the death of a cancer patient. No one questioned a corrupt doctor who didn't take his medical practice seriously. Only his mum. His protective mum, who could now finally rest in peace.

A new splash of water over his head quickly pulled him out of his reverie. The boy had lost patience. His eyes gleamed mischievously as he ran, wanting to be chased. Sebastian wiped the water off his face with both hands and lay back on the wet blanket that felt cool through his sweaty shirt. He smiled. The sun was baking. It was nearly horizontal, further down in the sky now. Soon, the beautiful orange sunset would flame up on the horizon behind the acacia trees. He was home. He was finally home.

59

Angolo woke him up. He had slept too long and didn't know what day it was at first. It was almost ten o'clock, and he sat up so quickly that Angolo was pushed down on the floor. Offended, the dog barked at him. *It's Saturday*, he thought, and he relaxed again. *Saturday!* They were due to meet the estate agent at the property in Skåde in an hour. Why the hell hadn't Irene called him. Oh, yes. He knew why. But she wasn't going to get out of their agreement so easily. He put some socks on, helped by Angolo who pulled them off him as quickly as he got them on.

"Stop it, you stupid mutt!" He snarled, but immediately regretted it when Angolo looked up at him guiltily. He patted the dog and went out in his dressing gown to see Irene in the kitchen. "Did you forget to wake me up? You remember, we're . . ."

"Yes, yes, I remember. But I thought you needed to sleep for as long as you needed to. And you have to collect Salvatore this afternoon, too."

Salvatore was flying to Copenhagen and continuing on to Aarhus Airport, where Roland had promised his aunt he would collect him. The unrest over the meeting rumbled in his stomach. Or maybe it was just the lack of breakfast. He took a shower first.

Angolo was lying in his basket when he came out of the bathroom and sat down at the breakfast table. Irene had made soft-boiled eggs, and the toast smelled delicious. He tried to picture Isabella in that role, but the image didn't fit. He would have to talk to her. She couldn't go around believing there could be something between them. The age difference would be his first argument.

"Bjarne Lund from the Canine Unit was over this morning to see Angolo."

He looked at her quickly. "So early—on a Saturday! So, what did he think of him?"

"He thought Angolo was definitely suitable," Irene said proudly, looking down at the dog as if it were a child who had got good marks in school.

Roland took a croissant and poured coffee for them both.

"Isn't the puppy too young for Bjarne to judge? It's not more than a few months old, is it?"

"Bjarne said that they start training puppies very early. Right now, Angolo is in what they call the 'socialisation phase'—where they learn who their boss is."

Roland finished chewing and laughed. "But that's you, Irene. It's *your* dog."

"I think he clings to you most of the time. And as a dog handler, you have to . . ."

"Irene. I'm not going to be a dog handler!"

She ate and looked inquisitively at him. "You were mumbling in your sleep again last night."

Roland's coffee went down the wrong way. He remembered all too well what he'd been dreaming about, but Irene certainly didn't need to know the specifics.

"You were mumbling something about unreported numbers, I think. You're not doubting whether you caught the real murderer, are you?"

Roland breathed a sigh of relief. So, he had also dreamed about that, even if he couldn't remember it. "He confessed," he deflected, looking at his watch. "Well, we'd better finish up so we're not too late."

Angolo stayed in the car. He watched them through the side window as they walked. There were two other cars on the road in front of the driveway.

"It's nice here, isn't it, Irene?" He took her hand and they walked towards the property like a newly-in-love couple. There was not the slightest damage from the hurricane, and now that the sun was shining and highlighting how well maintained it was, there wasn't much Irene could object to.

"Yes, Rolando. But it's also a lot of money."

Still, her eyes shone with wonder, and he was almost sure everything would go as it should when he saw the couple standing with the estate agent in the yard. He wanted to let go of Irene's hand, but instead, he squeezed it hard.

"Are you okay, Rolando?" Irene spotted the couple, too. "Oh, isn't that Mikkel? Why didn't you tell me he had a girlfriend?"

Roland didn't answer, but waved stiffly back to Mikkel, who had also seen them.

"So, you're out to look, too," Irene said, shaking hands.

Mikkel introduced his companion to her.

"My girlfriend, Isabella Munch."

Isabella had her arm under Mikkel's. She smiled at Roland in exactly the way she had done from the door that day. His own smile cracked a little at the edges, then he put his arm around Irene's shoulders and looked directly at Isabella. "And this is my beloved wife, Irene Benito. I had no idea you were interested in the property and not at all that you are a couple."

"We have been for some time. But don't tell the chief superintendent. He doesn't want romances in the workplace," said Mikkel, shyly running a hand over the fluff on his round head.

So that was the reason for the secrecy. For a moment, Roland wanted to spread the gossip, but Mikkel was one of his best people, and it would have consequences. It would probably hurt Isabella most of all, and he didn't want to lose her, either. She had proved to be more skilled than he'd expected.

"Are you on your way home? Have you seen enough?" he asked, hoping it didn't sound like he was chasing them away.

"We haven't just looked. We've bought it." Mikkel laughed, patting the estate agent on the shoulder.

He nodded. "I'm sorry, Benito. But nowadays it's first come, first served. It's not as easy to sell as it has been. Especially not this kind of property. And you couldn't put in an offer before selling your house, and in these times, so . . ."

Irene clenched his hand. "It's okay. We weren't in complete agreement on whether to buy or sell. It's my childhood home, and we've always loved that house," she said.

Roland forced a smile and nodded. He shook hands with Mikkel and Isabella. "Well, congratulations on your purchase," he said, a little moved.

Isabella held his hand a little longer than he liked, and he thought her eyes offered a note of apology.

"We can't wait to move in, and you can come and visit us," she said instead.

Only when he was sitting in the car on the way to Tirstrup in the afternoon did he feel the shocks subsiding. Which of them was the greatest, he couldn't tell. Maybe they were both just pipe dreams. How could he have believed beautiful Isabella would fall for an old fogey like him when charming Mikkel Jensen had worked closely with her from the time she started? He shook his head, glad they had gone out to view the property, otherwise he wouldn't have learned of their relationship, which could have got him into an extremely embarrassing situation. They had been very discreet. Like Leander and Julie. There was probably a lot of that kind of thing going on in workplaces that only the parties involved knew about.

When his bruised ego was somewhat comforted, the case resurfaced in his thoughts. Sebastian hadn't been found. He had quit his job, and the apartment on Klostergade had been rented out to a young couple. Sebastian must have left the country. Surely travelled to Africa where no one would waste time and effort looking for him there when they had a confession. Olsen's many conversations with Knud Engtoft had given no answer as to why the doctor and the waitress had to die, and why he killed his wife and threw her into the bog twenty-five years ago. He refused to comment. The surveillance in front of the nightclub hadn't revealed what time he—or Sebastian—had entered, but if you didn't want to be seen, it was easy to avoid. They only had the foster parents' word that Sebastian was left alone in the car that winter night. It wasn't mentioned in the old case files. And Sabrina Dahl, why was she covering for him? She claimed she fell into that tank herself. Said she couldn't remember when and neither could she explain how the cover was put back on and why she had even been at the cottage. Of course, she was also influenced by Knud Engtoft's confession and probably didn't want to expose Sebastian to more. She had lost her unborn child; perhaps that was also affecting her judgement. He had to see the case as closed, like Kurt Olsen said. So, he was reduced to mumbling about unreported numbers in his sleep—for as long as needed—and as long as he didn't start mumbling about anything else.

Having to find a parking spot at Aarhus Airport changed his train of thought.

It took a while before the plane landed. A cigarette would have been nice, but he chewed some gum and looked at the exhibits instead.

He stumbled across a stack of the *Daily News* and only looked at the front page. "Murdered Danish doctor practised euthanasia in Africa" was in bold type over a picture of Helge Vangberg, which Anne Larsen had seemingly unearthed from somewhere. It was taken in Africa. He was standing next to an African who was dying of AIDS. She had managed to report the story from a different angle. The murder case was no longer top news. Nothing was probably more boring to the press than a confession.

He watched people rushing off with their suitcases on their way in or out of the country. The global world, open borders, more motorways, bridge connections, faster air and train travel—new types of murderers from all over the world. He tried to forget the case and think of the new challenge that taking care of a boy that age would bring. The teenage years were difficult. He remembered that from his daughters. But the many questions of the case kept interrupting. Why had Knud Engtoft confessed? What had Sebastian said to him? And the murder weapons—where were they? Maybe they would turn up one day. For him, the case was not closed. That knife and that ebony rhinoceros would always haunt him.

He sat down on a step and waited for Salvatore.

ABOUT THE AUTHOR

Inger Gammelgaard Madsen is a prolific Danish crime writer best known for her Rolando Benito detective series. Ever fascinated by police work and forensics, crime fiction was a natural fit for Madsen when, after working for some time as a graphic designer, she decided to return to her first love: writing. She is also the author of the Mason Teilmann series, which has been published in four languages.

DISCOVER
STORIES UNBOUND

PodiumAudio.com